Dragonswood

Dragonswood

BY *Janet Lee Carey*

Dial Books

AN IMPRINT OF PENGUIN GROUP (USA) INC.

Dial Books

An imprint of Penguin Group (USA) Inc. • Published by The Penguin Group
Penguin Group (USA) Inc., 375 Hudson Street, New York, NY 10014, U. S. A.
Penguin Group (Canada), 90 Eglinton Avenue East, Suite 700, Toronto, Ontario, Canada M4P
2Y3 (a division of Pearson Penguin Canada Inc.) • Penguin Books Ltd, 80 Strand, London WC2R
0RL, England • Penguin Ireland, 25 St. Stephen's Green, Dublin 2, Ireland (a division of Penguin
Books Ltd) • Penguin Group (Australia), 250 Camberwell Road, Camberwell, Victoria 3124,
Australia (a division of Pearson Australia Group Pty Ltd) • Penguin Books India Pvt Ltd, 11
Community Centre, Panchsheel Park, New Delhi - 110 017, India • Penguin Group (NZ), 67
Apollo Drive, Rosedale, Auckland 0632, New Zealand (a division of Pearson New Zealand Ltd) •
Penguin Books (South Africa) (Pty) Ltd, 24 Sturdee Avenue, Rosebank, Johannesburg 2196, South
Africa • Penguin Books Ltd, Registered Offices: 80 Strand, London WC2R 0RL, England

The publisher does not have any control over and does not assume any responsibility
for author or third-party websites or their content.

Designed by Jennifer Kelly
Text set in Stempel Garamond

Printed in the U.S.A.

3 5 7 9 10 8 6 4

Library of Congress Cataloging-in-Publication Data
Carey, Janet Lee.
Dragonswood / by Janet Lee Carey.
p. cm.
Summary: In AD 1192 on Wilde Island, Tess, the daughter of a cruel blacksmith, is accused of
witchcraft and must flee, but when she meets a handsome and enigmatic warden of Dragonswood
who offers her shelter, she does not realize that he too harbors a secret that may finally bring about
peace among the races of dragon, human, and fairy.
ISBN 978-0-8037-3504-0 (hardcover)
[1. Dragons—Fiction. 2. Fairies—Fiction. 3. British Isles—History—12th century—Fiction.
4. Fantasy.] I. Title.
PZ7.C2125Ds 2012
[Fic]—dc23   2011021638

To my sister of the road,
DANA PANDEY.

We didn't run away disguised as lepers,
but we hitchhiked everywhere together,
which was perilous enough. Thanks for
watching out for me in our travels.

Contents

Fire, fire flaming bright,
Golden in the autumn night,
Warn me with your eldritch sight,
What danger comes, and what delight.

Prologue

I AM SEVEN years old. My father takes me to a witch burning. He runs in close enough to throw sticks in the pyre. The fire roars. The woman, Jane Fine, screams, flames snaking up her gown. Loud cracks of wood or bone. I am crying, choking on the smoke, the burning flesh. Too late Grandfather forces his way in, picks me up, and races back through the mob. I knew Jane Fine. She made pretty candles with flower petals pressed into the sides. They said Jane's candles blazed with hellfire; that she danced with Satan in Dragonswood. Grandfather holds me close. I weep in his strong arms, bury my head in his cloak. Jane is consumed by fire.

I AM TWELVE years old. I run away, after my father breaks my arm. I creep into Dragonswood, though it is against the law to go there. I have come here before to escape my life, to scale a pine tree and feel the wind. This night I cannot climb; my broken arm is still in a sling. Brilliant shining specks swirl deep in the wood, will-o'-the-wisps fly ahead—tiny fairies, cousins to the ones that are human-sized. I laugh, chasing them. I am filled with a deep longing I have no words for. They dance in magical patterns as I run. In this moment I am free from my raging father, from my mother, who can't protect either one of us from his anger, from my fettered life in town. I am wild as the fey.

I am laughing. I am crying. The fiery wisps vanish.

I AM SEVENTEEN years old. The sexton is burning a leaf pile in the graveyard. We have come to bury my baby brother, Adam. There are six other graves here, all my baby sisters from years past. My eyes are swollen from crying. I am holding my mother's hand. I am her only living child. With her other hand, my mother rubs my back. Across the tiny grave my father stands, head down, his first and only son gone to earth. I glare at the midwife whose useless herbs did not save my brother.

Sparks whirl up from the burning leaves. The firelight draws me in. I grow still as still. I cannot feel my mother's hand. The churchyard fades. All is flame. I know I am being pulled into a fire-sight. I have had visions before. When they come I am transfixed and I cannot look away.

In the pulsing blaze I see a man swinging a sword. His body shimmers, green in the flames. I cannot make out his face, all dark shadow in the fire. Light flashes from his sword, cutting bright across my face and chest. I feel the blade's icy light.

PART ONE

Witch Hunt

Chapter One

Wilde Island, AD 1192

I SEE VISIONS in the fire sometimes, images of the past or what is yet to come. The fire-sight does not lie. But I did not see the witch hunter who would ride in to scour our town of sin, so I did not know to run.

The whole of Wilde Island had been in an uproar all summer. King Kadmi Pendragon died in June. His eldest son and heir was away on crusade. A king's regent, Lord Sackmoore, ruled until his return. In July, thieves crept into Pendragon Castle and stole the royal treasure: crown, scepter, jewels, and all. For the rest of that summer, the king's younger son and his knights searched everywhere for the treasure. The army swarmed in and tore up our town. But it was the one who rode in next, the one we welcomed with open arms, who did us the most harm.

I start my story the day the witch hunter came. It was a misty September morn a week after we buried my baby brother, Adam. I'd been shut away in mourning. Hunger, lack of market money, and the need to make soup for our table drove me out. Basket in hand, I left town with my friends to gather wild onions. Meg wore her newly woven cloak, a russet red that matched her hair. Poppy bedecked her blond braids with fleabane flowers.

My empty stomach was coiled tight as a snake. "Do you think we'll find enough onions for soup?" Meg and Poppy didn't go without, but my family had nothing to eat that morning, and free food was hard to come by.

"I saw a good patch. Plenty growing there," Poppy said. She looped her arm through mine. "You should let me help you with that." She peered at my black eye—a gift from my father, the blacksmith.

"I'm all right."

Meg and I were pretty enough, but Poppy struck men dumb. They saw her soft curving shape, her milky skin and honeyed hair. I saw the friend who'd played fairy princess with me when we were small, who'd tried to pull my first wiggling tooth out with a string.

The trees in Dragonswood rustled in the wind along the boundary wall. Mist blew up from the sea and swirled at our feet like witch's hair. I looked to the pines, longing to scale one.

"When's the wedding, Tess?" Meg said.

"What wedding?"

"You're to marry Master Percival soon," Meg reminded me.

"Never."

"You're seventeen. If not Master Percival, it will be someone else."

I'd had other suitors; none were rich enough to please my father until this latest one. He wanted to rope me to an older man with money, one who kept his wife in the same fashion he'd kept his own. Master Percival had grown children. He'd outlived three wives already. I'd seen their bruised faces when I'd met them at the town well. The welts on their arms just like mine and Mother's.

"Wedlock is a hangman's noose," I said.

"Tess!" Meg gasped.

Poppy tugged my brown hair and giggled.

"Wedlock—a telling word; women are locked in, the husband keeps the key." I spun around. "Give me a man who never beats his wife or child, who lets his wife ride out when she likes, who buys her ink that she might draw or write, books that she might read, who walks beside her, not before her, and does not make her empty his piss pot." *Who does not mind that she slips into Dragonswood to see the great old dragons and glimpse the fairy folk,* I thought, but did not say. "A man who listens when she speaks and enjoys her conversation, and I will marry."

Poppy hooted.

Meg laughed enough to shake her curls. "You ask for the stars! Why not add that he's young and tall, well-muscled, with straight teeth, a deep laugh, and a dimple on his cheek."

"That too." I nodded appreciatively.

Meg went on, "Pale-skinned—"

"No, sun-darkened," I said.

Poppy bowed to me. "Beautiful Princess Tess, will you marry me?"

I liked that she called me beautiful despite my black eye and my left ear that Father had boxed so many times the skin was puckered like a cauliflower. I was almost completely deaf on that side.

"My lady," I said, putting out my hand. We dropped our baskets and danced.

"You'll both end up as nuns," Meg warned, but she danced with us till we were all out of breath. A ray of sun fell across the road. We'd been friends all our lives. I did not know then how much I would hurt them both, and how soon.

"So you see, I'll never marry."

"You have no romance in your heart." Meg was disappointed. She was lucky to have wed Tom Weaver when she was fourteen. Tom was a youth with little means who lived with his mother and his father, Old Weaver. He'd never beaten Meg or their daughter, Alice, to my knowledge. Tom was the exception.

I touched my puffy eye as we walked on. So many women in town wore the dull, downtrodden look that went with cuts, bruises, and broken bones. Ah, I'd noticed the tipped heads and hunched shoulders. I recognized the same look in my mother's pinched face, and in my own after Father broke my arm.

Poppy glanced at Meg. "Tess thinks to live alone and make a living scribing or with her artwork."

"Poppy! That was between you and me." I'd not told Meg, knowing what she'd say.

Meg cocked a brow. "Men paint and scribe for a living, not women." Mother had said the same, though Grandfather had taught me how to draw, write, and keep sums, and I'd kept accounts for Father's blacksmith shop for years. My sums were tidy, our finances were not. Mother's midwife drained our purse. Father drank up what was left. Thus our outing for this day's onions.

Meg went on. "A young woman does not keep to herself and earn her own way. Do you want to end up burned for a witch like Jane Fine?"

"She sold artful candles, Meg. I draw."

"What's the difference? Living by your lonesome without a man to protect you? They'll call you a witch and burn you."

"Jane Fine stole into Dragonswood and danced with Satan there," Poppy reminded. "Tess would never do that."

"She made us go over the boundary wall once," Meg argued.

"To gather blackberries," I said. "What's the harm of that? No one saw us go in."

"Are you sure?" We'd seen my father in Dragonswood with Tidas Leech that day. They'd broken the law, slinking into the king's protected lands to hunt deer. But we'd hidden from them.

"Here," Poppy said. We waded through the long wet grass to the onion patch she'd spied earlier. My mouth watered. I pulled two and ate them. I couldn't help it. After that I gathered in earnest for my family's table. The patch was just beside the stone wall. The evergreens whispered over us, casting a filigree of shadows on the ground. Poppy was wrong. I'd crept in many nights. Not to dance with Satan, never that, but to run, climb the trees, listen to the singing wind, see the moonlit world from up on high.

I loved the sanctuary that Queen Rosalind Pendragon and King Kye made long ago. They'd restored the heart of Wilde Island, once home to dragons and fey alike, by giving them their own reserve. *My place too.*

Trying to keep away from Dragonswood only increased my longing. I could barely breathe in our house above the shop. At night I'd pace in my upstairs room with pricking skin, leaden lungs, until it was dark enough to flee. Then out my window, down the oak tree, I'd loose myself from town, racing hard till I reached the sanctuary. Not even my closest friends seemed compelled to climb the boundary wall as I did night after night to run and run and run. Times I felt I must go in or die. And when I was away from it, I drew what I'd seen there in the moonlight: dragons, deer, foxes, owls, the shining will-o'-the-wisps, and the fey folk I'd been lucky enough to glimpse.

Meg hummed a tune. I dug up another onion, green as

dragon scales. Last week I'd spied a mighty dragon wing-
ing over the moonlit wood. A long, jagged scar traced
down his neck. He didn't see me hiding in the branches
when he wheeled down, scoring Harrow River with his
fire. The river, dark blue in twilight, glittered like spilled
gold with his flame.

"Tess," Meg teased. "Where have you gone?"

"She's always dreaming," Poppy said.

Horse hooves pounded down the road. "Hush. Someone is coming."

Knights rounded the bend. Riding along in their splen-
did livery, two men blew their trumpets. The herald behind
them called, "Hear ye! Hear ye! Come all ye citizens of
Harrowton and gather in the town square!"

Meg jumped up. "Let's go."

I gripped my basket. "If I don't have enough onions for
supper, I'll be beaten for it."

"We'll come back later, Tess," Poppy said. "You can't
refuse a royal summons."

"They already ransacked our town for the missing
treasure."

Poppy stood. "Maybe they've come to say it's found.
Or announce Prince Arden's come home from the crusades at last."

"To be crowned our new Wilde Island king," Meg
added.

A royal summons was rare enough. Knights had to ride

south along Kingsway Road, tracing the edge of Dragonswood down the coast from Pendragon Castle fifty miles to the north down to our town of Harrowton, at the southernmost tip of the reserve. Ah, and they'd have to ride hundreds of miles south after that to spread their news, for our isle is long and slender as a man's riding boot, stretching four hundred miles top to toe.

"Well?" Poppy said.

I plucked a handful of buttercups, washed my filthy hands in the wet grass, stood. If Prince Arden was home, I didn't want to miss the news. As we raced back down the road, Saint Cuthbert's bells clanged so folk as far off as Old Weaver's shop on the edge of town would hear the summons.

Townsfolk poured from shops and cottages. We joined the people in the northern half of town heading for the market square, crossing the stone bridge over the Harrow River that split our town in two. Halfway across the bridge, I spied a tall young man standing on the far side at the water's edge. Hands on hips, he stared past the coming crowd and back down the road at the approaching cavalcade. Mist rising from the river swathed the man in pearly light. I knew the folk in Harrowton. I did not know him.

"Come on, Tess." Meg tugged my hand. My feet obeyed. Gusting wind blew the dark youth's hair back from his high forehead. I caught his firm jaw, and crow-wing brows. He wore a sword at his side, and a black armband around his right arm in mourning for our dead king. The crowd was thick along the bridge. I slowed my step, watching him. His tunic was green, the color woodwards wear. The Pendragons hired woodwards to help the dragons and the fey guard Dragonswood and boot intruders out. We had our own man patrolling the south end of the reserve (though he'd not yet caught me!). What was this woodward doing here? Had he come with the riders? I saw no horse.

My breath caught when he glanced my way, his eyes pale gold as cinnamon. I glimpsed his keen expression before he pulled up his hood, turned, and vanished into the crowd. Fey folk can disappear that swiftly and that well, but I did not think he was fey.

I was still trying to spot him when I was swept into the throng.

Chapter Two

U P HERE." MEG climbed onto the stone bench skirting the well. Poppy and I hopped up. From there we could see above the crowd. People jostled for position close to the stage beside Sheriff Bollard's jailhouse. I scanned the gathering, trying to find the man I'd seen at the water. So many feet stirred up the common street stench. Folk tossed garbage out their windows day and night, and emptied their sewage pots onto the cobbles below. The muckrakers were sorely overworked, trying to keep up with it all. My nose was schooled to the odor; still, a brisk sea breeze wouldn't be amiss just now.

Mother pushed her way through the mob with my father and Master Percival.

"There's your betrothed," Meg said, spotting him too.

Goose-necked, middle-aged Master Percival carried a fat purse. My father would prosper from the match. "Let my father marry him if he likes him so much."

"Tess!" Poppy laughed.

Meg's husband, Tom Weaver, pressed his way through the crowd with little Alice riding on his shoulders. He joined us at the well. The red-haired weaver was taller than most folk, so three-year-old Alice had the best view of all atop his shoulders. She glanced back at her mother, then pointed to my black eye. "That's sore," she said.

"Hush, Alice." Meg patted her daughter's small back. *Alice lived,* I thought. *Some children live. Why not Mother's?* Why was I the only one to survive when all the rest died even down to Adam? I touched Alice's strawberry curl so lightly, she did not feel it and did not turn around.

On the other end of the square I spied Tidas Leech with his plump, sow-eyed sister, Joan Midwife, who'd lost every child my mother birthed. A sour taste came to my mouth.

Poppy pointed to the bridge. "Look."

A shout went up: "Lady Adela!" People cleared a path for the horses, waving and calling her name. At the end of the procession, a pimply boy drove a cart with the lady's trunks and three stately deerhounds with red velvet collars.

I'd been in bed with fever the last time Lady Adela came to town, so I'd not seen her myself: never seen her royal escort or the Gray Knight sent by her uncle, the king's regent, Lord Sackmoore, to guard the lady. The red plume atop the Gray Knight's helm bounced in time with his horse, and the black swan of the Sackmoore family crest was painted on his shield. But among the riders, it was Lady Adela who caught my eye and kept it.

Sitting tall in the saddle, she straddled the horse like a man even though ladies both highborn and low- were all taught to ride sidesaddle so as not to split their skirts. Astonished at her gall, I watched her as she steered her horse toward the stage that served as a speech platform, players' stage, and hanging gallows.

The youthful lady was all opposition in her dress, both plain and fancy. A short gauzy veil covered the top half of her face. She wore a proper black armband about the sleeve of her gray gown just like the woodward had. Yet for all this, her belt was jeweled, her sword ruby-studded.

Here's a woman who has mastered the world of men, I thought. *Unfettered by marriage, in command of her own life.* How had she risen to a man's post, commanding eight knights?

I had to admit I'd expected to see a more downcast woman, knowing her sad tale. As the story went, witches kidnapped Lady Adela four years back, when she was just eighteen. On the night of the Black Sabbath they tortured her in Dragonswood, slit her ankle tendon so she could not run, burned her with hot pokers, and worst of all, put out her left eye.

The lady knew violence from witches; we knew violence from our fathers and husbands. Still, she was more than conqueror now. *Draw her,* I thought. I did not render people well, yet my fingers tingled, thinking how I'd ink the straight line of her back.

I tossed her my buttercups. Three thin stems caught in her horse's mane. She took two in her free hand. A smile bloomed below her veil. I was glad I'd thrown them. As she rode past, one blossom fell from the white mane and was crushed under her horse's hoof.

Anon she dismounted and took the stage walking with a slight limp from her witch-wound. Above us all, she raised her hand. "Good citizens." She paused for silence.

Had they found the treasure? Was Prince Arden home to be crowned?

The town was still, waiting. "We have all been in mourning for our noble Pendragon king. God rest King Kadmi's soul," she said.

"God rest his soul," we all said, crossing ourselves.

"And we are an isle without its royal treasure until young Prince Bion and his army find the thieves who stole it."

She let the words sink in. The treasure was still lost.

"But I have not come here to speak of sadness or missing treasure. I have come to ask you, people of Harrowton, to stand with me and make ready for Prince Arden, our future king!"

"Make ready for King Arden," we cried.

She drew her sword and held it up. A ray of sunlight glinted from the blade. "Prince Arden has risked life and limb these past four years fighting in the crusades. Should our God-fearing prince come home now to find his beloved island crawling with Satan's spawn?"

"No!"

"Never!"

"Then," she cried, "let us scour our island clean of all wickedness before our new king returns!"

People raised their hands shouting. I felt a fervor growing in me. Even old Blind Cropper hollered, holding up his walking stick. Townsfolk gazed up at her in that spreading light as if she were an Angel of the Lord come to purify us.

When the shouting abated, the lady sheathed her sword and pulled back her veil, revealing the black eye patch covering her glass eye. The sight sent a soft, uneasy moan through the crowd. We'd all heard how King Kadmi asked the fey folk to create a glass eye especially for the lady after she'd been attacked. Some said the eye was magical, that it empowered her to winnow out a witch.

The lady stepped forward. "How do we know a witch?"

Quavering, I drew my hood up. Was this what she was after? Another witch hunt? She'd come to Harrowton four years back, right after her abduction. I did not know she was still on the hunt.

One man joked, "Witches be the toothless hags what stink up the room!"

Lady Adela said, "How easy that would be, sir. But witches are more cunning than that. Any woman standing in this crowd with us today could be a witch. They are not always old crones. Some are young and lissome." She paused and lifted her eye patch.

Now her fey eye was on the crowd. We all of us gasped. The sound came in a wave. I sucked a breath in and could not let it out.

"Could she be your neighbor, the baker's daughter? Is she the girl at the well? A friend who has herb skills? Does she look innocent and yet she harbors secret powers?"

Sweat slicked my back. Only Grandfather knew I had the fire-sight, and he'd warned me to keep the power secret. The visions came when I was alone, so I'd managed to keep it to myself—until the day we buried Adam. In the sexton's burning leaf pile by the grave I saw a flaming man all green and shining in the fire, swinging his bright sword. Later that same day I ran to Joan Midwife's house to demand our money back. I found her cutting eel for her stewpot.

"Pay me back for the sticklewort we bought to cure Adam, or I'll spread the word, Joan Midwife."

"What word?"

"Adam died because of you, filthy hag. You're not fit to handle infants. I'll spread the word about you. No one will ask you to be their midwife now!"

"Was it me made Adam die? I saw you staring at the fire, didn't I? In a trance, you were in the graveyard." She poked her gray tongue through her gapped teeth. "What witch spells were you casting, girl?"

"Who is the witch?" Lady Adela asked again. "Look to any girl seen entering Dragonswood. She goes there after Satan. In secret places she joins her coven to torture her victims; she even sacrifices children, stewing their bones for the power it gives her. She's a woman with a devil's heart!"

Poppy took my hand and Meg my arm. Both were frightened, though they'd only come in once with me for berries.

"No one saw us," I whispered to Poppy. But her wild-eyed look asked, *Did your father maybe on that day, or the leech?*

"We're exposed so high up here," I said. "Let's get down."

Meg managed to squeeze in next to Tom, but he could not make room for Poppy or me with the mob backed all the way up to the edge of the well. I tried to force my way down onto the cobbles and felt a crushing weight as my foot was pinned against the bench. I grunted with pain, tugging my leg, and barely managed to pull my foot back.

Up on stage Lady Adela turned her head slowly left to right. "A witch brings pestilence to your town, and death. Are your elderly safe from her, are your children? A witch need only give a babe the evil eye for it to sicken and die." Oh, that went to my heart, thinking of my brother newly in the sod. I was not the only one, for next I heard Father's booming voice.

"She's a witch!" He pointed through the crowd. "Joan Midwife! She poisoned our newborn son and made him die!"

The midwife shrieked, and I screamed, "No!" I tried again to clamber down and reach my father, whose arm was out, finger pointing. I knew he was still crazed over losing Adam.

I'd cursed Joan Midwife to her face a week ago when she wouldn't pay me back for her useless herbs. I might have called the midwife a witch when I fought with my father later in the backyard, but I hadn't meant it. Surely he knew that?

I had one foot on the ground and was still pinned up against the well when I saw my father moving like a great muscled bull forcing his way through the throng, shouting, "Witch!"

"Stop him, Mother!" She couldn't hear me above the din.

One man called, "Midwife's a witch?"

Then another, "A witch surely. I lost my child after she tended the birth!"

"She gave my girl the evil eye!"

"Makes a man pay whether they live or not."

"Get her!"

My shouts of "Stop. She's not a witch!" were swallowed up with all the rest. The excited crowd churned like a tide pool. Some coming closer to the stage, some trying to back away from it as Midwife Joan and her brother, Tidas Leech, fought their way toward a side lane trying to escape.

Father was still bounding for Joan with his fists up when two of Lady Adela's knights caught the woman from behind and dragged her toward the sheriff's house.

"Let me go!" she howled. "The man's a liar!"

"Witch! Witch!" people called. I couldn't believe how quickly they'd let my father's single outburst poison their minds against her.

"You want a witch?" the midwife screeched. "Look to yer daughter, John Blacksmith!" Joan was dragged inside the sheriff's house. The heavy door slammed shut.

Struggling, I tried to push through the throng.

"Tess," Poppy called from somewhere behind me. I could not stop for her. The alley was hidden by the pressing bodies, but I knew it was there. Get to it and I could run. Hood on, head down, I forced my way through, rammed into the fishmonger, stumbled. The crowd swirled around me. More shouts. *Witch? Where? I know Tess. She was here.*

There she is.

I ran, was knocked to the cobbles. On all fours I tried to crawl. Scratch my way to the alley. Where was it? Which way? Gowns, pant legs, stench. I stood, pushed past the man I'd seen earlier at the river.

More shouts. *Tess! There she is!* Heart in my throat, I

reeled for the alley, ran past the baker's, cobbler's. Large hands grabbed me. Tidas Leech. "Call my sister a witch, Tess, Blacksmith's daughter, and I'll call you one!" His face was red as raw beef. Spittle foamed in the corner of his mouth.

I struggled against him. "Father doesn't mean it. He'll take it back. Let me go!"

He was thickly built, stronger than I. I screamed and fought as he dragged me back through the crowd toward the stage.

"I've got her now! Tess the witch! She's the witch! Not my sister!"

I stomped his foot, elbowed him, threw back my head to pull away.

On stage Lady Adela looked down. Her fey eye on me.

Chapter Three

I WAS NOT allowed to speak at my trial the next day. Fishmonger said I hexed his pregnant wife so his boy was born with a harelip—*Gave my wife the evil eye day before she birthed our boy.* Tidas Leech said he'd seen me dancing naked with the devil in Dragonswood, and *kissing Satan's arse.* His sister, Joan Midwife, was brought up from her cell. Her lies were the most foul. She said I'd hexed our cradle to lull all Mother's infants to deathly sleep, used witchcraft to kill all my baby sisters and my brother so that I could stew their bones to suck in powers.

I threw myself at her. The guards dragged me kicking from the room, and dumped me back into my cell. I prayed to Saint Thecla, who escaped death by fire when a storm put out the flames. I still remembered Jane Fine's ear-splitting screams.

I had clung to Grandfather's rough neck as he ran through the mob. I was seven. He still lived in the tipped cottage by the harbor then. Among his maps and papers,

I'd sobbed until I was sick, the smell of burning flesh still in my nose.

"Remember this," Grandfather said. "She was seen in Dragonswood. Remember it, Tess."

"I don't want t-to remember," I howled.

Taking me up again in his strong arms, he did something then he'd never done before. Holding me close, he hummed and danced around the room. A soft fire burned in the hearth, a kind one, not a killing one. Great shadows were thrown up on the wall as he danced me about the tables and chairs. When he set me down at last, I was quiet. The man knew I had the fire-sight, but I'd never spoken my fear aloud. "Am I a witch?"

He came down on one knee. "No, child, you're no witch. You have a power, but there's no darkness in it."

I believed him then. I still believed him. The fire-sight wasn't evil, though why I had the gift was a mystery. He'd been right to tell me to keep my power secret, right to warn me not to be seen going into Dragonswood. I should have listened, but after Grandfather moved north, I'd had nowhere else to run for refuge nights after Father beat me. Against all reason, I'd gone to Dragonswood.

THE NEXT DAY I was taken to a larger cell with shackles on the walls. The place stank of sweat and vomit. Hooks and winches hung from the ceiling. Hammers lay neatly beside vises on a rough-hewn table. In the corner a long poker leaned against the burning brazier; the iron chair to its left sported thick leather bands to bind the prisoner down.

The room had the look of my father's blacksmith shop. But I was the metal here. I was the one to be burned and bent and pressed. I nearly wet myself seeing all the torture implements.

Lady Adela ordered the guard to tie my hands behind my back and hang me from the ceiling hook.

"No, Lady Adela! Please. I am innocent!"

She left the room as the guard did her bidding. I thought my arms would tear away from my shoulders. I screamed and screamed, but they left me there. I could not say how long I hung in agony. Afterward a jailor came and lowered me to the floor. I wept with relief. The man helped me up, not out of kindness, but to strap me to the iron chair he called the witch's chair. He tightened the straps around my waist and upper arms, clamped my legs in metal vises, then set a tray before me and strapped my wrists against it.

Lady Adela returned. She wore no eye patch. Her good eye seemed cool and deep as an evening pool, and there was life in the look, but her fey eye was cold even with the torchlight reflecting in the glass.

My shoulders and wrists still throbbed with pain from hanging. Dry-mouthed, I begged, "Please, Lady. Some water."

She took out a metal vise. The jailor jammed my thumbs between the nine-inch-long metal bars. Wrists tied to the tray, thumbs wedged in the thumbscrews, I could not pull my hands back. "Mercy. Have mercy."

A man came in with a notebook to write my confession.

"Why did you hex your mother's children?" Lady Adela asked.

"I didn't!"

"Yet they all died. Tell me why." She turned the screws, crushing my thumbs.

"Stop! The midwife—"

"Go on," she said, leaning in.

The thumbscrews sent shooting pains through my thumbs, up my arms. *Say she's the witch.* "My father blamed her for my brother Adam's death. She blamed me. It's . . . all a mistake."

"Tidas Leech saw you dancing with Satan in Dragonswood."

"I didn't."

She tightened the metal screws.

"Ah!"

"When was the last time?"

I gulped air.

The lady clicked her fingers. "Evidence." The note taker put down his pad, brought her a stack of parchment. She held up one of my dragon sketches, produced a second drawing of a fey girl riding on a dragon's back.

"We found these hidden in your cupboard. Yours, Tess. Don't deny it."

"I . . . sketch. It doesn't mean—"

"You could not have drawn these from your imagination, nor rendered the dragons and fey so well if you'd not seen them with your own eyes. And we found this."

She held up my drawing of the green-flamed man—the swordsman I'd seen in the fire-sight.

"You say you've never been with Satan, yet you draw him burning with hellfire."

Lady Adela dropped my artwork to the stone floor, the green man half covering the dragon. She tightened the screws.

"Stop!"

"Admit you're a witch."

The room tipped. My head fell. Blackness.

I awoke to horrible pain. The jailor's hands on my forehead. He stood behind the witch's chair, holding my head up.

"I will let you go when you confess," Lady Adela said coolly.

My body shook and shook.

"I'm not a witch."

She tipped her head, considering. "You say you're not a witch." For the briefest of moments I thought she might be coming round to believing me, then she said, "There are two reasons a girl enters Dragonswood. Either she goes to join with Satan, or she's drawn in by the fey." She glared at me with her glass eye. "What are your powers?"

"I . . . I don't have powers." The lie hung raw in the air between us.

She tightened the screws again. Blood spurted from my thumbs.

"Stop! Oh, God!"

"Name the other girls who joined you in Dragonswood."

Other . . . girls? "No one came with me."

"So you *have* gone over the wall. You admit it! Name the others."

I shook my head. Vomit filled my mouth, dripped down my chin.

She turned the screws again; blood pooled on the tray. "Tidas Leech said he saw you in Dragonswood with two other girls. He could not see the others well enough to name them. Tell me who they are."

"Loose the screws!"

"Name them and the screws come off."

I fainted again.

I awoke, already screaming.

"Name them!"

"Meg! Poppy! But they're innocent!" I sobbed. "We only went to pick berries!"

Too late to take it back.

Lady Adela smiled as she loosened the screws. The man wrote the names down.

Back in my cell, my bleeding thumbs swelled. I held them against the cold stone wall and cried myself sick. Would Meg and Poppy be arrested, tortured? God have mercy. What had I done?

MY CONFESSION WAS not complete. Within the hour I was hauled outside, trussed like a chicken with my wrists tied in front and palms pressed together, and tossed into a dogcart. The jailor drove me through town. My arms and shoulders ached from the hours I'd hung from the ceiling, my thumbs, purple black as leeches, throbbed against my chest as the cart bounced along. "Where are we going?"

"Millpond fer yer water trial," he said.

Chapter Four

FOLK FOLLOWED THE cart out of town to see me thrown into the pond. By law, if I should float, I would clearly be a witch. Sink, accepting the waters as any good Christian does in baptism, and I'd be deemed innocent, though dead if left under too long.

Clouds mounded up and rain pricked my face by the time we reached Miller's Pond. The noise of the bumping cart sent the geese flying and honking over our heads. I searched the crowd for Meg and Poppy. I'd named them an hour ago. Were they already caught? *Please God, let them be here, give me a chance to warn them.*

The jailor lifted me down from the cart, and, there! I spied Poppy sobbing into her hands, Meg trying to tug her back toward the yew trees at the edge of the assembly. I wanted to shout, *Run!* But that would only turn the crowd's attention on them. I struggled with my bonds. The jailor boxed my ear and passed me to Sheriff Bollard. "Make way!" the sheriff said. The crowd rived in two as he marched me toward the millpond.

Fishmonger called, "Witch! She gave my boy a harelip!"

That got others shouting. One man leered at me. "Too bad, she's such a pretty thing."

Mad Jack raced up giggling. Folk said he lost his mind after he was fey-struck. "Oh my sweet," he crooned, then he planted a snotty kiss on my cheek. Tidas Leech pulled him back and kicked him in the groin. Tidas hacked and spat at me. The gob stuck to my face.

"Enough," said the sheriff, and, "Back away!"

The witch hunter rode to the pond, flanked by three men-at-arms and her Gray Knight. She wore a pale blue cloak against the rain, the hood up, shadowing her face, but I saw she did not wear her eye patch. Her left hand rested on her sword's hilt.

The sheriff forced me through sucking mud, wet grass, and goose droppings. Rain pocked the gray millpond. I wept as he removed my cloak and tossed it by the tall rushes. He untied my wrists as another man pressed my arms down hard. The jailor wrapped a thick rope around my arms and waist, pinning my arms against my sides.

How could I escape now to warn my friends? "The rope's too tight."

He cinched the knots, and I swelled up to fatten my belly like a toad, hoping to give myself a little more room later on.

More folk had come down the road and my father was among them. Oh, why did he have to come? At least

Mother wasn't here. It would break my heart to see her. The mob pressed in closer behind us, knocking us into the shallows.

"Get back, rabble!" Sheriff screamed. Pulling his foot from the mud, he led me like a leashed dog to the end of the dock where the water was deep.

Poppy and Meg were still behind the rabble. *Run. She'll come after you next.*

The people sent their farewells.

"Throw her in why don't ye?"

"Let's see if the witch can swim!"

"She's innocent. Let her go!" Father shouted in his gruff voice.

"Curse the witch. She kissed Satan's arse." The leech's voice was the last thing I heard before the sheriff pushed me over the side of the dock.

The chill pond sucked me down. I held my breath and heard muffled cheering from my few friends as I went under. Sinking proved I wasn't a witch. The weight of water pressed in. I tugged and tugged trying to free my bound arms. Then I popped up to the surface, gulping air.

Cheers from the wretched folk who thought floating proved me a witch. I sank, sucked in my stomach, tugged. I did this two more times, popping up and down in between, and glory—the rope did loosen enough to pull one arm free!

I floated upward. The sky had of a sudden gone crimson. Screams on shore. Gasping for breath, I saw townsfolk running for the bushes. A dragon winged over with yellowed scales and a long neck scar. The one I'd seen in Dragonswood after Adam died. Skimming down, he dropped a large stone in the water. The splash sent waves. I went under. In the green gloom I fought the bonds, squirmed the rest of the way out, and looped the rope around a rock. I kicked against the muddy bottom, waved my arms, did not rise. I flailed, kicked. Nothing. God! My lungs would burst!

A stone swam up. Not a stone, for it had a face and stunted arms. I grabbed hold of the large turtle shell, watched his short green arms paddle. Angels. Mercy. He swam me to the surface under the dock. I grabbed a post. Sucked in air. My feet touched the bottom. Unseen under the dock, I breathed and breathed. The turtle blinked at me as if to say, *Safe now?* I nodded gratefully, and he left me with a quiet splosh.

The dragon had sent me this turtle. I knew it in my heart, though it seemed too large a thing to believe. How had he known to come? There was no time to wonder at it. I had to get away and warn my friends.

From my hiding place under the dock I could see the townsfolk reassembling back at the water's edge now the dragon was gone. All heads were turned, all eyes riveted on the pond where the rope still dipped.

My father shouted, "It's all wrong! Bring Tess up afore she drowns!"

Tidas Leech called, "Let the witch be. She'll float up soon!"

Father dove for Tidas and punched him in the jaw. Both men went down in the mud, rolling and fighting like dogs. The townsfolk gathered, cheering the two men on. While backs were turned, I slithered through the rushes, grabbed my cloak that the sheriff had dropped. While he and his men ran in to break up the fistfight, I darted to the nearest juniper bush, ran bush to bush around the edge of the crowd all the way to the thick-trunked trees.

Behind a prickly hedge, I made a hissing sound. Meg and Poppy had their backs to me. Poppy had her cat, Tupkin, in her arms. The black cat peered back, curious. I threw a stone, missed. Threw another and hit Fishmonger's wife. She grunted and walked toward me. I dove into the scratchy greenery.

"The rope moved," Poppy screamed.

Fishmonger's wife retraced her steps. "Is she comin' up?" She headed closer to the water to get a better look.

I threw another stone and hit Meg's rear. "Ouch!"

I popped up enough to show her my face. Meg gasped, grabbed Poppy's arm, and dragged her behind the juniper hedge.

"Tess!" she said in a hissed whisper. Both crouched low with me.

"Thank God, Tess," Poppy whispered. "But how did you—"

"Quiet." I peered through the foliage. The boisterous mob moved in a wave around the fighting men. But higher uphill, Lady Adela sat in the saddle, focusing hawk-like on the rope in the millpond, the place her prey went down.

Wet as a dog and shivering, I hurriedly confessed what I'd done under torture.

Meg's freckled face grew blotchy as I told them both I'd named them, how sorry I was, that I hadn't meant to, and that I'd do anything to take it back. Her eyes went colder and harder with every word till she right out slapped me.

By the saints! I slapped her back! And we rolled in the grass behind the hedges. All the venom I had for Lady Adela seized me. I had Meg by the hair, tugging at it mightily till Poppy cried, "Stop it now."

We froze. Peering through the bush, I saw the miller turn toward us.

"Go, Poppy," I whispered. "Make it right with him."

Poppy stepped around the hedge.

"What's going on, girl?" he said, suspicious.

"I . . . I said stop it!" she pleaded. "Make those men stop fighting before someone gets hurt!"

"Look away then, wench!" the miller said, then went back to the skirmish. Poppy returned, heaving a sigh. I checked again. Lady Adela had ridden closer to the shore, accompanied by her Gray Knight. The sheriff had come up from the dock to speak with her.

I turned to my friends. "I'm so sorry. I never meant to give you away. You have to believe me." Poppy shook her head, still reeling with the news. There was no forgiveness on Meg's face, only fear and hardened anger. Even the sight of my swollen purple thumbs did not move her to pity, but we'd no more time to talk other than to make swift arrangements. "You can't stay here in Harrowton any more than I can now. Both of you will have to come with me."

"Come where?" asked Poppy, grabbing her cat.

"Into Dragonswood for now."

"Dragonswood?" Meg snorted and tugged my wet hair. "A pox on your plan, turncoat!"

She'd never called me a turncoat before, but then, I'd never set a witch hunter on her.

Meg stood up. "I'll run home to Tom."

"No time for that."

"My Tom will know what to do." She darted to the next tree before I could argue more with her.

Poppy and I raced behind, tree to tree, heading for Tom at Old Weaver's cottage on the edge of town.

In the cottage, Tom was weaving on his loom. On the floor at his feet, Alice spun a red top. "Mama!" She leaped up.

Tom saw Meg's tears, me in my dripping clothes, and stopped his work. "Meg? What is it? What's happened?"

I hurriedly explained. He pushed me up against the wall. "Woman, you have ruined us!"

"Tom!" Meg cried. "What are we to do?" Tom swiftly locked the door. "Hide," he said. Alice was crying, "Mama! Mama!"

I shook my head. "They'll find us, Tom. We have to run away. Now."

"Run? They'll catch you!" he shouted, slapping his hands up to his face. "God!"

There were shouts from down the road outside. "Witch vanished. They pulled up a stone!"

"Hurry!" he cried. Then, "Wait. Here!" He grabbed a pile, threw robes at us. "Leper's robes I was weaving for Saint Cuthbert's infirmary!"

We swiftly put them on.

"I don't want to go!" Meg cried, hanging on to him. Alice clung to her mother's skirts, sobbing. We heard more shouting down the lane. Doors slamming.

"They'll do a house-to-house search," Tom said, pushing Meg away. He grabbed Alice. "Go. Into the woods! Now!"

We raced out the back door and ran for the trees.

Chapter Five

I'M STARVING, TESS." Meg glared at me across our
small fire. We'd gathered greens and berries, raided
stinking midden piles for scraps our first four days on the
run; still we curled up each night morbid with hunger.
Tonight we'd made camp on the cliffs above the town of
Hessings Kottle, shared a dead songbird I'd wrested from
the seagulls, chewed seaweed.

"Try not to think of food," Poppy said. Tupkin was
curled up on her lap, purring. "At least we are alive."

"For now," Meg snapped, throwing back her leper's
cowl and combing her tangled hair with her fingers. We'd
have been caught straightaway if it weren't for the leper's
robes. People feared contagion and kept their distance
from us. And we tied rags over our noses as lepers do to
cover gaping holes where their noses had once been. My
friends had no sores to show, but my oozing purple-green
thumbs were enough to give anyone a fright. Donating the
robes to the monk's hospital would have earned Tom one

year and forty days' indulgence for the forgiveness of his sins. What sins Tom sought indulgence for I didn't know, but we owed our lives to him.

Thunder boomed in the distance. Lightning lit up the sea. No rain fell. Meg sniffed. I shifted uncomfortably on my log. She'd cried every night since we'd left Harrowton, missing Tom and Alice.

"How much longer till we get there, Tess?"

"Another three days or four if we travel fast," I guessed.

"Hasn't all this walking counted for something?" She rubbed her grimy ankle. "Are you sure your grandda can help us?" Her voice wobbled. I braced myself for tears. "What if he doesn't? What if we have to wander on and on as lepers with the witch hunter always at our backs?"

Poppy put her arm around Meg. She shrugged it off.

My grandfather worked as a mapmaker north in Oxhaven and had friends in many ports who might hide Meg and Poppy from the witch hunter. Our hope lay in him.

I broke a stick over my knee. Always, after the year my father broke my arm, the snapping sound reminded me of breaking bones. I added the kindling to the blaze and watched the flames lick the wood.

Meg was still in tears. She left the fire. When Poppy stood to follow her, I held up my hand. "I'll go. It's my fault we are here."

I found Meg leaning up against a boulder crying into the crook of her arm.

"Meg?"

"Go 'way."

"Meg. It will be all right. I promise."

"Go before I slap you, Tess!"

"Hit me, Meg."

"It won't help."

"Pull my sore thumbs."

"Shut your gob. Leave me be!"

I put out my hand but she drew back. "When Grandfather finds you a new home, he'll see to it Tom and Alice are sent for. You'll be together again. I promise."

Meg wept into her hands. I held her and felt her shudders shake me to my core. Angels in heaven, how could I promise her such a thing and be sure of it?

Back at the fire, Meg scooted close to Poppy, seeking comfort from the friend she still trusted. I hated myself for breaking up her little family, for dragging her and Poppy into my troubles.

Later, when they curled up to sleep with Tupkin between them, I kept vigil by the campfire. The road was different for me, though I did not say so to my friends. I was frightened enough, and hungry, but fleeing Harrowton I'd slit the cords that bound me to my life under my father's roof. Gone were his fists, his marriage plans for me.

Years I'd longed to run away to Grandfather's. Only love for Mother made me stay. I'd feared Father would beat her more often if I left. Now I'd been forced to run. On my own with my friends, in constant danger, I'd never felt so alive.

If I could truly escape, start again, might Grandfather help set me up in my own business, scribing for a living, or better still, illuminating manuscripts? A cottage near Dragonswood would be my choice. I would be at home under the whispering trees, with a view to the mountains where the fey folk dwelled.

Even now I felt the forest's pull. Dragonswood was just across the road from our camp here in the cliff. I'd tried to convince Meg and Poppy we'd be safer walking inside the refuge. Dragonswood's eastern wall traced Kingsway north to Oxhaven, where Grandfather lived, and beyond that all the way to Pendragon Castle. But my friends wouldn't go over the wall. Poppy feared we might be fey-struck like Mad Jack, who'd gone off hunting one day, and returned a week later, singing, snarling, and pissing in public. Meg believed the gossip that the fey cruelly punished trespassers, casting spells on them and turning them into *Treegrims.* All the years I'd gone to Dragonswood, I'd never seen a dragon or a fairy harm a man or find a person magicked into a tree. Still, in our four days running north, I'd stayed on this side of the wall.

We'd not gone far enough; spent too many hours searching for food, begging in our leper's garb. Tomorrow I would make my friends walk faster no matter how hungry we all were. I was thinking this, stirring the coals, when a woman's high-pitched screams cut through the night. We all jumped up, alert and trembling.

"Where's it coming from?" Poppy cried.

We raced to the cliff edge overlooking town and harbor. Far below us, smoke rose from the town square. At first I thought a cottage was alight. Thatch roofs easily catch fire, and when they do, the house burns swiftly. But from our lookout spot, I focused on the rising smoke and saw now it came from a witch fire in the middle of the town square.

Townsfolk dressed in black moved in a great, slow circle around the bonfire. The girl they'd bound to the stake shrieked louder as the blaze raced across the logs, catching her white gown at the hem. Up on the cliff under the hawthorn trees, I clung to Meg and Poppy. Her screams ripped through us.

Two mounted figures rode in, the bonfire bathing them in golden light. Meg saw who it was and yelped. Poppy quickly covered her mouth. "The witch hunter can't see us so far away up here," she said. "And these trees and bushes will hide us."

From behind us, I heard the deep woofing sound of pumping wings. A massive shadow swooped overhead. Against the night the dragon's scales seemed black. Tail whipping in the wind, he dove for town. At first the townsfolk did not see him, so when the dragon swept into the square, tearing the girl and staff straight up from the burning pyre, the folk below had little time to run. Some few scrambled into shop doorways. Most dropped to the cobbles, covering their heads.

The dragon spooked Lady Adela's horse, who galloped off full speed, the Gray Knight racing behind. High above the town, the dragon dipped up and down awkwardly, trying to reach the sea. The tip of his left wing burned, and so did the girl in his claws. He made it just beyond the harbor. Skimming but a few feet above the bay, he dipped both girl and wing in the water, and put the fire out.

Meg and Poppy stayed by the hawthorns, but I stepped out a little, watching the great dragon. Twice lit by the moonlight above and reflected in the sea, the dragon was the same old one I'd spied from the branches, the same one who'd dropped a turtle in the millpond. His yellowing scales and the long neck scar confirmed it.

His flight was so ragged from his damaged wing, I feared he might drop the girl, yet he kept aloft. Over the sound of waves, I heard the girl sobbing. She was injured from the fire and, no doubt, feared her rescuer, but I was sure the dragon meant to save her. I saw how he pressed her against his coppery chest scales as he soared closer to our cliff.

Somehow the dragon had unbound the stake the girl was tied to. He dropped the charred pole, and I jumped back as it hit the grass, tumbled off the cliff edge, and landed on the rocks below.

Too late the church bell down in Hessings Kottle rang out a dragon warning. He had already flown back to the sanctuary.

The bonfire burned. The girl was gone.

Chapter Six

WE FLED HESSINGS Kottle, walking all night north on Kingsway Road.

"Why would a dragon take her?"

"To save her, Meg. That's plain enough. Saint Thecla escaped from burning at the stake when God sent a storm to put out the flames," I added.

"Would God send a dragon?" Meg argued.

"God can do anything he pleases, Meg," said Poppy wistfully.

"But where would the dragon take her?" Meg had gazed left toward Dragonswood.

"Someplace safe?" I suggested.

"But why? Why would the dragons care to rescue anyone?"

Had they not seen the dragon drop the turtle into the millpond? We'd never spoken of it. Perhaps they thought as I had at first that he'd dropped a stone.

Poppy said, "Maybe it was the fairy riding on the dragon's back who wanted to help rescue the girl."

I stopped her on the road, staring hard at her face. I could not read her expression well in the pooling moonlight. "It's not like you to jest about such things, Poppy."

"I'm not. I saw a rider. A fey man on his back."

Meg offered, "I didn't see anyone."

Nor had I. "It was dark," I argued gently. "I think you mistook the ridge along the dragon's backbone for—"

"It wasn't a ridge, Tess! I saw a fey man clearly. His hair was as red as Meg's!"

We could not tarry any longer to bicker over it.

By dawn we were worn and hunger-gripped; still, the horror of what we'd seen drove us on toward the safety of Grandfather's. At midmorn a laborer rumbled past on his oxcart. We begged for bread.

"Contagion!" he called. "Get back, lepers!"

Wind whistled through the trees. I was cold even in my leper's robe.

"Sing a song to cheer us, Meg," Poppy said.

"I can't," Meg said. "It's not in me."

Poppy tugged her arm. "Please Meg, you sing so well. It will help me walk."

Meg grumbled. But at last she began. Meg had a sweet voice and loved to sing. Poppy croaked a tune as well as any toad.

In the enchanted woodland wild,
The Prince shall wed a Fairy child.

Dragon, Human, and Fairy,
Their union will be bound by three.

And when these lovers intertwine,
Three races in one child combine.
Dragon, Fey, and Humankind,
Bound in one bloodline.

"You think it's true?" Poppy asked.

I considered a moment. "It's just a song. Grandfather's tales never mentioned any marriage between human and fey."

Meg fingered her tangled hair. "Fey men take lovers."

"And leave a girl alone with child." We'd heard the tales that began with dancing under the moon at Midsummer Night's Fair. They did not end well, not for the girl, at least.

"A Pendragon prince might wed a fey maiden," Poppy said. "And she might go to him. The royals are different from the rest of us."

We Wilde Islanders were proud of our royal family. No other rulers in all the world had dragon's blood in their veins. They had since Queen Rosalind's day, the first Pendragon born with a scaled finger and dragon's talon. It was said her children had scaly green patches. Her son, King Kadmi, had a patch on his wrist; his two sons bore scales hidden on neck or arm. Even King Kadmi's daughter, the smallest Pendragon princess, had scales, though folk did not like to speak of her.

Poppy hummed the tune off key. "Maybe after Prince Arden sails home, he'll seek a fairy princess for a wife," she said. "It's not like we have other princesses lining up here on our island. Think of it." Her eyes sparkled. "A fairy princess for our own Pendragon queen."

"It's only a minstrel song," I said again.

"It was Alice's favorite," Meg said.

Days when we used to meet down at the river to wash our clothes, Alice always asked her mother to sing. I'd pound wet cloth on the rocks, loosening the dirt and keeping rhythm with Meg's song while Alice twirled round and round on shore. Last time I saw Alice she was crying, clinging to Meg's skirts.

THAT AFTERNOON THE sky was gray as boiled pig meat. The sun hung pearl white behind it as we headed north, eating a few wormy chestnuts.

We found no food when we reached Margaretton, where a riot broke out in the market. Outraged townsfolk overturned sellers' tables, angry over the king's regent's new grain tax. A pack of men stormed the Dragonswood wall with bows and arrows, shouting, "Meat! Meat!" We fled as fast as we could, but still we saw the sheriff's men leap the wall on horseback, and hack the rioters to pieces.

I'D PROMISED MEG and Poppy Grandfather would hide us, that he'd find a way for Meg to be with Tom and Alice again. But when I stood trembling at his seaside inn in Oxhaven two days later, the innkeeper's wife said, "He's not here. Old man's gone off to sea on some mapmaking expedition."

A knife went through me. "When will he be back?"

"Never, I should think, the old salt. Who wants to know?"

WRETCHED, WE HID that night in a cave just outside of town. Poppy would not speak to me. Meg wept.

Alone, I sat by the fire in our small cave. Gone. Without a word. Grandfather loved the sea, but I was desperate for his help. I needed him now. I cried for the first time since we'd fled the witch hunter, covering my mouth with both hands so my friends wouldn't hear.

Sometime past midnight, the fire popped and sparked, pulsing with life the way it did when strange visions slid into the flames. In the heat my skin went chill, and though the sea was nearby, the pounding waves hushed as my world grew small and still around the fire.

The lulling flames changed from gold to green where the man's figure emerged swinging his bright sword. Sparks flew in flurries over his head as if his sword stirred stars. His face was all in shadow, and look as I might, I could not make out his features, but I'd seen him once before in the burning leaf pile the day we buried Adam. Another shape grew and I saw someone before him in leper's garb. My heart chilled. I wanted to pull away from the blaze, but I could not move when the sight was on me.

The girl in the fire had her back to me, but the fire-sight never lied. I knew I was seeing myself at some future time. Why wasn't I running from the green man? Why stand there dull-witted as he threatened me with his sword? I'd not been in the vision the first time I'd seen this swordsman. Again he swung his weapon as if to slice me in two. No sound came. If I screamed on that future day, I did not hear it now. Our bodies faded. Orange flames bloomed where the green ones had been.

Chapter Seven

LOOKING BACK, WE should have kept moving after that and never stayed near town. But it was harvest time; the tempting fields were rich with wheat. Manor lords were bound to bring the harvest in before Michaelmas, for the weather was already changing. We watched the reapers swinging scythes. Folk followed after, gathering the wheat into sheaves.

Meg slipped into the bushes by the wattle fence and stripped off her disguise. "I'm gone," she said.

"Gone to where?" asked Poppy.

"Landlords pay folk with food after a day's harvest," she said, nodding at the wheat field.

"You can't, Meg. The witch hunter's looking for us."

"She looks for three girls. I'll be alone."

Poppy ducked in beside her and shed her robe. "Now we are two." Her blond hair and pale face stood out amidst the green brambles.

"Wait." I tugged Meg's sleeve. "Think of the danger."

"I'm sick of midden scraps and mushrooms!" she shouted.

Her cheeks were sunken, her eyes ringed. We'd all grown thinner on the run. "What if Lady Adela comes?"

"I'm too hungry to care. She knows your face, Tess, not ours. Poppy and I can work in the field. We'll blend in with harvesters."

Poppy took Meg's hand. "Let's go."

"No one is going. It's too dangerous. We'll find food another way!"

Meg hopped over the wattle fence with Poppy close behind. Tupkin slunk through the wheat. I was furious. "Think of Alice, Meg! What if something happens to you?"

Meg linked arms with Poppy as they headed for the reapers. "You should have thought of that before you gave our names to the witch hunter, Tess. Today my name is Hester, and, Poppy, yours will be Violet."

I hid my leper's robe in the bushes with the others. In my own cloak I'd worn underneath, I jumped the fence and crept into the field to keep an eye on them and make sure they were safe.

Children raced by. Barking dogs chased rabbits through the field. I fingered the wheat, which was the color of my mother's hair, thought of her at home and ached. Her face was often pinched from the hard life she led, but her eyes were blue as day. She used to sing to me when I was small, her voice raspy and low for such a slender woman. Was she safe? Was Father beating her more often now I was gone?

Chewing raw grain, I followed my friends, hidden in the tall rows, anxious all through the day till the work was done, and the harvest king sat atop the cart. A broad-shouldered youth with sandy hair, he grinned down at the laborers, who shouted, "Richard! Richard! King of the harvest!" They clapped, hooted, and sang on their way to the storehouse.

"And who be harvest queen?" one called.

Sunlight rinsed the fields, spreading a circle around them. Poppy shone as if she were a lissome fairy. She'd escaped men's notice in her leper's robe and cowl, but now . . .

"Violet!" he shouted down.

Poppy tried to get away. Workers pushed her forward, laughing and hooting. The king of the harvest scooped her up to sit beside him on the cart. Meg saw me hiding and shot me a fearful look as Richard crowned Poppy with a laurel wreath.

Folk escorted the harvest king and queen into the barn, where they jumped down from the cart to great applause. I darted inside and hid behind the hay bales stacked near the open barn doors. The tables in the barn were laid out for the harvest feast. At the high table, the manor lord presided over all. I reeled at the sight of so much food. I had to keep myself from grabbing. There was meat aplenty (ham as well as mutton), trencher bread and round rolls alongside waxen wheels of cheese, fresh butter, mounds of fruit and cakes.

The lord of the manor stood and said the blessing. "Good folk, let us be thankful to God for a plentiful harvest. God bless Prince Arden, our future king. Grant him safe passage home from the crusades, and swift."

"And may the treasure be found in time to crown him king!" a man shouted.

All said, "Amen."

Pipers and fiddlers played, some danced, others went for the tables first.

With my hood up, I took a mug of ale, stuffed cheese and rolls and apples into the lining of my cloak to share with my friends later, snatched a knife, then ate my small feast behind the hay bales.

A tall young man entered and slipped behind the haystack in the corner opposite mine. He hid in shadow, but I saw by his green tunic he was a woodward. I stared at him from behind my hay bale as I chewed my apple. Why was he holding back, not feasting or dancing like the others? These woodwards were curious. The one I'd seen by the Harrow River had kept apart too, before he'd vanished in the crowd.

He watched Poppy dance and flashed a wicked smile. Why keep in the corner unless he's no woodward at all but an outlaw, come to steal from the rich lord in his time of plenty? The man could have slit a woodward's throat, pilfered his purse and clothing. A woodward's garb would disguise a cutpurse perfectly.

A sunbeam slipped in through the open barn door and lit the man. I bit right through the apple core. It was he. The dark man with cinnamon eyes I'd noticed at the river. He'd spied me in Harrowton when the witch hunter came. If he saw me now, he would turn me in. I ducked deeper into the shadows, damp with sweat. His attention was on the dancers. He had not turned my way, thank God. His face drew me in as it had before with its wide brow and angular features, yet there was also an ease around his mouth as if he knew how to laugh. My fingers tingled. *A man to draw.*

A trumpet blared outside, announcing the arrival of a noble. Music stopped. Dancers paused, breathless. *Not her. Please, God not her.*

The crowd parted as Lady Adela rode in through the wide barn doors on her white mare.

Chapter Eight

MIGHTY GOD! WE were trapped! The witch hunter hadn't gotten a good look at my friends before we fled, but she'd been hunting the three witches who'd gotten away. She would be on to us if Meg or Poppy bolted suddenly. Their only hope was to blend in and play the part of harvesters as they slipped back slowly toward the barn door. Revelers opened the dance floor to the lady who steered her white mare right up to the lord's high table. Behind her, the Gray Knight rode helm down, the Sackmoore shield strapped to his back. Eight more armored knights marched in on foot followed by the pimply lad leading the lady's deerhounds on their long red tethers. The barn was silent now but for the horses' snuffing and the hounds' jingling collars.

Poppy and the harvest king were to the witch hunter's left, Meg to her right. I saw them catch each other's eyes. Fear in the looks, but all being still, they could not run yet. I gripped my newly stolen knife. *Merciful God, we've come so far. Don't let her take us now!*

The lord of the feast stood. "Good eve, Lady Adela."

Lady Adela drew back her hood. Her back was to me, so I did not see her eye patch but saw the thin strap above her dark plaited hair. She wore it now as she had the day she arrived in Harrowton. "Lord Norfolk. There's much work for all of us to do before Prince Arden returns. No time for idle feasting. Our isle's infested with witches and thieves. Is that something to celebrate?"

"My lady?" Sweat beaded Lord Norfolk's brow.

Poppy inched toward my corner, but Meg was still too terrified to move.

"Go," I whispered. "Now." Meg was like a stunned rabbit. Would I have to dart out and pull her back? Such abrupt movements would cause a commotion Lady Adela would be sure to notice.

I glanced left. The woodward had vanished.

The witch hunter said, "I've come to reward any here who could lead me to a band of escaped witches. Three of them together and all of them young. I am ready to pay up to fourteen shillings whether they are brought to me alive or dead."

My breath caught. Such a high bounty on our heads! Excited murmurs passed through the crowd. Fourteen shillings was more than two months' wages for a skilled craftsman like the blacksmith; to the peasants here, it was a fortune. Why hadn't I fought more to keep Meg and Poppy away from this cursed harvest?

Lord Norfolk frowned. "We've found no witches here in Oxhaven, my lady."

Bless him for saying that. The musicians moved uneasily on his right, checking their bows and gently plucking strings, awaiting his command.

Lady Adela was not finished. "No witches? You might be deceived in that, my lord. If not the three I seek, there are likely others. I look for ones with powers. Witches breed with Satan in Dragonswood," she reminded, "and their numbers grow."

Sighs and mumbled agreements came up in waves from both sides of the room. Lord Norfolk cleared his throat. "Our sheriff will know any news either of witches or thieves, my lady."

"I have already spoken with the sheriff, sir," Lady Adela said. "My company stays at his manor. I have inspected his new jailhouse and noted too many empty cells there. Your district is lax in our time of trouble, sir, but the cells will not be empty long."

I willed Poppy and Meg to step slowly and carefully toward the back door. Neither of them moved. Lady Adela leaned down and spoke to one of her knights, who marched outside. A servant followed him back in, leading a horse with a body hanging limp over the saddle. I could not tell if the man was alive or dead. His bloody clothes hung in shreds, a filthy hood draped over his head. He'd been dragged behind a horse for some distance, by the look of him.

"I have here a man who consorts with witches," Lady Adela announced, sweeping the crowd with her good eye. "His soul might yet be saved if the witches be found."

Meg was nearly to my hay bales now. I put out my hand. Seeing me, she clasped it. Poppy was now past the ale barrels and nearly to us. *Come on. Hurry.*

"Bring him forward!" ordered Lady Adela. Two knights pulled the man down and dragged him to the front of the room, where they lifted him onto the platform before the high table. Facing the crowd, they held the shrouded man up between them lest his knees give way.

Poppy reached us. Now we were all behind the bales ready to flee, but it must be done stealthily so no one noticed.

"Do you see any here you know?" Lady Adela demanded of the prisoner.

The man's head sagged. The knight to his left raised the man's head puppet-like first by yanking back his hood, then tugging on his matted red hair.

By heaven! Tom. It was Meg's husband, Tom!

Behind the haystack I clapped my hand over Meg's mouth, and felt her body's full weight against mine as she fainted.

"See you anyone you know?" the witch hunter asked Tom again with steely voice. The crowd moved under his gaze. Some stood straighter, some backed up slowly.

Tom moaned. Mouth swollen. Face bloodied. God. Oh, God. What would happen to us? We had to get outside, yet we couldn't move now. All eyes scanned the room wherever Tom was looking.

"Saints protect us," whispered Poppy.

Lady Adela leaned down from her saddle toward Tom. "Cooperate, wastrel, or hang!"

POPPY AND I were dragging Meg over the boundary wall when she woke from her stupor. Three times she tried to bolt and run back to her Tom. I kept my hand firmly pressed over her mouth as we forced her deeper into the trees. She kicked and clawed us every step of the way, mad as a wildcat fighting for her mate.

At last I shoved her down, and firmly tied her to an elm tree. I had no choice just then. Let her go and she would run straight back to Tom and give us all away.

On the ground she kicked and kicked, her skirts flying.

"Stop all your noise!" I hissed. "They'll find us!"

Meg wept, shook her head.

"She will not hang him, Meg," said I for the hundredth time. Meg's eyes were swollen nearly shut from crying.

"She will, Tess. You know she will!"

"I know she will not, Meg. Lady Adela is clever. She uses Tom as bait to draw us out. As long as we stay hidden, she keeps your Tom alive."

"And drags him from town to town," Meg cried.

"Keep your voice down," Poppy warned. "We're not that deep in Dragonswood here."

We'd grabbed our leper robes from the bush. Now

Meg was tied up, we had a chance to put ours on. Even in our costumes we had to be vigilant with the witch hunter close by.

"You know nothing about love," Meg said. "You're both just . . . just girls. Foolish little girls!" She glared at me. "It's your fault she's tortured him!"

I could not swallow. Tears stung my eyes. But I would not give in to the hurt. "Think, Meg," I said. "If we turn ourselves in to save him, we will all be hanged."

"Or burned." Poppy drew her hood up.

"Just let me go by myself, then," Meg pleaded, straining at her tethers.

"You think the witch hunter wouldn't torture you and make you tell her where the rest of us are?" I held out my purple thumbs encrusted with scabs. One black nail remained. The other had fallen off.

Meg grunted. "What about Tom? Doesn't anyone care what she's done to him? What she might be doing . . . to him even now? Oh." Eyes closed, she banged the back of her head against the trunk again and again. Poppy grabbed Meg's discarded robe and jammed it in behind her skull to cushion the blows.

I paced until Meg stopped banging. Meg was right. I had to find a way. We couldn't leave Tom with the witch hunter. Even now she could be taking him back to his cell. This very night Tom might be hung up from the rafters till it felt as if his arms would rip from their sockets.

Meg peered up at me, with eyes red as yew berries. "I . . . I have to go to Tom. Tell him I love him, and that I am sorely sorry he is hurt." She paused, gulped. "And ask him if . . . if my little Alice—" She stopped to sob, caught her breath, and went on. "If my . . . Alice is safe."

"Oh, the witch hunter wouldn't harm your Alice, dear heart," crooned Poppy. How Poppy saw the best in everyone I could not tell. Her lack of guile endangered us sometimes, but I wouldn't have traded her for any other friend at that moment. I saw her words calmed Meg a little.

I bent down to her. "I'll think of something, Meg. I promise. Just give me a little time."

Tupkin padded up in the dark, curled up on Meg's lap, and bathed his extended hind leg with his tongue.

"Get off, Tup," Poppy said.

Meg sniffed. "No, let him stay. He warms me."

Tupkin purred. Even *he* was kinder to Meg than I was being just now.

"I know it's my fault. All of it."

"That's true," Poppy said, not bothering to look up at me.

Meg sniffed and nodded, so all agreed. Guilt for what I'd done to my friends heaped up high as a hillside in me. If I couldn't think of a way to help Tom, how could Meg ever forgive me? How could I forgive myself? *You'll have to rescue him. Think.*

"Poppy, promise me you'll stay with Meg. Watch her and don't untie her. I have to come up with a solid plan."

"Leave us alone here in Dragonswood?"

"I won't go far."

"Dragons and fey patrol it. We're not safe, Tess."

"Safer here from the witch hunter than anywhere else," I argued. But a sight flashed in my mind. The swordsman I'd seen in the fire. My fire-sight did not lie. Would he come for us tonight? Would he find us and cut us down? I feared him most of all.

I pulled the knife I'd taken from Lord Norfolk's table. "I'll keep you in my sights. Just let me go and think."

Meg said, "Go then." No trusting look from her. She spat the words.

I ran but not too far. An owl took off, soaring brown-winged and silent, as I climbed a broad oak. Beyond the forest edge, the fields were empty. The sea was black. The cold night sky above was like a floor swept clean but for the broken glass of many stars. Holding the rough trunk, I pictured Tom's torn body. Had he glimpsed us in the barn? If so he hadn't let on, brave soul. The witch hunter would have thrown him in one of the sheriff's cells by now with men-at-arms guarding him.

In the tree I listed all I had on my side. The knife newly snatched, three leper robes, the love I had for my friends, and finally, justice, for surely it was just to set Tom free.

Chapter Nine

MEG AND POPPY hid in the juniper bushes with me at the sheriff's walled-off manor. "Saint Barbara watch over us," I prayed. Jailed by her wicked father, and later murdered by same, Barbara was avenged when God in his goodness struck the man with lightning for his crime.

Meg and Poppy crossed themselves. "Amen." Meg stripped off her robe. "Let me come."

"No, Meg."

"Give me your knife."

"What for?" This wasn't in my plan.

She put out her hand. "I only need it for a moment."

Shearing off a small lock of her hair, she tucked it in the hood and handed me her robe. "Tell Tom—" She couldn't finish. Crying soundlessly, she kissed me on the cheek. "Oh, Tess, thank you, Tess." Her kiss bolstered me as nothing else could. It also doubled my fear. I knew Meg would be deeply crushed if we failed. She might even do something foolish like turn herself in for the love of Tom.

"Ready, Poppy?" I whispered.

"I wish I had a basket for these rolls," she said, holding out the three I'd taken from the harvest table.

"You'll do fine." Pulling Meg's extra robe over mine, I felt along the wall, found a handhold, and started up. Once on top, I lay flat, taking in the sheriff's manor house, the lit windows where dark figures moved. The building was a long way from the wall, so the figures looked quite small. The stone jailhouse was set apart on the opposite end of the expansive yard. I knew it by the barred windows all at ground level.

Someone approached. Knife in hand, I held still and heard laughter as men passed through the rose garden, their feet crunching on the pebbles. In the distance, a door slammed. When all was clear, I held my hand down to Poppy. It took her a while to scale the wall even with my help, but she made it and we jumped down into the dark garden and raced through the roses with our heads low.

We waited behind a garden bench, where Poppy re-moved and hid her leper robe. Straightening her skirts, she boldly went up the stairs and opened the door.

"I brought some rolls from the kitchen. I don't think the sheriff will mind."

"Well now, isn't that nice of ye?"

The voice of a single guard. Good.

"Oh, I should've brought some honey along." The word *honey* was Poppy's signal that she'd gotten the guard to turn away from the door. I flew up the steps and slipped inside on silent feet.

"Well, you're sweet ta think of honey, missy. I'll wager you're sweet all round."

Even now his hands were on her waist. Poor Poppy. Still, she laughed and batted her pretty blue eyes at the man so I could snatch the key ring from the wall and slip down the steps for the cells.

The torchlight from the walls fell in piss-yellow pools on the floor. I peered cell to cell. Most were empty, but a few housed prisoners huddled on straw in a corner: men or women, it was hard to tell. Around the corner I spied a sleeper through the bars with a shock of red hair. Tom. My breath quickened. I fiddled with the keys, trying one after another with sweaty hand. At last the iron lock clicked. Inside, I closed the door quietly. Tom slept on his back in the straw with arms out wide like Christ crucified. I thanked Saint Barbara for guiding me safely thus far.

"Tom?"

A stirring in the straw, a head looking up, a disgusted gasp. "Unclean! Do they send a leper to infect me now?"

I ran to him, whispering, "Hush. It's me, Tess."

He sat up drunkenly, his torso swaying side to side, though wounds, not wine, caused the sway. "Tess? What now? Is Meg here?" It was a strangled whisper. "What cell did the fiend witch hunter put my Meg in?"

"Meg is safe," I whispered. "I'm here to rescue you."

Tom crawled back a little toward the corner.

"Trust me. I did not turn Meg in." On my knees I told him my plan. "Do you think you can walk?"

"I am a man." He was offended. Perhaps I should not have asked, but even in this gloom I could see his cuts and oozing sores.

Putting a hand to the wall, he stood, the hay coming off his person in hunks as he leaned against the wall for support.

I took off Meg's leper robe. "Put this on."

He stared at it.

I fished a curly red lock from the folded hood. "Meg sent this to you for luck." Tom kissed it once, and painfully put on the robe: His every limb was raw.

"What now?" he asked.

"Tear what clothing you can from beneath your robe." He tore easily. His clothes were already in shreds.

"Use this one to cover the bottom half of your face. I'll take the rest."

Tom hid his face in the smelly rag. I piled the straw again, laying the larger rags in clumps overtop in the appearance of a sleeping man. I helped Tom across the cell, whispering my plan to him, locking the door behind, then peered through the small window bars placed high in the door to satisfy myself the rag pile might pass for a prisoner. We crept round the corner for the stairs.

"You will see Poppy entertaining the guard above."

Entertaining? I thought, disgusted, but went on. "Follow my lead out the door, then do as we planned."

I waited on the top stair with Tom a step below. Poppy caught my eye. "Now you make a girl blush, sir." She opened the door as if to go.

"Aw, don't go just yet," said the turnkey. Poppy shrugged and deftly lured him to the opposite corner. With the turnkey's back to us, I hung the key ring and scurried out the open door with Tom behind. If we'd cleared out unseen, Poppy could leave soon after, but the turnkey spotted Tom on the stairs.

"Hey!"

"Now," I whispered.

Tom lurched back inside as if he'd just burst in from the cold. I watched his performance from the shadowy porch.

"Please." Tom thrust out his bloodstained hands. "Take pity on a leper. Put me in a cell."

Poppy backed away. "Get back, leper," she cried.

The startled turnkey shouted, "Unclean!" covering his face in the crook of his left arm.

"A cell," insisted Tom. "Have mercy, sir." He took another step toward the frightened guard. "I'm starving. Even prisoners are given bread."

Poppy fled out the door and down the steps; behind the bench she slipped on her robe and tied a rag about her face. Now if any more men should come upon us, we were three lepers here to beg for shelter, though Tom was the only one within. I drew my knife outside the door. The turnkey sliced the air with his sword. "Outside, leper, before I plant this in your chest!" Sweat melted a buttery slime down my neck. I envisioned Tom impaled at the end of the sword.

"Take pity on us lepers," I called from the door.

"Another one? By the saints, where are you vermin coming from? Get away now before I kill you all!"

Moaning, Tom backed up and stumbled down the steps with me.

"And don't come back!" The turnkey slammed the door.

Saint Barbara took pity on Tom, lending him the strength to make it through the garden. Poppy and I propped him between us. Feeling his weight, the metal scent of blood, I prayed lightning would strike Lady Adela for what she'd done to Tom just as God in his mercy struck Saint Barbara's murderous father.

Fresh blood seeped from Tom's wounds as we helped him over the wall, yet when we reached the bushes I saw such kisses as I'd never seen between man and woman. Poppy looked down, quietly giggling, but I did not turn away. Tom could barely stand, yet he had his arms about Meg and sought to hold her up as they kissed. The more I watched, the hungrier I became for what they had. But all hope of love between myself and a man had been beaten out of me years ago.

WE FOUR HID in a cave I found in Dragonswood. It was too dangerous for us to be so near Oxhaven with a bounty on our heads, but we'd no choice. Tom was too sick to move. I couldn't look at his festering wounds without my stomach turning. I was ashamed of my reaction, seeing how carefully Poppy and Meg tended him. *Poppy's used to it*, I told myself. Didn't I always come to her after a beating?

Poppy used her herb sense, though it was mostly guesswork. First she found thunderbesem to tie about Tom's neck to quell the fever. We searched for knapweed or oxeye. Finding none, she and Meg bathed Tom's wounds in water we'd taken from a nearby stream.

The sun hid all the next day. We finished the cheese and apples I'd pilfered from Lord Norfolk's table. Meg wouldn't leave Tom's side. Poppy searched again for healing herbs. Alone, I begged on the road. A boy threw stones. One cut me just below the eye. I returned hours later with only a few mushrooms and snails. We all gagged on the roasted snails. Tom couldn't keep his down. Rain froze in gray puddles, then snow drifted to the forest floor.

That night we were awakened by a dragon's cry that shook me to my bones. The piercing sound sharp as a kestrel's scream echoed through the wood. Tom moaned. Meg and Poppy sat up, hugging each other, shaking in the dark. I shivered, listening to the pumping wings some-where above our cave.

Was it the elder dragon who'd helped me in the pond, who'd rescued the burning girl? If so, should I run out and show myself, ask for his help? We needed help, especially Tom. He would die without intervention soon. Ah, God. I was all confusion huddling with my friends.

Another cry overhead. Meg and Poppy rocked. What if it wasn't the old dragon but another one out patrolling his sanctuary? We were trespassers. Under the law a dragon could oust us, leave us stranded on the road, where Tom would surely die and we'd be captured soon enough. Our fire had gone out. No telltale smoke rose from our hiding place. Rhythmic pumping wings drummed over us, then they diminished as the dragon flew away. After that we huddled in the dark, too fearful to start another fire.

More snow fell our third day of hiding. Poppy left for herbs. When she'd not returned by twilight, I began to worry. I searched the darkening forest, calling *Poppy?* in a half whisper, lest my voice carry all the way out on the road. I saw her figure walking slowly in the snowfall and ran to her, relieved. "Poppy, it's cold. Come back inside by the fire."

She did not seem to see me, could not hear me. Her eyes were wide, and glassy.

"Poppy?" I stopped her. She tried to push ahead. "Poppy, what's the matter, are you ill?"

"North," she said. "Come north." Her face was wet, her lashes flecked with snow. "Poppy, wake up." I shook her.

She blinked, began to weep. "Let me go, Tess. I have to go."

"Go where, Poppy?"

She put her face in her hands and sobbed. I led her back to the cave.

"What's wrong with her?" Meg asked, alarmed.

"I don't know, let her sleep."

Poppy curled up in the corner. She awoke an hour later, sat up, then went right to work helping Meg with Tom. The glassy look had left her eyes. I watched her, still troubled by what I'd seen out in the wood.

That night Tupkin brought us a mud-clotted dove, which I hurriedly plucked, cooked, and shared among us. Two morsels each and we sucked the tiny bones. Tom ate nothing at all. His fever worsened.

Meg asked, "Will you tell us one of your grandfather's stories, Tess?"

I shook my head.

"One about the fairies in DunGarrow," Poppy said, narrowing her eyes at me. *Meg needs a story now,* her look said. *Can't you see it? Can't you see Tom's dying?*

Poppy was right. Meg needed cheering. We all did. I could not bear the idea that Tom might die. But if we tried to move him and find help, we were sure to be captured.

Trapped. I tried to breathe. The smoky air was sour

with the stench of Tom's wounds. "Which story shall it be?" I'd tell them any story at all except one about a fairy turning a man to a Treegrim. I wasn't childish enough to think the fey were innocent, far from it. But my friends were scared enough hiding here in Dragonswood.

Meg said, "Tell 'The Whistler.'"

I cleared my throat. "This is the tale of a young girl who should have known better than to follow a bright bird into the forest, but follow him she did, for his song was like none she'd ever heard before, and she couldn't stop her feet from going after him. How far she walked, she couldn't tell, for day and night seemed the same to her as long as the bird sang. Her hair grew longer as she walked, and the seasons did no harm to her at all, neither rain nor snow bothered her as long as she followed the whistler north. In time she came upon a castle pressed up against a mountain with a waterfall tumbling right down the side of it."

"DunGarrow," whispered Poppy, her face open. I saw her yearning as she listened.

I'd taken up a piece of charcoal from the fire and had begun to draw as I told the tale. It was like being caught up in a dream, the drawing and the telling. I'd been sketching the castle spires when Poppy said *DunGarrow,* and my hand kept moving as I spoke—the story coming alive on the rough cave walls.

"And though she'd reached DunGarrow Castle late at night, she heard music playing in the high meadow across the bridge, and saw figures swirling under fairy lights." I drew dancing fairies as I'd always imagined them. Maidens with their twirling skirts, fine men in well-cut tunics. I even sketched the tiny will-o'-the-wisps. I longed for bright colors to fill in the charcoal lines. My friends' eyes were wide by the fire, and even Tom had one eye open as if he were listening. Where our doctoring had failed, the story might ease his pain.

"The song she heard from the meadow was the same tune as the bird's call. She looked up in the trees. For a moment she thought she'd lost the bird, and she nearly cried out for him, but he fluttered down, landed right at her feet, and grew into a man."

"Oh." Meg sighed. She'd always liked that part.

"He whistled the tune once more, then the fey man said, 'My lady, will you dance?'

"'I will.' She crossed the bridge to the meadow, and danced with the whistler."

"Tell us they married," Meg said.

"The story doesn't go like that," Poppy reminded.

"It should." Meg stroked Tom's blood-clotted hair.

I fumbled with the charcoal in my blackened fingers. As the story went, the girl danced through the seasons, but when she wandered home at last and reached her cottage door, she was a shriveled-up old woman, for a hundred years had passed while she danced with the whistler, and everyone she'd known in her former life had died.

Meg knew how it went. But when our eyes locked, I saw tonight she couldn't bear it. I found another bit of charcoal. "That very spring when the meadow was in bloom, the whistler, who had fey power to transform into a bird and sing any girl he wished to into the wood, chose the one girl who'd followed him so bravely and so far to be his wife. And she lived with him and the fey folk deep in Dragonswood in DunGarrow Castle, a place that blends into the mountainside and cannot be seen with human eyes unless the fairies will it so."

I drew the couple hand in hand, rough sketches on the cave wall; the stone wasn't smooth by any means. "She lived free among the fey folk and never wanted to return to her old life that had been full of hunger and sorrow under her father's roof."

I sketched what came next before I could think of it. "A dragon came to their wedding," I said, drawing his right wing so large, I had to use the ceiling. "He lit a bonfire to celebrate their union." I drew the left wing spanning over the couple in the meadow. "And they lived all their lives content in Dragonswood." I sat exhausted, longing for that girl's happy life over my own.

Meg bent her head over Tom. Her tears fell on his face as she whispered in his ear. Poppy gave me a little nod as if to say, *You've done well*. But changing the story did not change ours. We were trapped with no whistler to come along and sing us into freedom.

PART TWO

The Green Man

❦

Chapter Ten

AT DAWN I heard squealing sounds, hearty snorts, and snuffling. A stick whacked hard against a tree. A dog barked. A man's voice said, "Get on now."

I pressed my back up against the cave wall. My companions slept on, curled up on the hard dirt floor behind me. Should I run to the man for aid? If I did, would he turn us in for the bounty?

Undecided, I huddled inside. A brown-muzzled hound came sniffing. Next a pig poked his snout in and snorted. Poppy and Meg woke with a start. A man's boots appeared. "Move along," he said. The animals barring the entryway didn't budge.

Then the voice said, "Out with you, trespassers, and mind I have a sword at the ready."

We were caught and had no choice but to come out. Meg and Poppy propped Tom up between them. I ducked under the low entrance and stood squinting in the morning sunlight, my knife tucked in my belt under my leper's robe.

The man was not far from us, standing in shadow with his pigs and growling bloodhound.

"We came here only for shelter, Master Woodward," Poppy said.

He stepped from the shadow. It was the woodward I'd seen in Harrowton, and later in the barn.

The man drew his weapon. "I saw you at the harvest feast."

Sunlight speared the clouds, the single beam fired his green tunic, his sword sparked, the brightness burned my eyes. A chill tore through me. The green man from my fire-sight. It was he.

He sliced the air just as he had in my vision. My knees nearly buckled, but I held my place.

"You are in my part of Dragonswood," he said.

"We'll go," Poppy cried. "We promise."

"This man was in Lady Adela's custody."

"Don't turn us in, sir," Meg pleaded.

"Quiet, Meg," I warned. If he wasn't thinking of the bounty money she'd offered for us, he'd recall it now.

"You're the ones the witch hunter is after," he said, putting two and two together with Meg's help.

"We're none of us witches," she went on. "We aren't. We're innocent."

"Stay back!" I drew my knife. It was nothing to his sword, but I could not run and leave my friends here with Tom. *So that was why I didn't run when I saw this in the fire-sight.*

"Why draw your knife, lady?"

"Put away your sword!"

He didn't move. "Harm any one of us and I'll slit your throat," I warned.

"Lady leper," he said. "I have no intention of harming you or your friends if you vacate my wood."

The *lady leper* was in jest. He'd seen Meg and Poppy dancing in the barn and knew we were not infected. "We'll clear out. No one has to know you saw us here."

The woodward tipped his head, gesturing toward the distant boundary wall. "I'll escort you out."

We were less than half an hour's walk from Kingsway Road. I knew, for I'd gone back and forth from it to beg, but Tom was too ill to move his legs. Meg and Poppy grunted, dragging him between them. I would have offered to help, but I had to keep my knife handy in case the woodward turned on us. Our armed escort was growing more and more impatient with our slow progress. At last he stopped. "Your man looks half dead and the rest of you don't look much better." He frowned a moment. "You'll be arrested in a snap once you're exposed." He ran his hand through his hair, paced. "I should not do this, God knows."

Tom moaned. His head rolled forward.

"I'll shelter you four until you're strong enough to go," the woodward said.

I stayed my ground. I was desperate for help, but not stupid. Shelter us and he could lock us in, go off and find the witch hunter, and gather his reward. "Tell us first where you take us."

"The king's hunting lodge is not far off, a few hills over." He pointed. "I am called Garth. As woodward I guard the king's lands, as huntsman I stay in the king's lodge and tend the animals kept there year-round. Call me Garth Huntsman if you like, and come if you wish to stay under my roof until your man here has mended."

"Praise the angels," exclaimed Poppy.

The bloodhound inched up and sniffed my hand. The huntsman said, "Stop that, Horace." Horace stepped away with his tail between his legs.

I was still wary. This man had vanished from his corner when Lady Adela rode in. Still, he'd recognized Tom, so he must have slipped deeper into the shadows in the barn and stayed long enough to hear Lady Adela's offer to pay good tender for us. "How do we know you won't turn us in?"

"You can't be certain what I'll do," he agreed. "But your man will die without help."

"We'll go with you," said Meg hurriedly.

I stayed put, my hand on my knife.

"Tess!"

"Quiet, Meg!"

"Tess," he said, hearing my name and calling me by it for the first time. "By my troth, I won't turn you in," he said. "I will not feed the witch hunter any more logs for her fire!"

There was no trace of deceit in his face, his eyes fully fixed on me and his sword down now, his hand gripping the hilt, but gently.

"Not even for the bounty, sir?"

"Stubborn girl, my own grandmother was tried for witchcraft! She was made to walk the coals. Does that satisfy you?" His chin was high, and shoulders tense. He glowered at me for pushing him to this confession.

She'd made an old woman walk the coals? That practice was outlawed in Queen Rosalind's time. "I am sorry to hear it, sir," I said clumsily.

Garth Huntsman took up a stick and nudged the pigs out of their wallowing hole. "Stay here if you like. It's all the same to me."

"Tess!" Meg pleaded. "Think of Tom."

So it was we followed Garth Huntsman, his pigs and old hound, Horace, to the king's lodge. On the way the huntsman bid me herd the pigs so he could help Meg with Tom. "One of you was clever enough to come up with a way to break the law and spring your man here."

"That's Tess," said Meg proudly, nodding in my direction. The huntsman looked at me with something close to admiration. I felt my cheeks flush, and covered my unsightly cauliflower ear with my hair.

The king's hold was but a few miles from our cave. On a windy hilltop we gazed down at the fenced land where sheep wandered in the grassy fields. The large, central lodge was built of river stones, but barn, kennels, and other outbuildings were all of wood. No smoke rose over the lodge, though the day was chill.

I marveled that food and shelter was so close by. If the huntsman had come upon us a few days later, he'd have likely found four dead souls within. The thought sent cold fingers up my spine. We went downhill, through gate and snow-covered garden. A toothless old man leaning against the chicken coop smoking his pipe hailed us as we passed.

"That's Jim Cackler, or just plain Cackle if you like," said Garth Huntsman. "He keeps an eye on the animals for me." The bent man looked too feeble to walk much farther than from house to barn and back. He stood to bang his pipe bowl against the coop, the effort seeming to take something out of him; still, he took the stick from my hand and herded the pigs into the pigpen.

We crossed the muddy yard through scattered rugs of melting snow and waited on the porch for Garth Huntsman to pull out his iron key. The iced-over vegetables and herbs in the side yard had wilted in the unseasonable cold. The sight of any food, however spoiled, made my stomach growl. I blushed at the sound.

Tupkin saved me further embarrassment with a loud meow. He bounded up to the porch, ready for a cozy spot inside by the master's hearth. Horace bumped him aside and barked indignantly; that got him a loud hiss and a good scratch on the nose. The dog's surprised yelp made me jump. I bumped Tom, who moaned.

"Sorry, Tom," I said. "We'll have you in bed soon. See? We've arrived." Tom did not even have the strength to raise his head.

"Cat stays out," the huntsman said, pushing open the kitchen door.

"Oh, but sir," Poppy pleaded. "Tupkin meant no harm."

"Tell that to Horace."

Tom's room was close to the kitchen, the more to tend to his wounds with what ointments and herbs we might mix and boil. Garth built a fire in the room. Poppy and I turned our backs while Meg undressed Tom, so our host might view the full extent of his wounds.

"I've seen this type of thing before," he said. "Infection causes fever. We must cleanse the wounds to bring the fever down."

"Will he be all right?" Meg whispered.

"We'll do what we can," Garth said.

I went out to the well for water and hung my head over the side, breathing in the dark underwater smell. *Don't give in to this hospitality no matter how tired you are. Stay alert. Guard your friends.* I sucked in the damp air praying for courage.

It took two buckets full to clean the wounds. Meg and Poppy worked patiently. I stood aside, feeling useless as ever in the sickroom. I could have been helpful in some other way if this were my house, my kitchen, but it was not. Anon the huntsman used wine on the abrasions and spread egg whites on the sores. We left Tom sleeping soundly in the room.

On the bench at the kitchen table I sat with Meg and Poppy in my damp and stinking robes. Garth Huntsman and Cackle served us pears, some hard rye bread, and glory of all glories, cheese and honey! Before we ate, our host filled our fingerbowls with cleansing water from a copper ewer.

I imagined our Pendragon king and his grown sons using the slender-spouted ewer and the fine fingerbowls to wash their hands in before they supped. I rinsed my fingers humbly and tried to hide my unsightly thumbs as I did so.

The huntsman slipped outside with Horace and did not eat with us in the kitchen. Cackle followed him out, a hunk of honeyed bread in his fist.

"Huntsman's good to us," Poppy said with a full mouth.

"Maybe too good," I said.

Meg spread honey on her bread. "Why say that, Tess?"

"You know as well as I this could all be a trick to win our trust. He settles us in, then off he goes to the sheriff or to Lady Adela for the bounty money." I knew better than to trust a man. Even Grandfather had vanished in my hour of need.

"He wouldn't turn us in," Poppy said, licking the

honey from her fingers noisily. We needed his help. Tom most of all. I was just as desperate as they were for a safe haven. Still, I'd seen him in the fire-sight, not just once, but twice. Couldn't it have been a warning? I'd promised to bring my friends to safety. It was foolhardy to let go my vigilance now only to be trapped.

Meg went back to Tom. Outside, the huntsman was chopping wood by the shed. I stood in the doorway with Poppy watching as he swung his ax up high and brought it down with a loud crack. The wood split. The pigs ran in circles, squealing in their pen.

He raised his ax again. Dizzy, I clung to the door. The floor pitched like a ship's deck.

From far away I heard Poppy's voice. "Tess? Are you all right? Tess?"

All went black.

They must have carried me to the bed. It was dark when I awoke. I did not know how late it was, how long I'd lain in blackness. I gripped the covers, remembering the sound of breaking wood, the pigs squealing in their pen. It had taken me back to the last time my father had beaten me, the day after Adam died.

Through the open kitchen door, Mother and I had seen my father out in the backyard. He'd placed the baby's cradle on the low stone wall dividing our yard from Todd Shoemaker's. Grandfather had fashioned the pinewood cradle for me when I was newly born. It was smooth and deftly made with vines and playful animals carved around the rim, and I loved it dearly. I'd rocked many of Mother's babes in it. Adam was the last to sleep there. None had lived long enough to need a larger bed.

The heat from the backyard fire pit sent a polished shine through the air. My father's form seemed to waver in the warm air as if beneath a river. The darting flames hid his right side from me.

"What's he got in his hand, Mother?"

"Mallet," she whispered.

At the wall my father swung the mallet. The smashing sound as it hit the cradle rang across the yard. Shoemaker's pigs squealed and ran in circles.

"God's teeth! What's the fool doing?" I raced outside.

"Tess, don't!" Mother caught up to me outside and pulled my sleeve. "Come back into the kitchen before you're hurt."

He was in the mood to bash and would strike me if I weren't careful; still I tore myself away. The cradle rested lopsided now on the four-foot wall. I put out my hands, speaking as softly as I could. "You don't mean to do this, Father. You'll be sorry for it later. Let me have the cradle."

He waved the mallet overhead. "Get back, girl! A witch curse is on it. Come any closer and I'll clout ye!"

"The cradle's not cursed," I said in a coaxing tone. "Who told you so?"

Roaring, he pivoted on his heel and split open the side of the cradle. A foot-long splinter flew over the wall into the pigsty. The pigs scattered.

"Give it to me. I'll mend it." I darted forward, grabbed the cradle. Father dropped the mallet. With a mighty tug, he wrested the cradle from me. Hurling it aside, he punched me in the eye, knocking me onto my backside. I lay in the dirt, the sky spinning overhead.

"Tess. Oh, Tess." Mother knelt down. I covered my eye, the pain fierce and stabbing.

"Leave her be, Merriam!" Father warned, his looming figure swimming in and out of view.

"Get up," he said, kicking me in the side.

"John," Mother said. "Don't."

"Woman, don't defy me!"

I stood, swaying. "Who t-told you my cradle was cursed?"

"Joan Midwife."

I stepped back, reeling. A sob tore up my throat. Never had I let myself cry in front of Father no matter how hard he hit me. The sob turned to a roar. "Damn the flea-bitten hag! Devil take her! Adam's death has nothing to do with my cradle. It's her fault and I told her so when I demanded our money back for her useless sticklewort! She's the one who snores while Mother's in pain. She doesn't lift a hand to help Mother or see the babe is strong before she runs off with her fee. Then when the babe sickens, the biddy has the nerve to sell her useless herbs at a high price so she can buy fresh market meat."

The storm shook me to the core, but I couldn't stop till all was said. "What's it to her if the child dies?" I screamed. "Joan Midwife's the one to blame for Adam's death, his and all the others, Father! She's the witch!"

A week after we'd fought in the backyard, the witch hunter came.

I could not sleep for hours. How carelessly I'd used the word *witch* in my anger and my grief. The midwife had called me a witch when I'd gone after our money. But did it matter which one of us said it first? Between us we'd released hellfire.

Sometime much later in the night, I fell into a dreamless sleep in the unfamiliar bed.

Chapter Eleven

Here you are," said Poppy, coming into the room. "You gave us all a scare."

"I'm all right." I sat up slowly looking around. A warm fire blazed. A child's brightly painted rocking horse sat before shelves lined with books.

"How long have I slept?"

"All night and half the day. Garth Huntsman insisted we share the room that I might watch out for you and let him know when you awakened."

"Don't."

"Don't what?"

"Don't let him know I'm awake, Poppy."

She ignored my comment. "There's chamomile tea," she said. "I'll put honey in it for you. Oh, isn't it grand we're here, Tess?"

"I don't know," I said, confused.

"I'll fetch the tea and you'll feel better soon."

"Where is your leper's robe?" I asked her suddenly. "Where is mine? And who took my knife?"

I stood swaying by the bed, then had to sit again.

"The robes stink, Tess. We don't need them here."

"My knife," I insisted shakily.

"It's in the kitchen where it belongs, Tess."

"The knife belongs with me." Meg and Poppy were so ready to receive the huntsman's kindness, but was it kindness? How could we be so sure? I'd blame myself if he was only after the bounty money. "Where is the huntsman?"

"Here, why?"

"Did he leave while I slept?" I tried to calculate how long it would take to ride from this hunting lodge back to Oxhaven, but my mind was still too hazed with sleep.

"He was gone this morning."

"For how long? Was he on horseback?"

"On foot, and why are you asking so many questions? You have me reeling, Tess."

"I won't be tricked, Poppy."

"He's been nothing but honorable since we came here."

"We need our disguises," I insisted. "What if we have to run? Tell me where they are."

"Oh for God's sake!" Poppy marched out and returned to heave a reeking bundle on the floor by my bed.

"Here!" she said. "You can have them all. And the knife you insist on having. And now you're awake, you can make your own tea and see if I care!" With that, she slammed the door.

I'd have stayed in the room, but I needed to use the privy.

I'd slept in my black kirtle, and the rags I'd wrapped about my blistered feet while on the road. I got up and waited for dizziness to pass. I'd grown thin on the road and was as much a shadow wraith as a girl. I checked the tall wardrobe and was relieved to find my cloak inside. Wearing the leper's robe over my cloak while on the run had protected it so it wasn't fouled with dirt. I slid my feet into my shoes.

It was raining hard outside. The wind was chill. I returned from the outside privy, walking soft-footed (or so I thought) through the long corridor, when I heard a voice call, "Tess?"

In the room on my left, three stuffed chairs were drawn up by the fire. The voice came from the largest, high-backed chair.

"Sir?" I leaned against the doorframe. I was still soul tired and wanting my bed, if not to sleep, at least to rest and think. I needed to come up with a sound plan to save my friends if this man betrayed us.

Garth Huntsman said, "Come here and sit awhile."

I went to the hearth, but did not sit.

The huntsman sprawled comfortably in his stuffed chair, a finely embroidered one that King Kadmi likely used at one time. Horace slept at his master's feet, his long, soft ears spread on the floor like wings.

The man eyed my dripping hair. "Wet day out," he said. I did not reply. I wasn't about to say I'd had to go outside to the privy.

A book lay open on the table by his pewter mug. So the man could read? The woodward who patrolled our southern section of Dragonswood was a simple man, some said a lazy one, who couldn't read or write. More books filled the shelves by the window. Thin volumes of poetry, thicker works on history, castle defense, and weaponry, things such as a king or his grown sons might read. The poetry, I thought, might have belonged to Queen Lucinda. It made me sad to think of our queen who died in childbirth four years back.

The huntsman poked his thumb in and out of the pewter mug handle like a turtle peeking out of his shell. "Tell me, how did you manage to spring Tom?"

I curled my toes in my wet shoes. The clean room made me all too aware of my sour, sweat-stained kirtle. I drew my hair over my marred ear. "Why do you wish to know, sir?"

The huntsman looked up. Again I was surprised by the contrast of his light eyes against his sun-darkened face.

"Poppy and I climbed over the sheriff's manor wall, sir." I edged my damp shoes closer to the blaze. The path between lodge and privy was icy. My feet were very cold.

"You need not call me sir. Call me Garth," he said. "You both went over the wall. Then what did you do?"

"I filched the keys while Poppy entertained the guard."

His brow went up at the word *entertained.* I ignored it and told him how I'd gone to Tom's cell, then how Tom had tricked the turnkey disguised as a leper.

"Ah! Fear of contagion!" He laughed. "Tom begged for a cell and the frightened man pushed him right out the door."

I smiled a little. "The leper's garb is a good disguise."

"Until now," Garth noted. "Lady Adela will have heard all about Tom's clever escape. She'll be looking out for lepers now."

I felt the shock of what he said, but of course it was true. The stinking pile by my bed was useless. We couldn't guise ourselves that way again. Now what would we do?

Low flames burned russet in the hearth. Garth extended his long legs and crossed them at the ankles. There was an ease of confidence in him as if he knew he was strong and did not have to prove himself to anyone. *It's well he's our protector if that's what he truly is.*

The huntsman leaned forward and pumped the leather bellows. Sparks skittered up from the burning logs. "You know I break the law bringing you and your little mob to the king's lodge," he said as he pumped. Ah, he'd been too rash, and regretted his decision now. I couldn't blame him.

"I wouldn't endanger you after your kindness to us, Garth Huntsman." Trembling, I made a quick decision, and spoke before I weakened. "Now you've fed us and all, I'll leave before dawn and take Poppy with me. We are both strong. But if you would keep Tom a while longer?" My knees were putty. "And Meg too, being that she's his wife. If you could let them stay on so the man won't die on my account."

"On your account?" He stopped pumping and gave a startled laugh. "I saw what the witch hunter did to Tom. Was it you who captured him, tethered him to a horse, and dragged him through the streets?"

My legs folded. I sank into a chair. I might as well have beaten Tom myself. But I'd not say that to the huntsman. He was not my confessor.

"I've upset you. Are you hungry? Do you need something to drink?"

I shook my head. Still Garth left for the kitchen and returned with an apple and a mug of ale. I took the ale gratefully, drank too fast, and belched into my hand.

"Sorry, sir," I whispered.

"It seems you were thirsty after all."

I put the mug down and ate the apple.

Garth swished his beer. "Lady Adela thinks she'll clear the island of witches, but there are too many accused, and too many burned."

I'd thought the same myself. I didn't doubt there were witches abroad who practiced evil spells. Hadn't a coven tortured Lady Adela? Put out her eye? But still.

"I've thought many of the women aren't witches at all." I blushed saying this. We three friends had discussed this on the road, but it was rash to convey such radical ideas to a stranger.

Garth looked at me for a long while. Rain pounded the windows. My mind raced as I tried to think of ways to soften what I'd said. No words came. Then he surprised me.

"The townsfolk seem eager enough to point out all the witches to Lady Adela. Why do you think that is?" he asked.

"Folk are angry with their lot."

"And what is their *lot* as you see it, Tess?"

Was he teasing me? I couldn't tell. It might be incautious to say more, but I was numbed by my long journey, eased by ale, and it seemed too late to turn the argument to another course. At home I'd get a split lip for voicing my opinion, but unlike any man I'd ever known, he appeared genuinely interested in what I had to say. "Many people are hungry. Men can't feed their families. With hunger comes disease. You've heard of Lord Sackmoore's new grain tax?"

"I have. Not a wise move in these times," he added.

"We saw men die in a riot for food. They rushed into Dragonswood to hunt game and were slaughtered. Brutally so."

His face hardened. "If they'd come in here I would have booted them out, by God."

His flash of anger was all too familiar. *Run if you have to.*

"But there was no need to kill them," he added. "Lord Sackmoore has a lot to answer for. King Kadmi wouldn't have put such a strain on his people."

My hands were filthy on the armrests; I put them in my lap and tucked my damaged thumbs in. "Suffering is not a new thing. Children sicken. Babes die—" Remembering Adam, I nearly choked on the words before managing to continue. "Men lose their children or their women when they die in childbirth—"

Garth gave a start and set down his mug. "Go on, Tess."

"I won't. I've troubled you." Had his mother died birthing him or a younger sibling? Or was he thinking of Queen Lucinda? Garth was twenty or twenty-one by my guess, and would have been a young man of sixteen or so when the queen died.

"Do go on, Tess," he insisted. "It's been a long while since I've spoken to anyone by this fireside, so I mean to hear your theory out."

"All right." I'd not reached the meat of my argument, the reasons why folk produced witches in every town. "Seeing their loved ones sicken and die, folk look for someone to blame so they say, 'The midwife's a witch' or if the cow sickens and the milk sours, they say, 'Yon girl hexed our cow and stanked the milk.' They're careful to pick a weak old woman or an unwed girl who's poor. Not the wife of a powerful man in the town." I thought of Jane Fine, whose only sin that I could see was that she chose to live alone and make a living by selling her pretty candles. I'd looked up to her as a girl and wanted to be like her.

"Or," Garth added, "if a child goes sick, the mother might point and say, 'That woman hexed my little boy and gave him the pox.'"

I nodded. "That sort of thing. So by this they cast all their woes on a single soul and burn her. As if that will make their hardships disappear in the flames."

The muscles in Garth's jaw worked as he stared at the poker. "The witch hunter should be reined in," he said. "If I had the power to do it . . ." He squeezed the rim of his mug as if to strangle it. I was very close to him in my chair, and tensed. I knew how a man's anger built up sometimes slow, sometimes fast, but by degrees. First came the tight-jawed talking under the breath, then fists forming, muscles rippling down the arms, after that came shouting and blows.

He's angry with Lady Adela, not me, but I'm handy. Get out of the room. No. Fearful looks and sudden bursts for the door might intensify his rage. One time when I'd tried to run after Father discovered I'd forgotten to empty his chamber pot, he'd grabbed me hard enough to break my arm.

The door is but fifteen paces back: If I rise slowly and creep out even slower . . .

My soaking shoes steamed by the fire. Garth noted my shivering—whether from fear or cold or both, I couldn't keep still. His eyes followed the steam rising from my shoes.

Of a sudden, he went down on one knee. "You're cold," he said, pulling one shoe off and then the other.

Speech left me. A husband might touch a girl's ankle,

remove her shoes. I hardly knew this man. The stinking cloth wrapped round my feet against the cold hung in gray shreds. Horrified, I grabbed my shoes and made for the door.

From behind he called, "If I keep those two I might as well keep you and Poppy. The law does not change whether I harbor two fugitives or four."

I wondered why he would risk so much for us. I turned and spoke from the hall. "You're under the king's protection living here as master of his hunting lodge."

Garth rubbed the armrest. "The king won't be coming here again," he said in a low voice. He stood and turned his back, arms crossed, one hand covering his black armband.

I bit my cheek for bringing up King Kadmi so lightly. There was a brutal long silence between us broken only by crackling noises from the fire.

"Go back to your friends," he said at last.

I fled down the hall, chastened.

Chapter Twelve

THE NEXT MORNING at dawn, Garth Huntsman rode out to fetch a healer. He said he knew someone who might have the skills to save Tom. I roused Poppy. We cleaned the filthy kitchen, chased the mice with the broom, dumped the flour fouled with mouse droppings, and used the rest to mix bread dough.

By forenoon Tom's fever worsened. Red-eyed, he spoke to the shadows in the room. There are strange tales of shadow wraiths in our land, spirits that haunt the dying and steal the very life-breath out of them.

Meg looked at me, her eyes wild with fear.

"Tom's babbling is fever-driven," I said. The dark patches creeping along the walls could be only lack of sunlight in his room. I swiftly drew the drapes to let in the October sun, weak as it was. Sweeping the cobwebbed corners, I also said a prayer to Saint Agricola, defender against misfortune.

We made a hearty lamb-bone soup, and Tom sipped a

little of it. After lunch, Garth still hadn't returned with the healer. Our worry increased to agitation. Egg whites on the sores had failed. We had no agate stone to place upon Tom's forehead to draw out the fever. I brought Meg and Poppy cold, wet cloths, and a little wine for Tom.

Garth had told us all to stay indoors, *for our own protection,* he'd said, but after bathing Tom's burning skin, Poppy went out to gather herbs. I did not try and stop her, I was that worried over Tom. Returning to the kitchen breathless, she dropped stinging nettles she'd carried in her skirts on the sideboard.

"We'll seethe the nettles, strain the liquid, and let Tom drink it from a wooden spoon."

Tupkin tried to sneak inside. I shooed him out and shut the door. Drink nettles? I knew the stinging welts nettles left on the skin. "How came you by this remedy?"

Poppy shrugged, her pale hair in tangles and a bit of moss hanging from the tips.

"I've not heard tell of the cure," said I. "Did Beulah teach you this?" Her housekeeper had the simple healer's knowledge of women raised out in the countryside. It was from her that Poppy gleaned herb-sense.

Poppy shook her head.

"Then who did?"

"I can't remember, Tess." She tugged the moss from her hair and stared at it.

We'd relied on Poppy's knack for finding wild onions

and mushrooms while on the run, and many times my friend had salved my abrasions, and helped Beulah set my broken arm. But Poppy's remedies were guesswork as often as not. Once back home when I gave Mother licorice root boiled in vinegar as Poppy had instructed, Mother turned green and vomited. We could not afford to sicken Tom.

"If you can't remember where you heard of it, how do we know it won't harm Tom?"

Poppy kicked the table. "Would I do that? Would I ever?" Her pink face grew pinker.

"Not purposefully," I said, "but Tom's too sick to take chances on—"

Poppy snatched a pot and went to the well for more water. She would boil the nettles herself, and press her cure on Tom.

"We shouldn't risk it!" I called through the door. Tom might be dying, and the wrong cure could be fatal. Outside, Poppy grunted as she yanked the well rope. Tupkin paced at her feet.

Cursing under my breath, I swept Poppy's muddy prints from the kitchen floor. How much longer before Garth returned? He'd ridden out on the black stallion leading the blond mare on her tether, a second horse for the healer, I supposed. But I wondered once again if we'd been too trusting. The man had told us to stay in the lodge. Was that to protect us, or did he mean to trap us? The green man swung his sword just as I'd seen him do in the fire. He hadn't killed us then. Could it still have been a warning?

I swept the dirt outside in three broad strokes. *The law does not change whether I harbor two fugitives or four.* How long did he mean to hide us? Garth had an occupation and did not seem needy. But might he lose his post at the hunting lodge now King Kadmi was dead? In these times when work is hard to come by and hunger isn't far from any door, a man with no hope of future wages might be tempted to collect a handsome bounty.

I set the broom against the wall and wiped my damp hands. *Garth's also a king's woodward.* Even with the hunting lodge in disuse, there were animals to keep (with little aid from Cackle, I was sure), and woodwards were needed year-round to guard Dragonswood. More had been hired to ride through the forest and search the caves after the king's treasure was stolen. I imagined that was part of Garth's job now, though he hadn't mentioned it to us. Perhaps he'd come to search our cave the morning he found us? Four starving waifs appeared instead of gold and jewels.

The bread was done. I took it from the oven and set the steaming loaves by Poppy's nettle pile on the sideboard. If he had only gone for the healer, we should stay.

But I'd seen him the first time down in Harrowton. What was a woodward from so far north doing there?

Why come the very day the witch hunter arrived? Why had I seen him the second time only minutes before Lady Adela rode through the barn door? He could be a spy in her pay. If he'd gone after the law, we should run while we had the chance. *But Tom is too sick to move. And Meg will keep by him no matter what.* By the saints! I fairly boiled with indecision.

Feeling I'd go mad in the oven-warmed kitchen, I gathered Poppy's nettles in my skirt, careful not to touch them, raced out, and dumped them in the mud behind the privy.

Back out front by the well, I spoke with Poppy.

"We can't run off!" she argued.

"I know Tom cannot, and Meg won't because of Tom, but what if it's a trap, Poppy?"

"It's not a trap. Why are you so distrustful, Tess?"

"And why are you so trusting after all that's happened to us? I'm the one responsible and I tell you I'm wary."

"Leave, then." Poppy turned her back and ladled water into the cook pot.

I marched out to the henhouse to confront Cackle.

"What is your master's plan, Cackle?" I demanded.

He looked up from his whittling. "Plan, missy?"

"Has he gone to fetch a healer like he said, or gone for the sheriff?"

"Why'd he go ta sheriff?" he asked, perplexed. I could see Cackle knew nothing of our situation. Fuming, I raced for the barn. All I could think to do was to hide there.

Should the huntsman return to arrest us, I'd escape unseen and come after my friends wherever they were jailed. A flimsy plan, but for what it was worth, I squatted in the corner, to peer out a low knothole.

Tupkin padded in and settled purring by my feet. "You'll come away too, will you?" I whispered, but even he would stay with Poppy if it should come to that. In the straw I waited, spying foreyard and lodge till our host returned.

AN HOUR BEFORE sunset Garth rode in with the lady leech. How glad I was. I'd give the woodward a thick slice of freshly baked bread this eve. I was surprised the leech was a woman. Most leeches were male, but Mistress Aisling inspected Tom's wounds and she went right to work.

Meg stood and swayed, exhausted from her long vigil with Tom. Crying with relief, she stepped away from the bed and leaned against me. I eased her onto the bed on the opposite side of the room, where I removed her shoes. Poppy rolled up her sleeves and helped Aisling without a word between them as if they'd often worked together. The lusty leeches on Tom's chest grew fat with foul blood, sucking out the corrupt humors. Would God they might restore Tom's health.

Garth entered the sickroom, leaned against the corner wall, and watched us with arms crossed. He was completely still, yet his eyes darted from Poppy's face, to her profile, to her small waist and round backside. The man stared hungrily at her as if she were made of pudding. I knew Poppy's seductive beauty worked like a love-hex on most men.

The room grew hot. I headed for the well. Steam rose from the fresh horse droppings on the muddy ground. In the sty, Garth's pigs rolled joyous in the muck. I should be glad Garth was besotted with Poppy. If he liked her well enough to wed her, I'd have one less friend to worry about. Poppy would be safe here at the hunting lodge, and didn't she deserve this after all I'd put her through?

At the well I breathed in the pine-scented wind. Morgesh Mountain towered in the distance. The fairy realm lay somewhere in those foothills. All this time as I'd run from the witch hunter, I was drawing closer to Dun-Garrow. The thought eased me a little.

"I am glad Garth likes her," I said to myself as I filled the pitcher.

I returned to the sick chamber, where Poppy thanked me for the wet cloths for Tom's fevered head.

"Will Tom strengthen?" I asked.

Aisling set a third leech on Tom's shoulder, and shrugged off her shawl. "We will see."

Now her shawl was off, I was surprised at the quality of her deep blue gown laced up the front with leaves embroidered on the sleeves. Truth be told, the only female leech

I knew lived with her ailing husband by the docks, grubbing what coins she could for her service. Folk mostly used Tidas Leech, trusting a man's powers over a woman's. But Mistress Aisling was no ordinary healer. With full lips, blond hair touched with gray, and dark eyes, she was uncommonly pretty.

"Will your husband miss you while you are away?" I asked.

"I'm not married. I live alone and travel as I please."

She'd chosen leeching over marriage and motherhood? How had Mistress Aisling managed to ply her trade without arousing suspicion? Jane Fine made her own livelihood without a man. She burned.

I cringed as she dropped a bulbous leech in the bowl. She might be independent, but I couldn't bear such a profession. Poppy's face was calm, even interested. She was at ease around blood and pus. I was sickened by it. Back in the cave while she and Meg had doctored Tom, I'd scrounged for food, kept the fire going, told tales, sketched pictures on the rock wall to entertain them, anything but tend Tom's seeping wounds.

Mistress Aisling pulled a jar from her pouch. "Have you a wooden spoon?" she asked. I ran to fetch it, glad for the coolness of the kitchen. When I returned, Meg was awake and by the bed with Poppy and Aisling. Garth had stepped deeper in the shadows. The man liked corners and was standing still enough to gather dust.

Poppy uncorked the jar, sniffed the mixture, and frowned. "Can you tell us what is in your posit, Leech Aisling?"

The leech took my wooden spoon and listed her ingredients. She was not secretive about her mixtures as some are.

"Nettles?" Poppy narrowed her eyes at me.

The leech nodded. "Seethed an hour, then strained and cooled. It's a fine cure."

It was the very thing Poppy had suggested earlier. Her eyes said, *See? See, Tess?* Blushing, I left the room.

GARTH FOUND ME in the stable.

"The stallion's shoe is loose," I said. I'd come to the stable to curry the horses after their day's journey, saw the black stallion's awkward stance. The huntsman poked his head in soon after.

"I see which hoof it is. There, there, friend," Garth said, patting the horse's muscular shoulder. "We'll fix that." He went out and came back with a hammer. "You have a good eye, Tess."

I stepped away so he might fix the shoe. "I grew up above a blacksmith's shop. All the horses in Harrowton were shod there. I came to know them all by name."

"Well, that explains it." Garth skillfully lifted the stallion's leg. "Just needs a new nail. Could you hand me one?" I found a nail and watched him pound it into the horseshoe. "His name is Goodfellow," Garth said. "And she's Seagull." He pointed with the hammer to the blond mare in the next stall. She nodded at him as if to say hello, and we laughed. I liked the name well, her coat gray white as an ocean gull's.

Garth shelved the hammer. "I can finish currying Goodfellow," he said. "I was in a hurry to bring Mistress Aisling in to see to Tom, but I can tend to them now."

I kept the brush. "I don't mind doing it." The stable was open to the air, the horses pleasant, and I'd spent too many hours between kitchen and sickroom today. I ran the brush down Goodfellow's shoulder; his silky mane was as black as the huntsman's hair.

"How good a rider are you?" he asked.

"I rode a few times returning horses to their masters after they were shod. Goodfellow's a beauty," I added.

"He is that." In the next stall, Garth used a pick to clean the clogged dirt from Seagull's hooves. "They're strong. You wouldn't think we'd ridden close to twenty miles today by the look of them."

"Is Aisling's home to the north?"

"Aye, she's from the north. Why?" He gave me a curious look.

"No reason," I said. "She doesn't dress like a leech."

"How do leeches dress?" he asked wryly.

I huffed. "You know what I mean."

"Not really, Tess."

I could not say more. She had the demeanor of a fine lady, and a costly gown a wealthy husband might afford, yet she'd led me to believe she'd paid for it with her own earnings. I would not share my curiosity over her with Garth Huntsman, who only seemed amused by it. What did he know of a woman's fortunes? We are trained up to wed, enter the nunnery, or become servants. None of us can live alone and earn our own bread without suspicion, yet Aisling had done so and prospered. I would like to know how she'd managed it. Were women freer up north? Was there some small chance I might do the same, only with my art? Monks drew leaves and animals illuminating holy manuscripts. What if I plied my craft illuminating books?

I'd been lost in thought when Garth said, "Tess?" He pointed to my brush. "If you're done with that, toss it to me, will you?"

I finished my last few strokes and heaved it over the stall. Garth caught it with his left hand. He'd not rolled up his sleeves to work as most men do. His muscles would not be as thick as my father's, who daily beat hot metal into submission, but muscled still, I thought.

"I like a lady who can ride." Garth's back was to me now and his head tipped as he swept the brush along Seagull's side in a wide arc.

Give me a man who lets his wife ride out when she likes.

I'd said that once; still I imagined the sort of ladies Garth was speaking of: rich maidens who rode delicately sitting sidesaddle. Mistress Aisling had ridden so this afternoon. To my mind dangling one's feet over one side made for an awkward perch. Long skirts and modesty made it necessary. I'd seen two females sit astride as a man does: the witch hunter, and a fey maiden I glimpsed, riding a dragon one night in the refuge. I considered my own short jaunts through Harrowton. "I'm not a skilled rider, sir," I confessed.

Garth laughed. "So no fox hunts for you."

"None for me no matter how well I'm saddled," I said gruffly.

Garth said no word, but finished currying Seagull, shelved the brush, and left.

There was something of the wildwood in the man who came and went illusive as moonlight moving through the branches.

Chapter Thirteen

MORNING SUNLIGHT GLISTENED on the frozen puddles. The wind smelled of pine and coming snow. I walked around behind the lodge. The pond in the open field was iced about the edges. Water trembled in the middle. Ducks flew down and skated across the ice, fluttering and skidding. It made me laugh. Some blackbirds sang on the icy edge. I could hear it only in my right ear, not my left. My hand went to my cauliflower ear. It did not hurt. Not anymore. But I'd have the reminder of my father's punishments all my life. Garth appeared walking Horace and saw me rubbing my ear.

"I've been wondering who did that to you," he said.

I wondered if he meant my thumbs, still misshapen, the nail still missing on one. But he was looking at my ear.

"My father. He used to beat me."

"Men who beat the weaker sex are brutes."

"We are not the weaker sex," I snapped.

He put up his hands in mock surrender. "All right, Tess."

He looked at me again. I glanced away, surprised by my own outburst. Turning, he led Horace out beyond the pond and disappeared in the oaks.

I'D BEEN RUDE to our host early in the morn when we were the only ones awake. Later at the breakfast table, I thought to catch his eye, and say a word or two, hoping he'd forgive my rudeness. Garth ignored me and watched Poppy as he spooned more jelly. Morning sun poured through the window, sweetening Poppy's hair and face.

"Poppy," I said, "did you tell Aisling how you helped us forage food in the wood?" She'd worked well with the leech. She might become Aisling's apprentice if the woman needed the help.

Poppy blushed at my praise.

"It's true," I went on. "She senses where to find herbs, mushrooms, and berries. What food there is, she finds. And," I said, looking at Aisling, "Poppy brought nettles here wanting to make the very tincture you have in your jar for Tom."

Aisling wiped her mouth. "Where are the nettles?"

"I threw them out," I confessed.

"A waste," Aisling said sternly. She looked fondly at her helper. "Tess is right. You have a gift. And your hands are steady with wounds. Any eye can see it."

Garth asked, "Tell us where you learned this, Poppy."

"Sir, I can't say as I know. It . . . comes to me." She batted her eyes. The two would be wed within the month if she continued looking at him thus. I cleared the table and went outside for air.

That night I made a tasty stew from the dried peas and meat bone I found in the cupboard and turnips from the garden. There was food aplenty here compared to our kitchen back home, where Mother and I were always scraping meals from nothing. Each day we were anxious, fearing we'd not enough to satisfy Father, who'd pound us for the meager meals. It mattered little that Father drank most of our market money, that we took in sewing and scribed letters for pay so we could afford to buy more food.

Stirring the savory stew, I thought of Mother and wondered how she was doing back home without me. Steam wet my face, and tears. I said a little prayer for her safety.

When all was ready, I was glad to serve the hot dish. For the feast day of Saint Placid, who was saved from drowning and invoked against chills, hot stew was a proper meal.

"Mm," Aisling said. "You're a fine cook, Tess."

Garth ate, but did not say a word. Aisling, Meg, and Poppy put their heads together, talking over Tom's condition. Meg took him a steaming bowl of stew. I could not offer medicine, but I hoped the meal would strengthen him. Later, when I'd finished scouring the pot, I headed down the hall with a gift for Horace. Garth was in the library with his hound. I paused at the doorway, suddenly uncertain.

"Come in, Tess. What is it you want?" It was not a warm greeting.

Horace met me with wagging tail and snuffed the back of my hand. I produced the soup bone and his tail wacked the table legs.

"He'll be your champion forever now," Garth said. I smiled to hear a softer tone from him at last, and at the idea of the old bloodhound as my champion. By the fire Horace gnawed the bone. I edged to the desk and touched the feathered quill.

"Do you wish to write something?"

"Sir? No, I—"

"You don't know how," he said matter-of-factly.

Many people, even lords and ladies, did not know how to read or write, so I shouldn't have taken offense; still, I barked, "Of course I know how! I can read and write and do mathematical sums. I used to keep my father's accounts; the clodpole couldn't do his own."

"Pardon me, mistress."

I blinked down at the floor. *Leave now before you embarrass yourself further.*

"You're welcome to take a few pages." Garth met me at the desk. "You might like this." He pulled a small ink block from the drawer with an elegant dragon carved along the top. "Just take a little black powder from the edge like this . . ." He demonstrated for me, using a pen-knife to scrape powder into a small dish. "Add water and you have ink."

Give me a man who buys her ink that she might draw or write, books that she might read . . .

"It's wonderful," I whispered. "I've never seen anything like it."

"A traveling man's ink, no worries over spilling the ink bottle. What will you write?"

I looked up at him. He was tall and lean, though muscled in the right places and his shoulders were broad. His dark hair curled about his ears. My skin tingled strangely. A feeling I'd not had before and one I couldn't name. I wanted to say I had no plan to write a letter, but to draw. "M-may I mix the ink now?" I stammered.

"You have a lover you wish to send a note to telling him you're safe now?" Garth asked, arms crossed. My hand slipped, I spilled the ink dust from the dish onto the table. "Oh, sorry. So clumsy of me." Garth smiled and swept the dust back into the dish, the side of his hand blackened.

"May I go?"

He turned back to the fire. I rushed from the room, took a little water from the kitchen bucket. Behind my door, I breathed hard. Why run from the library like a coward? Cramps came as I drew. My courses would be here tonight. I would have to gather rags to catch the blood, find a private place to wash them out. I supposed this huntsman was not familiar with women's troubles. The cramps strengthened as I filled the parchment page, but I was soon lost in the picture forming under my hand.

I was halfway into the first sketch before I saw I was drawing the great old dragon rescuing the burning girl. He winged over the sea, dipping her in the water to put out her burning gown. I showed her flailing in his claw, screaming, as I remembered her, though he meant to help her and not harm her. I added the dragon's long tail and arched neck with its jagged scar, the moon above, the fishing boats to his left, the harbor. I did not sketch the fey man Poppy saw.

I still did not understand how Poppy spied a fey man on dragonback when I did not. I was the one who'd slipped into the sanctuary night after night, hoping to glimpse a fairy or a dragon.

When the page was full in every detail, I quickly hid the work behind the wardrobe. All the art I'd done back in Harrowton was in the witch hunter's hands. Had she kept the dragon sketches, the drawing of the green man?

One page left. My hand knew what to do if my mind did not. A man sprawled comfortably before the fire with his faithful dog beside him. Garth's face was less challenging in side view. I caught the way his brow tipped when he was deep in his own thoughts, the small ridge high on his nose, his strong chin and cheekbones, his mouth, which turned up a little. He could go very quiet, then of a sudden, rush into action. *He is like the deer that way.*

My hand flew. But I found I could not capture the man's mysterious nature, his readiness and ease. Some ink pooled near his boot as I drew his long legs crossed by the fire. I paused, not completely happy with my sketch.

You have a lover you wish to send a note to telling him you're safe now? Why presume that? What I did next confounded me. Did I mean to prove I was not writing a lover? Why else would I find myself again at the library door with the parchment in my hand. Garth was gazing out the window. I nearly ran off again, but he turned and crossed the room.

"It's not finished," I said, blushing. *Then why did you bring it here?*

"You're an artist, Tess," he said. There was no jest in his tone. He took the drawing and set it up on the mantel above the hearth. "Look Horace, you're in it too." Horace lifted his head, tail thumping at the pleasant sound of his master's voice. I leaned up against the wall by the window. Garth's brown eyes questioned. *You didn't want the quill to write to a lover?*

Only to draw with. "I'd write to my mother if I could, and tell her I am safe, but a letter from me would only endanger her. There's no way to send her one anyway."

He joined me at the window. "You're right to protect her."

Even if her worry over me is breaking her heart?

He was standing close enough for me to catch the scent

coming off his skin and clothes, a mix of wood smoke, horses, and evergreens. A goodsome smell and not at all like my singed, ale-breathed father. New beard growth darkened his cheeks. I'd shadowed his face to show this in my drawing. He'd skipped his morning shave to ride out early after the leech.

"I've meant to thank you," I said.

"For letting you use a little parchment?"

"For fetching Mistress Aisling."

"A fine healer," he said. "I hope we're not too late." We were quiet a moment, thinking of Tom. Garth pointed above the trees. "Look." He opened the window. "There."

Stars hung shining over the wood.

"Stars are jewels, my mother used to say. Heaven's treasure free to anyone from prince to peasant if they have eyes to look."

I liked his mother for saying that. They *were* free for anyone who cared to look. No one owned them, yet even as I gazed up I felt the need to capture the heavens on parchment as I drew other things I loved, to hold the vision and keep it with me always—a kind of ownership, I supposed. Perhaps I was not as generous as Garth's mother.

"Free to all," I agreed. "And these jewels can never be stolen."

Garth frowned. No doubt he'd been asked to look for the king's stolen treasure. All woodwards had to scour their sections of Dragonswood. He gripped something in his hand. Seeing my curious look, he spread his fingers. A thin gold chain coiled in his palm with a single pearl on the end.

A large pearl. "Does it belong to the king?" I whispered. Garth handed it to me. His fingers brushed my palm as he let go. I trembled near him, framed at the window, the fire behind him, darkness outside, and wind. I tried to give the necklace back. "I have never touched anything belonging to the king."

His brows went up. "Haven't you? The dishes here, Tess, the quill you used just now, the chairs by the fire." He nodded at the chairs behind us with their finely patterned needlework. "The feather beds—"

"The king slept in our room?"

"His sons did."

"The princes?" I stepped back. Well, that explained the rocking horse at least, though Prince Arden and Bion were grown men in their twenties now.

"The hunting lodge is not as big as a castle, Tess. Not many slept in these walls. Servants and men-at-arms stayed in the outbuildings beyond the barn."

"Why didn't you put us there?" I accused. "Won't the king—" I checked myself. "Won't the princes be angry?"

He shook his head, smiling a little. "I think not."

"Do you know them that well?" I still had the pearl held out. He seemed reluctant to take it back.

"As well as any boy raised at Pendragon Castle. I am

a nobleman's son, not eldest but a second son, so I was a castle page before I became a knight, and served here as His Majesty's huntsman."

The pearl felt cool and silky. "How did you come by this?" Such a slender gold chain might have been lost under a bed and the huntsman would have opportunity to thieve it, I supposed.

"You're quite inquisitive, aren't you, Tess?"

He laid his hand across mine, the pearl shelled between our palms. I looked up at his face quite close to mine, then glanced away, dizzy with lack of sleep or too long a journey in the woods or . . .

"You think I stole it?"

My mouth went dry.

"I didn't, Tess. It was my mother's pearl." His throat sounded thick with emotion, and I guessed his mother was dead. Perhaps the black armband was for her and not for the king as I'd first supposed.

He took the pearl, closing his hand around it so even the chain was hidden. The night wind from the open window blew my hair against his arm where the sleeve was torn. If it tickled through the tear he did not move to draw his arm away. I could not think what to say to comfort him. I'd nearly lost my mother many times to the perils of childbirth, but each time she'd strengthened and recovered.

He broke the silence. "Why were you accused of witchcraft, Tess?"

I looked at the hunched willow by the garden wall. "Why do you want to know that? You'd have turned us in by now if you planned to collect the fee."

"There, so now you trust me that far at least," he said.

My small shiver made him shut the window. We moved to the fire. Garth pocketed the pearl. The room closed in the way a flower folds its petals at nightfall. We did not take the chairs but stood in the circle of the red glow.

"You were there in Harrowton that day. I saw you."

He nodded.

"What were you doing so far south of here?"

"You evade my questions, Tess."

"I have questions of my own."

He smiled, looked away. "I'd come to see your woodward. We check in with each other time to time. I found him sleeping on the job. The man is too lax to notice intruders in his part of Dragonswood."

I'd been one of the intruders he was too lax to notice.

Garth added a log to the fire and poked it into place with the tongs till it spat sparks. "I came to speak with your Sheriff Bollard about him, to ask that he be replaced with another man more watchful at his post."

It made sense, I supposed. Though it was less dramatic than the wicked role I'd cast him in before I'd come to trust him, when I'd imagined him to be one of the witch hunter's spies, first showing up in Harrowton the day she arrived, then at the harvest feast just before she rode in.

"The midwife accused me."

"Hmm," he said. "After she herself was captured by the guards, as I remember."

I nodded. "It was my father who'd accused her."

He raised a brow. "Then you were tried."

"At my trial the fishmonger said I hexed his pregnant wife so his boy was born with a harelip."

He laughed. "What powers you have, Tess."

I put my hand on the stone hearth. Recalling the trial did not bring me to laughter. "May I go now?"

"I offend you," he said. "I'm sorry for it. Go on with your story if you would."

I'd not talked about my trial to anyone but my friends, who blamed me for all their misfortune, so it was a burden and not a release when I'd told them. But I told him all. I do not know why, perhaps because he'd let me hold the pearl and spoken so tenderly of his mother, or because he had asked and was willing to listen. The fire warming my skin, the huntsman at my side, I went on.

"Tidas Leech said he'd spied me in Dragonswood dancing with Satan." I shifted on my feet. I would not mention his accusation that I'd danced naked and *kissed Satan's arse,* as he'd put it. I nearly choked when I recounted Joan Midwife's chilling lies that I'd murdered my mother's infants one by one that I might suck powers from their tiny bones.

Would Joan have said so at the trial if I hadn't blamed

her for Adam's death and called her a witch myself? She'd pointed at me in order to take the charges off her own back, so all was a tangle of lies.

Last I told him how the witch hunter had me hung up by my arms for hours, and twisted the agonizing thumb-screws while I was strapped to the witch's chair. I caught him staring at my thumbs. This time I did not try and hide them.

"Go on," Garth said in a gentle tone. He could see this was painful for me.

I did not speak for a long while. At last I confessed in a low whisper how I'd betrayed my friends to the witch hunter.

"You named them?" he asked, astonished.

I nodded miserably.

The room fell silent.

He'd asked. I'd told.

Garth's face was hard. An odor filled my nose. Rotting meat. My skin. My clothes. The smell of what I'd done to my friends. Garth would not speak nor look me in the face.

I left.

The next morning the huntsman was gone.

Chapter Fourteen

I T WAS A full week before he returned. Mistress Aisling stayed with us and doctored Tom. He was still fevered, but she said he was ever so slowly improving. I made meals, minded the kitchen, and when my work was done, walked alone in Dragonswood.

I did not feel as constricted in the musty hunting lodge as I had at home. Still, I am a girl who prefers trees over walls, the sky over a roof. I breathe more freely in the wood, so I took my chance and left to explore a part of Dragonswood I'd not been in before. The forest was all mystery in October. Long moss bearded the branches. Through the greenery I spied a family of deer. The underbrush crackled as they sped away. The buck had brought his good wife with him and a little fawn. I saw the white flick of the doe's tail. How I love the deer. Their quietness and quickness is like the water, placid and cool until stirred, then they rush and rush.

We were farther from the coast in this part of the wood,

but when I climbed a tall pine, I thought I caught a scent of the sea. From on high I took in snowcapped Morgesh Mountain, the northernmost point of the refuge. The fairy castle DunGarrow was somewhere at the base of that mountain. I tried to imagine the fey kingdom. Did the fairies dance in the high meadow under the stars like the stories said? I'd seen only a few fey patrolling the refuge on dragonback. Now I was in their wood by day, the part Garth Huntsman watched over for them. Perhaps they had no need to patrol the woods here.

My longing to be alone in the wildwood increased. The second day I rushed through my chores, scrubbing the flagstone kitchen floor with such speed, Poppy stood in the doorway laughing. "Why in such a hurry, Tess?" she asked.

"I'm not," I said, not bothering to look up. I could not explain my longing even to her. I did not understand it myself. I planned to explore a little farther my second day out, and could not wait to leave.

At last I pocketed an apple and quit the lodge. At midday, mist still hung over Dragonswood. I ran and ran until my lungs ached, then stopped to eat my apple. Taking secret paths, I crossed a crooked stream. All along I noticed my surroundings so I could find my way back. Climbing a hill, I followed a songbird, hopping branch to branch like the girl in "The Whistler." My cauliflower ear began to hum like a hive of honeybees, or was the sound coming from somewhere deeper in the forest?

As I climbed, the humming turned to a whisper. *Tessss . . .*

I looked about in the wavering shadows.

Come away.

The boughs seemed to pull me farther in. *Tess. Come north.*

"Who calls me?" I whispered, though the voices came only to my crippled ear, and they weren't likely to be human. My feet followed a narrow path where pale sunlight patterns fell.

Tessss . . .

Prayers whispered in church sounded thus, but this was not God's holy house. Were fairy folk moving invisibly through the woods? In my wandering, I might have passed beyond the huntsman's domain. I was alone. Trespassing. Would I be drawn in only to be fey-struck or turned into a Treegrim as Meg feared?

"Show yourselves."

Sounds like stray breezes hissing through grass, blowing in me and through me. *Tessss.* Skin tingling, I could not disobey the call, but followed. I willed it so and could not turn. *Tessss.* On I walked, damp ferns wetting my skirts.

The voices faded. My ear went deaf again and I found myself alone. My body ached, full of strange longing. Why would the fairies tempt me only to leave me alone again?

I brushed against a hunched crabapple tree, bare and

fruitless. Not a Treegrim. Still, I was frightened. I turned and ran back toward the lodge, fleeing from myself or the wilderness or both.

THAT NIGHT WE ousted Cackle from the kitchen and boiled water so we might take turns bathing in the great metal tub. "I'll go last," Meg said, preferring to sit at Tom's bedside with Aisling.

It took a great deal of boiled water to fill the tub. Poppy and I added just enough cold to get the temperature right. I washed Poppy's hair while she hummed, poking and popping the bubbles.

"You have gentle hands," Poppy said.

I was still stung by Garth's rejection, still shamed by his silence and by his leaving the very next morn. *He rode off to be apart from me.* Poppy's kind remark touched something raw.

"I'm sorry I dragged you away from home," I whispered.

"I know," Poppy said. I poured a cup of warm water over her tipped head to rinse her soapy hair. Her eyes were closed. She did not see my tears.

The tub had cooled when she was done. We added more hot water. Poppy did not offer to scrub my hair, but stayed in the kitchen to talk, the steam rising between us. I had a deal of trouble getting the dirt off my arms.

"Like trying to remove dragon scales," Poppy said.

I scrubbed at the dirt till my arms were cherry red.

Poppy gave a nod. "Scales gone. I wonder what the princes' arm scales look like?" she mused. "They can't just scrub them away, you know."

"Grandfather said the Pendragons' scales are a mark of their power and their bond with dragons."

Poppy frowned. "Not everyone admires them."

Was she expressing her own opinion? I wasn't sure. "I wouldn't mind scales so much."

"Tess. You don't mean it. Think of . . . *Princess Augusta*." With the whisper of her name, shadows moved along the kitchen wall. Queen Lucinda's last babe—the one that killed her.

"Do you think it's true what they say about her?"

"It must be."

No one on Wilde Island had ever seen Queen Lucinda's youngest child. But it was said that she had scales on her face, dragon eyes with slit pupils, and clawed hands. Folk said Augusta killed her mother, scratching her insides with her claws as she was being born. That very night four years ago the babe was whisked away to Dragon's Keep. She'd been there ever since.

The bathwater was chill when Meg came in, worn from tending to Tom's needs. Her skin pallid, dark rings around her eyes. Poppy and I said not a word, but boiled up more water, that Meg might bathe in warmth as we had. Together we washed her hair.

Meg slept after her bath. Poppy and I dried our long hair in the study by the fire.

"Do you think Queen Lucinda ever came here?" Poppy asked.

I held my damp hair close to the fire's warmth. "It's a man's refuge."

"And a boy's," Poppy said.

I thought again of the rocking horse in our room and nodded. Soft light spread through the study. There were a few poetry books on the shelves. "She might have come here, I suppose."

"Ask Garth Huntsman what the queen was like," Poppy said, fluffing her hair.

I shook my head. "You ask him when he returns."

"He talks to you, not so much to me."

Not anymore he won't.

Poppy sighed. "They say she was beautiful, with flaxen hair and deep green eyes. Sad to think she died in child-birth."

"Even a queen is a woman like anyone else," I said with a heavy heart. So many died that way. I thought of how strong Mother was even though she appeared so frail.

Prince Arden left for the crusades right after his mother died. Broken-hearted, people said. We were all sad to lose her.

We roasted chestnuts in the fire.

"I dreamed of the fairy kingdom last night," Poppy said. "I often dream of it. All your stories you've told me,

I suppose, but this time . . ." She paused to pull a steaming chestnut from the fire. "The dream was brighter than ever before. The fairies were dancing. I heard no music, only the soughing wind through the trees, and there were beasts circling, owls in the sky, deer and foxes down below. A black bear came right up to me," she said.

"And then?"

"That was all." Her large blue eyes were on me, questioning.

"We're closer to DunGarrow here than we've ever been before. Maybe that's why you dreamed of it."

Poppy offered me a nutmeat. We ate by the hearth, the fire tilting with the night wind blowing down the chimney.

GARTH RETURNED A few days later and went straight-away into Tom's room to see how the man was improving. He was cold when I came into the room, and would not look at my face.

He avoided me all the next day and the next. One morn he came in from the chicken coop with straw in his hair and fresh eggs crooked in his arm. He did not say a word when I thanked him for the eggs.

I was familiar with a man's anger and knew how to duck a fist. This chilly silence was new, and baffling. *God's teeth. If he does not speak with me soon, I'll shout.*

We breakfasted in the kitchen; all but Tom, who was

still too weak to join us. Meg's head drooped over her platter. "Alice dearly loved an egg," she said. Her lip trembled and her eyes welled up.

"Now, now, Meg," said Poppy. "You are overtired. Let Tess seethe you some chamomile tea."

I'd just sat down to my breakfast, but as the one who'd separated Meg from her little girl, I sprang up to make the tea. When it was hot I filled Meg's cup. Her eyes were still puffy from crying when she left the table.

"Come, Poppy." The leech threw on her cloak and took her helper out to search for herbs, nettles would be my guess. I was glad to see them go, but once they were out the door, I felt Garth's eyes on my back, and was loath to turn around. I filled his ale mug, sloshing some on the table. When he'd seen me as the hero who'd rescued Tom, he'd enjoyed my company, and even let me hold his mother's pearl. Now I was a low worm, a betrayer who'd given my friends over to the witch hunter. I'd likely never live it down. Why had I told him? I'd have given anything to take it back now.

The bowls needed scrubbing. Tying on an apron, I pulled the wash pan from its hook.

Garth said, "Tom is better. I'm glad for it." So we were speaking again? I stood with the wash pan. Suddenly dumb as a toadstool.

He drummed the table. "Is Meg always so tearful?"

"Meg? Why, no. It is only that she misses Alice."

"Who's Alice?"

I told him.

"Tom and Meg have a child?" he asked, surprised.

"Alice turned three this summer."

"So you broke up their little family when you betrayed her to Lady Adela."

"I did." I was surprised it did not hurt to say this honestly and true. It was like the relief of a splinter coming out.

"Is the child in danger?"

"I do not know." The question struck me with force. I'd worried so much about my friends, the danger I'd put them in, and then over Tom's illness; I'd had no time to think of Alice.

Garth went outside. Paced. Was Alice safe with her grandparents? The witch hunter wouldn't go as low as to take Alice as bait the way she'd taken Tom, would she? Turning clumsily, I knocked a platter to the floor. *Not Alice.* My hands were awkward as I scooped spilled egg onto the platter. *Not little sunny-faced Alice.*

Garth came back in. "We are friends?"

"If you like," said I, looking up at him confused.

He took my wash pan and headed for the well. The larks in the yard abandoned the puddles as he rushed by. I cleared the rest of the table. I did not care about my spilled breakfast now. My throat was closed. I wouldn't have been able to swallow it.

Garth returned with the wash pan, sloshing water on

the sideboard where he set it down. He took up his ale, emptying the mug in three gulps, and then stood halfway in, halfway out the door, arms crossed and back against the frame. I was all over hot and prickly. Why stare at me that way? Why not just leave?

All through breakfast I'd wished he'd look at me instead of Poppy. His eyes were on me now, gold brown and all too clear. *He studies me as a man might inspect a market fish to see if it's spoiled.* But what he said next surprised me.

"How much do you want to amend the wrong you've done to your friends, Tess?"

I PULLED MEG out of the sickroom to speak with her. She wept with joy when I told her the huntsman and I would ride back to Harrowton for Alice. We'd forged a plan together. Garth had business in the south, he said, and wouldn't mind a companion on the trip, a small rider coming back. I had not asked him what his business was, I didn't care. Brightness filled me as we laid out our plan, as if I'd drunk a tankard of sunshine.

Poppy joined us in the hall. "But won't you be in danger?" she asked.

I could not deny it, but was happier than I'd been in ages. I'd hungered for a chance to make it up to my friends and sweep my soul clean of its crime. I hugged Poppy, smiling for the first time in a long while. "Garth will keep me safe. Never you worry about it." Then Meg embraced us both so the three of us were in the hall, arms around one another when Mistress Aisling left Tom's side to see what all the noise was about.

Garth planned to ride out as a cloth merchant. I took some amusement in it since it was my former suitor Master Percival's profession. The trade had been my idea. It seemed to suit our needs. Cloth merchants will sometimes ride town to town investigating new dyeing methods or visiting weavers of repute. For my part I must go as his wife. A man does not ride alone with a woman unless she is his wife. I was willing to play this game for a short time—the closest I would likely ever come to marriage. My black kirtle, though newly clean, was unsuitable for a guildsman's wife. Mistress Aisling kindly offered her fine blue gown and her fur-lined riding cloak besides. I refused at first, but she persuaded me, saying she had a second gown in her bags, and she could use my cloak while I was gone.

So it was we left the hunting lodge next day on a windswept October morn. It took a week for three leper girls to walk along the coastal road from Harrowton to Oxhaven, but we'd spent a deal of time each day begging and searching for food, so our progress was slow. Garth and I planned to make haste on horseback. Three days' journey down and three back, if the weather didn't hinder us.

Packing food aplenty in the saddlebags, the huntsman also brought coin to pay for a meal or sleep under a tavern roof if a storm drove us in.

I was jumpy our first day out, unused to the saddle and wary to be back on the road. The witch hunter still looked for me, so I went hooded, riding sidesaddle like a lady. I refrained from looking up or speaking when we met folk traveling on Kingsway. Once we were alone again, I began to ride astraddle so we could progress more quickly. Garth agreed.

On the road Garth treated me with the same chivalry alone as he did when riders passed us by, as if he did not care to shed the hoax, not even for a moment. This made me glad and uneasy in turns. From childhood I'd learned never to trust a man. He'd been kind thus far, but he was a man and his temper could flare. A part of me waited for this, the moment I would see his darker side.

Midday we heard thundering hooves from around the next bend. Garth signaled, and I steered Seagull behind him to a high hedge, where we dismounted and stroked the horses' necks to keep them quiet. Garth was stiff-backed as the troop passed with clanking armor and shields glinting in the sunlight. At least the men were riding north, while we were heading south.

When Kingsway was clear we mounted and left our hiding place. A biting wind hit us, stripping red maple leaves from the trees. I was glad for Aisling's cloak. "How long do you think it will take them to find the Pendragon treasure?" I asked.

"Lord Sackmoore's men look diligently enough," he said, which was no real answer.

I remembered rumors I'd heard back in Harrowton. "Some folk say it must have been taken by magic, that the fey folk stole it in league with the dragons."

Garth glanced back sharply. "Is that what you think?" he snapped.

I swallowed and gripped Seagull's reins a little tighter.

Anon Garth shook his head. "Sorry, Tess. I shouldn't have barked at you."

"If you want to know," I said, bringing Seagull up to ride alongside Goodfellow, "I think it was only gossip. People couldn't understand how thieves took it from the strong room, so they started saying it was done with fairy magic."

Garth's head was bowed, lost in some troubling thought. He guarded Dragonswood. With rumors that dragons or fey took the treasure . . . "Do you worry about the sanctuary?" I asked.

He didn't answer. I adjusted my position in the saddle. Rain pricked my skin. It was not raining in earnest yet, only spitting drops from passing clouds. But the clouds were gathering and the wind was still strong.

"You said Lord Sackmoore searches. What about Prince Bion? I heard he's anxious to find it." I'd wondered why our younger prince would leave Pendragon Castle even if it was to search for the treasure. Wouldn't he want to oversee some of the affairs of state till his older brother took over?

"Prince Bion will see the treasure's back in the strong room once his brother's crowned."

"How do you know that?"

Silence again from Garth. He'd met both the princes. Maybe he didn't like me questioning the younger prince's ability to locate the treasure in time. We'd only just started our ride south. Would he treat me to so many moods and silences all the way down to Harrowton?

I patted Seagull's neck. "Some think Prince Arden's nobler for going on crusade. But I like it well that the younger prince chose to stay home with us. Only I wonder why he lets Lord Sackmoore rule when he could rule in his brother's stead until Prince Arden's home. He's old enough."

"You want to know why?" Garth asked.

"I wouldn't have asked if I didn't."

Garth kept his head straight, his eyes fixed on the road ahead. "If Prince Bion tried to rule Wilde Island even for a day, Tess, he'd be accused of wanting to usurp his brother's throne. King Kadmi appointed Sackmoore king's regent to take temporary rule until Prince Arden returned to ensure peace between his sons."

Grandfather had taught me some history. I knew thrones were often gained through bloodshed. "Two brothers and one throne," I said.

Garth's face hardened. "I can't blame the dying king for his decision. I'm sure he didn't know how dangerous Sackmoore could be." Goodfellow clopped along, his head held high.

I said, "Even King Richard the Lionheart has been challenged by his younger brother, John."

"Where did you learn this?"

"English traders down at Harrowton Harbor said so."

"It's true Prince John's been acting as if he were the rightful English king while King Richard's on crusade, turning on the men still loyal to his brother and treating them as outlaws." Garth flicked his reins. "It will not go that way here on Wilde Island," he said. "As to Prince Arden's return, I say Godspeed." With that he kicked Goodfellow to a trot and rode ahead.

Clouds amassed all day, some gray, some dark as char. At dusk a thundershower drenched us. When the storm did not subside, we were forced to sup at a tavern in Margaretton, the very place where I'd seen the sheriff's riders cut men down in Dragonswood.

"Is it safe?" I'd asked.

"As safe as anywhere these days. I'd planned to stop here anyway, Tess."

Garth was careful to choose a corner table where we both might sit in shadow. He raised his hand, calling for meat and ale, and I saw the stitches where he'd mended his sleeve: a man's needlework, all crooked and clumsy. He caught me considering his sleeve. I raised my mug to hide my face till the beef tray arrived.

The room we were shown had a goodsome hearth. Garth placed our saddlebags that were full of our travel gear in the corner, and added logs to the fire. Golden light illumined his face, his neck and chest. I could not take my eyes from him, but I was agitated, seeing the single bed against the wall.

"That business I mentioned," he said. "I'll take care of it tonight. You'll be safe enough here at the inn while I'm gone."

I'd not asked what his business was about before we left the lodge; now I was both curious and frightened. Who was he meeting in Margaretton? Why leave me alone here on this stormy night?

He saw the way I held my cloak around myself, but misread my thoughts.

"Have no fear." He nodded at the bed. "The bed is yours, Tess. I will sleep in the chair."

He changed his clothes behind the screen. I watched his shadow moving, the broadness of his back and his strong arms. I should not have looked, but it was only shadow. Tossing his riding shirt across the back of the chair, he straightened his woodward's tunic. Wherever he was going, he was going as himself. Smiling, he said, "Sleep well," and left me in the room.

I took the chair by the fire. The man was on business.

What sort of business? He traveled quite a bit, hadn't he left us in the lodge for days at a time? And he'd never said where he'd gone or what he'd been up to, nor had we felt it proper to ask.

I'd confronted him only once.

You were there in Harrowton that day I saw you. What were you doing so far south?

I spoke to Sheriff Bollard about your woodward, asked that he be replaced with another man more watchful at his post. Who watched the wood near Margaretton? Did Garth plan to speak to his fellow woodward about the riot I'd seen? Maybe, maybe not. I could not hope to guess, the man came and went so much. I should be used to it, but I wasn't. I leaned my head back against the chair, felt Garth's rumpled shirt against my neck.

Since I could not yet sleep, I went downstairs, and borrowed a needle from the innkeeper's wife.

Back in the room, I tore out Garth's man-stitches and mended the tear. A womanly duty, but I did not mind it. He'd not cuffed my jaw, shouting, *Mend my shirt, wench!* the way Father did.

The mending didn't take long. The shirt smelled of Garth and Goodfellow and the damp green of the woods. I rubbed my aching legs. It had been a long ride today.

I must have slept. Next thing I felt was a soft wind blowing across my face warm as a summer breeze. A voice came on the wind. *Tessss.*

I opened my eyes. Garth was kneeling by the chair; the fire at his back cast a halo round his head like Saint Peter's stained-glass halo in our church back at home. I blinked, hardly breathing.

"You need not sleep in the chair," Garth said. "I told you earlier the bed is yours."

He lifted the mended shirt I was still clutching. I scurried to the bed.

Draping the shirt back over the chair, he poked the fire. "You can change behind the screen," he said. "Or shall I leave the room?"

"N-no," I sputtered. "I'm fine." I lay on top of the bed in Aisling's gown, the only one I had with me. Garth did not know this. He'd not been privy to the things I'd packed or did not pack for the journey. Garth took the chair and heaved a contented sigh. He slept soon, and heavily. I lay on my side on the bed a long while looking at his sleeping form, his hand dangling loosely from the armrest. Something glinted there. The sewing needle was much too close to his wrist. Move and he might jab himself. I rose, crept toward him, and reached slowly for the needle. I'd nearly got it when he caught my arm in a tight grip. The movement of a man under attack. I caught my breath.

Seeing who I was, he let go.

I leaped back.

"Tess? I'm sorry. You startled me. I didn't mean to—"

I pointed at the needle. "I thought it might jab you in your sleep."

"I see," he said, picking it up. "Such a small weapon, but sharp. Here." He handed it to me. I carried it back across the room in my open palm as if it were a living thing and set it on the bedside table. "A blanket," I said. "Do you need one?"

He eyed me carefully. "If you have one to spare."

Heart pounding, I stripped the top one off my bed and gave it to him.

I quickly got into the bed. Garth was quiet across the room. Sleeping? Awake? I decided not to look. Under the covers at last, I found the bed truly welcome. Shadows played across the ceiling. I'd been raised the daughter of a lowly blacksmith. Garth Huntsman knew the royal family, had served them personally. What was I doing here, pretending to be his wife? It would not be such a sham to wear the wife's guise if I were nobly born.

The bed was welcome and the dreams that came even more so. I dreamed of DunGarrow, a place I'd never seen but hoped to see. My hope painted it for me, the castle set against Mount Morgesh, the rushing waterfall at its side.

I walked or floated across the bridge spanning the river (indeed it felt like floating) and just like in the tale of "The Whistler" I arrived at the high meadow where the fey folk danced. Hovering at meadow's edge I wept in my dream, seeing my mother dancing with a fey man in the crowd.

Like the girl in the tale, she danced freely. The man spun Mother round, her loose hair flying out without scarf or braids to bind it, and she wore a fine green gown with gold trim like the one I'd seen on the first fairy maiden I'd spied riding a dragon. How beautiful she looked.

"Mother," I called. "It's you!" The words *it's you* made me cry all the more. I was seeing her joyful as I'd never seen her in my life. She'd exchanged her threadbare kirtle for the dazzling gown, freed herself from my father's hold, unbound her hair, let go her cares, and danced.

My eyes were damp when I awoke. Garth had left the room. I put on my cloak and went to look for him.

Chapter Fifteen

THE DAY WAS chill as we left Margaretton, but the heavy storm had passed in the night. Puddles on Kingsway Road caught clouds and sunlight both. Seagull was fidgety all through the morning ride and kept stopping by the roadside to tear up hunks of grass. Garth saw we'd fallen behind, turned and clicked his tongue. "Now Gull," he said. "You were fed at the inn stable and you know it." She shook her head, but minded him like the good mare, coming back up alongside Goodfellow at a trot. I adjusted my grip, caught Garth staring at my discolored thumbs and hid them in Seagull's mane. At least they were no longer swollen or pussy.

"She wasn't always like that," he said.

"Who?"

"The one who did that to you."

"You speak as if you know her." The trotting horses made our speech choppy.

"We both dined in the Great Hall at Pendragon Castle,

she with her uncle, Lord Sackmoore, who serves as king's regent now, while I ate nearby at the knight's table. More than once she watched me joust at the tourneys."

So the man jousted? I pictured Garth dressed in tourney armor gripping battle shield and lance. If I'd been a noblewoman in the crowd I'd have tied my scarf about his arm, claiming him my champion. I would have liked to see him joust. But I was bound to Harrowton then, engaged in my own demanding sport shielding Mother from my father's meaty fists.

Garth told me earlier he was a nobleman's son, a second son who would not inherit land, so he was a castle page as a boy, a knight before he became the king's huntsman. Of course I should have thought of it before. The knights we'd seen yesterday on the road would have known him from his time at the castle. "So that's why we hid from the garrison." The quick retreat wasn't only for my protection. They might have questioned why he'd abandoned his post at the hunting lodge.

"I'd rather not explain why I'm riding south with a lady," Garth said.

My mood shifted at the word *lady*. He was a nobleman's son. I was a lowly blacksmith's daughter. I made a soundless sigh. No, Aisling's fine blue gown and riding cloak was a costume as much as the leper's robe had been, surely Garth knew that?

We rode through a swarm of gnats and when one flew

into my mouth, I discreetly spat it out. "I'll wager Lady Adela liked seeing men bloodied at the tourneys."

"Would you wager that? With what coin?"

"It is an expression, Garth. She's a fiend." I steered Seagull closer. "How can you think her anything but a devil, knowing what she did to me, and worse, what she's done to other women?" My angry voice startled Seagull, who reared back.

"Easy, Seagull," Garth said. "Easy now." From his saddle he reached over and patted her neck to calm her. "You say she's a fiend, Tess, but I knew her before she was kidnapped. The torture she underwent changed her. They hobbled her ankle, put out her eye, she—"

"I know what they did. Does that excuse what she did to me or to Tom? Or what she is doing, even now, to other girls?" I was breathing hard; the cold air stung my throat.

We rode a while under the boughs, letting only the wind speak for us. It was a long time before I could say, "You knew her before she . . . before the witches stole her," I said. "Is that why you are not afraid of her?"

Garth snorted. "Who said I'm not afraid of Lady Adela? She is full of righteous anger. Such women are to be feared."

He watched me as he said this, a half smile on his face. Was he implying I had righteous anger?

"I'm excused from such company," I snapped. "God knows I am not righteous!"

"Now you're angry?" he said with a huff. "How is it you turn everything I say to an insult?"

He raced ahead. Goodfellow's pounding hooves sent crows flying from the ash grove, peppering the sky before they settled in the trees farther down the road.

Seagull followed at a trot. I did not try to catch up to the man. How could he have the smallest ounce of pity for the witch hunter? His own grandmother was tried for a witch, and worse, made to walk the coals.

We stopped briefly to rest the horses and share dried plums, wine, and cheese. Garth gave me a goodly portion, but no word passed between us. The wine sent fire down my throat.

We mounted again, still silent. As we rode south, my body felt a strange tugging as if invisible hands pulled my skirts, or a rope was about my waist. I'd felt it earlier, but it was stronger now, harder to ignore. Wind twisted my hair, whispered in my ear.

Tess. Turn around. Come north.

I leaned forward in the saddle. *Tessss. You are going the wrong way.*

Seagull's ears pressed back. She tried to turn about. I gripped her reins. "Stop this," I whispered. "Obey me." Looking straight ahead, I pressed Seagull on.

Tall pines graced the edges of the road. We climbed a steep hill. Seagull puffed as we came down the other side. Rolling clouds gusted in from the ocean, thick and white as mounded wool. Then the clouds blushed red as they blew over Dragonswood. It was midday and not yet time for sunset. I tensed, recalling the old saying *Red clouds without the aid of sun. Traveler beware. The dragon comes.* Trees shook. The air about us darkened as if we were riding under a crimson sea.

Seagull whinnied and glanced back at me, the whites of her eyes showing.

"Garth?"

At the sound of my voice he spun Goodfellow about, riding toward me, his black hair flying back as the tempest swept in. I heard the thunderous, beating wings coming from Dragonswood where the treetops bowed.

Chapter Sixteen

THE DRAGON SKIMMED over the canopy, her long, blue-green tail swam fishlike in the sky. The startled horses bolted. I ducked my head and hugged Seagull's sides with my knees as she sped behind Goodfellow. With an angry cry the dragon dove at Garth, driving Goodfellow headlong into the bushes. We weren't in her sanctuary, why attack us on the road? No time to wonder more, for she'd already wheeled about flying open-jawed toward me. Her heavy wing strokes agitated the branches; her teeth were dagger sharp, her eyes a brilliant blue.

I yanked Seagull's reins in a frantic attempt to turn her about. The terrified horse bucked me off. I flew back and hit the road hard, tumbling through dust and stones, ending painfully on my backside.

"Tess?" Garth was shouting from somewhere up the road, but the hard landing had knocked the wind out of me. I struggled to draw breath. The creature dove again.

I felt the heat of her wings, her copper belly became my sky as she skimmed overhead with her foreclaws stretched out. I did not know dragons could extend or retract their talons like a cat's claws, until I saw her black talons jut out suddenly, twice their former length, as if to catch me. Stunned from my fall, I could not pull my knife to defend myself, could not scream or roll away.

Garth raced back, shouting and waving his arms. The dragon flew upward, spitting red fire before she darted back to the wood.

Garth was at my side, his face drawn with concern. The dust still swirled around us. "Tess? Are you hurt?"

My spine ached. There were many stones on the road; at least one poked into my back. I sat up dizzily. "Only bruised, I think. She was angry with us, Garth. Her cry sounded angry." I looked at him. "Why is that? We were not in her wood."

"Can you walk, Tess?" He wrapped his arm around me. I'd known the back side of a man's hand, the crack of a man's fist. But this new, tender touch surprised me. He helped me to my feet and I stepped away, confused.

"I can walk." I dusted off Aisling's riding cloak and saw the tear in the hem. "Aisling won't like the state of her cloak."

"It's not her cloak I care about."

Blushing, I glanced down the road where Seagull waited, thrashing her flaxen tail across her rump. She was still unsettled and I couldn't blame her. Garth's well-trained stallion was calm compared to her. Head down, Goodfellow chewed the patch of dry grass beside us. Garth led Goodfellow along by the bridle as we went to fetch poor, startled Seagull.

"Now, now," I said, stroking her sweaty neck.

Garth rubbed her nose. "It's all right, my girl. No one's going to hurt you."

His words melted me. I put my face against Seagull's neck, and felt the heat rising up my own.

"You did not scream when the dragon flew over, Tess. Most maidens would have."

I had to fight to take possession of myself. I was all knots inside over the dragon's attack, over Garth's tender touch. At last I said, "I have seen dragons before."

"Many folk still scream mightily when one flies by, even if they've seen one before."

"That's true." We led the horses on. The reddened clouds turned gray brown overhead. More blew in from the sea, bringing sheets of rain, and we were forced to shelter under oak boughs overhanging the boundary wall. "I didn't tell you earlier. We all saw something while we were on the road."

"Go on." Garth adjusted Goodfellow's saddle, which had slipped askew in the attack.

"A dragon rescued a girl from a witch burning back in Hessings Kottle. He pulled her from the fire just in time, and his wingtip was burned in the rescue."

"How badly burned?" Garth asked, alarmed.

Did he care for dragons? "I don't know. He flew the girl to the bay to douse her burning gown, and dunked his flaming wingtip also. His flight was awkward with his singed wingtip. He struggled even after he managed to put out the flames. But he did not drop the girl."

"And he took her—"

I answered, nodding at Dragonswood. I'd watched it all happen from the cliff that night, but I'd missed some things. "Poppy saw a fey man riding on his back, but I did not."

"Fey can vanish in the blink of an eye," Garth said.

True he might have done that, and I'd only just missed him.

Garth said, "We should move on." The rain had lessened, though smaller pinprick drops still fell.

I glanced about. "Will she attack us again? I'm worried about Seagull."

"I don't think she'll return." Garth cupped his hands. His hood fell back as he helped me up into the saddle. His black hair was tangled, and I had the urge to straighten the lock hanging over his eyes, smooth the worried wrinkle from his brow. I combed Seagull's mane instead.

OUR RETREAT THAT night was an enormous boulder leaning strangely to the left, providing a goodly overhang.

The evergreen beside it arched over like a giant's bow. Shielded from the weather beneath boulder and tree, Garth tried to light a fire. When the damp sticks were not responsive, he pulled a black stone from his saddlebag. This time the fire took.

"Burningstone? Wherever did you find it?" I'd dug alongside my father many a time in search of the rare rocks said to be made of ancient dragon bones. Burningstone would have done wonders for his smithy, heating the ovens without costly wood, saving him the chore of making his own charcoal. We'd never found any.

"It's around if you know where to look," Garth said.

"Could you show me?" I asked timidly.

"Too dangerous to ride so far in these times, Tess." He sounded somewhat apologetic, as if he might like to take me there. The flames grew steadily, but my damp back was still chilly. I drew my cloak in tighter. "Are you sure it's safe to camp in Dragonswood?" I'd asked him the same thing earlier when we'd entered the sanctuary for the night. It was the first time we'd gone inside the wall.

"Safe as it's ever been. I'm allowed in here as a king's woodward."

"Yet we were attacked today." I knew he was also upset by the dragon's attack, but he'd been reluctant to talk of it all afternoon. I watched him blow into the flames to encourage the fire along. He wiped dirt from his palms, and caught an airy bit of floating ash.

"The dragon's gone now, Tess."

"I still don't see what we did to offend her."

Garth kicked the back of his boot against the rock to knock the mud off. "We might have ridden too close to her den," he suggested. "If she has hatchlings, she'd be on high alert."

Was this what he really thought, or a reason he'd taken all afternoon to come up with? Still, it could explain her strange behavior. Angry birds dove at my head when I'd gone too near their nests. Even larks, usually so sweet, had attacked me once to protect their young.

Garth took his crossbow and left me to tend the flames while he went to hunt up some dinner. I placed the stewpot on the fire to boil, and finding a clean, flat stone, used my stolen knife to dice an onion. The knife was the only weapon I'd ever owned. It comforted me to have it here in the darksome forest even if I used it now to chop an onion. Soon my eyes were streaming. I leaned against the boulder awaiting Garth's return and stared long at the flames.

The burningstone added a spicy scent to the fire. Colorful sparks flew up from it. Whether it was the strangeness of the burningstone, the long day's ride, or the blue-green color the stone added to the yellow flames, I cannot say, but in time my body went very still, my breath grew shallow, and my pulse slowed. The fire-sight came on.

In the wavering light I saw a fey woman riding a dragon

across the sea, the water glowing red with dusk where it was not white-capped. The dragon wheeled, rising and falling in the heavy gusts as they winged silently into the distance. Flames roared, but the fire was not done with me. I saw a girl strolling down a beach. Her back was to me. How old she was I could not tell, but she was small in stature and her step was as lively as a child's. She wore a strange kirtle, copper colored as a dragon's chest scales, and indeed the pattern of the cloth was scaly as if the gown were sewn with dragon scales.

The girl ran. Waves crashed, but I did not hear the sound. Down the beach I spied a woman holding a babe. The woman shouted, yet like the waves, I could not hear the shout, only the coaxing whisper of the fire, and the strange bubbling and whispering sound that sometimes troubled my left ear. The girl with her back to me ran closer to the woman with the babe.

I saw the woman's face and it was mine. My heart thumped against my ribs. But I could not move hand or foot, entranced by the fire. Was this some future event? Where was this beach? Whose babe was in my arms, and why was I shouting? The girl snatched the babe, and when she turned about, I saw her monstrous face and screamed. Green scales covered half the girl's forehead, and her eyes . . . her eyes were golden dragon eyes with black diamond pupils. She'd snatched the infant, my babe! Ah, God. What was she about to do?

The fire-sight faded. Teeth chattering, I backed away from the flames and ran.

Garth must have heard my scream earlier; pounding up with his crossbow, he dropped the rabbit he'd shot. "What is it, Tess?" he asked, looking left and right. "What's happened?"

"Nothing," I said, shivering. "I . . . had a wicked dream."

He sighed. "Come sit down, then. I can see I made you ride too far today."

Back at the fire, I averted my eyes, fearing more fire-sight might come. Garth skinned the rabbit and put it in the pot with the onion. When the stew began to seethe, he asked, "What did you dream?"

"It was nothing."

"Nothing does not usually make a lady scream as you did. Were you dreaming of the dragon that attacked us today?"

I shook my head. "I have night terrors," I admitted.

"What sort of night terrors?"

"Mostly about my father." Without thinking, my hand crept up to my cauliflower ear. I dropped my hand, but he'd seen me covering my ear.

He broke a stick over his knee. "You know what I think about that," he said.

Men who beat the weaker sex are brutes. "I know."

I watched the hot steam rising between us.

"So you fell asleep and dreamed about your father," he said. "What happened in the dream?"

I cleaned the onion juice from my knife blade. Tossed the brown onion skins in the fire. I'd often had nightmares of my father beating me with his mallet, trying to pound me into shape, but I'd only spoken of it now not wanting to confront the images I'd just seen.

Garth must have sensed my reluctance. He said, "I sometimes dream I'm falling from a high cliff, but I wake up just before I'm smashed to pieces on the rocks below."

"A good time to awaken."

"Indeed."

"Are you pushed?"

"What?" He gave a startled look.

"Does someone push you off the cliff in your dream?"

"I don't think so."

"Then you jump?"

He frowned, watching the bubbling stew. "Maybe," he whispered. "Maybe I jump."

Then I told him what had made me scream, as if it were a dream and not a fire-sight, I described the hideous monster who'd stolen my child.

"Hideous . . . monster?" Garth jumped up with such violence, he nearly kicked over the stew. I huddled like a hunted creature. He towered over me and I saw the mounting, inexplicable anger I'd known all my life.

This time I'd not wait for a beating. I grabbed my knife and fled.

Chapter Seventeen

"TESS?" GARTH'S HEAD was thrown back to peer up at me in the branches. "Why scurry up a tree? The stew will be ready soon. Won't you come down?"

I gripped my knife. Why had I trusted him? I knew better than to trust a man. "You're angry with me."

"No, I'm not."

"Don't lie; I know anger when I see it." He looked so small standing far below. Like a grounded blackbird.

Seagull trotted up to him and whinnied. Garth patted her neck. "Now see, you have Seagull worried."

"Tell her I am happy up here in the tree."

"She is happy up there in the tree, Seagull."

I smiled a little. "Tell her I am tired of sudden anger, of punching fists, black eyes, cuts, and bruises."

"She is tired of sudden anger, fists—"

"Punching fists," I corrected.

"Of punching fists, black eyes, cuts, and bruises."

Seagull huffed and nodded. Garth and I laughed.

"Will you come down now and have some dinner?"

"You go ahead and eat. You must be famished." I felt gnawing hunger but would not admit it. The man did not obey. Instead he climbed. My breath caught. What was he doing?

Garth positioned himself on a thick branch across from me and slightly lower so his head was not quite as high as mine.

"This is my tree," I said.

He poked a pinecone. "So you own it?"

"I didn't mean it like that."

"Do you plan to cut a branch?" he asked, looking at my blade.

I didn't answer. A squirrel leaped pine to pine, then raised his brushy tail, calling *Cheet! Cheet!*

"He thinks your tree belongs to him," Garth said.

"Sir Squirrel," I said, "you can have your domicile back soon enough."

"So you mean to come down eventually?"

When I did not respond he added, "Do you want to know what angered me?"

I fingered the blade.

"You dreamed of Princess Augusta."

"How do you know it was she?"

"I told you I was a castle knight. I did not mention my father was a friend of the royal family. My father, my brother, and I often traveled with them when I was a boy."

"Did you go with them to the hunting lodge?"

He nodded. "The lodge in fall, the castle on Dragon's Keep in summer. I played with the princes when we were boys."

"Then you've . . . seen their little sister?"

"The one you called the hideous monster? She is but four years old now. I visited her a few times with Prince Bion, though Prince Arden has never gone to see the child."

"He's been busy on crusade," I said.

"Busy? Is that what he's been?"

I felt his irritation raising the hairs along my arms, but Garth had climbed the pine to speak with me, not thrash me. "The girl in my dream was more than four years old. It might not have been Princess Augusta."

"You described her face, Tess: the scaly half of her fore-head and her copper-colored dragon eyes. It was her."

I swallowed, remembering the girl had snatched a baby from my arms. What did it mean?

"What is she like?" I asked cautiously.

"Like a four-year-old girl," he said. "She is no more a monster than the rest of the Pendragons whose scales are hidden on wrist or neck or arm. She did not ask to be so marked, but it's too much for most folk. Even her father could not look at her."

I thought of King Kadmi rejecting his youngest child. Was it only for her looks? "There might be other reasons." I told Garth that Poppy's mother had died birthing her.

That her father had resented her because of it and kept her as a man does a thoroughbred animal for its value and not for love.

Garth was silent. I could not read his expression in the dark. The pine swayed in the damp wind. We held our branches, riding the gusts. *He seems as much at home as I am up here,* I thought. I liked him well for it.

"If you're such good friends with Prince Bion, why aren't you with him searching for the missing treasure now?"

Garth rode another gust before answering. "He asked me to guard that part of Dragonswood."

"Why that part?"

"Bion fears the sanctuary walls there might be breached. The sheriff in Oxhaven is a powerful man and one who would like to see the boundary walls come down. He'd use the excuse of hunting for the missing treasure for a start."

"Then it's dangerous for you to leave and ride south with me."

He shook his head. "I have allies, Tess, and they guard that part of Dragonswood while I'm away."

"And what's Prince Bion doing while you and your friends guard the wood?"

The wind had quieted. I felt the night wrap around me as I waited for his answer. "Other than combing the isle for the treasure?" he said with some rigidity. "If you want to know, Prince Bion has to keep an eye on the king's regent, Sackmoore, a crooked man if there ever was one."

Crooked? I considered the man who had funded Lady Adela's hunts. Garth was watching his tongue in my company. There were baser words to describe the demon.

The gusts had swept the sky clean of clouds. Garth clutched the branch, straightened his arms, and leaned back to spy the stars through the greenery. The moon was like a half-gone pie.

"Nice up here. How often do you scale trees?"

"I cannot say."

"Cannot or will not?"

"Will not."

"Often then," he guessed. "You surprise me."

"I'm glad."

He laughed outright. "Are you ready to come down?"

"I might like to taste your stew."

"So hunger wins," he said.

I slid my knife in my belt and climbed down after him. When I jumped from the lowest branch, he caught me, and held me a moment. The touch sent a clean wind through me, sweet and strong. If I could have stayed there all through the passing night, I would have. But he let me go and we trailed back to the boulder and the warm rabbit stew.

UNBUCKLING GOODFELLOW'S SADDLEBAG, Garth pulled out two wooden bowls. Wolves howled somewhere in the distance. Our eyes locked. "We'll keep the fire going throughout the night," Garth said. "And if they come closer we can always climb yon tree," he added with a teasing smile.

The howling continued. How could he jest about such a thing? But behind the light talk, I saw caution. Scrambling up the tree would keep us from the wolves' jaws. I thanked God we'd seen no bear scat in the woods. Bears are veteran climbers.

"How clearly did you see the dragon who rescued the girl from the fire?"

"It was night, but I saw he was very large."

"An old one then," Garth said, filling my bowl.

"An old one," I agreed. "And one I'd seen before."

"When?" He did not try to hide his curiosity, but had stopped mid-pour, holding the bowl up between us and looking at me through the rising steam.

I'd told him about my witch trial back at the lodge the night he'd showed me the pearl. But I'd not detailed my escape from Harrowton. He handed me my bowl. I was about to tell him how the old dragon rescued me, dropping a turtle in Miller's Pond, when I felt as if a cold hand encircled my throat. *Don't speak of it.*

I glanced down and blew on the hot stew. *I already told him the dragon rescued the burning girl, why not mention my rescue?* The invisible hand seemed to tighten. I fought against it, sipped the stew to bring warmth back to my throat. Was this my own caution or something else preventing me? *Tell him about the other time.* "I saw the same old dragon one night when I'd climbed a tree."

"In Dragonswood?"

I nodded.

"So you were also a lawbreaker, Tess."

"I never hunted in the wood," I said. "I just went there to be alone and think."

"And recover from your father's blows?" he guessed. His look was kind.

Again I nodded. "I saw the old dragon the night before we buried Adam."

Garth's look asked *Who was Adam?* but he waited for me to say more.

The cold hand was no longer at my throat. I could eat from my bowl; still, I was finding it difficult to speak. "Adam was my baby brother," I whispered. "I'd gone to Dragonswood to cry. Seeing the dragon . . . helped. He breathed a stream of fire over the Harrow River. It was beautiful," I added.

Garth nodded. "Dragons can be wiser than men, though they're wilder." He tasted his stew, and ate some more.

"Did you meet dragons on Dragon's Keep?" He'd only just told me of his boyhood travels. I was trying not to be jealous. "Have you ever spoken with one?" I added eagerly before he could even answer my first question.

He nodded. "I have, and I can tell you this. The dragons wonder that we, the weaker race, should have taken over the world, driving them from their wilderness in the last few thousand years."

I knew the dragons died without vast hunting ranges. I also knew the jealousies the sanctuary provoked. "Men like my father want the dragons and the fey booted out. He often talked of tearing down the walls so he could hunt and fish and harvest the timber there for his forge."

"A common sentiment," Garth said. "Men high and low want the wood back, the lords no less than commoners. The king's regent knows it too. In fact he counts on it. Sackmoore would destroy the sanctuary if he had the power."

"Then Prince Arden best hurry home," I said.

"Amen to that," he whispered. Garth sat cross-legged on the ground in his mud-stained jerkin. A proud man and strong, he was concerned for his section of Dragonswood, I could see that, yet he'd taken us in. Now we were on a mercy mission for Meg. "Why have you been so kind to us?"

He shrugged. "I knew from the first you weren't witches." He sloshed more stew into his bowl. "I could not leave you out there to die, could I?"

"Some might have." I studied his face, half in light and half in shadow, the fire and night taking what they may. "Was it because . . . did it have to do with what Lady Adela did to your grandmother?" I asked cautiously, knowing it might upset him.

"The witch hunter didn't harm my grandmother."

"But you said your grandmother was tried for witch-craft."

"She was. I would not lie to you about that, Tess, but it was years and years ago."

"Was she . . ." I fought the bile coming up my throat. "Did they burn her at the stake?" I pictured Garth as a small boy, seeing his grandmother taken, perhaps witnessing her death. Some people took their youngsters to witch burnings. My father brought me when I was just seven.

"No, Tess. She was lucky. She lived."

He would not tell me more of her, though I asked not only from my heart, but because I wanted to know how she'd gotten away. I'd heard of no other women aside from myself and the one the dragon rescued who escaped after their witch trial.

Garth finished his meal and left the fire. I did not follow him. I could tell the man needed to be alone. The stewpot sat cooling near my feet. The fire's heat silvered the air above. I watched Garth brushing Goodfellow's mane as if through glass. The burningstone greened the fire; flames moved like living dragon scales. The green man I'd first seen in the fire-sight long ago continued to surprise me. I sat very still, my body at rest, my heart full.

Chapter Eighteen

THE LAST NIGHT before reaching Harrowton, we camped again in Dragonswood. Garth fried three trout for dinner and when the meal was done, he whittled a woodblock he'd loosed from the edge of the fire. Scraping all the charred black wood from the surface till it was clean and white, he'd cut grooves in the sides, trimming the wood into a roughly human shape.

"What do you make?"

"A doll for the child." His cinnamon eyes were fixed on the poppet. I studied his face, so stern with concentration as he worked the blade. Such fine articulated attention almost made me jealous of the woodblock. I dismissed my absurd feelings as I watched him shape the doll's head and peel curling layers thin as parchment to form her small chin. Hands blackened with char, he paused to rub the bridge of his nose and left a black smudge behind. Not once did he look up.

I stood.

"Don't go in too far," Garth said. "I spied bear scat earlier."

"I won't go far." *Give me a man who does not mind that she slips into Dragonswood.* Stepping a little way into the forest, I tramped under the night sky. The stars appeared like snowflakes caught and never falling, held by God's hand, I supposed, or suspended by his breath. It was easy to gather moss hanging from the oak branches. The doll's hair would be thick and curly as my own.

Night wind blew against my face as I tugged away the moss. A hissing sound came to my left ear, *Tessss*

I spun round, peering into the dark. *Tess, you are going the wrong way.*

I drew my knife. "Show yourselves. Who are you?"

Come north.

"Leave me be. I am going south with Garth."

Wind swirled a maelstrom of leaves torn from the trees. Bright specks of light twirled in the distance—will-o'-the-wisps flitting through the forest? It couldn't be anything else. I'd seen the tiny fairies only once before. Each was the size of my little finger with translucent wings, and all were lit up golden white from the inside. Dipping in and out of the branches ahead, they split apart, swirled in dizzying patterns, then came together in one bright orb as if the moon were bobbing through the forest.

I was filled with longing. I ran toward the dancing light, my arms stretched out wide. I raced through the bracken until my lungs were winded, and nearly reached the fairies.

They vanished.

In the gloom, I hunched over, panting, the knife loose in my sweating hand, the moss I'd gathered for the doll, gone. I'd wanted to catch up to them so much, wanted desperately to go with them. I sobbed, suddenly overcome with feeling as if I'd lost something precious. I wiped my nose and tried to steady my breath. The ache in my heart would not leave. What had come over me? Why so desperate? At last I stood up in the chill forest.

Don't be such a clodpole! It could be some kind of trick. I turned full circle. The woods were coal black. Trees grew so thick here, I could not see the sky. Worse, I couldn't see Garth's campfire. Had I run only for a few minutes, or was it hours, years? Fairies liked to toy with a person's sense of time. My heart thumped. Spying a single moonbeam ahead, I raced for it, then leaped back, gasping at the illumined man-shaped tree. The Treegrim's arms were stretched out, twiggy fingers splayed. Hulking like an oversized scarecrow, a bird's nest crammed in its hollow belly: The look of horror in its black eye pits and craggy face was caught forever in wood.

I screamed into my hands, swirled round, and shouted, "Garth!"

"Tess? I'm over here."

I scrambled toward the distant call. It seemed to take forever in the dark, but at last I caught the scent of smoke. Garth ran toward me with his sword drawn. "Did you see a bear?"

"No bear." I tried to laugh, nearly choked. *Had he missed me? Was I gone very long?*

"I . . . was a little lost."

He sheathed his sword. Standing close he was shadow dark, yet with all in shadow there was firmness in his stance, protection.

The moss I'd picked was gone. I pulled more from the branches as we went back to the fire. Seated again, I handed him the moss, then tugged a little sticky sap off the nearest pine.

He stared at it, wondering.

"Hair," I said, giving him the pitch to glue it on.

"Green hair?" He cracked a smile and picked up the carven doll. "She will be a woodland girl, like yourself," he noted.

He did not catch my expression. I loved the trees. I never wanted to become one.

I added another log to the fire and watched the sparks fly up. *Why will-o'-the-wisps tonight? Were they the ones who'd called to me all along?* Why would tiny fairies bother to say "You are going the wrong way"? Did they want to keep me out of Harrowton? Had they led me to the Treegrim to show what the fey could do to me if I disobeyed their summons?

I watched Garth carve the doll's legs. I knew it was foolhardy to enter Harrowton, where I was known for a witch, even if we did plan to sneak in at night, even if I was disguised as a cloth merchant's wife.

"You're very quiet." He'd stopped his work to look across the fire.

"I was just thinking about tomorrow."

"We'll be in and out of town fast, Tess. I'll protect you," he added.

"I know." And I did know it. My body warmed. Garth would do all in his power to protect me when we went after Alice.

"If you'd rather wait outside of town while I go in—"

"No. We've talked of this already. Old Weaver and his wife won't give up their grandchild to just anyone. They know me. More importantly, Alice knows me." The child would likely scream loud enough to raise the dead if Garth tried to take her away all by himself, and I wouldn't blame her. "The only chance we have is if I assure Old Weaver and his wife that their son is safe, that he and Meg asked me to bring their daughter to them."

"All right, but if you change your mind—"

"I won't."

The doll was ugly and might frighten the child, but Garth wasn't finished with it yet. "Tell me more about Princess Augusta."

He slid the blade down the doll's side, the "woodland girl" growing thinner by this. "Think, Tess," he said. "Who are the monsters? Dragons do not think men are comely. To them we appear thin-skinned, wingless, hair-less—"

"We have hair," I argued.

"Not fur like the animals have," he said. "Besides that, we are tailless, clawless, flat-toothed, flat-footed—"

"Enough," I said, laughing. "Are we so plain?"

"To them we are." He adjusted his seat on the thick branch and scratched his arm. "The dragons think our royal Pendragon family handsome, at least the part of them that's scaled."

"Did you ever see Prince Arden's or Bion's scales?" I asked.

"I have."

"What are they like?"

"Like dragon scales, only much smaller. About the size of your fingertips."

I wiggled my fingers, studying them in the soft firelight. "I would like to see that."

"Would you? The dream you had frightened you more than a little." He tugged a pine needle out of his hair. "You said Princess Augusta was hideous. But I tell you this: The dragons think she is the most beautiful human in the world."

AT NIGHTFALL WE reached the outskirts of Harrowton. Hail pelted the rooftops and danced along the cobbles. We'd left the horses tied up just outside of town and crept in quietly on foot. I hunched on the porch as Garth pounded the weaver's door. Old Timothy Weaver opened the door a crack, and started when he saw me.

"Tess," he hissed. "Because of you the witch hunter took our Tom away!"

"I know, Master Weaver, but your son is safe now. He and Meg are safe."

"Who's there?" came his wife's voice. "Who's come at this hour?"

"Let us in, good man," pleaded Garth. "We come to help you in your need."

"How do I know it's not a trap?"

Muffled steps inside. "I asked you, Timothy, who comes to our door?'

"Blacksmith's daughter, Tess, and some other man."

"Lock it!" she cried.

I jammed my foot in the doorsill. "Mistress Dulcy!" I spoke in a low tone. The street was abandoned so long after curfew; still, there were other shops and houses down the lane. I had no wish to alert anyone to our presence. "We have good news about your Tom, if only you would let us in."

At this the old woman flung the door open. We entered the cold room, the fire having long since been doused, for Old Weaver and his wife had gone to bed. Weaver held a guttering candle; in its inconstant glow we four huddled in the entryway, barking words, our breath white with the cold, till Dulcy led us into her kitchen and lit the fire.

I spied Alice sleeping in the corner on the kitchen settle. She looked cozy under her thick blankets and did not waken when the fire was lit nor when we argued at the table. Garth said Tom and Meg were safe, though he did not say where they hid. This was for the old couple's safety as much as our own. The weaver looked relieved, but his wife went fitful when we said what we'd come for.

"You mun not take the child," Dulcy cried, standing between us and the settle and spreading out her arms.

I stepped closer, my feet stirring the rushes on the floor. "Alice belongs with Meg, Mistress Dulcy. You know she needs her mother."

"And what do we say when folk ask where Alice has gone?" asked Old Weaver. The man had a brain.

I laid a hand on his table. "You know the abbey south of us in Brigidshire? Say she's gone to live with the nuns there at Saint Brigid's Abbey."

Weaver's wife grabbed the poker. "Out!" she screamed. "Now!"

The noise woke Alice. Sitting up, she pulled the coverlet to her chin and peeked out like a frightened little mouse. "Gamma?" she moaned to the old woman, fat tears sliding down her cheeks.

"Hush, now, Alice," "Gamma" warned, waving her poker at us.

"Hear us," I insisted. "We have a good plan that will be safe for all. You are caring grandparents, I don't doubt it, but Alice must miss her mother. I know Meg and Tom miss her desperately. Let us take her to her parents. For your part, you can't say she simply went away, or Lady Adela could send the law to track her down and find Tom. Think on it," I urged. Then in a whisper so as not to fright the child, I said, "Say you took her to Saint Brigid's. You know the law could not touch her there." The abbey was famous for having schooled Queen Rosalind's mother; still, for all its fame, it was a safe place set aside for God's work and cloistered from the world.

At the table Old Weaver tugged his wool hat down over his ears. "Put the poker down, woman," he ordered. She did, though with a grunt. Later, whilst the two men planned it all out, we sat with Alice between us. The child stuck to her grandmother like a limpet.

"Mistress Dulcy," I said, "have you seen my mother?"

She nodded. "On washing day down at river."

I used to bring our washing to the riverside. Mother had to do it now. *So soon after childbirth and she's not strong.* I felt a pang. "Does she . . . look well?" I had to know if Father used her as his punching bag now I was gone.

Mistress Dulcy put her hand on my arm, smearing char from the poker on my sleeve. But she understood my question. "As well as ever," she whispered over Alice's head. "You might go see her."

Could I risk it? I sorely missed her, wanted desperately to see her, but I'd thought it too dangerous to stay any longer here than we had to, to fetch Alice. Now she'd said it, my heart ached. My father would be at the Boar's Head this time of night. I might just sneak in, hold her in my arms, tell her not to worry, that I was all right. Across the kitchen Garth was awash in dim firelight. He put his foot up on a stool and rested his forearm on his knee as he spoke earnestly with the weaver. How strange it was to feel safe with a man yet not be confined by him, a feeling I was only beginning to grasp, one I was sure my mother had never known.

"I will try, mistress."

She nodded.

I gently clothed Alice. Dulcy sniffed as she packed her a small bag; the child did not own much. By the time I tied her cloak and put up the little hood, Alice was half asleep again, her little body slumping against me.

When I picked her up to go, Dulcy gripped my arm. "When you see Tom, tell him he's a good boy," she said. "And tell him to come home as soon as ever he can."

"I will." Tom would never come home. How could he? But I wouldn't hurt her mother's heart now she'd opened it to me.

ALICE WAS ASLEEP again when we left Weaver's. The hailstorm had ended, rain fell, but softly. Outside, I told Garth what I wanted to do.

"Are you sure, Tess?"

"It won't take long, I promise."

We made a quick plan and stole through town with the sleeping child. Down the alley by our house, I pointed to the woodshed below my upstairs window. "You can hide here out of the rain and look out for my father. If you see him coming, toss a rock up to my window to warn me."

"How will you get out, Tess?"

I nodded at the oak tree. "I have a way down. I've used it lots of times before." All rested on Father's nightly excursion to the Boar's Head. I knew his habits, how long he stayed. I didn't think he'd turn me in, but I wouldn't visit long enough to risk his beery wrath. I'd never let him hurt me again.

Through the kitchen window I caught Mother mending torn breeches by candlelight. My eyes welled seeing her at her sewing. I knocked. She opened the door and fainted straightaway. I caught her before she struck her head against the doorframe and quickly drew her back inside. When she woke, she whispered, "Tess. Thank God. Oh, thank God."

We were both crying for joy, but I knew we hadn't much time. Leading her up the stairs to my room, I opened the window a crack, peered down at the shadowy figure holding a sleeping child. Quick as I could I told Mother of my journey north with Meg and Poppy. For her own protection I did not say where we were hiding, only that we were all safe for now.

I looked closely at her in the spare candlelight, and was relieved to see no welts or bruises on her face.

"You look well," I whispered.

"And you," she said, fingering my fur-lined cloak and pretty gown. "You're a lady now."

I shook my head. "No, Mother. Borrowed clothes."

"Borrowed?"

"Don't ask more. I can't tell you. For your own good, I can't say more." Rain pattered the window—or was it a stone? I poked my head out. Garth stood quiet down below. "I came to assure you I'm all right to ease your heart, but I can't stay. Others are relying on me and anyway, Father will be home soon." I held her hand tightly.

"Wait. I have something for you." She left the room and came back. "Your grandfather sent us a letter and a package for you. They arrived a few days after you ran away."

She handed me a small unopened parcel. I tucked it in my belt. Her eyes fell on my blackened thumbs.

"Oh, Tess! What you've been through. It's my fault." She took my hands and, weeping, kissed my thumbs.

"Not your fault at all, Mother. It was mine, partly mine. I stole into Dragonswood. I was seen there." I said it to ease her. She wasn't to blame.

"Sit down, Tess. I have something to tell you."

"I haven't time."

"Sit," she pleaded, so I did.

"I knew you went to Dragonswood," she whispered.

"You did?"

"Out the window and down yon tree. I knew why you went."

I peered up at her. "I don't understand."

"It's to do with your father."

"I know all I need to know about my father," I snapped, jumping up.

"No, you don't. There's something I must tell you, Tess. Sit down."

"Whatever it is it has to wait. I'm endangering more than myself staying here so long. I have to go before Father—"

"He is not your father."

The room went white and hollow as a cockleshell. "What?"

I began to sway. She gripped my arms to hold me up. "If I'd told you this before, none of this would have happened. I waited too long," she said. "I was afraid."

She looked at my face. "Do you understand what I'm telling you? I was with child when I married John Blacksmith."

"I . . ." She swam in and out. *Don't faint.* "Does the blacksmith know?"

She shook her head. "He can never know."

Mother wrapped her arms around me. I could not feel them. I was in some deep cave, abandoned. Alone. "Who . . . am I, then?"

"You are yourself still, Tess," Mother whispered.

"Who is my father?" I drew back to search her face. Red shame streaked her neck. How had it happened? Had he forced himself on her? Was that why she'd put off telling me, waiting until I was a grown woman who would understand such things? "My father didn't hurt you or force you to lie with him, did he?" Suddenly I was desperate to know he hadn't harmed her.

"No, Tess. It wasn't like that. We danced at Midsummer Night's Fair. He was . . . kind." She blushed.

There was love in her blush. I felt a sob coming up my throat. "Then why? . . . Why didn't he marry you?"

"I could not go with him. We lived in different worlds."

A pebble hit the window. We both jumped. "The blacksmith's home!"

The door slammed down below.

"Woman?" The sound of his heavy boots came up the stairwell. "Woman, where are you?"

"Hurry, Tess," Mother said.

"But you haven't told me—"

"Quick!" She pushed me toward the window.

I barely made it out before the door flung open. Halfway down the tree I heard the demanding bellow from above, "Wife, why didn't you answer me when I called?"

I fled with Garth back down the alley. Alice stirred but fell asleep again. Garth and I took turns carrying her wrapped safely in our cloaks. The going was slow with the rain slicking the cobbles.

Once we were safely out of town, Garth led the horses back to the road, but we made little progress in the storm. Alice woke and cried. I tried to comfort her, saying, "Hush now, don't be afraid," and "We're taking you to see your mother." The child had known me all her life; still, she was frightened to be on a dark road with me on such a stormy night traveling with a grown man who was a stranger to her.

A cold wind whistled through the forest by the time we'd made a bit of shelter. Garth strung the wax cloth tarp between two trees for a tent. Wood and tinder damp, he produced a chunk of burningstone to start a fire. Alice whimpered, so I rocked her. She was three and no infant, yet I sang her the lullabies I used to sing to Mother's babes. All the while I thought, *I am not the blacksmith's child. He is not my father.*

THE STORM HAD passed in the night and the rising sun spread vermilion over the sea. Fishing boats were leaving the bay for the deeps beyond, their sails as red as the water. By morning Alice was braver and she laughed when Garth held her up to me in the saddle. Seagull stomped, impatient to be gone, but Garth spoke to her with a "Kush, kush, now." Then he wrapped a soft cloth round Alice's middle and mine so the child would not fall off.

On the road over the next two days we played our parts, the husband riding protectively ahead, his wife and child behind. I kept my hood up at first, but took it off once we were a goodly distance from Harrowton.

Alice grew more used to the ride and bounced impatiently in the saddle, squealing, "Wide fast, Tess!"

Her glee reminded me of when I was three or four bound to my mother's waist the same way. We didn't own a single horse, so Mother must have been taking a newly shod mare back to its owner and brought me along for the outing. I remember riding down to the dock in Harrowton Harbor, and another time trotting along Kingsway.

How high up in the world I was riding with Mother. Like Alice, I'd laughed when our horse began to trot. It delighted me to feel my mother's warmth against my back, and to smell her scented hair.

Small as I was, I do not think I was at all afraid when we rode together. By then I was already well acquainted with fear, and had learned to hide behind the settle when the blacksmith beat Mother, so I was relieved when we could both escape.

Garth rode up ahead and as we followed him around a bend, the robins splashing in the puddles took flight. Alice laughed and threw up her hands as if to catch one. Holding her close, her small body pressed up to mine, and her plump arms spread out to the birds, I ached in the light of her laughter. For the first time I wondered at my mother. With all my efforts to protect her, she'd still taken her share of blows. Never could she stand up to her husband. Yet I knew deep down I could never be like her. I'd never let a man hit a child.

ALICE WAS STURDY for her age, but she grew bored with the long ride.

"Sing," she said one afternoon with a yawn. Meg's voice was fine. I could not sing the way her mother did, but I would try.

> *Lady, come ye over,*
> *Over the sea.*
> *And bring your heart with you.*
> *And marry me . . .*

"Not that one," Alice said rudely.

Garth looked back at her and laughed.

"Sing 'Fey Maiden,'" she insisted. Meg had told me it was her daughter's favorite.

"Say *if you please*, Alice."

"Please, Tess." She tipped her head and smiled up at me.

"Very well."

> *In the enchanted woodland wild,*
> *The Prince shall wed a Fairy child.*
> *Dragon, Human, and Fairy,*
> *Their union will be bound by three.*

I sang the second verse. If there was a third, I did not know the words. My voice was not as sweet and clear as Meg's had been when she'd sung it to us the night we fled the witch burning.

You think it's true? Poppy had asked.

It's just a song. Grandfather's tales never mentioned any marriage between human and fey.

Fey men take lovers, Meg had said.

"Sing it again," Alice pleaded.

"I'm tired. Perhaps Garth Huntsman will sing it for you."

"Sing," she called happily to Garth, clapping her small hands.

He drew Goodfellow back to ride alongside us. "I should tell you the song has been outlawed."

"Why?"

"The king's regent called it dangerous."

"It's just a song," I whispered.

"Is it?" His eyes searched mine.

I tried to make light of his look. "You don't think a fairy maiden would wed a Pendragon prince, do you?"

"Not one from DunGarrow to be sure, but a half-fey girl might."

Half fey? I remembered Grandfather's tales of girls who went with fey men, how they ended up with child out of wedlock, and had to raise the half-fey child on their own. Not happy tales.

Garth said, "The fey folk would like to have their bloodline represented on the throne. A half-fey girl might not have many fairy powers, but she'd be drawn to Dragonswood, she'd want to protect the refuge."

Not many fairy powers, but one, maybe one. Fire-sight.

Was it true? Could it be true? My breath came fast and shallow. The boundary wall moved in and out, and the trees behind it tipped as I tried to fight the dizziness.

"Tess?" Garth's voice came from far away.

"I need . . . I must get down."

"What, here?"

"Please, take Alice."

Dismounting, he led the horses to the roadside and took Alice in his arms. I jumped off the saddle and ran hard into the trees.

I was with child when I married John Blacksmith.

Who am I, then, Mother? Who is my father?

Climbing over the boundary wall, I did not stop running. Why had the old dragon rescued the burning girl? Why had he dropped a turtle in the pond for me? He would not have rescued ordinary girls, or flown a witch to DunGarrow. Fairies would not harbor witches.

A half-fey girl might not have many fairy powers, but she'd be drawn to Dragonswood, she'd want to protect the refuge.

I ran and ran.

I knew you went to Dragonswood, Mother had said. *Out the window and down yon tree. I knew why you went. It's to do with your father.*

I'd seen the love in Mother's eyes when she'd spoken of my father.

Why didn't he marry you?

I could not go with him. We lived in different worlds.

Different worlds. Our human world. The fairy kingdom; ah, they were different enough.

"Tess?" Garth called in a worried tone.

I did not answer or turn back. The woodland welcomed me. Greenery bowed, branches waved. It all fit. My longing for the wood, my secret power, Mother's confession, the dragon's rescue from the pond. I knew it in my body. In my bones. I'd known it long. I'd known it always, but never understood till now. *My father is a fey man.*

Poor Mother had run home and married the first man who asked her so she would not have to raise a half-fey child alone.

Chapter Nineteen

ALICE!" MEG RACED outside, swung her little girl down from the saddle, and hugged her, crying with joy. My arms felt suddenly empty, my chest where Alice had leaned her head on the long ride went cold. I could only watch mother and daughter from atop my horse, Meg's arms around her girl, and Alice squealing, "Mama! Mama!" Kissing her cheeks the way a small child does, clasping Meg's face between her pudgy hands.

Soon Poppy and Aisling ran out from the kitchen, their hands still wet from washing up. Even Tom came out, eyes shining with tears.

Alice called, "Da!" and he took her in his arms. Tom had improved greatly while we were away. Aisling and Poppy's ministrations had strengthened him, but it was Alice who brought color to his cheeks.

Garth helped me dismount and led the horses to the barn. His head was slightly down and his steps weary. It had been a long ride. I was watching him go when Meg flung her arms around me. "Thank you. Oh, thank you Tess!" She kissed me wetly.

"Thank Garth. He's the one who—"

"I will," she squealed, her voice as high-pitched with delight as her daughter's, but I noted she did not go to the barn to seek him out immediately as I would have done.

Later that afternoon we ate Meg's hearty stew and bread trickled with honey. God bless the bees for it.

I had been content to play the family when we were together on the road. And I'd thought Garth felt the same, but the man shed the guise of marriage and fatherhood like an old cloak when he joined us at table. Had it all been a game? The long talks we'd had in the saddle or at the fire, the attentiveness he'd shown me when I'd played his wife? I'd only tasted the stew and bread, but my hunger had already vanished.

Taking an apple, I went out to the stable.

Things had changed between us after I'd sung "Fey Maiden." I'd been quieter on our ride, lost in thought, the hoofbeats echoing *fey, half fey,* in my head. Even Alice noticed my strange moods and had ridden with Garth part of the time. Had he looked at me differently after I'd run off from him and Alice? Did he suspect something?

Seagull's blond neck was smooth under my stroking hand. "You understand, don't you, my lady?" She eyed me quizzically, chewing the apple I'd brought. Garth stepped in and re-saddled Goodfellow. "Tess, will you give Cackle a hand and see the animals are fed while I'm away? And if you can, help him walk the dogs?"

"We only just got home this morning." The word *home* had slipped in without my thinking. "Where are you going?"

"I have duties," he said, cinching the saddle a little tighter. "They've been sorely neglected while we went for Alice."

"Do you regret it?" I asked. I hadn't meant to say that, only it slipped out.

"What? No, Tess. I don't regret it." He slid the bit into Goodfellow's mouth. Out near the pigsty, I heard Alice laughing. She'd come out with her father to watch the pigs.

"I've not thanked you yet for helping me fetch her," I said.

"That's thanks enough." He pointed at father and daughter across the fenced sty.

I wanted to say more and keep him with me a moment longer, even if I was still smarting over the way he'd ignored me at the table, but Aisling appeared with a lumpy burlap sack.

"This should help," she said. Garth slipped it into the saddlebag. Food for the journey? How long would the man be gone? Garth bid me hold Horace's collar as he rode off. The old dog howled and strained, wanting desperately to go with his master. I felt the same, yet had to restrain myself as much as I restrained the forlorn hound.

FOUR DAYS PASSED with no sign of Garth. I helped
Cackle with his daily chores, feeding the pigs and chickens,
and walking the dogs two at a time. Garth's favored hound
came along. Horace was older and quieter than the rest
and did not require a leash. The first day out, the freckled
pointers were not well-mannered. Tails wagging, they
tugged their tethers and pulled me off my feet. I allowed
this but once, before shouting and taking a firmer hand.

Returning the dogs, I went out a second time alone,
but for faithful Horace. After a goodly walk, I took out
Grandfather's small parcel and undid the string. I'd expected a letter, but unfolded a small painting I'd done
when I was a child. A picture of DunGarrow Castle all
colorful and bright. My name was at the bottom in a child's
hand, and by it one word Grandfather must have written
just for me. *Remember.*

A chill came reading that one word. He must have
known about me from the start. I thought of all the stories
he'd told me of the fey—his way of providing me with
my family history. He'd learned some tales firsthand from
the fey folk he met crossing the sea. They'd come from all
manner of places in the world in search of safety and freedom in Rosalind's refuge. I knew he'd cherished his meet-
ings with the fey folk on their voyage to Wilde Island.

Grandfather had offered what he could, arming me with

knowledge of my father's people while honoring Mother's secret. Along with the little painting, he also sent a lady's handkerchief. The rose-pink cloth was smooth and sparkled in the sunlight. I'd never seen anything so fine.

His one word whispered through me. *Remember.* Perhaps he'd longed to tell me the truth about myself. But it was Mother's news to tell. He had to respect that. "She waited much too long," I said to the child's painting, the handkerchief.

I tucked his gifts away. On the path I listened for any whispering voices in my deaf ear. All was silence from the fey world since I'd learned who I was. Did they still want me to come north? If so, why not call me now? But part of me wasn't disappointed. I knew I could not go quite yet. In my heart I was waiting for Garth's return.

While I'd been away south with Garth, Poppy had washed our old leper robes. In the evening we cut them to make new short cloaks for Meg and Poppy, and a little cloak and smock for Alice. All were green, for we had no dye. We took pleasure sewing together by the fire. Mother and I had done some stitchery for the tailor to make some extra market money, but Meg was the better seamstress.

We settled in the three stuffed chairs by the hearth, warm, dry, and barefoot with the golden flames so near us. Poppy was in the chair Garth liked to sit in to read with her eyes on my ink drawing.

I felt myself blushing. *I should have taken it down.*

Poppy said, "It's a good likeness of him."

"Do you think so? I didn't quite capture his—" *Ease, charm, complexity, stubbornness, secretiveness . . .*

"His what?" Meg's eyebrow lifted.

"His . . . expression."

"He would be difficult to draw," Poppy agreed. "Garth Huntsman keeps very much to himself."

"Yes," I said, relieved. "That's it." *Can we talk of something else now?*

"And did he keep to himself on the road?" Meg inquired.

I threw my garment piece at her. Meg laughed and tossed it back.

Poppy snipped the clean cloth spread over her knees. "It's almost a shame to cut them up."

I was surprised. "I thought you hated your leper robe."

"I did, but this big cowl"—she held it up—"hid my face. I found it a relief."

"I don't understand." She'd been angry with me the whole time we'd hidden out as lepers, though not as vocal about it as Meg.

"No one saw my face while we were on the road. I'm tired of men only liking me for my looks. Even my father cared for me only because of what I might win him."

"A noblemen for a son-in-law," Meg said with a nod. Lord Bainbridge had a handsome castle and vast farmlands. People did not marry below their station; still, the wheelwright had noticed how the lord's eldest son, young Richard Bainbridge, had eyed his beautiful daughter.

"Father hated me when I was a child. It was only later when I grew up and he saw the woman I was becoming did he—"

"He didn't hate you, Poppy," Meg said.

"He did! I felt it all my life. He hated me because Mother died the night I was born."

"That wasn't your fault." I wasn't sure Poppy believed me, if she even heard me at all.

"I prayed nightly for my father to have a change of heart, that he might love me." She teared up a little, and clipped threads, searching for composure.

I knew the kind of prayer she meant. So many years I'd prayed for my stepfather when I was young, begging the man would grow in faith, drink less, or if he must drink, that the ale would not work to loosen his rage. Lips bruised and swollen, I'd beg. I spoke of those old prayers as we three stitched together. Eyes fixed on my sewing, I confessed my deep disappointment when I'd heard no answer from God.

Meg asked, "Do you doubt God?"

The fire's light and shadow wavered around us. Even with all that had happened I felt something holy in the world. *Perhaps we are all too small-minded to glimpse creation, even our little corner of it.* "I doubt my understanding of God," I said at last.

Meg crossed herself and gave me a look of deep concern. Tom's health was better. Alice was with her again. Was her faith stronger than mine, or was it that her happiness was close at hand? I was glad for her. I still had my questions.

"Does prayer ever work to change a man's heart?" Poppy asked "My father changed his opinion of me, but not in the way I'd hoped. When I showed signs of becoming a woman, he became suddenly attentive. Still, he did not like me for myself."

I thought she might cry more, but she sat with a straight spine, squinting with concentration as she snipped. "I liked all the attention at first, the way the boys and men stared at me when I went to mass or shopped at market. I'd been lonely before that time, except when we'd played together—you and Meg and me," she added. "But soon enough I was tired of all the glaring. Eyes followed me everywhere."

We'd been good enough friends for me to know she'd grown tired of men's reactions to her, but she'd not talked so openly of it before. I was surprised by how much it had bothered her. Meg seemed surprised too. She'd stopped sewing to listen.

I wanted to ask if Poppy minded the way Garth had watched her sometimes. He'd seemed less intent on her since we'd come home with Alice, but then, he'd only been home a few hours before he left. I decided not to ask, feeling closer to Poppy now than I'd felt in a long time. "Someday you'll find the right man to marry," I said, hoping the right man wouldn't be Garth.

"How will that change anything?" she asked.

Meg huffed. "It will change everything. Your husband will not want other men ogling at you all the time. He'll protect you." She smiled to herself, thinking of Tom, I supposed.

"There," I said. "Your new cloak." I stood, holding it up for her. "And see, I've kept the cowl as large as you like it."

Poppy smiled and jumped up to try it on.

In the morning, Alice wore her new green smock when she followed me outside to feed the chickens.

"Me," she said, holding out her hands. I gave her a little feed. She threw it in a wide arc. Hens cackled and scampered over. "Oh, you're very good at it," I said.

"Me," she said with her hands out again. When the chore was done, Alice shouted, "Catch me!" as she ran for the maples. I chased her to a leaf pile out beyond the kennels.

"I've got you!" I tickled her sides, then swung her round and round. Meg stepped outside to watch. Dusting flour from her apron, she crossed her freckled arms and laughed. Tom joined her. He wasn't strong enough to swing his Alice around just yet, so he took Alice's small hand in his larger one, and went looking for Tupkin.

When I was three did my fey father spy me laughing?

Did he hear my laughter, long to pick me up, hold me, and smell my hair?

Am I not his daughter?

I WAS ELBOW-DEEP in dishwater and peering out the kitchen window when Garth rode in. Before the huntsman could leave the saddle, Horace bolted through the door, barking. Tom followed the old dog out. The door was left open, so I overheard the men conversing in the yard.

Garth dismounted and patted Horace, the dog's tail whipping his legs. "Cackle's good with the hens," he said. "But I could use another man about the place. There's much to watch over here."

Walking Goodfellow toward the stable, he asked if Tom and his small family might stay on more permanently. "I know you're a weaver by trade, but if this sort of occupation suits you—"

Tom interrupted to happily accept the offer. I scrubbed and dried the pot, keeping busy so I would not rush outside. When Goodfellow was back in his stall, the two men hastened to the kennels. The excited hounds howled and jumped up and down when Garth freed them. In a mass of wagging tails they followed Garth and Tom over to the pigsty. The animals all seemed joyful at their master's return, and though I was still at my work, I too felt a gentle warmth glowing outward from my heart as if Garth lit a candle there.

I'd set a warmed platter on the sideboard, as I had every meal since Garth left in case he returned hungry. It was all I could do to keep myself from running outside with his grub. The pot was clean, but I scrubbed harder so as not to make a fool of myself.

Leech Aisling stepped up and peered out at Tom, who'd squatted down to pet one of the dogs. "My work is done here."

I nodded. "You have done a fine job with him, Mistress Aisling."

"Poppy was a great help." Before she left the room, she glanced at Poppy, who'd come in to dry the dishes.

"What was that look for?"

"I'm to ask you something," said Poppy.

"Well, what is it?"

"Mistress Aisling says I have the gift of healing."

I nodded, knowing it was so.

Poppy put up the dry bowl and took a wet spoon from the cutlery pile. "Aisling asked me to come live with her at her smallholding. She's been looking for a new apprentice since the former one ran off to marry without her leave. And she promised to teach me all manner of things a healer needs to know," she concluded.

I pulled my hands from the suds and turned to my

friend, water dribbling down my arms. "Is that . . . what you want, Poppy?"

She did not look at me, but watched the dancing dust in the window light between us. "She is very kind, and I like the work, Tess."

"Look at me. Say yeah or nay. Tell me if it is what you want."

A blush pinked her pale neck. "I want it."

It had been my dream to earn my own way in the world without the need of a man, not hers. *Earn my way through my art, not handling leeches or tending wounds.* Poppy had always doctored me, and she'd helped heal Tom. She had the healer's touch, only she'd been unschooled. This was a good choice for her.

Suddenly I wanted her to stay. Not to leave me. "You should go with her."

"You don't mind?"

"It's what we've wanted, isn't it? A safe place for you to live far out of the witch hunter's sight?"

"And we can still visit," Poppy said. "Mistress Aisling's smallholding is but a day's ride from here." Her face shone.

"Aye, it's not too far away." I hugged her, my wet arms staining her kirtle, but it would dry again and I did not care.

"Don't cry, Tess," she whispered.

"I'm happy for you. Go and tell Aisling your news."

Poppy dropped her towel. Treading on it in her nervous excitement, she left me with the sudsy water that was barely warm now.

The next day Meg filled Aisling's basket with cheese, bread, and onions. She kissed Aisling and Poppy on the cheek for healing her Tom. I hugged Poppy tight. My arms were dry this time, so I held her long. I did not know when I would see her again.

Poppy and Aisling were mounted on Seagull, who was large enough to carry both with little trouble if they rode slowly and let the horse rest when she needed to. Behind us the hunting dogs yowled for their master to let them out. Garth paid them no mind, leading Seagull out beyond the gate. There he paused, his hand moving up a little as if he might speak. Then he turned as they rode on. A small furry shadow followed Seagull: Tupkin trotting down the path with his tail up. I think the cat was glad to leave a house where he'd never been welcome.

Back in the lodge, I sat awhile looking out the window, then went out to hoe the garden. One friend gone, and the one remaining was full content now Tom was well and little Alice was back in her arms. The two I'd betrayed were settling in at last.

THAT AFTERNOON GARTH was outside more than in, touring the grounds with Tom to show the man his new duties. At mealtime he was pensive, and taking down a rushlight when darkness flooded in, he excused himself to read alone by the fireside. I walked down the hallway more than once, but he did not call me into the library as he'd once done.

Next day he made ready to quit the king's lodge again, filling a bag with a bit of food, and his water skin at the well. I went outside before he left. Garth would not say where he was going, or when he would be back.

"Might I go along?" I asked, trying not to blush.

Garth did not look me in the eye. "I have my duties," he said crisply.

I watched him go off alone on foot, without even Horace for company, slipping between the rowan trees and out of my vision.

I am not wanted here.

Back in the kitchen, Meg said she'd like to cook now that Tom was better. Even that duty was taken from me.

I retreated to the shadowed corridor.

You let your guard down, let yourself be duped into thinking he might love you. You are half fey. You've known that since the day before you returned with Alice. It's time to go.

The room I'd shared with Poppy was empty. Her bed was neatly made.

I shouldn't vanish without a word. I should write to him at least. I sat on the bed trying to think of what I might say. No words came. *I'll take parchment with me on a walk, write a letter in the woods, then leave it here for him before I go.*

Before I could change my mind I went to the library where we'd talked so many times together, took a quill, an ink block, and parchment from the desk. In the kitchen I packed my writing supplies, water pouch, and food into a rucksack. Circling back to my room I paused to finger Grandfather's handkerchief a moment before folding it and slipping it into the pack along with my traveling knife. I'd be back only long enough to drop off a letter, then on my way again.

The pewter sky foretold snow. Gusting wind blew my hood off as I stepped out the back door through the garden. No one called or tried to stop me. They'd seen me go out to walk the hounds often enough. This time I passed the howling dogs cooped up in the kennels to leap over the back fence. My noisy landing startled the blackbirds from the holly. For a moment I could not move, surrounded by a sudden wild flurry of black wings.

Chapter Twenty

I T SEEMED A day of birds, for even more accompanied my walk. Passing a pond, I saw a bright kingfisher dive in beak first and bob up with a minnow. A mile deeper into Dragonswood, gulls screamed overhead, crossing the sky like torn strips of white sailcloth as they winged toward the coast. Hearing their cry made me think of my grand-father sailing warm waters somewhere across the world. Perhaps his ship would cross paths with Prince Arden's on his way home from the crusades.

It was chill outside. The air had the scent of coming snow. I came to a sunlit spot. *First sit here to write the good-bye letter.* Garth's quill, ink block, and parchment were tucked in the rucksack. But I needed some water to add to the black dust I'd scratch from the block. I'd crossed a little stream earlier. I was making my way toward the stream when I spied a moving figure through the trees. He was some distance from me, but I knew Garth's singular stride, the way he threw each long leg out in movements both casual and quick.

Where was he off to? I wondered again why he'd been so firm about going off alone. Was he already missing Poppy? Perhaps the food he'd packed was meant for Mistress Aisling's table. I saw his steps took him north toward the leech's house. *We can still visit,* Poppy had said, *Mistress Aisling's smallholding is but a day's ride from here.* Her eyes had sparkled when she'd said it.

I shouldn't follow; still, I crept behind, curious.

A soft snow fell and the brisk wind made the going cold. I thanked Saint Scolastica it was not yet snowing hard. I can step quietly as a deer if I have a mind to. By this, and the noisy wind whistling through the branches, I shadowed Garth undetected. After an hour or more the path narrowed to a deer trail thick with brambles. Up ahead, Garth used a stick to beat the brambles back. I could not do the same, since whacking sounds would give me away.

My cloak snagged in the evil thorns. I had to stop numerous times to free it. My hands were scratched, my fingers pricked.

I followed until Garth disappeared into a dark cave on the far side of a steep gully; smoke curled from the entrance.

I caught the smell of herbs on it, fennel and another bitter smell I could not name. Crouching, I waited outside, peering intently at the dark opening, as a cat will watch a mouse hole. A deep growl brought me to a run. I clambered down to the base of the gully and up the other side to the mouth of the cave, where I peered out from behind a rock.

Twenty paces from me, Garth looked straight up into the face of a dragon.

Half the dragon's bulk was hidden in the deeper chamber behind. The creature's triangular head loomed over the huntsman. Garth stood very still below. He'd told me he'd seen dragons up close on Dragon's Keep, but up *this* close?

Now my eyes adjusted to the dark, I saw the blue-green scales of a female. Her neck was not fully extended; still, it looked long as a pine sapling, near ten feet by my guess. All this I noticed in a moment, for now I could see her eyes were blue, a color rare in dragons. This must be the one who'd attacked us on the road.

Another rumbling sound and I saw what I'd taken for a growl before had been a kind of speech. I listened, keeping well behind the rock.

". . . to Harrowton?" the dragon asked huskily. "And on the road?"

"We went to gather a child," said Garth.

The dragon huffed, enveloping Garth in smoke. He went ghostly for a time and coughed till the smoke rose to the roof. "Should I do nothing to help the women Lady Adela hunts?" he asked.

My knees wobbled. He'd told the dragon about us?

The she-dragon tipped her head. "Are they witches on the run?"

"They are no more witches than my grandmother was."

Both went silent as if in reverence, though how this

dragon would have known Garth's grandmother was beyond me.

"Do any of the girls have fairy blood?" The dragon's tongue flicked out, furling and unfurling.

Garth did not answer straightaway. My heart sped.

Finally he said, "Half fey you mean? How can a man tell that?" With one hand on his hip, he pressed the other against the cave wall and leaned against it, crossing his legs. An astonishingly carefree pose before a powerful dragon. What would he do next, start whistling?

The dragon blinked, then smiled or snarled, I could not tell which. "Are they gone now from your lodge?" she asked.

"One is gone with the leech. Four guests remain, counting a husband and a child."

"Put them out, Bash!"

Bash? Had he lied about his name?

The dragon flicked her tail. My ears pricked to a tinkling sound coming from behind her. Peering harder into the dark well of the cave, I caught a glint of gold.

"I should not send them away, Ore."

Another name I knew from Grandfather's history lessons. Ore was a she-dragon hatched under Queen Rosalind's care, the smallest female of the clutch, and one with uncommon blue eyes. Might this be she? I wanted time to ponder it. Rosalind's Ore was raised on Dragon's Keep and might have met Garth there in his visits. There was no time to tease it out while they argued.

"How can I put them out when the man is still recovering and they are all penniless besides?" argued Garth, or Bash, or whoever this huntsman was.

The dragon swept her tail behind her. Gold coins tumbled out, rolling past her enormous clawed hind feet and settling near Garth's boots.

"Give them that. Then send them off."

"And where should I say I found the money?"

"Bash!" She gave a warning growl. Garth backed away.

"Before you leave, young sir, give me what you stole last time."

He wiped his sweaty forehead with the back of his sleeve. "It's mine, Ore."

"We agreed I would guard it all."

"You do."

"All but the pearl in your pocket, boy."

"Shall we spar for it?" he asked, drawing his sword. The dragon reared back, extending a sharp black talon. I nearly screamed and raced out, but Garth jumped back, smacking his rapier against her talon as she matched parry for parry, breathing short, concentrative plumes of fire. It was like a tourney—both fighting for the contest but not the kill.

Throughout the match, the dragon used only one talon against her smaller opponent. But her eyes were narrowed on Garth. She had no expressive brows, yet her eyelids wavered up and down as when a woman concentrates over difficult needlework. Garth avoided talon and flames, jumping onto higher rocks.

"You hold back!" he accused, leaping to another ledge.

"I do not, Bash!" She turned her scaly arm, clanked against his sword.

"You could have me for supper!"

"A puny snack!"

Ore knocked him flat against the cave floor, flicked away his rapier, and imprisoned him under five long, black, fully extended talons.

He sat up coughing in the dust, and laughed. "Touché, Ore. Let me out."

"Give me what you stole last time."

"I keep it only as a remembrance." He spoke quietly, gripping the black curved bars. Though he knelt in her jail, nothing but his body knelt. Garth would not bow to her power. I wondered at it.

"And you've shown it to no one since taking it?" Smoke now, not fire. I guessed she was trying to keep her temper, but she would not let Garth go till she had what she was after.

"One saw," he admitted.

More smoke from Ore's nostrils. "And what did you tell him?"

"Not him. It was a girl."

"Why did you show her the pearl?" This came out like a moan, if dragons moan.

"I'm sorry, Ore. The girl, she . . . she—"

"Attacked you? Held a knife to your throat?" said Ore. "What?"

Yes, what? I thought behind my rock. *Why did he let me hold it?* My heart pounded.

"I see," said Ore at last.

See? What did she see? A look? A gesture? Garth's back was to me. What did I miss? It was all I could do not to show myself then and insist the man finish the speech he'd started.

Ore released him.

He took the necklace from his pocket. "I thought you would not begrudge me keeping this one pearl," he said.

The dragon held the necklace in the air between them and spread a thin carpet of blue fire under it.

Behind my stone, I held my breath. The pearl glowed atop the blue flame like a tiny sun.

"She was so beautiful," said Garth.

Outside, snow whipped in the wind. Trees leaned toward the cave where we three hid. Still, it was day within. The fiery stream from the dragon's mouth made a sound like rushing water, spreading light around the pearl.

Ore lowered it again. "I know you'd like to keep it, Bash. But the crown jewels must be guarded."

Chapter Twenty-one

THE CROWN JEWELS! Garth had struck me as an outlaw from the moment I saw him. How had he fooled me, fooled all of us? Garth or Bash or whatever his true name was, was no more than a common thief.

When he quit the cave, I followed him down the snowy ravine and up again, fighting through the thorns behind him.

The time we'd hidden from the king's troop on the road? The man hadn't done it to defend me; he'd done it to protect himself!

I kept him in my sights for an hour as I worked up the courage to confront him. I didn't get the chance. He was suddenly accosted by seven knights of the realm. They surrounded him with such speed he'd no chance to defend himself. Next they made him mount a horse. A part of me wanted to rush out in his defense, but the other wanted him to get what he deserved. Just before they rode off, Garth spotted me through the greenery. He looked somewhat stunned to see me. Before he glanced away, he shook his head, warning me to stay hidden.

The royal troop rode off in swirls of snow and mud, Garth's dark hair clinging to his cheeks. He'd warned me not to show myself, but I couldn't let him go so easily. I darted through the wood after the troop. The horses' easy trotting pace in the thicker wood turned to a canter as the trees gave way to wider paths. The captors rode too far, too fast. At long last I gave up the chase and stood, breathless in the falling snow.

I hadn't written Garth a good-bye letter. Pointless now. His name wasn't even Garth. He'd lied to me from the start.

I wandered deeper in the wood, paying little attention to my steps as my mind repeated the same words over and over. *Garth. Bash. Huntsman. Thief. Garth. Bash. Huntsman. Thief.*

Three days I journeyed north. DunGarrow drew me toward itself. The tugging sensation was stronger with each step as if I were in an invisible river.

At first the foothills seemed farther and farther away as if I chased a moving land, but on the third day, Morgesh Mountain loomed ahead. Snow melted under a warmer sun, falling from the boughs in slow, heavy drops. Even in my weary state, I sensed a difference in the air as if I'd crossed some invisible boundary and entered the fairy realm.

Reaching a small clearing on the third night, I fell exhausted. By my count it was All Hallows' Eve—a night to keep watch. All manner of spirits are loosed on the

Witch's Sabbath when covens meet to sacrifice the innocent and seethe a stew of human bones. I was wary to be in Dragonswood on such a night. It took a long while to light a small fire in the damp, even using the last of the parchment I'd taken from the study. Finally small flames licked the torn page and caught the kindling.

As I squatted, damp and shivering, holding my hands out to the fire, darkness weighed down over the world like a hushed, black wave about to fall. I was far from humankind, yet I felt I was being observed like an insect under a mage-glass. I glanced about. No eyes glared from the woods. I heard familiar scuttling noises of small forest creatures and the dry, dusty sound of flitting wings.

Still I sensed something else. *Who watches?* I looked left and right.

Then in that hour light came, thrown like a ball to the base of a tree. One circling flame falling, then another, and another. I screamed as the light orbs piled up on all sides. Heat washed over me, drying my damp clothes to the stiffness of brown leaves. The rushing sound of flames hushed all else in the night wood. In brightness, I was lifted, swung, paraded through the forest on waves of living fire that did not scorch or burn, but sang beneath me:

Eshkataa breelyn kataa. Bring her in, her in, her in.
Fairy bound in human skin. Bring her in, her in, her in.

PART THREE

Fey Folk and Foul

Chapter Twenty-two

L ET ME GO! Put me down!" I shouted as the company of will-o'-the-wisps bore me over the night wood. Mighty in number, they flew on and on, all heat and light and whirring speed.

They raced me toward a castle that appeared at first to be made entirely by nature's own device, rising in a series of gray-black pinnacles against the mountainside with a waterfall riving it in two and gushing right down the middle. The scalloped terraces on the pointed towers were edged with green. The ferns were all a-dance in the swirling mist sent by the fury of the central waterfall.

My frightened screams were as nothing to the whirring of the wisp wings, and soon the rushing water drowned out all other sounds. I was flown through an open window in one of the many towers. They careened down a maze of hallways to a large room with a central, steaming pool, stripped off my stinking clothes, and threw me in the water. I thought I'd drown till I extended my legs and found I could stand in the shallows. Making me sit again, the tiny fairies washed my hair.

Straight from my bath they flew me naked through more passages leading down to an inner room with one wall made entirely of hives stretching floor to ceiling. The wall hummed with what I supposed were bees. The whole of it was the glassy gold of Tupkin's eyes. In the middle of the room a plump, milky-skinned woman sat on a throne made of vines.

I did not think the woman was a fairy; she was like none I'd spied anyway. White-haired, white-browed, and white-gowned besides, she seemed bleached of all color. The leaves sprouting from her chair looked vivid green by contrast.

Dripping wet and shivering, I faced her. I'd crossed into the fairy realm. Trespassed. Was that why they'd stripped off my clothes? Had they brought me here to torture me? I held one arm across my breasts, and one hand covering my most private part.

The woman appraised me without pity. I near fainted then and there.

"Turn about," she said. I could barely hear her over the humming bees.

"First, my cl-clothes, please." My teeth chattered. I tried not to whimper.

The woman's gown swished about her ankles as she got up to pluck a needle hanging, point down, from the ceiling. In her chair again, she repeated her command, this time with a sigh. There was no anger in her voice and no love in it either. Afraid to cross her, I turned about as I was told, covering my behind as best I could when my back was to her, then bringing arms in front again to face her. "What are you doing? What do you want?"

"Mind me and we'll get this done quickly."

She had power I could sense from where I stood. Even now my flesh had begun to dry in the heated room. White as snow, this woman was all heat. She turned her attention to the glassy hives. "Grass green," she mumbled. Pricking herself with the needle, she let out a little snarl of pain before pressing the bleeding finger into the wall. A long needle-thin green line bled across the glassy hexagonal orbs. Transfixed, I watched as it branched in all directions. It was like a map with a tiny blood-fed river crossing a golden landscape.

Then the green-winged insects flew out and swarmed overhead. Hundreds on hundreds. They looked like bumblebees but for their longer legs and strange color.

"Stop!" I screamed. "Do they sting?"

She laughed. The swarm descended. I flung my hands up, waved them off, then turned and ran down the long passageway. A few will-o'-the-wisps followed me out, though not enough to shed any real light. The green swarm was in chase. The woman shouted from her room. "I'll call the flits back. Go naked to the fairy king if that's what you want, half-blood!"

"Fairy king?" I paused, blushed at my condition, swore, and raced back inside. She'd called the insects flits. I'd not seen or heard of flits before. Why had she released them? The woman pointed to a flat stone pedestal three inches off the floor. "Stand there. Hold your arms out a little."

"What for?"

"Do you want a gown or not, Tess?"

She knew my name. "Y-yes," I stammered. "A gown, please."

"Hold your arms out. No, not that much. Yes, that much. Now be still or be stung!"

The humming noise was deafening as the flits swirled down in a winged wheel spinning silken green threads from their abdomens. With wriggling legs they wove soft cloth about my neck and shoulders. Spinning down each arm, in a tiny windy gale that tickled as they wove shimmering green sleeves.

"Oh, beautiful," I said all in a breath. I made to scratch a tickle and screamed. One of the little beasts had stung my forefinger. It throbbed.

"I said be still."

"I am!" I shouted, and was stung again, this time on the neck. Tears ran down my cheeks, but I froze then and there. Two angry stings were enough for me, if all the flits should sting . . .

The woman watched me cry; seeming satisfied at last, she told me, "I am the fey called Morralyn," she said. "Mistress of the Hives.

"Gold to set it off," she said, her forehead wrinkling with concentration. She pricked her finger, fed the hives, and new flits swarmed and spun, adding golden patterns to the green.

They fell to the floor when done. I could not tell if they were dead or only sleeping, but as I touched the silky cloth I saw my green gown had the same golden stitchery I'd seen Mother wearing in my dream the first night I slept at the king's lodge. This was the very gown. What did it mean? Was it myself I'd seen and not my mother? I whispered what I'd said to Mother in the dream.

"It's you," I said, blinking back the tears.

"Hungry?" asked Morralyn.

"I . . . I . . ."

The hive mistress sucked her pricked finger and frowned. "Did I waste my flits on a dull-wit?"

"No. I am hungry, mistress, thank you."

"Good," said she. "You've made me late to the feast as it is."

Chapter Twenty-three

W MADE OUR way through the long corridor. Few torches burned along the walls, but will-o'-the-wisps flew ahead for light. In the busy hallways we were greeted by fairy children running to and fro with food platters. Each waif stopped to bow, holding the trays steady as they did so. Mistress Morralyn dispatched them to their duties with a nod. Climbing a spiral staircase, I thought of what lay ahead. Would I meet my father at last? What would I say to him here in the fairy kingdom? He'd not come to me in my world. Left me on my own for seventeen years. Would he even wish to see me?

"I'm not ready," I blurted. "My hair's still wet."

Morralyn drew back. Her chest swelled, then she blew a stream of warm air. The hall torches sputtered in her wind and I broke into a sweat. My hair is thick and curly, often taking an hour to dry, but her breath nearly crisped it.

"There," she said. "Ready?"

I had no excuse now. The last and longest passage

opened to a Great Hall. A clear stream rived the room right down the middle. Fairies used the flower-spangled bridge to cross side to side. *I'll cross the bridge just like the girl in the tale "The Whistler."* I paused a moment. *Would God I won't return to the human world an old woman after a hundred years have passed.* Mistress Morralyn urged me across the running water.

Crowded feast tables lined both sides of the enormous room, snaking through a high archway all the way out to the meadow. Only days before I'd been with my friends and Garth, and now here I was, about to dine with the fey.

I'd never seen such beauty or such variation. My fingers itched to draw them, even more to paint them in full color. All were richly dressed, yet it was not their clothes that captivated me, but their vivid faces, their smooth skin that varied from a rich black to light brown to a creamy pale (though Morralyn was in extreme the palest of all). Grandfather had said fey folk live hundreds of years, yet with exception of the smallest children who raced about in twos and threes playing with the will-o'-the-wisps, and the older children serving the repast, I could not begin to tell their ages.

As we moved among them, I scanned the Great Hall for my father. I was sure I would know him at once. I cannot say how. I checked the highest table, where the fairy king was slitting an apple. He was blond-haired, rosy-cheeked, and merry. He'd surrounded himself with beauties, a short, pale lady on his left, and a taller, dark-skinned lady on his right. Mother was blond like him, my hair was curly brown. *Not my father,* I thought. The bearded king leaned right, kissed the taller lady on her cheek, and raised his goblet to her. All the fairies in the room held their goblets high.

The lady was glowing. "Is she the fairy queen?" I asked.

Morralyn said, "For tonight."

"I don't understand."

Morralyn urged me onward. Ladies turned their heads as we passed. They hadn't a care for me, but many tugged the hive mistress's sleeve, begging for a new gown. She ignored them one and all.

As many fey dined without as within. Knowing how cold I'd been outside, I wondered that they should choose to eat outdoors, but these were fey folk, accustomed to forest life. And although a frigid breeze blew through the meadow, my silky gown kept out the cold. I noticed no one wearing cloaks against the night, a testament to Mistress Morralyn's art and to the flits' shining weave.

Three deer stepped round the tables, regal in their gait, the males' antlers adorned in green leaves and red berries. There were foxes too, and wolves, which frightened me more than a little, but not as much as the brown bear scratching his side against a tree. The fey folk seemed fearless in their company, and indeed one small boy had the gall to order the bear about, saying, "Get out of my way, ya great oaf!" To my surprise, the bear stepped aside. I remembered the bear in Poppy's dream. She'd been right; here the bears came right up to you.

Morralyn sat on a pink-cushioned bench under a spreading oak and took a platter from an impish boy. Behind her bench I rocked on my feet. How could I find my father in such a crowd?

Then I saw a man's back, and started. The dark hair and broad shoulders were like Garth's. *It's not him. You know he's been locked up.* Still I went for his table. The fey man turned just before I reached him. His striking face was more handsome than Garth's, but I found his unworldly perfection less to my liking. I shied away, circling back to Morralyn.

An urchin, beaming and filthy, brought me a platter stacked with food. I eyed the bright orange cheese suspiciously. There were no farmlands in Dragonswood that I'd heard of.

"How came you by this?" I touched a wedge.

"The farms near Oxhaven."

"Stolen?" I whispered. In Harrowton farmers came to market complaining of missing eggs, or cows milked dry; they'd blamed the fey for their troubles, but I'd not believed the gossip.

Morralyn stuffed cheddar into her mouth. "Stolen, if you like, but cows milked by fairy hands never sicken."

She chewed thoughtfully, washed the cheese down with

wine, and banged her chalice on the table. The empty chalice rang like a bell. A girl raced up puffing; she carefully poured Mistress Morralyn's wine, then filled her second cup with honey. No one else seemed to be drinking honey, but then, Morralyn was plumper than most.

Why hadn't I seen him yet? As I took my seat on the bench, four minstrels passed playing pipes and mandolins. A sweet song, if a little haunting, that made me wish I could hear as well in my left ear as my right.

I'd not yet taken a bite. Eating fairy food caused one to be fey-struck.

Morralyn eyed my platter. "Eat, Tess. You're a fey man's daughter. It won't enspell you."

I tried the wine first. I'd had an overpowering thirst; the coolness of the drink addressed my jangly nerves even as it lightened my head. I drank more, sighed, then tried one of the little cakes. I'd never tasted such delights. The round-faced maiden to my left with steel-gray eyes and bluebells in her dark hair looked me up and down as I ate, her lip curling as if my human smell offended. She leaned in a little. "I know you," she whispered. "I saw you on the cliff."

My mouth full of cheese, I peered closer. I remembered her too, though last time I'd seen her she was flailing in the old dragon's claws. So the dragon *had* brought her here to DunGarrow. "It was dark that night, but I saw you also."

She'd been burned before the dragon flew in. Were her

legs very damaged? The fey had helped her, no doubt, and she was well enough to join the feast, but I'd yet to see her stand. I'd have asked about her burns if it weren't so callous to do so.

"I am Tess," I said.

"Tanya," she said with a nod. "Half fey," she added in a whisper. We looked at each other. I wondered what her story might be, how long she'd known, what the realization meant to her. Had she longed to come to DunGarrow? Had she heard whisperings? Felt strange tugging? But I couldn't ask her such things here.

By now many tables were deserted and folk were dancing. All the harder to find Father, I thought glumly. A motley juggler who'd swiped a stack of empty platters from two urchins tossed them in the air, first three, then four and six. Throwing out his hands, he let all fall in a loud crash. The fey children screamed, but the juggler laughed and snapped his fingers. Clickety-click the platters mended themselves and leaped into neat stacks. The fairy children clapped, the juggler bowed, his red curls bouncing like springs.

When the juggler left, I saw my father at last, and no mistaking. He was the tall, broad-shouldered man in belted leather tunic and dark breeches, dancing with a lovely dark-skinned maiden in a shimmering purple gown. As Father turned his lady round, my heart sped. My curling hair is his, as are my green eyes, also my oval face and thick brows, which accentuate his merry eyes but hunch broodingly over mine.

"There you've marked him," said Morralyn.

"He looks as noble as the king," I whispered.

"It wasn't long ago Onadon *was* our king," she said. "But Elixis rules now." She pointed through the torch-lit archway into the Great Hall where King Elixis dined. I'd known him for the king at once when we'd passed through the Great Hall.

My eyes were on my father again. *Onadon.* I heard magic in the name. *Onadon of the water. Onadon of the forest.*

Morralyn took the uneaten food from my platter. I didn't care. Here was my true father, the one I'd wondered about since I'd learned Mother's secret. I wanted to go to him. Greet him as a daughter greets a father, but he'd not yet looked my way. Lithe on his feet and laughing, he danced with a new partner now. The fey folk changed partners often, but never mind that, my chest ached just watching my father, and my heart felt too large in my breast.

Morralyn drank honey and said in a sticky voice, "If you look for some special affection, child, you are all too human."

"What do you mean?"

"Fey men are fathers of all just as fey women are mothers of all."

The tune changed, Onadon switched partners again. The fey children dashed about, most now clearing the tables, stacking platters one upon the other in dangerously steep piles. "Don't fey men know their own children?"

"They might. Does it matter?"

"Matter? Yes it matters!"

Morralyn gave a little huff and licked her fingers to capture the last crumbs on her platter. "You have lived too long with humans," she said. "We should have brought you here years ago."

"Why didn't you then? Why let me grow up apart from all of you? Instead you abandoned me to be raised by a brute."

I stopped. I wouldn't bare any more of my troubles here. Tanya scooted away from me, disturbed by my outburst, but Morralyn looked unimpressed.

I tried to steady myself. "How can a man not know his offspring from another's when his own wife bears them?" I asked.

"Fey men do not own women, nor do fey women own men. Wedlock is a human custom."

I wanted my father to stop dancing, to turn and look at me with kind eyes, then tenderly cup his hands over my shoulders and draw me to him. I wanted him to hold me and welcome the girl he'd lost, the daughter he'd longed to meet but could not until now. Still he danced, and did not look around.

He's only thirty paces from me — a short walk. I stood, wavering. *I will go to him, curtsy, and meekly say, "I am your long-lost daughter, Tess."*

I could not move my feet.

Onadon's new partner danced with her back to me. Morralyn had made her an exquisite gown embroidered in red and pink roses. The pale yellow bodice matched the fey girl's hair. I could see her gown was much finer than mine. Why had she been favored so?

Onadon spun his pretty partner round.

I gasped and ran.

Chapter Twenty-four

Poppy. Dancing with my father! I raced across the meadow toward the castle. Morralyn sent a fey lad chasing after me to escort me to my solar. The guest room was not unlike the huntsman's quarters, with two beds, a small, round writing table, and a mirrored wardrobe, though this one was high off the ground with a balcony overlooking the meadow.

Alone with the fire lit, I paced bed to bed. *Saints! What is she doing here? She can't possibly be half fey, yet here she is prettily gowned and dancing with my father!*

My head swam. I kicked the rushes on the floor and tried to piece it all together. Poppy's mother must have wed the wheelwright as soon as she knew she was with child. Beelzebub! Did my mother know? Had both girls slept with fey men and made a pact to keep the secret between them?

Poppy's mother died in childbed. Her secret died with her. I felt cheated to have the information come at me unawares when my only thought had been for my father.

What fey power did she possess? Did she have fire-sight? Could she envision the future in the flames? I was sure she did not have my power. What then? Were there clues I'd missed? She did see the fey man riding on the dragon the night Tanya was snatched from the fire. And looking back, I remembered the time I'd found her walking in a trance through the snow. When I'd called, she did not hear me, and when I'd shaken her gently awake she'd cried, "North. Come north," her eyes glassy, her lashes flecked with snow. So she'd heard the voices too, but powers?

I went out to the balcony. Across the river, folk still danced. I couldn't make out if Poppy was still there. My friend had herbing sense and healing skills. That could hardly be called a fairy power. Aside from that she was startlingly beautiful even in comparison to the fey maidens I'd seen tonight.

Her beauty stunned men. We'd all witnessed her seductive allure, something fairy magic might explain. Even Garth had been drawn to her before we'd gone after Alice, though he'd seemed less taken with her once we returned. My heart softened a little. Perhaps Garth had only been enchanted like all the others. Could he have helped it if it was her fey power?

I'd stepped back inside and closed the glass balcony doors when Poppy burst into the room.

"Tess! Isn't it wonderful?" She threw her arms around

me. She was damp with sweat, and her breath smelled of sweet mead. "Aisling said you're half fairy too, and that you might come to us here in DunGarrow soon. I didn't believe her at first. I couldn't imagine you a fairy's child!" Hand over her mouth, she giggled.

"I was just as surprised to see you," I said.

Two black paws poked out from under the bed. Tupkin slunk out. Rump up and front paws extended, he stretched, yawned, and jumped to Poppy. She swayed as she cuddled him. "There you are, my little soldier. Have you been good while I was out? How good, tell me, sir?" She'd drunk too much mead, I could see, and was babbling more than a little.

"What's your fey power, Tess? Is it your gift for drawing?"

"What?" I'd never thought that a form of fey power, but it was a "gift," as she'd put it, I supposed. Were there fine artists and craftsmen here? I glanced at the flowering vines painted around the wardrobe mirror.

"Maybe," I said. I was still stunned over finding her dancing with my father. She'd spoiled the moment when we were meant to meet. I wiped a disappointed tear from my cheek before Poppy could notice.

Poppy put Tupkin on her pillow. "How many gowns has Morralyn made you?"

"One."

"I have three." She spread her arms wide. "Morralyn

said I am the prettiest of all the fairies and the only one who can do her gorgeous gowns justice," she said with a happy blush. Then out of concern for me: "You only just arrived, Tess. She will have the flits stitch you more gowns, I'm sure."

"Why?"

"Sister, you're a fairy princess."

Sister? Could it be? Dizzy, I sat on my bed.

"It's wonderful, isn't it? I didn't guess I was half fairy, but I always knew or felt there was something . . . I mean," she said deliriously, "but I never dreamed—"

"Poppy," I blurted. "Who is your father? Tell me. Is it . . . Onadon?"

"No, my father is Elixis," she whispered in wonderment. "King Elixis. Can you believe it? Not the wheelwright!"

I sighed, relieved. "Not the wheelwright. And not the blacksmith for me. Have you spoken with your father?"

"Oh, aye, a little. But he is busy being the fairy king." Poppy flopped down onto the covers. *She's terribly drunk. I should tuck her in her bed and talk with her in the morning.* I stood to do just that and had reached the writing table between our beds when she said, "I'm going to marry King Arden and be the next Wilde Island queen."

"What?" I gripped the chair back.

She sat up. "You know the troubadour's song about a prince marrying a fairy child? Turns out it's true, all of it.

It's an old fey prophecy foretelling an alliance between the humans and the fey, and the fairies turned it into a song and gave it to a troubadour who thought he wrote the song himself. He sang it all across Wilde Island to prepare the people for the day when a fey girl should marry the prince." She paused. "A half fairy, anyway. And it wasn't the fairy's fault that the king's regent hated the song and had the troubadour hanged," she added.

"Hanged?" I was aware I'd been reduced to barking single words as Poppy went on, but it was all too much. My head pounded. I eased into the chair.

Poppy said, "When my father, King Elixis, told me the troubadour was hanged, he said it was a terrible crime and humans are cruel. I told him I wasn't cruel, and he said he knew that."

Hopping up, she studied her reflection in the oval mirror on the wardrobe door. "The fairies have been watching me all along," she said, "gathering what news they might from the will-o'-the-wisps, or spying invisibly from Dragonswood, waiting for me to grow up and fulfill their wish for me, and here I am getting ready to marry King Arden."

If this song was a prophecy as Poppy said, had the fey intended for Poppy to grow up to fulfill it? Why bring me into it then? Why bring Tanya? I'd also heard their voices calling me north. And the dragon had dropped a turtle into Miller's Pond to save me.

Poppy talked on to her dim-lit reflection and mine, since she could see us both in the glass. "And since I'm going to marry him, you can marry his younger brother, Prince Bion, if you like, because you are half fey too, and we can all live together in the castle."

"You don't know what you're saying, Poppy. You've had too much mead."

"I know exactly what I'm saying, Tess. Mead has nothing to do with it. Didn't anyone tell you the plans they have for me?"

"I just arrived."

"Oh." She whirled around and dropped back onto her bed. "That's true." Poppy leaned against her pillow and yawned. "Well, now you're here, you can learn all the courtly dances with me before I'm presented at the castle." She sighed. "I danced and danced tonight," she added.

"I saw."

"You were at the feast?"

"A short while."

"You should have stayed and danced too, Tess."

"I didn't feel much like it."

"Oh." Poppy looked confused.

I walked out to the balcony, thought of her poor mother, who'd married the wheelwright, just as Mother married the blacksmith. They'd no choice but to marry straightaway, knowing they carried a half-fey child. Poppy's mother died never getting the chance to know her daughter.

Back inside, I asked, "If this is all true, weren't you even a little angry to learn that the fairies had a plan laid out for you from the beginning? A plan you didn't ask for or want?"

Poppy turned onto her side. "Who says I don't want it?"

"But did you ask for it? Were you consulted?"

"Don't spoil it, Tess."

"I don't mean to spoil it. I'm happy you're so content, only—"

"Only what?" Her blue eyes held the candlelight.

"It seems the fates have woven our futures without our knowing or asking. I don't want to be a part of someone else's plan. I want—" I choked up, unable to say what I wanted aloud or even to myself.

Wind blew in from the balcony, bringing in the forest scents and the clean wet smell of the waterfall. The candle guttered and went out. I knelt by Poppy's bed, loving her and fearing for her. She was like a girl dancing on a cliff's edge. I saw the fall she might take if the fey betrayed her, only she couldn't see it herself.

At last the fairy's mead caught up with her and my friend fell asleep. I covered her and sat on the edge of her bed with Tupkin. The fire was dead, the room dark. There were at least three half-fey girls, Poppy, Tanya, and me. Why so many? Was it insurance? One girl to replace another if she failed?

Chapter Twenty-five

IN THE FLIT room, Morralyn inspected my new red gown. Satisfied, she said, "You're to meet Onadon by his fishing spot."

"Where?" I asked anxiously.

She waved her hand. "The will-o'-the-wisps will show you. Go on."

We walked a long way past the waterfall, the river trail bending this way and that following the Harrow. It amazed me to think this same water flowed south another fifty miles or so through Dragonswood before it left the sanctuary, wending through Harrowton on its way to the sea.

The current slowed where the river grew wider. In this quieter spot where the glassy surface mirrored the blue sky, I saw him. The will-o'-the-wisps flew off when I did.

My father stood with his back to me, shin-deep in the river, a net dangling from his left hand. He pointed at the sparkling surface and wriggled his finger. A trout jumped in an arc and fell with a splash. More movements, more jumping, till Onadon chose one he liked, pointed to his net, and the fish leaped in. I leaned on a willow, watching him, a fey man, strong and trim and merry (or so he seemed when he danced), and nothing like the oily blacksmith.

Speak. Say something. I did not move. I lingered by the willow tree, watching him use his fairy power to fish. The river's current wedged around his legs making *clork, clork* sounds. Midges buzzed about his curly head. He swatted a little.

I stepped away from my tree, opened my mouth, closed it again, my voice caught like a rabbit in a trap. Still, he turned and saw me. Wading to shore, Onadon stood barefoot on the strand while I peered at him from the grassy riverbank. Sand stuck to his wet feet like sparkling boots. I need only jump down and run to him. A sudden shyness held me.

"Tess." His voice was deeper and smoother than I'd imagined and filled my cupped ear like cream. More than this, he'd said my name.

"You are my father, I think?"

Instead of responding, Onadon clicked his fingers. A boy sprang from the air, startling me.

The fairies have been watching me all along, Poppy had said, *gathering what news they might from the will-o'-the-wisps, or spying invisibly from Dragonswood, waiting for me to grow up and fulfill their wish for me . . .*

A second child appeared in the shallows. How many

more fey folk skulked by the river where my father fished? I whipped my head around, peering through the greenery.

Onadon spun the net and knotted it above the trout. "Take this to the kitchens, Branki. Hurry on now and earn your due." Branki fled up the bank and vanished mid-leap, boy, net, fish, and all.

"You too, Susha. To the kitchens now. Go on."

She vanished.

Father brushed sand from his legs and called his boots. They walked over to him, black and wrinkled from use, the tops waiting, openmouthed. Fingering the sand out from between his toes, he slid them on and climbed the riverbank. "Shall we walk?"

"Are we alone now?"

He laughed. "A former fairy king is rarely alone, but you can speak freely."

I saw more footprints on the sandbar. How many would follow us?

Father took the grassy trail along the bank, walking in long, even strides. I matched his pace in my full skirt. The grass blew where the wind tugged. Trees let go their leaves in red and yellow swirls.

Onadon asked, "How is your mother?"

My cheeks burned. He could have known the answer to that anytime he wished to, couldn't he? Why had he stayed away from her, from *me*, seventeen years?

"She is well."

He glanced at me with a wary look, or was it mocking? "Good for her."

I won't be angry. I don't want to be. He'll tell me why he had to stay away so long if I ask him. We turned at the river bend, keeping to the narrow trail along the edge. I cleared my throat. "Is it true fairies do not marry?"

"Who told you this?"

"Mistress Morralyn said so last night. I came to the feast. Did you know?"

"I learned so, but you were gone by then."

"I saw you dance with Poppy," I added bitterly.

Onadon ran his hand through his hair. The bangs pulled back showed a receding hairline that bespoke his age, though he had no gray. Fey folk live longer than humans. I could not guess his age.

"Poppy is a lovely girl," he said.

"All men think so."

He laughed at that, and clapped his hand against a trunk as we passed. "It's true we do not marry, Tess," he said, returning to my earlier question.

"Is that why you abandoned my mother?"

"Listen to yourself, Tess. 'My mother,' you humans say. 'My father.' 'My child.' Do you own her? Does she own you?"

"No. But we . . ." A lump caught in my throat. "We belong together."

"Still, you left her."

"You left her, Father! I didn't." I took a long breath, eyed the river loping and curling below, and tried again. "I had to run."

"I know."

"How is it you know?"

"We know much of the goings-on in the human world. I kept an eye on you."

"Kept an eye on me? You saw me running from the witch hunter. Then why didn't you intervene?"

"I couldn't intervene. You had to be drawn to us by your fey blood, by your longing. We could not make you come."

"I heard voices."

"Still, it was up to you to decide to follow them and try to find us."

"But the will-o'-the-wisps flew me in."

"We could help once you'd made it to the border of DunGarrow. Until then it was up to you."

"Some kind of test of strength?"

"You could call it that. You took a while, but you got here, didn't you?"

"What about Poppy?"

"She reached here before you."

"And Tanya?"

"Inquisitive, aren't you," he said with a sidelong glance.

"Some think so." The blacksmith slapped my mouth for my outspokenness, but I'd learned to speak more freely with Garth.

"Tanya would have died if Lord Kahlil hadn't flown in and rescued her. She stays here, Tess, but she's of no use to us now."

No use to us now? Bitter words. I tried to calm myself, listing to the river talk, the birds calling from the trees as I followed Onadon's steps. We nearly died on the road. It still hurt to know the fey had watched us and done nothing to help us. *Think of something else to say.* "Why is it you're no longer king?"

"My throne was challenged. Elixis won."

"Is a fairy kingship so easily lost?"

"Easily?" Father gave a little whistle. "There was some danger in it."

"So there was a battle?"

"Not with swords, if that's what you imagine, Tess, but with magic. Still, one of us could have died."

Men and their battles. I thought of the elks I'd seen in Dragonswood clashing horns in mating season. I had to ask, "Could you challenge him again and win back your crown?"

There were excited sounds behind us, fey folk whispering over my question, I supposed.

Onadon flipped a stick up with his foot and snapped it. "I could challenge Elixis if I wished."

Louder whispering behind us and above us in the trees.

"I don't want to," he added, tossing the broken stick in an arc toward the river. It landed with a gentle splash. The voices fell silent.

I turned about. By the saints! Couldn't a girl speak alone with her father? "Who follows us?" I challenged. "Come out. Show yourselves."

"Let them be, Tess. Would you leave me unguarded?"

"Who would harm you?" I felt my waist for my knife, but it wasn't in its usual place. I'd forgotten I was in my new red gown, not my old black kirtle. My hand dropped empty to my side again, but Father had seen me reaching for a blade.

"You're a strong lass, Tess." He flashed me a smile. Glory! If I could hold such a thing and keep it, I would.

Onadon went on, "I think now Aisling might have judged wrongly by choosing Poppy for the next Pendragon queen."

So their plans for Poppy were true.

"Aisling didn't know I was also half fairy," I suggested confidently.

"She knew," he corrected.

I sped up. My red gown caught in the thorn bushes. Beelzebub! In my urgency to free it, I tore the hem. "Aisling . . . knew?"

"She was fairly sure when she met the two of you. But she bided awhile, healing the man, Tom, and waiting to see."

"See what, Father?" I liked saying the word *father* walking here with him. I'd let all the poison go out of the word now I was free forever from the blacksmith.

"Aisling knew the half-fey maidens would be drawn to us. That each must follow their yearning and come. She is half fey herself, though more than twice your age."

Half fey too? I'd sensed something different about her from the first. Now I knew why.

Onadon continued, "Aisling was not surprised when Poppy told her how she longed to go north."

How his words hurt. "I was drawn to DunGarrow. I'd longed to go deeper into the wood. Only I couldn't come until my friends were safe and settled." And because I'd wanted to be with Garth, only I couldn't say that.

"You took much on yourself, Tess, looking after them."

"Would you have had me abandon them?"

He didn't answer that but noted, "You say you were drawn to us, but Aisling saw you willingly ride south, away from us, not toward us."

"To fetch Alice! That's why I went." I'd heard the voices whispering, *Turn around, Tess. You are going the wrong way*, but I'd ignored my urges.

Onadon paused and turned. "Shall we try, then, Tess? It would be interesting if you should win."

I looked up, torn hem in hand. "Win what?"

"What have you been told thus far about why you were drawn here?"

"I was drawn here—" I could not say the rest. Because I sought you, because I wanted to find my true father once I knew I was fey, to find a place where I might belong.

He tipped his head in the slanting light. "Do you know anything of our plan?"

"Only what Poppy said last night."

"Very little, then."

"Because you are holding back from us."

"Because the girl's head has been full of dance steps and pretty gowns since she came here."

I had to smile at that.

"Tell me what you've learned from your friend thus far, Tess."

Chapter Twenty-six

ONADON CONFIRMED POPPY'S story, even supplying the song "Fey Maiden" in its entirety. He sang it in a rich baritone, the invisible fey trailing us, harmonizing with him so it was as if the river also sang. I knew the first two verses well, but I'd forgotten the last verse until he sang it.

> O bring this day unto us soon,
> And forfeit weapons forged in strife.
> Sheath sword, and talon, angry spell,
> And brethren be for life.

The fey had high hopes indeed. Onadon smiled at me once when the song was done. I returned the smile politely but not wholeheartedly. A fey maiden marrying a prince, was this the sole reason I'd been born? And Poppy and Tanya as well? Were all men the same, whether human or fairy? Must they all use women for pleasure or some scheme?

Not all men. Garth had fed us and sheltered us with no gain to himself that I could tell. He risked the ride all the way to Harrowton just to bring Meg her little girl. He didn't seem at all annoyed to travel with me as a wife, and Alice as his daughter. I stopped myself. Garth wasn't who he said he was.

"Well, Tess, what do you think?"

I didn't know what to think of my father's elaborate plan, whether I fit into it or didn't. I needed time. "How old is the song 'Fey Maiden'?"

Onadon pulled a holly leaf. "It wasn't a song to begin with. We added the melody to the prophecy written by King Ambrosius, who was our fey ruler in King Arthur's day. But we'd kept it to ourselves for hundreds of years. Merlin believed in it. Still, even the fairies could not see Ambrosius's vision ever coming to pass until recent times. Wilde Island is the only land whose sovereigns have dragons' blood. A Pendragon need only marry a half-fey girl for the prophecy to come true."

"Why half fey, why not a fairy maiden?"

"We don't marry, Tess. We already discussed that."

"Not even to wed a future king?"

"Not even then. It's not in our blood to marry. Wedlock is for humans. We live free here."

Wedlock—a telling word, women were locked in, the husband kept the key. I'd said those words myself. The fey lived free. Hadn't I always said I wanted that, to live without need of attachment to any man? *Because you feared he'd beat you. Beat your children.* I sighed.

"What if that's what I wish too?"

"What do you mean?"

"Not to marry."

"You're half human, Tess. You'll long to be some man's wife. Why not let it be a king?"

Father tossed his holly leaf and used his finger to guide it higher till it settled in a treetop. I wanted to ask, *Did you love my mother? She loved you in a way she can never love my stepfather. Do you have any idea how cruelly you treated her by sending her away?*

He turned to me. "We had hoped Queen Rosalind's son, Kadmi, might choose a half-fey wife."

"Did the fey hope Aisling might be queen?"

Onadon laughed. "You've a quick mind. She might have won Kadmi, but the man chose Lucinda."

I was glad to hear the fey hadn't used magic to force a match, that they'd let King Kadmi choose. "So you had to wait for Kadmi's son."

He nodded. "For Arden to become a man, or Bion if something should happen to his older brother."

"Nothing's happened to Prince Arden, has it?" I said, alarmed.

"No, the prince is on his way home. A long sea journey to be sure, but he should be here soon."

"Poppy said Lord Sackmoore hanged the troubadour

who sang 'Fey Maiden,' and he's outlawed the song so no one can sing it now."

Onadon kicked a pebble. "The hanging was just one of Lord Sackmoore's many crimes."

He also funds Lady Adela's bloody witch hunts, I thought. We'd entered a stand of fruit trees growing alongside the river. I peered up, spying what I'd thought were peaches and found I was mistaken. A will-o'-the-wisp flew inside an orb, lighting it up from within. More lit up as wisps entered; some glowed yellow, some blue, some cherry red.

Seeing my wonder, Onadon said, "Wisp dwellings," as he plucked a few blackberries.

The glowing orbs were like no houses I'd ever seen in the human world. The orchard seemed hung with hundreds of colored lanterns. I took in the sight, breathed in the forest air. How I loved it here. Why should I have to leave?

My father offered me the first handful of berries, a thing the blacksmith never would have done.

Farther along the trail, Onadon jumped down from the embankment and led me back to the water's edge. The shore was strewn with round gray rocks the size of goose eggs and larger. I steadied myself to traverse it in my slippers. Reaching the narrow sandbank at the riverside, I ate the berries Father picked, savoring each.

"I once brought my friends over the wall to pick blackberries in Dragonswood."

Onadon popped two into his mouth. "You were seen that day."

I nodded. "A dragon with a fey rider came to boot the blacksmith and the leech out of the wood," I said with some delight. I appreciated how dragons and fey worked together guarding their sanctuary.

"Do the dragons want a half-fey queen?" I asked.

"This is their wood as much as ours." Onadon skipped a stone along the surface. "You know they live long, more than a thousand years, and they are mighty creatures all. But dragons have one or two clutches at most in their lifetime, and that's if they even find a mate. Their kind would have died out without this stronghold. Here they have caves to raise their young in safety, and a hunting range expansive enough for such large creatures to survive."

I knew it was true. Hadn't Grandfather told me? Hadn't I felt it myself? The last of their kind were mostly here on our island, in the safety of Dragonswood and some caves on our smaller sister island, Dragon's Keep. Some renegade red dragons were said to live far south on Mount Uther. The live volcano was much too fiery a place for men. "The red breed?" I asked.

"They're few enough. They keep to themselves."

"And the fey?"

My father turned. "You've seen us, Tess. By looks alone you must have noticed we've come here from every corner of the world. The fairy folk have been driven out of every land no less than the dragons. But Wilde Island was ours long before England conquered it. We returned home thanks to Queen Rosalind."

"The Pendragons still protect you." I knew King Kadmi had done his best to guard the wood.

"Our hope is less secure with each new generation. Prince Arden was never as fond of dragons or fey as his younger brother and sister."

Princess Augusta, the one with scaly face and dragon eyes. Father didn't notice my shiver.

"We'll see where he stands once he's crowned. Until then, Lord Sackmoore and those like him want to reclaim Dragonswood. One of Sackmoore's troops felled part of the boundary wall out along our western border. Armed villagers raced in, killing game and cutting trees."

"When?"

"Just days ago." Onadon stared at the water's surface. Shadows from the trees on the far side sent dark spires across the river that wavered in the swift current. I knew my stepfather would have relished such a raid, stealing in to kill a deer and fell the trees so he'd have venison for his table, free firewood for his blacksmith forge.

"They tried to keep the raid secret, breeching the wall in the west where there are fewer folk. But it's only the beginning. Plenty of men want the walls down."

I told him of the riot I'd seen, the men racing into Dragonswood shouting *Meat! Meat!* after Lord Sackmoore issued the grain tax.

He nodded. "I'd heard of it."

"What will you do?"

Onadon skipped another rock, but he was angry; the rock bounced but once before it sank. "Rebuild the walls when they're breached. Double our patrols."

"And you have magic," I reminded.

"That we do, but too many men breach our walls and come to take what's ours. How many do we turn to Treegrims or send home fey-struck before the whole island turns against us?"

I hadn't thought of that. Mad Jack, the only fey-struck man in Harrowton, wandered aimlessly about, babbling, dropping his breeches and exposing himself. How many such men would a town tolerate? Cupped shadows on the sandy river bottom looked distant and haunting as the Treegrim's black eye pits. To my mind it was better to turn a man into a tree than to run him through with a sword as I'd seen the sheriff's men do in Margaretton. At least a Treegrim was alive; still, did the hunchbacked thing I'd seen with the nest crammed in his belly have any memory of his life before his strange punishment?

Onadon spoke again. "Prince Bion sides with us. He tries to keep Lord Sackmoore from misusing his authority before Arden's crowned."

"Not an easy task, I should think." I rolled two blackberries in my open palm. "Things will be better once Prince Arden's crowned."

Onadon chose another stone, one worn from the river with a hole in its center. "Perhaps, but he's been away a long while now, fighting what he calls 'the heathens' in the holy land. Will he come back to call us fey folk heathens? We are different and do not live under the same laws the humans do." He rubbed the stone with the hole, thinking aloud, it seemed, for he spoke out to the water. "Lord Sackmoore had great influence on the prince when he was younger. If his influence remains strong once Arden's on the throne, we may still lose our sanctuary."

I looked up at him, startled. "Where would we go?" I'd said *we* and meant it. I was with my kin now.

Onadon shook his head.

"What about Dragon's Keep?"

"Dragon's Keep will be as much King Arden's domain as Dragonswood, Tess. If he takes away our sanctuary here, we'll be scattered to the winds again." He hurled his last stone high in the air so it hit the water with a splash. "We might have been safer if Queen Rosalind hadn't set our sanctuary so close to the harbor towns."

"Why did she?"

"She didn't want to isolate us. Besides, she wanted Dragonswood nearby so she and Kye and their descendants could visit us when they liked. Pendragon Castle's but a few days' ride from DunGarrow."

Light and shadow moved about me. *Garth is imprisoned just a few days' ride from here.*

Onadon turned. "This is all we have, Tess. This is our home."

Now by the windy river I was truly warm. "*Our* home," he'd said. I saw a sudden red flash as a bright kingfisher flitted out and dove for a fish. He came up with his wriggling prize, then darted back into the trees.

"Will you agree to help us?" My father looked down at me, a drifting cloud in the blue sky crowning his head. I was stunned to have his full gaze.

I understood the urgency now for an alliance between the Pendragons and the fey. Still, I found the idea both daunting and ridiculous. Until just recently I'd been Tess, John Blacksmith's daughter, a homeless girl on the run from the witch hunter. Hardly the stuff of royalty. Did this fey man even see me? "You know where I came from," I said.

"I know exactly who you are and where you came from."

"You really want me to be Wilde Island queen?"

"I'd like nothing better."

He did not say *Because you are my daughter,* but there was a glint in his eyes, or was it only a reflection sent by the river? I wanted to say *Yea,* but I wasn't sure.

"Poppy's my friend. I don't want to go against her."

He nodded. "Let it be a contest between friends, then."

Hadn't he also admitted to the contest betwixt Elixis and himself? Perhaps his wish wasn't driven so much by fatherly love or need to protect his magic wood, as by a strong competitive desire to win out over the one who'd seized his fey crown?

Onadon awaited my answer. The sun sent a ray down, missing me, hitting him in the chest where the leather jerkin was water-stained.

I ate the last blackberry I'd saved, crunching the tiny seeds. I'd come here to learn more of my origin, to be with my father and my father's people if they'd welcome me, not to marry a man I didn't know, even if he *were* destined to be king. Still, I saw how the marriage would protect the fey, and my father said he needed my help. How could my heart not warm to that?

"Poppy's set on the crown, Father, and men adore her. How could I compete with her?"

"Her seductive allure is a strong fey power, but I would see you try, Tess. I think you have the fight in you."

So it was true. Poppy's extraordinary seductiveness was a fey power. No wonder men panted after her and followed her about, cow-eyed.

"What if I refuse?"

Silence from Onadon. I think he was trying not to scowl. Oh, I didn't want his anger. I'd come too far to be with him for that. "Think, Father. I only just stumbled into all of this. I mean, I meant to come here as soon as I learned who I was. But I came to stay, not to be sent away again."

"You know how to speak your heart, Tess. It is not always the wisest choice."

I was fighting off tears and barely winning. Could a daughter not speak her mind to her own father?

"I have to think on it," I whispered.

He smiled. "The day after tomorrow I ride out to the edge of Dragonswood. Come with me. Tell me your answer then."

He vanished. I watched his footprints cross the sand. Thick ferns shuddered where he passed and the end of a spider's web blew broken.

Chapter Twenty-seven

I WAS TENSE when Tanya showed us around Dun-Garrow the next day. I had a single day and night to think over Onadon's offer. Still, I tried to be attentive, even civil with our guide; after all, she was taking special care to give us a tour of the castle and grounds. Tanya started with the busy kitchen, where cooks baked delights and roasted meats in the many roaring ovens. Hot as the blacksmith's shop, the place was a-run with fey children doing the work of kitchen scullions. One wall flowed with fresh water diverted from the waterfall; by this there was no need for the children to fetch well water. "Very handy," I said, pointing to it.

Tanya shrugged. "Oh, that's nothing, Tess. Let me show you more."

Fey children worked everywhere we went. Their childhood appeared to be as cramped with chores as mine. For years I'd envied the fairy children, imagining them scampering through the woods, playing night and day. The truth was they lived like little servants here.

Tanya took us to more flit hives, where fey children worked on great, long sheets of silken cloth the size of sails. The humming in the room was deafening. Like Morralyn's cloth, the work was all done by hand, or rather by pricked finger. I watched the waifs pointing with puffy, red fingers, directing the flits where to weave. Perhaps the most talented among them would grow up to be hives mistress or hives master.

"What is all the cloth for?" I shouted over the buzzing.

"Walls," Tanya shouted back before bringing us down another hall.

"Walls?"

"You'll see." She gave me a mischievous smile before leading us outside.

Tanya stays here, Tess, but she's of no use to us now. Cold words from my father. Entangled in these thoughts, I rammed into Poppy when Tanya stopped beyond the meadow to point up.

"Ouf!" Poppy said, and laughed.

I laughed too. "What is it?" I asked, crooking my neck to see what Tanya was pointing at. And there! I *did* see fairy houses high up in the branches. So not all the fey lived in the castle as I'd supposed. The tree dwellings were akin to small, fairground tents. The cloth walls shimmered green as sunlit leaves and were yellow with that same light where they were not green, so they appeared and disappeared from view. I'd challenge any human to see them at all.

"Walls," I said. "Are they sturdy enough?" It was a bright day, but how would they hold up in a storm?

"Let me show you mine." We followed her into the trees, where she climbed an oak. Poppy came last, unused to climbing, but I was up the friendly branches in no time and through the shimmering door. We stood on a wooden platform, hidden by leafy branches below, the floor firm underfoot. The silken flit-cloth walls wavered in the wind. I ran my hand along the surface, smooth and soft as a flit gown. *Home,* I thought. This was like the place I'd searched for years and years when I'd climbed the trees in Dragonswood. How lucky Tanya was.

It was nearly sundown, and growing colder by the minute, yet it was cozy inside. By this I guessed no fire was needed—the cloth working as I'd found the gowns to work against cold weather. The room wasn't tidy. White coverlets on the unmade bed were piled up like cream, shoes and stockings littered the floor, a blue gown was draped over the small wardrobe. But I liked the simple furnishings and the clean smell of the forest that scented the air.

A single purple iris graced the small table. The vase caught my eye. I touched the cool, clear glass shaped like a long teardrop.

Tanya nodded. "I see you like that too. Fey artisans work wonders with glass."

"Wonders like Lady Adela's glass eye?" I said. I felt

uneasy now I'd loosed her name in the room. Still, I added, "Why should the fey favor someone like her?"

"The Pendragons asked them to," said Tanya.

A simple answer. "Do you think her fey eye is magic like they say, that she can use it to spy out witches?"

Tanya returned my look. "She picked us out, Tess. Are we witches?"

So she knew my story, part of it at least. I asked how she'd been arrested and why. She too had been seen in Dragonswood. "But I'd been careful not to show anyone my fey power," Tanya added.

"What power?" Poppy said. I was as curious as she, but would not have asked.

Tanya focused intently on the vase and a bright bouquet appeared with roses, lilies, and daffodils.

"Oh," Poppy said, clasping her hands. "You can glamour things. Lucky you."

"I'm getting better all the time since coming here," Tanya said with some pride, "but I'm not as good as the full-blood fey."

"Maybe you will be in time," Poppy said.

"You're kind to say so, Poppy." The glamour faded, leaving the single iris behind. My eye lingered on it as I compared Tanya's fey gift to mine. She controlled her power. I had no mastery over fire-sight. If I stayed here, would I learn to see more? Call visions from the flames? It would make deciding on my future that much easier. Or would it?

I sent a breath that made the iris petals tremble. What if seeing my future in the flames constricted my freedom? What if once I'd looked ahead, I had no choice but to follow what the fire showed me?

Tanya said, "Hiding my power did no good in the end. After I was seen in Dragonswood, the townsfolk accused me of flying there at night on my broomstick. Imagine that," she said with a sharp laugh. "William Carter said I'd hexed his son and made him fall into the well and drown. It wasn't me," she added hastily. "His boy had fits, but no one listened to my arguments. They called me witch and were eager to see me burn!"

I heard the venom in her speech. But Poppy, who did not like to dwell on such sad things, said, "It's a pretty home you have, Tanya, though a bigger room would be even nicer."

I disagreed. "I think it's just right. Nothing else is needed."

Tanya smiled. Her eyes lit up. She was uncommonly pretty when she smiled.

I was glad to speak no more of witches in her lovely house. I took a chair, resting the back of my hand against the teardrop vase. I'd said nothing else was needed, but if I lived in this tree house, I'd want another to sit in the chair opposite mine. And the man I'd want was the one I'd once seen reading in a king's chair before a fire, a man who liked to put his long legs out and cross them at the ankle. I'd been trying to push him out of my mind since coming to DunGarrow; now I let him inside, pulling back the silken door as Tanya had done when we'd stepped in. He'd once climbed a tree to talk with me. I'd watched him lean back to look up at the stars. I thought he'd like the little house high up in the branches as much as I.

It would be time to dress for dinner soon. We made ready to leave. Poppy fingered the pearls on the blue velvet gown draped over Tanya's wardrobe. "You should wear this tonight." She tugged it down and tossed it to Tanya. She was being playful flinging it to her, but her action uncovered the full-length mirror and we saw our reflections there.

In the brief instant before Tanya cried out and threw her dress over the mirror again, we saw her burn scars in the glass. I glimpsed the mottled red and white skin on her neck and jaw, the branching scars on the right side reaching just below her ear.

She must have more scars up her legs and front, I thought, but those were hidden by her dress. I'd assumed fairy medicine had healed her completely, but the mirror told the truth. She'd had to use a glamour spell to conceal the scars.

Poppy whispered, "Sorry. I'm so sorry." She tried to take Tanya's hand. "Does it hurt?"

"Get out," Tanya snapped.

"Please forgive me," Poppy insisted.

"You're a fool!" Tanya shouted. "You don't deserve to be Pendragon queen!"

"She didn't mean to upset you," I said in Poppy's defense.

"Leave!"

We both scrambled down the tree.

"She'll never forgive me," Poppy cried on our way back through the meadow.

"She will. She was just upset with you for revealing her secret so suddenly."

"You know I didn't mean to. I'd help her if I knew the right herbs for such terrible burns." She sniffed and looked at me. "I don't understand. Why couldn't the fey heal her?"

I couldn't answer. I was as surprised as she to discover their limitations. Was their magic less powerful than I'd supposed? I found the thought unsettling.

TANYA DIDN'T JOIN us at the feast table. Nor did I see Onadon anywhere in the high meadow. I thought I might take Tanya up some food, but Poppy said she'd go. I watched her heading for the tree house with honeyed bread and golden plums as a kind of peace offering. I hoped Tanya would accept her gifts.

Food was plentiful as always here. After a few bites I was too unsettled to eat more. Onadon expected to hear my decision tomorrow. The tour had kept all my questions at bay. Now I had to think it all through.

I quit the meadow to be alone in my solar awhile before Poppy returned. Outside our balcony window, the stars glittered in the autumn night. Beyond the meadow the treetops lined up like black arrowheads below the peaceful heavens. Hearing a whisper of cloth behind me, I spun round just as a fey child winked into view. I jumped, still unused to the fairy folk's sudden appearances.

The child smiled wickedly at having surprised me, then cleared her throat. "Mistress, I'm to take the red gown you tore down by the river yesterday to be mended. You'll wear this meantime."

It was the girl I'd seen in the shallows. I could not recall her name. I looked at her outstretched arms and saw no gown there.

"Take it, mistress," she said, as if the air she held was heavy. She was indeed a slender thing, near as pale as Morralyn, though dark-eyed with a thatch of short, brown hair. I reached out. A rough gray robe appeared between us. She smiled shyly.

"You're quick with your magic," I said.

She curtsied. "Thank you, mistress. I am a second tier."

"Second tier?"

"I already know comings and goings."

Comings and goings, she called it? She'd shown me her

prowess—vanishing before my eyes at the river yesterday, appearing suddenly before me now.

"Embellishments," she went on, "and I'm learning filching and food fabrications."

"By filching you mean stealing."

"Never, mistress. It is an art to take and make things well. A fey-touched hen's a mighty layer. More eggs for all by it."

I had to smile. "What is your name, child?"

"Susha, mistress."

"Well, Susha, turn about whilst I change, will you?" She did. Struggling out of my torn red gown, I slipped on the robe. The weave was rough and scratchy. An ill-made thing and surely not flit spun. "Who sent this?"

"Morralyn, our Mistress of the Hives."

I nodded. No doubt she'd sent the poor excuse of a robe to punish me for damaging her lovely creation. "You may turn about now, child."

I gazed down at her. She was eight or nine in human years, if they were not the same in fey, and small as a wild bird. *She is hungry,* I thought, *and sups little. So much for "food fabrications."* I wondered who cared for her.

"Tell me, Susha, who is your father?"

"Mistress?" She covered her mouth and giggled. But she saw I meant my question. "King Elixis is our Father King and the rest of the masters are our All Fathers."

It was what Morralyn had said; still, the words *All Fathers* did not sit well. I'd stayed a short time at DunGarrow and did not understand their society. As a fey man's daughter, I was but one among many. This child, Susha, might well be one of Onadon's offspring, my half sister. The thought sent a dull ache through me.

"You call the fey men masters. Are you a servant, then?"

The child stuck out her chin. "I am no servant, mistress. I am fey!" Her brown eyes sparked dangerously. "We all of us start out climbing the tiers, acquiring magic on the way."

The fairy folk might be born with the capacity for magic, but it seemed the children had to study and undergo years of discipline to master their powers. This wasn't much different from the human world, where boys apprenticed themselves from age seven to carpenters or stone masons to learn a trade. The blacksmith had put off having a young apprentice. *I'll train up my own son,* he'd said. My heart tightened thinking of Adam.

The child was swinging her hands. "So when you are a grown-up, Susha, what happens then?"

"When I am grown, the younger fey will do my will," she said with a greedy look. "I will be in my full powers and an All Mother." At this she turned and walked regally from my room, my torn gown thrown over her shoulder, lank and floppy as a dead man draped over a horse.

THAT NIGHT I lay sleepless, staring at the ceiling. Tomorrow I'd have to speak with Onadon. Was there something wrong with me? Wouldn't any maid, especially one who'd lived with hunger and distress as I had, go giddy with the thought of being a queen? Wouldn't most girls feel joy to be so chosen?

The room seemed too close with the high, four-poster beds and the hulking wardrobe against the wall. I put on my slippers, and in my scratchy dun-colored robe, went out to our balcony. Many fey were still awake and a few danced out in the meadow. The figures seemed small from my high place; still, the meadow was well-lit with swirling wisps and hanging colored lanterns, and I had no trouble spying Poppy dancing with a red-haired fey man. I did not see Onadon with the revelers.

A couple left the meadow and climbed a tree. I would have chosen a cozy tree house over this solar, but no one had bothered to ask. Tugging my old cloak from the wardrobe, I went out. A few will-o'-the-wisps followed me down the hall, but I did not mind it; I wasn't running away, just going out to a more open place. I wanted to climb a tree and think, but the fey tree houses blended in so well, I couldn't be sure which trees were vacant in the dark, so I chose the waterfall.

Here was the great waterfall Grandfather had spoken of so often, the very headwaters of the Harrow River. Rushing water roared like a happy crowd, or a fierce wind, so the sound could be a glad one or an angry one, depending on who listened. Tonight I heard ferocity in it, that being my mood.

The fey had cut a black stone stairway beside the falls. The going was steep, the steps slick with water, but a hand-carved wooden rail went alongside. I climbed until my chest ached, cupped some water from a little side pool where a rock shelf jutted out, and drank. It was early November, not yet winter, but a few icicles hung thin as reeds from the ledge.

I found a small alcove near the top where I might sit away from the swirling mist. I watched a spider spinning her web across the entryway. The mist hung in droplets from her silk, each drop seemed to catch fire as the wisps sped past.

Onadon already had marriage plans in mind. How was that any different from the blacksmith who eyed me like his raw metal he could shape by force? Was one father's magic much different than the other's mallet? *I am not property.*

I touched a droplet on the web and let it gather like a small, clear pearl on my fingertip. The fall's roar was thunderous and deep. The will-o'-the-wisps' high-pitched laughs sounded like bells as they dared one another to fly closer to the spray.

What if I said no? I'd seen Onadon's cold look when I'd asked that. If I didn't do his will, would my father reject me?

If I agreed to his plan, I'd be closer to Garth. I pictured him sitting in the filthy straw of the jail cell, knees up and back pressed against the wall, his hands dangling empty in the dark before him.

Was Garth warm this night, or chill? Could he see the sky through the dungeon bars?

We'd looked at the sky through the study window. He'd shown me the necklace and said it was his mother's. How could he lie about such a thing? Had he lied about everything? Was he not a woodsman at all? Did he really know the royal family?

Garth was a man of corners and secrets, but I'd kept secrets from him too. I'd never told him the truth about my fire-sight, nor mentioned who I was after I'd learned I was half fey. Both of us had lied.

Would Garth have abandoned me if he discovered I lied to him? He'd seen me dressed as a leper, hungry and stinking in a cave. He'd known me as a costumed criminal on the run, even known I'd betrayed my friends to the witch hunter, yet he'd not judged me harshly. Might there be more of his story I didn't yet know? Should I judge and condemn him without knowing all?

Even if he was a thief, he was my thief.

I could not push him away anymore.

Chapter Twenty-eight

THE NEXT DAY, as Onadon had said, we rode bareback through Dragonswood, he on the black mare he called Lady, and I on the sorrel, Gideon. I was unused to riding bareback, so I held handfuls of Gideon's mane while trying to assume a dignified composure. I suspected Onadon knew my discomfort and was amused.

We'd ridden silently, skirting Morgesh Mountain, going eastward toward the sea. Anon I left off concentrating so hard on the horse and peered at Onadon, trying to read his face. I was nearly beheaded for it. Gideon sped under a low branch, forcing me to duck. I felt a sharp pull on my scalp as the branch snarled a goodly hunk of hair.

"Mind!" I shouted, yanking the sorrel's mane. He shook his head, affronted at my grip. I did not loosen it. I could not.

Onadon pulled over and waited for me to catch up. "You have an answer for me, Tess?" he asked.

"I do."

I'd not tell my father why I'd chosen to agree to his plans. Poppy was welcome to win Prince Arden. She'd be a beautiful queen, both thoughtful and kind. For my part I'd join the fairy delegation as a means to get inside Pendragon Castle so I could locate Garth and free him if I could.

"I'll go with you, Father."

"Good girl." Onadon turned Lady and cantered down a grassy knoll.

I followed, disappointed, milking the words *good* and *girl* for all their worth and finding them dry—he'd said them with little feeling. Even so, I'd seek Garth's cell as I'd found Tom's. I had no wish to join him as an outlaw, but what if I convinced Garth or Bash to give the treasure back?

If he and the dragon Ore returned the king's treasure as secretly as they'd taken it to begin with, he'd not have to live on the run from the law. I'd seen a strong man at the hunting lodge, a learned man who could read and write (a thing even most guildsmen in Harrowton could not do). He had skills enough to start a new life. A life with me? I could not count on that, but a good life anyway, and a free one.

I ran my hand along Gideon's muscled neck. "One thing troubles me, Father. I've heard Lord Sackmoore's niece, Lady Adela, is often at court. She accused me of witchcraft. She'll burn me if she catches me."

"Lady Adela won't be an impediment, Tess. The Gray Knight will keep her away."

"How do you know that?"

"Believe me. It is true."

My father began to whistle happily. The sound haunted me. I'd set about to trick my father, a powerful fey man. What happened to girls who tried to trick fairies? Nothing good, I suspected.

He expects you to carry out his plan.

I'm his daughter. He won't hurt me.

You've not yet seen him when he's angry.

I was familiar with my stepfather's rages, what of Onadon's? I gripped Gideon's mane a little too tightly. The horse drew his ears back in annoyance.

AFTER A BRIEF rest, Father said, "We need to move with more speed. Are you ready for a little magic?"

"What sort of magic?" I asked, excited and wary both.

"Just some aid for our mounts, Tess." Helping me up on Gideon, he said, "Hang on to his mane and keep your head low. You'll be all right."

I had no time to ask what he meant to do before the horses took off again. The rough ride became smooth as glass. The trees around us blurred. I tried to look down to see if Gideon's hooves touched the earth and could only see more brown blur below.

Riding thus, we reached a little clearing at the edge of Dragonswood in no time. There was a lake just inland from the sea with a dense green isle at its center. I'd heard of an enchanted lake with the isle God's Eye in the middle. "Is that Lake Ailleann?"

"The same," answered Onadon, riding ahead.

I stared at God's Eye, where Merlin had stayed to study wizardry more than six hundred years ago. Merlin came here as a young man when our island was as wild as its name, a magic place with dragons and fey folk, Euit tribes, and a few magicians. In later years when England used it as a prison colony, the ancient magic was driven underground. Queen Rosalind and King Kye built the sanctuary walls hoping to restore some of the lost magic, though the native Euits were all but gone.

God's Eye was thick with evergreens, but I saw a few maples shedding leaves near a dark rocky hill that stood out black as a pupil.

"We visit God's Eye," Onadon said. "There is someone I want you to meet." Hopping down, he gently turned Lady's head toward a bough, and pointed. By this the mare seemed tethered to the branch, though he had no rope. She nibbled the grass amiably, used to invisible tethers, I supposed. Helping me down from my sorrel, my father used this same magic to hold Gideon in place.

How would it be to point to a tree or bush and bind my mount with no true binding other than my will? Did my father have such power over men? If I had that fairy power, I could bind the jailors right up when I went after Garth.

"Might I learn to do that?"

"Do what?"

"Bind animals in place." *Or people.*

"Why?"

I did not answer.

Onadon said, "We walk from here."

"Who are we meeting, Father?"

"You'll see."

I kept up with Onadon's stride, my limbs awkward, my eyes sandy from a sleepless night. The hills were empty but for a shepherd boy and his flock. Halfway to the lake, Onadon stretched out a finger, picked a sheep from the boy's herd as he had picked his trout, and lo, the sheep crept off from the rest.

Anon we met the stray sheep standing mud-deep in the rushes. How he'd walked to the lakeside so quickly was a mystery, but then, he'd come by magic. At water's edge, Onadon shrouded us with mist. A rowboat answered Onadon's "come hither" finger the way the sheep had.

My father climbed inside, sat on the bench in the stern, and took up oars. I clambered in after the sheep, wetting both slippers and gown, though I'd tried to keep them clean. The sheep stood between us, spreading his legs wide and bleating so pitifully I felt sorry for him till he nearly overturned us, at which time I slapped his rump.

"Why bring him?" I asked once we were ashore.

Onadon only beckoned again. Were we to dine on this fat, scraggly woolen creature? My stomach was already in protest of this, though I was hungry enough. The sheep came away at last, mud-coated and sandy-legged, his top half white and bottom brown and dripping as a rain cloud.

We zigzagged through trees. The land was so densely green we had to work our way like fleas across a hairy dog. God's Eye had not looked overlarge from shore, but seemed to grow the more we walked. Midges overtook us, and flies. I waved both arms about. It did no good. After endless walking, we reached the rocky hill. I would have missed the cave altogether if Onadon hadn't walked right in. For a moment I thought he'd vanished.

I entered also, though I like to think I was not as docile as the sheep. If the dark inside annoyed me, the stench was worse. Couldn't Onadon smell it? Did the fey man have a nose?

Pinching my nose, I used the other hand to feel along the wall. Deeper in, a faint glow appeared and guided us. The putrid smell came also from there.

"Lord Kahlil," said Onadon. A flame leaped out. In the single flare, I saw a great dragon's head rising from its resting place on his outstretched claws. The wrinkled lids drooped over large, sleepy eyes that were pink-streaked where they were not copper.

"Onadon, the once fey king." His voice was lower than

the female dragon's, crackling and roaring like fire in the blacksmith's forge. Lord Kahlil coughed a cloud of smoke, then yawned, exposing teeth sharp as javelins, though much yellower. Three teeth were missing from the red and swollen gums. If a dragon can live over a thousand years, this one had already lived well beyond his nine hundred and ninety-ninth.

Spewing another flame, the dragon lit a fire between us where logs were piled up on the floor. Like the smaller dragon, Ore, much of his body hid in the recesses of the deep cave so that even with the firelight, I could not see all of him. But when I spied the jagged scar down his neck, I knew he was the dragon I'd first seen from a pine tree, the one who'd rescued me and later Tanya. Up close he seemed too weak to perform such feats, but then, he'd only just been sleeping.

Onadon went down on one knee, bowing to the drag-onlord. I knelt as much in greeting as in thanks. This old one had saved my life.

"I see you have brought a sacrifice," said Lord Kahlil.

Sacrifice? My skin iced, but only for a moment. Looking back, Onadon beckoned to the sheep. The creature baaed and stumbled unwillingly toward the dragon. I was halfway to my feet when Lord Kahlil crushed the sheep in his claws, then stripped his wool quicker than a shepherd shears. Skewering his kill on one of his talons, he flame-roasted it and popped it into his mouth.

I stared at the pile of wool at the dragon's feet. Not a single drop of blood was on it. My knees wobbled. The beast still relished his meal, chewing noisily. I studied his high ridged back, very long and thin with age or disease or both. I also met the source of the rank smell. Yellowing scales hung here and there between the healthier green scales along his sides. Many hung by fibrous strands from his bony frame. Dried blood traced their edges.

Lord Kahlil scratched his side with his back leg; one scale tore off and drifted leaf-like to the stone floor. I noticed then a goodly number of shed scales littering the floor around his feet.

The dragon swallowed his meal. "My hunter has not come these past weeks."

Onadon said, "I should have brought you fresh meat sooner, my lord." He added a log to the fire. "I will send you a hunter until you're well."

Lord Kahlil smacked his jaws in agreement.

Until you're well? Was the skin disease so bad? Then I remembered the dragon had a burned wing.

Lord Kahlil picked his teeth with a talon. "King Elixis already visited here with Poppy. He boasted of her stirring beauty and sexual allure. He was certain she'd charm the future king. I took his word on this. Our eyes do not judge human or fey beauty. You are all worm-like to us, if you pardon my saying so."

I remembered Garth saying dragons thought us ugly.

To them Princess Augusta was most beautiful of all with her face scales and dragon eyes.

"Elixis is right about Poppy," Onadon said. "She'll attract any human male, but I say there should be two contenders. More chances to win the future king's heart that way." He nudged me to step forward. "Tess also came to the outskirts of DunGarrow on her own as was agreed. Drawn by her fey blood, she arrived only two days after Poppy."

Father had already mentioned that half-fey girls had to come on their own. If not for that, this dragon could have flown me to DunGarrow the first time he spied me in the tree.

How different that would have been. I'd have skipped my trial, had no witch hunter at my heels. Poppy might have stayed at home and never gone north herself, living alone and unhappy with her father, or been forced into a marriage she did not want. And Meg would still be crammed in with her small family above Old Weaver's shop instead of ruling her own kitchen at the lodge.

We'd been through a deal, yet strange as it was, I saw both Poppy and Meg were happier now than they'd ever been in Harrowton. And if the dragon had sped me straight to DunGarrow that first night, I would have never met Garth. Much as I was still angry with him for lying to me, to us all, I couldn't imagine never having met him.

Wandering thoughts had kept me from my father's conversation. I picked up the thread again.

". . . not just the fire-sight, Tess can read and write. The girl is cunning."

"Cunning?" I glared at Onadon. Was this flattery or insult? The dragon coughed or laughed, I couldn't tell which. The sound was alarmingly loud.

"King Elixis did not bring me a sacrifice," the dragon said.

The sheep was a point in Onadon's favor. The hint of a smile visited my father's face. Lord Kahlil whipped his head around to chew under his right wing so violently it started to bleed.

"It looks worse, my lord," said Onadon. "Aisling made more salve." He pulled a jar from his waist pouch. "Go on, Tess," he said, handing it to me.

"Sir?"

Lord Kahlil blinked down at us, a torn scale hanging from his teeth.

"Open it," Onadon urged.

The greenish balm inside had a vaporous scent that made my eyes water. There was pine in it, and mint, and some sweet flower. The powerful smell was not an ill one. The dragon's nostrils flared, sniffing the fumes.

"Rub it on the raw places," said Onadon. "It will ease his itch."

I was speechless, but went to the scored spot below the right wing.

"Not where it bleeds, Tess," my father hissed. I jumped

back. Of course, a bloody wound would sting with such strong ointment. I'd been too nervous to think of it. I would be more cautious. Jar in hand, I inched along to a withered scale. Father had not forced me, which is to say I was not compelled by point of finger. I had stepped up on my own.

Grandfather once had an old hound named Padrick, whose vile skin disease made his fur fall off in hunks. The wrinkled balding spots itched the poor hound fiercely. He scratched and stank like this dragon. I'd salved his sores many a time, so it was Padrick I thought of as I tread the fallen dragon scales carpeting the dusty floor. Some sloughed scales were dingy yellow, but many were a healthy green or brighter golden chest scales, not fallen from disease but shed in season.

All dragons shed as they grow. Long ago Princess Rosalind made a gown of shed pip scales, and gathered more hatchling scales to write on, making herself a book. *If I had a book made of dragon scales, I'd draw in it.* The book she made when she was forced to live alone with the dragons on Dragon's Keep was under glass now at Pendragon Castle. I might see it myself soon.

The thick, cool ointment spread evenly over Lord Kahlil's raw spots. I was careful at first, fearing it might sting even here, and was ready to jump back, perhaps even run, but Lord Kahlil let out a long sigh of pleasure, and that encouraged me. The salve's scent overcame the rotten smell, and that pleased me also.

My doctoring seemed to seal things betwixt Father and the dragonlord. They talked easily now about my future and spoke of other matters. I listened intently, working my way along. Strange. I'd been useless when it came to helping Tom. His weeping sores upset my stomach, so I'd backed away like a coward, leaving Meg and Poppy, and later Aisling to do the work. Why was it I could tend Grandfather's dog, and now Lord Kahlil's sores without the same repulsion? I did not understand myself at all sometimes.

The old dragon's scales were surprisingly smooth. It was like salving a wall, so high was his bony frame, but a living wall, and breathing one, and warm.

Kahlil said, "Prince Arden's ship will arrive next week."

"So soon? We are not ready."

"Ready or not, make your move, Onadon. Lord Sackmoore will present his daughter, Lady Lizbeth, straightaway to Arden."

"Bucktooth Betsy? Lady Lizbeth doesn't stand a chance."

"Do not underestimate Lord Sackmoore," said the dragonlord. "And the other lady might still be in play."

"She was just a boyhood fancy, my lord. I'm sure Prince Arden is long over her."

So Prince Arden had a lady love before he left on crusade? My hand stopped mid-salve. "What lady?" They ignored my question.

The dragonlord went on. "I wouldn't discount her. Time does not always lessen affection. You know the woman has the spine to be a queen."

"But not the beauty," argued Onadon. "She's lost the flower of her youth."

The bucktoothed daughter of the powerful king's regent; an old lover who'd lost her beauty; and me: None of us had a chance against Poppy. Still, Onadon was driven to smash Elixis in this fight, and I was his mallet.

Lord Kahlil shook his head. The scale wall moved under my hand. "You bring up beauty again. What of courage? Strength? Is beauty so precious to a man?"

Onadon laughed. "Very precious. The new king must think his wife beautiful if he's expected to beget an heir by her."

I paused and looked at my father. "If beauty surmounts all, Poppy will win." It had to be said.

"You are beautiful," Onadon remarked. I blushed, drawing more ointment from the jar.

On tiptoe I applied some to a yellowed patch. Suddenly the dragon's back leg lunged at me with long, sharp talons.

"Tess!" Onadon shouted.

Chapter Twenty-nine

ONADON DOVE UNDER the beast's mighty jaw to find me huddled, arms over my head.

"Excuse me," Lord Kahlil said as Father helped me to stand. I was shaken but began to see what had happened. Old Padrick had scratched his itchy side violently when I tended him. The dragon had done the same without conscious thought to harm me.

"You are all right?" His eyes swiveled on me with concern. Unlike the smaller, blue-eyed Ore's, his irises were golden. And now that he was fully awake, no longer drugged with sleep, they glowed like molten metal.

"I'm unharmed, my lord." I held up the jar. "The ointment is half gone already."

Onadon cupped my shoulders with his hands, proudly as a man might bolster his brave son after battle. "Do what you can with it, Tess."

I went back to work, rubbing the dragon's wrinkled elbow, soaked in the knowledge that Onadon had leaped to my rescue, as a father would a daughter. Still, I'd done my part. I'd had the reflexes to dart backward. I'd learned that maneuver long ago.

Had Onadon seen something of my strength? Not all women need rescuing. Some prefer to look both man and dragon in the eye. *I am becoming more to him than a plan or a prize.*

Finishing the right side, which was by far the worst, I slipped under the dragon's long neck to his left side.

"Lean down a little, Lord Kahlil. There is a place I cannot reach."

Roaring laughter echoed through the cave. I reared back again, alarmed, but two were laughing, my father and the dragon.

"Well, she has spine enough to give orders to a dragon!" Lord Kahlil snorted.

"I'll say that for her." Onadon wiped his laughter-soaked eyes, and sighed.

"Come by me again, Tess. I will lean down as you asked." Lord Kahlil's voice was gentle, if a sound that is deep and rough as a rocky gully can be called gentle. He lowered his head. "Climb up on my wing if you need to reach the upper back."

I hesitated. "Isn't it still damaged at the tip?" I'd seen it burn when he rescued Tanya.

"The tip still troubles me. Avoid it there, but the upper wing is sound."

"The burned tip is why our good lord cannot fly," Onadon added.

"It will heal," snapped the dragon.

"My pardon, lord." Onadon made a quick bow.

"Would the salve help?" I asked cautiously.

"It might, child, but the scales are tender there."

We all moved a little ways toward the mouth of the cave. Lord Kahlil needed room to unfurl his left wing without scraping the wall. He was a very large dragon even in such a sizable cave.

The scales were blackened at the tip, and there was a painful-looking red spot where one scale had fallen off and new ones had not grown in.

"New scales grow, Tess," he said, sensing my concern. "I'll fly again soon enough. Try the salve, but gently."

I did so, rubbing carefully as I might rub a babe, so tender were the burns. Lord Kahlil let out a great sigh. When the wingtip was done, I removed my slippers and climbed up on his inner wing to reach the yellowing scales higher up on his back. The upper wing scales were warm on the soles of my feet. My hands smelled of minty ointment. Strange contentment filled me as I eased his lordship's pain.

One discolored scale peeled off as I applied the balm. A healthier green scale lay beneath, but the edge was prickled and inflamed. I knew better than to spread the balm there. Climbing higher on the wing, I saw the uppermost part of the dragonlord's back. There was a space at the base of his long neck where one or two fey riders could sit comfortably astride him. But he seemed too noble a creature to be ridden so.

There were still sore places on his left side. I was sorry

the jar was empty. Climbing down, I put on my slippers and joined my father by the fire. Lord Kahlil lowered his cupped eyes, inspecting me. Such mirrors these. What did they see? The dark slit pupils were the length of my hand. The golden irises were like bright curtains drawn back to a diamond-shaped night window.

"Come closer," he said, smoke coiling from his nose.

He pointed with a single talon. "Turn around, Tess."

I sighed. The blacksmith bid me turn around, inspecting my soundness for marriage. Morralyn asked the same when I was naked in her flit chamber. Now the dragon wanted me to turn. What did turning have to do with anything? Was there something telling about my back or buttocks I should know of?

I obeyed, my slippers crunching in the pebbles.

After a long pause, Lord Kahlil flicked his tongue. "King Kadmi has two sons."

"Only the older will be king, my lord," said Father.

"Can you see the future?" asked the dragon testily.

"I cannot," admitted Onadon.

"Better for all of us if both princes marry girls with fey blood, Onadon. More mixed-blood offspring that way." He appraised me a little longer. "I've known Arden and Bion from children. I watched them play on Dragon's Keep. This girl of yours came closer to me than the one called Poppy. From the time he was a boy, the younger prince Bion showed no fear of dragons. The same cannot be said of Arden. I say Tess is better suited to Bion."

My father looked startled, but bowed his head quickly, replying, "As you say, my lord."

I clamped my teeth. I'd not met either prince, yet every man, every male creature for that matter, seemed to think he was my matchmaker. Did any one of them consider asking me what I thought?

"We will send both Tess and Poppy," he concluded. "Make sure to school them well before they go. Whoever becomes queen will have to speak for all of us and for the sanctuary."

Onadon nodded.

"All right. Here is what I told Elixis. The Pendragons might be willing enough to take you in, but the king's regent will turn you away at the gate if he knows you're fey. In the beginning introduce Tess and Poppy as Irish princesses. Arden would welcome princesses from his mother's homeland. And many lesser Irish kings squirm under England's boot. An alliance with Wilde Island would be to their advantage."

"We would have to come by sea to bring it off," said Onadon irritably.

Kahlil blinked. "No doubt you can guise a ship, and your flits can weave a proper Irish flag."

"And later when the truth comes out, my lord?"

"The truth must come out, Onadon. Prince Arden has to know he's choosing a half-fey girl if he takes Tess or Poppy. You only go as an Irish delegation to get past Sackmoore."

"Ireland it is, then." My father bowed.

Chapter Thirty

I CAME LATE to the high meadow many nights later, having missed the meal once again. Since returning from God's Eye I'd been trapped day after day learning courtly dances. When not gliding on my feet or colliding with my instructor, I was sent along with Poppy to learn a bit of fey history. We were schooled enough to speak with confidence for our people. Whoever became queen would have to hold her ground and protect the dragons' and the fairies' rights to this sanctuary.

When not busy dancing or studying, I was sent to Morralyn. Poppy had eight elaborate gowns ready for Pendragon Castle. Onadon was determined I'd have just as many. Thus I was made to stand still in the humming hives when my feet ached and all I wished to do was to sit. I held my arms out just so while the flits spun new gowns. (Still I was all over stung!) Seven complete now, my favorite one was flame-colored. The red-orange cloth shimmered like living fire. I knew I'd save it out for something special. One more visit with the flits on the morrow, and I'd be done.

My newest gown spun this day was a soft rosy pink. It reminded me of something. Up in my solar I'd pulled out Grandfather's handkerchief and pressed it against the new gown. The sparkling rose cloth matched perfectly. *Flit-made*. No wonder it was so fine. He must have gotten it from one of the fey friends he'd met at sea. I tucked it into my sleeve before going outside.

King Elixis was dancing with his "queen for the night." He'd been angry to learn Lord Kahlil approved of me as the second fey princess. He'd expected to bring only Poppy to court. He and Onadon argued long. It seemed like a pointless discussion after Lord Kahlil gave judgment. The dragons and the fairies had to agree on the half-fey girls with the sanctuary at stake.

Sipping wine and gently rubbing a drop on my flit-stung elbow, I watched couples dancing in the meadow. The fey were tireless. I was worn out from the lessons and dress fittings, and too exhausted to dance.

Fey men and maids swung round and round, moving close and closer. On the edge of the crowd, I saw partners slip off toward the treed fairy houses to couple for a night. How different their society was. I was learning about it in our daily lessons; still, I wasn't used to it. Men and women coming together one night, parting again the next. Mothers bore the children. I saw imbalance in that. Men were free, but were the women here? And the children seemed little more than servants, minding their All Mothers and

All Fathers. Still, if marriage is abhorrent, certainly my mother's was, there was something to be said for this way of life.

Poppy made her way through the dancers. "Nice gown," she said. "Pink becomes you."

She sat by me, a little breathless. "You have a matching lady's handkerchief," she noted. "Morralyn hasn't made me any. I'll ask her to."

I quietly fingered the cloth and was considering how to tell Poppy it hadn't come from Morralyn when she pointed into the crowd.

"Do you see him, Tess?"

"See whom?"

"Jyro, silly. Over there." She drew my attention to a lanky fellow with ginger hair as curly as sheep's wool. The youth stood out from the others not in his handsomeness, for that was common among the fey, but in his quick, playful movements. He was the one who'd juggled the platters to amuse the children my first night here.

"The juggler."

"He's a fun dance partner," she said. "And you know I saw him long before we came here."

"What? When?"

"I told you the fey man I spied on the dragon's back the night they rescued Tanya had hair as red as Meg's."

I remembered. I'd been puzzled she'd seen a fey man when I had not.

"It was him," she said breathlessly. "Jyro." She stepped away from me. Already Jyro was running across the lawn to claim another dance with her.

It was only later the next evening while packing for our trip, Poppy startled me with her news.

"He loves me, Tess."

"Who does?"

"Jyro. He said so." She swatted her pillow to plumpness so she could curl up on her side and face me. "He is a wonderful man."

"A fey man," I reminded.

"Fey," she sighed. "Aye, fey, so much better than human men, don't you think?"

She smiled up at the ceiling.

I should have sensed she was falling for Jyro. Hadn't she danced with him exclusively the night before? Frowning, I folded another gown and placed it in my trunk. I'd been with the Mistress of the Hives in the afternoon and had come away with three new flit stings, two below the knee and one new inflamed one on my wrist. "You should get up, Poppy. We need to finish packing."

Poppy took a yellow gown from the wardrobe and twirled with it a little before laying it across her bed. "Jyro wants to marry me." She did not look me in the face but kept folding.

I went to help her fold. "Poppy," I said softly. "You know fey don't marry. Jyro didn't mean it the way you think."

"He meant every word. He wants to marry me. He said he'd find a way."

Would Jyro go against his own fey king, against their entire fey way of life here?

I thought not, but I could see she cared for him. She'd never fallen for any man before, at least not that I knew.

I took her hand. "I know how it feels to be lied to by someone you care about." I could say no more then; the thought of Garth suddenly stopped my throat. When I could speak again, I said, "I'll stay by you."

"I don't want you," she laughed. "I want him."

"What about Prince Arden?"

"I don't care about being a queen anymore. I told you, Jyro loves me."

I leaned against the wardrobe, the cold mirror at my back. "You know as well as I Jyro can't marry you. Marriage is against their way of life."

"Jyro's different. He promised me he would." There was a desperate tone to her voice that frightened me.

"Maybe he said that so he could kiss you, or even more than that, so he could—" I saw her shy smile and stopped. She was wrapping her pretty combs so they wouldn't break on the journey. Her hands working with speed as if she were in a race. So Jyro had already gone further than kissing?

"Poppy, what if he gets you with child, then leaves you the way both our mothers were left?"

"Jyro wouldn't do that." She swept up her combs hurriedly, then dropped them all. On the floor together, we gathered them up again. The wrappings had come off but only the bright blue one was broken, the one that matched her eyes. Her hands shook as she put the two pieces together as if to join them by force.

Jyro had used magic to mend the platters he'd dropped, breaking them for laughter's sake, and fixing them as soon as broken with a playful wink. The man stood out from the other fey, entertaining the children who were too busy at their chores to stop long for a little fun. "I do not think Jyro is a liar, Poppy," I said, "but he's something of a trickster."

Her eyes lit up. "He makes me laugh more than anyone."

On the floor I leaned against my open trunk. "Even if he married you, where would you live?"

"Here in DunGarrow."

We rewrapped the combs again, keeping out the broken one. We'd studied the fey together, all part of our queen training. "You know if you lived in DunGarrow, you'd lose your man to another fey woman at the dances. They don't stay with one partner long."

Poppy stuffed the combs in the trunk and took out her blue gown to fold. I opened our balcony door, remembering the waif named Susha who'd come in to fetch my torn gown, the determined look on her face as she'd boasted she was now a second tier. Childhood here was full of tests, it seemed, with no particular mother or father to claim you. Could Poppy live with that?

"What about children?" I asked her cautiously.

"They'd have Jyro's red hair, I think," she said dreamily. "Like little Alice."

A cold foreboding crept along my skin. "You know you would have to give up any children you and Jyro might have," I said, "watching them live as little servants till they earned their fey powers and their freedom." I saw her face changing, but I went on. "You would be an All Mother with no real family of your own."

"Stop it, Tess." Throwing the gown over the open trunk, she went out onto the balcony. Poppy stood with her back to me, her spine rigid as a birch. The last light of the day spread over the woods, a rosy hue washed round her. I let her be. I knew my words disturbed her, but I'd said it for my sake as much as hers. This too would be my fate if I chose to live in DunGarrow. All the fey men would have a husband's rights, yet none of them would show any special care for me or my children.

I went out and put my arm about her. "I've said too much. You know as well as I the way they live here." I paused, gazing out at the meadow. "It's only I'm afraid."

She did not look at me. "Afraid of what?"

"That you'll be cheated in some way. That Jyro will hurt you the way Onadon hurt my mother, the way Elixis hurt yours. And if not that, then I worry you'll stay with him only to be unhappy here."

Her shoulders eased. "Tess. You've always worried overmuch." She put her arms around me, the wind coming down the mountainside chilling the air as it sang through the pinnacles.

"What will we do now?" I said.

Poppy pulled back. "Jyro said I should go to Pendragon Castle as planned. He'll come along so I won't be alone. He promised he'll think of a way for us to be together."

Poppy still had the broken comb in her left hand. Jyro might have the magic to fix it in a wink the way he'd fixed the platters, but hearts and lives were harder to mend. How could he interfere with the fey plans for an alliance without endangering their sanctuary?

"I thought you would be pleased for me to step aside," Poppy said. "It means you can marry Prince Arden yourself."

I gripped the railing, leaning out into the wind. I wanted to tell her the real reason I was going with the fey, but could not press a single word past the lump in my throat. I knew Poppy wouldn't tell a soul, but my hope to free Garth seemed like a dream, a bright reflection in the mirror that looks warm in the light and turns cold when you touch the glass. I was sure if I spoke, I'd see all the ways in which it could never work. It's one thing to spring a prisoner from a small jailhouse set apart from a sheriff's manor, another thing to free a man from a king's dungeon guarded by well-trained knights, and escape from a castle fortified with towering guard walls and a moat.

BECAUSE WE HAD to arrive by sea as a royal delegation from Ireland would have, our party of fourteen rode southeast for a place called Swanebrook Harbor to find a worthy ship. Morralyn came along to act as Poppy's lady's maid, Aisling as mine. Other men and women joined us, including King Elixis and Onadon, who would be called Lord O'Malley and Lord McLaughlin in turn until we were past Sackmoore's guard. So we left with our entourage, our lordly escort. And of course, Jyro.

Now that Prince Arden was at court, both Onadon and Elixis were anxious to reach Pendragon Castle. We hadn't ridden long before my father resorted to magic.

"Shall we speed it up?" he asked.

Remembering our ride to meet Lord Kahlil, I sensed what was coming. "Hold on," I said to Poppy, "and keep your head low."

In a rush, the horses sped through the greenwood. It was rough going at first, then just as before, the ride became smooth as silk and everything became a blur. Riding thus, we reached the boundary wall quite soon and took up our journey again on Kingsway. I was nervous at first to be traveling so conspicuously on the road. I soon found I needn't have worried. Everything—all the fey, their horses, and the cart—completely disappeared when humans were near.

My first dizzying experience of this came after Elixis's scout spied a tinker's wagon up ahead, a man and his family rolling wares to the next town. They'd not yet seen us. Elixis waved his hand, and in a wink, we all vanished. I let out a startled scream. No sound came. All was silent in the fairy spell so Tinker and his family would neither see us nor hear us approach.

I did not know how quick the fairy's senses were, but I was deaf within the spell and could not hear the jingling wagon, his horse's hoofbeats or our own. All the clopping rhythmic sounds that had drummed the roadway only minutes before went dumb. Only our telltale hoof prints on the snowy road gave evidence of us.

As my eyes adjusted in the spell, I caught a glimmer of myself and my companions all wavering pale as sunlight through mist. But I knew the humans could not see even that. I became less anxious and began to ride along comfortably like a quiet flame suspended in midair.

A girl of five or six peered out of the back of her father's wagon. Mouth open, she pointed at our new-made hoof prints appearing in the snow. The excited child tugged on her brother's cloak and was ignored.

When we'd ridden far enough down Kingsway, the spell faded and we came into ourselves again. I was a little numbed by the magic. Jyro rode near Poppy, consoling her after her first vanishing. I saw him speaking softly, but he did not touch her. As it turned out, the tinker's family was the first of many encounters. So Poppy and I had to adjust ourselves to the vanishing spell as we rode on. It came to me this was the way the fey had always moved through the human world when it suited them. I wondered how often I'd passed them by myself.

Swanebrook Harbor looked deserted in the moonlight. It took little time to "borrow" a ship, as Morralyn called it. Sailors watching the harbor were gently enspelled to sleep. Soon fey men hoisted sails aboard the newly christened *Malarkey*. Jyro unfurled and raised the flit-spun Irish flag.

A light snow fell on ship and harbor as I made my way across the dock. Many fey were already on board. King Elixis helped Poppy over the icy gangplank. On shore my father directed the horses to return to Dragonswood, and onward home without us. Other fey men carried trunks and heavy bundles across the plank. I decided to cross the steep gangplank on my own. Halfway over, I slipped on the ice, fell facedown, and screamed as I felt the sharp nail gouge my chin.

Onadon was at my side in an instant, his eyes full of fire. He gripped my upper arm so fiercely, I knew there would be a bruise there later. He pulled me up, saw the deep cut, and said, "Now look what you've done, clumsy girl," his eyes backlit with anger. He had yet to call me *daughter*, but *clumsy girl* came easily enough.

King Elixis snickered as Father helped me onto the ship's deck, which was slippery wet but not as icy as the plank. "She bleeds like a stuck pig," Onadon complained.

"And it's running all down her gown!" Morralyn added, horrified.

No one but Poppy seemed to care that I was hurt. "Poor Tess," she said, offering me her new kerchief.

"Thank you, Poppy, I will be all right." My teeth chattered as I pressed her gift over my bleeding chin. Onadon gave strict orders. "Take Tess downstairs and fix her face."

Snip-snap, Morralyn and Aisling led me down the creaking steps to a tiny cabin, and helped me onto a straw-stuffed pallet. Morralyn lit the lamp while Aisling ran off to fetch the bags. Once back she dribbled one tincture after another onto a gray sea sponge.

"What is that?" I asked, afraid.

"Poppy juice, hemlock, a touch of bryony, gall from a castrated boar—"

"That should knock her out," Morralyn said, opening her bag.

"Leave me be."

Aisling hushed me. "You don't want to feel the stitches, do you, Tess?"

"Stitches?" I tried to sit up. "Can't you spell the cut away?"

"You're half human, Tess. It's not as simple as that." Aisling pressed me firmly down and cupped the sponge over my face. The ship's cabin rocked—whether it was the motion of the boat or the tincture fumes, I could not tell. Morralyn pulled out a long needle. I have never screamed into a sponge before, but there is always a first time. Before darkness fell, I heard the two arguing.

Aisling said, "The stitches will show for days and days, Morralyn."

"We will have to glamour her face."

"Not possible. Prince Bion made us swear we would not glamour our fey maidens or use any love spells to win his brother's affection."

I was surprised to hear Prince Bion knew so much about the fey plan, enough to place his own conditions on it.

Morralyn threaded the needle. "Our agreement with Bion restrains us from making Tess more beautiful, but should she enter court with the face of a warthog?"

Warthog was the last word I heard as the tincture filled my nose.

HOURS LATER I awoke to a throbbing and swollen chin prickly with stitches. Sickened but needing air, I half stumbled across the tilting floor to the porthole window. It was open a crack, enough to let in the frigid breeze.

Above deck, pipes and fiddles played. My ceiling boards drummed with the fairies' rhythmic, pounding feet. I was hungry and terribly thirsty, but I knew I would not go upstairs where Onadon was. My gash had bled, and I'd seen no care in his face, only anger, disappointment, even . . . disgust.

He is not the blacksmith. He yanked me up harshly, he shouted, but he didn't strike me.

I watched the snow falling above the sea, then stuck my fingers out the inch-wide opening and caught a snowflake. It was colder than the pearl Garth let me hold, but just as white before it went clear and turned into a droplet on my finger.

I gently touched my stitches, disappointed they'd not used magic. It had been the same for Tanya. They'd done their best to heal her burns, it seemed, but their medicinal magic was for fairies, not for those of us who were just half. The longer I stayed with my father's people, the more I learned about their powers and their limitations.

The tune changed upstairs. They danced to "Fey Maiden." Already King Elixis and Onadon were celebrating an alliance between the Pendragons and the fey kingdom. They had no idea Poppy's heart was set on Jyro, mine on freeing Garth. Neither man had bothered to get to know his daughter.

The ship rocked on the night sea. I shut the porthole window and heard a knock. "Enter."

Poppy came in with a water goblet and some hot peas porridge. The porridge was not the kind of food the fey would eat, but seeing as how I couldn't chew without pain, I welcomed the bowl.

The water dribbled down my chin as I drank. I winced.

"It must hurt awfully," she said, sitting by me on the pallet.

I nodded. How many times she'd said that in our childhood back in Harrowton when she'd seen a new bruise forming on my lip or eye, or when she'd laid a fresh poultice on my boxed ear.

"I've been dancing with Jyro." Smiling, she looked down at her hands.

"And no one noticed?"

Poppy knew what I meant. Couldn't others see the growing love between the two? But she assured me they were careful, and no one had seemed to know. I listened to her talk while I ate, trying for small bites so I wouldn't move my chin. She loved him, I could see. Every word she said was love-lit.

What would King Elixis and Onadon do if they knew their daughters' hearts? One set on a thief, another on a fey man? We were in a mess, surely.

Chapter Thirty-one

WE MADE LANDFALL the next afternoon to great fanfare. How the fey managed to have a cheering crowd greet us in Dentsmore Harbor was beyond me. Prince Arden had ordered a royal escort down to the harbor. This time Onadon himself helped me across the gangplank. He wouldn't tolerate any more mishaps.

I was still counted as one of the "Irish princesses." It had been agreed among the fey that Morralyn would charm my stitched chin in public. By this I would not be a warthog.

The castle escort took us north along Kingsway Road. I was glad not to have to ride bareback; still, my sore chin throbbed in rhythm to the bouncing saddle. I sat regally as an Irish princess in her fine gown, and thought about Garth and my challenge ahead.

Snow covered the rolling hillsides and the woods beyond. I heard hammering in the distance, and rounding the corner, I saw the Lord Faul Amphitheatre crowning the hill. Built in Queen Rosalind's day, it was named after the dragon she'd served as a girl on Dragon's Keep. I did not think there was another land in all the world that could boast an amphitheatre named after a dragon.

There was much ado about the place. On the large stage below the ringed seats, carpenters sawed and hammered, building a tall wooden structure as a temporary roof.

The castle escort riding just ahead of me said, "They'll be working straight through to finish the roof in time. Prince Arden's coronation's to take place there three days from now on Saint Dyfrig's feast day."

"An auspicious day for the new Pendragon king to be crowned," said Lord McLaughlin, *Onadon*.

I silently agreed. Arden was a Pendragon, and Saint Dyfrig was the famed bishop who'd crowned Arthur Pendragon King of Britain.

We rode in slow procession so I had time to take in the great gray castle overlooking the sea. Right away I counted four towers at each corner of the immense structure, and four more towers in the corners of the outer guard wall. The palace was surrounded on three sides by a stone wall and a deep moat, and on the backside by sheer cliff and sea. A sour taste came to my mouth. How in the name of all the saints would Garth escape once I freed him?

I was the last to arrive at the drawbridge. All the kings and queens of Wilde Island had crossed this very bridge. Now I crossed. Tess of Harrowton, blacksmith's daughter.

Tess of DunGarrow, fey princess. I bared my head and let my hair fly back.

Horse hooves pounded the planks and echoed down below. The spiked portcullis gate hung over my head like a monstrous jaw, the iron spikes sharp as dragon's teeth.

The courtyard swarmed with castle guards, lords, ladies, servants, and dogs. In a glance I spied a falcon's mews, stable, kennels, a buttery, and henhouse. The rest of the outbuildings were not so easily defined, but one beyond the mews and garden might be an outer kitchen, judging by the rich scent of roasting meat.

All of this was nothing compared to the castle itself. Larger than DunGarrow, it loomed over all like a watchful grandfather with a hundred eyes, and all the eyes were windows. High and low, the windows were barred from attack; many were arrow slits just wide enough for archers to shoot through, though some higher up were bright with stained glass. The few I saw at ground level were dark even in the late afternoon sun. *Dungeon cells.* Black and desolate as the Treegrim's eye pits. Fixing on those barred windows filled me with dread. Was Garth down there? How could I reach him? What condition would I find him in? Please God not beaten. It had been hard enough discovering Tom raw and bloody in his cell; I didn't think I could stand to see Garth that way.

"Your hand, my lady." A groom helped me from the saddle and led my horse toward the stables along with

Poppy's. Poppy struggled to keep Tupkin hidden in her cloak.

A sallow-skinned lord stepped out with his guards, wearing velvet robes with golden neck chain and golden belt. His feet were clad in red pointed shoes curled up at the toes. *Lord Sackmoore,* I thought. *It must be.* He was a man of fashion sure, but his sunken cheeks and puffy eyes told me he knew little sleep.

A young noblewoman with protruding teeth had stepped out with him. Also clad in velvet, she wore a gown of pale blue that showed her ample bosom. The lady sucked her lower lip as she studied us. I remembered Onadon's remark about Lord Sackmoore's bucktoothed daughter, Lady Lizbeth.

Onadon, or Lord McLaughlin, as he'd be called here, introduced our party. Sackmoore fixed his eyes on the ornate treasure chest in his arms—lavish gifts for Prince Arden from the Irish king. Sackmoore bid his attendant reach for it, but my father held firm. "I was told to deliver it to no one but the prince himself, my lord." His voice was quiet, but stern, looking the king's regent squarely in the face.

Lord Sackmoore backed off and turned his attention to the Irish princesses. If he was annoyed by my pretty face and comely figure, he was truly stunned by Poppy. Even with a smudged cheek and hair tangled from our windy ride, she was as beautiful as ever. The lord steeled his face, recovering his composure, but not before I saw his quick marriage plans for his daughter undone. He would have some work to do now the competition had arrived. Elixis and Onadon looked gratified.

A trumpet blared above. Prince Arden stepped out onto his high balcony and hailed us down below. This was the first time I'd seen our soon-to-be king. I was struck by his strong frame, his dark skin, which came from his great-grandmother, who was herself a woman from the holy land, and his broad smile as he took us in: a handsome prince indeed. I noticed Poppy thought so too. A moment later she eyed Jyro, and blushed.

The prince's finely embroidered coat still missed a left sleeve. The tailor who'd come out on the balcony with him was measuring his arm. The prince ducked back inside a moment later.

Lord Sackmoore bid us come inside. "An awkward time for you to visit," Sackmoore complained to my father. "With just three days left to prepare for the coronation. The palace is in an uproar."

I saw at once what he meant. Servants scurried past us in the halls. In each adjoining room, I saw them sweeping, scrubbing floors, or laying down fresh rushes. In the Great Hall, a stout man perched on a high ladder replaced the candles in the enormous chandelier. I'd heard this chandelier held a hundred candles. I believed it now. The man whistled through his teeth as he dropped the spent candles to the floor, stubs the blacksmith would have made us burn. There was no such thriftiness here.

Lord Sackmoore did not show us the busy kitchens, two inside and one out, he said, where thirty cooks were baking, roasting, mixing, and boiling for the coronation feast. We passed an alcove where I had to stop, though the party in front continued on ahead.

Two castle guards stood on either side of a glass case. No jewels on display here, but what a jewel Princess Rosalind's book was to me. Here was the very one written on dragon pip scales while she was on Dragon's Keep. By clever device, one could turn a page without touching the book. A bellows embedded in the glass case allowed the reader to pump air into the enclosure, blowing a page over. Ah, I'd read, and if allowed, I'd pump. The guards stood stock-still. I scanned the page, read:

Mother knifed Tess.

I swallowed, seeing my name, but this was a Tess from long ago. I went on reading. *She scrawled witchery in blood across her hut, and let the angry crowd rush to Morgesh Mountain to burn Demetra for the crime. Marn, Tess, Demetra. Three deaths I knew of to keep my claw secret, were there more I knew nothing of? Was it only a blizzard killed the midwife on my birthing day?*

Before I could read more, Morralyn marched back and hauled me away. I'd grown up beaten by the blacksmith, hating the man I thought was my father. But this island queen had a mother who was a murderess. How had Rosalind borne it?

Down more halls, past more castle uproar. The noisy palace annoyed me. I'd only just come in and already wanted out. The windows on this level were but arrow slits made for defense, not to gaze out. Saints. How could the Pendragon family live with the constant, noisy bustle? If forced to stay here, I'd straightaway adopt the highest tower overlooking the ocean and let the crowd swarm far below.

All through the hurried tour, I thought of Garth. Could he hear our pounding feet overhead? With so many kitchens here, wouldn't they give their prisoners more than stale bread or day-old porridge? Was he cold in his dark cell?

Before a servant showed us our rooms, I spied one promising stone stairwell leading down to the castle underbelly. The sentry guarding the door gave me some small hope it might be the dungeon stair.

At last our party broke up to be escorted to our separate rooms. Servants hefted my trunk into the solar I was to share with my lady's maid, Aisling. The second-story window was on the back side of the castle overlooking the sea. We were high up, but not so high that I couldn't hear the waves pounding the cliffs below. Door shut, Aisling heaved a sigh, then waved her hand, removing the glamour from my chin. Half fey like myself, she'd mastered glamour spells just as Tanya had. In the dull white window light she cupped my jaw. "It's still swollen and bruised. With all your stitches showing, you'll not be tempted to stray." Saying this, she pulled a vial and sponge from her bag.

"You would knock me out?" I asked, alarmed.

"I would give you rest while we wait for your formal introduction to the prince. The pain keeps you awake, am I right?"

"It does hurt, mistress. If you leave it here I will take a dose if I need to."

"Two drops at most, Tess," she cautioned. "Onadon will have my head if you sleep through your first court occasion."

Due to my unsightly wound, Aisling did not see the need to lock the door. Her mistake. Once she was gone, I slipped outside and took the corridor for the dungeon stair.

PART FOUR

Human, Dragon, and Fairy

Chapter Thirty-two

IN THE SHADOWS, I decanted the sticky fluid, added three drops to the sponge just to be sure, then creeping up behind, clapped it over the sentry's nose and mouth. I heard a grunt, felt his heavy weight fall against me as I lowered him into a seat by the stair. He slumped over, head and arms hanging down, but I had no time to straighten him.

The turnkey below gave a muffled cry when I tiptoed behind him and shoved the damp sponge over his face. He fell hard against the wall, struggling before he went down. Saints. What would I have done without the potion? For the first time I was glad I'd cut my chin.

Swiping the keys, I went down the hall, peering cell to cell. My heart pounded, thinking I would see Garth soon. I'd rehearsed my speech while I was still half drugged and in pain aboard the *Malarkey.* Words fled now. So far none of the prisoners down the first long hall proved to be Garth, but in the last cell round the second corner, I spied a man lying facedown in the straw. He was up against a shadowed wall. Too dark to see who it was, but he was the only prisoner left. It must be he.

The fourth key opened the heavy timber door with a loud click. Praying under my breath, I looked about. A woman moaned from another cell in the corridor. A rat scuttled by. But no sound came from the turnkey. He still dreamed down the hall. I slipped inside, closing the door just enough to touch the wall behind me and no more, then went to the sleeping man all worried and whispering, "Garth? Is it you? Did they . . . hurt you?" Gently, I turned him over, cradling his head. A toothless old man squinted up at me.

"Angel?" he said. His face was ravaged. Fleas played about his hair and beard. Yellowing curds seeped from the corners of his eyes. I was repulsed, but since the man was fevered, I carefully placed his head back on the straw.

"I am no angel."

He pointed at my stitches. "Who cut you, dear?"

He was far older than my grandfather, but his eyes sparkled like a boy's. "No one, sir, I fell."

"Down Jacob's ladder." He spoke gibberish in his fever. I felt sorry for him, but I was in a hurry. Another castle guard might be downstairs at any moment, see the turnkey sleeping at his post, and discover the keys missing. I had only the potion sponge and my knife strapped to my belt to defend me.

"I am looking for a friend. Garth or Bash, some call him."

"Bash," he laughed, and coughed. "Clever dragons."

"Do you know where he is, old man?"

"He came here. Then he didn't. Do you have him?"

"Have him?" Did he think I carried the man about in my pocket? "Is Bash in a cell somewhere?"

"In a cell?" He looked surprised. "Sackmoore. Bastard." He raised a shaking fist, coughed some more.

"You said Bash came to visit you, so he was jailed here awhile. Where could they have taken him?"

"Oh, high up."

"The tower, you mean? There are four in the castle and four in the guard wall. Which one has a cell?"

"I come with you now, Angel."

Beelzebub! I couldn't be encumbered with an old man when I had to reach the tower. Already he was sitting up on the straw, the muscles in his skinny arms twitching as he struggled to stand.

"Sir, I cannot take you. I will try and come back for you if I can."

"I am Soothsayer Osric. Old Osric, they call me, but not much longer." He laughed at his own joke, then wheezed from laughing. "Help me, Angel." His hand was out. I took it. He trembled violently.

Three breaths in and out, and he was gone, dead in my arms.

I laid him on the straw and sat awhile, stunned. I was still in a daze and weeping when I locked the dead man in. Hitching the keys back onto the sleeping turnkey's belt, I stumbled upstairs. *God have mercy on the soothsayer's soul.* I wiped my hands on my gown, the feel of death too fresh on them. Near the topmost stair, I peered out. Two knights marched up to the sleeping sentry.

"Will you look at the fellow?" He kicked the man's boot.

"Drunk on the job. Hey, Rufus!" The second knight shook him. "What a clodpole! Come on and take his other arm." They dragged their friend down the hall. Another guard would be posted there soon enough. I slipped out the door while I had time, hurrying past a kitchen scullion with a dish tray littered with half-eaten food.

Which tower held my thief? I darted up and down stairways, lurking in the dark and listening. I was about to approach the fourth set of spiraled steps. Around the corner I spied an armed guard at the base of the stairs.

The door above was partway open. And I heard voices from within. I flattened myself against the wall and decanted five drops onto the sponge. He was a large man and would need full strength. *I'm nearly out. If I'm wrong and this isn't the right tower, I'll have wasted these drops.* Still, I crept up. The man was looking right at me. "Sir," I whispered. "I've lost my way. Can you help me find my room?"

"I cannot leave my post, mistress." He was frowning at my stitches. My richly embroidered gown and rose-colored cloak told him I was nobility, but my swollen chin gave him pause.

"Oh," I said in a startled whisper, "is that a mouse there?"

I pointed into the shadows. As he bent down to look, I shoved the sponge over his face. He was strong enough to fight the potion longer than the rest had; I barely managed to hold it to his nose and mouth. At last he crumpled to the floor and I eased him up against the wall by the bottom stair.

Up the steps the door was ajar. Through the narrow door slit I saw Prince Arden with his arms crossed, frowning down at the prisoner on a low stool.

Even from behind, I knew the seated man was Garth. I'd seen him in chair, saddle, and by a campfire. I'd known him running with his hounds, grooming his horses, leaning back to look at the stars from the branches of a pine tree, hunched with concentration whittling a doll, carrying Alice through a storm, and even sparring with a dragon. A woman will know a man from all sides after that.

All these thoughts washed over me in a flood as I hovered at the door. The first chance I got, I had to make my move. The dusty tower was filled with player's costumes and giant masks close to five feet tall. The kind players carried on poles. A straw-stuffed serpent hung from the rafters.

Prince Arden leaned over his prisoner. "Damnation! You know it goes against my mind. But as long as you insist on this, you'll stay here in the tower."

He turned his back on Garth. I used the moment to dart inside and duck behind a black-horned devil's mask leaning up against the wall. To my right, a giant mask of God stood by a tall wardrobe, his curly hair and shining beard made of gold-painted rope. I heaved a quiet breath and stuffed the sponge and potion vial back into my waist pouch.

My hiding place was full of dusty cobwebs. I brushed them aside. Through the devil's eye slits, I saw three candles burning in glass jars on the small table. Golden light glazed Garth's face in profile. *No torture marks, and his hands and feet aren't bound.* He could burst out the unlocked door and run if he had a mind to, though no doubt he assumed the guard downstairs was armed. He had no way of knowing the man was in a stupor.

Garth sat silent and very still. Above him, Prince Arden loosened his collar. Telltale greenish dragon scales peeked out from under the cloth, evidence of his dragon's blood passed down from Queen Rosalind. I gaped behind the mask.

Where was the younger brother Prince Bion right now? The dragonlord thought Bion a better match for me. Not that I planned to follow through with his marriage plans any more than I planned to obey Onadon's. Still, if the younger prince had agreed to have the fey party come here, why hadn't he bothered to greet us in the courtyard?

"So you refuse to confess what you know and choose the tower still?" the prince asked.

Garth answered, "Where else should I go, Ardy?"

Ardy? How forward Garth is to call our future king by a nickname! He jerked his head, indicating the door. "Shut the door completely that we might speak in private," he said.

Prince Arden's clenched jaw mounded into two small, royal molehills. Storming past my mask and throwing back the door, which clanged against the wall, he shouted down the stairwell, "Get up, man, and stand guard as you ought. I'm closing the door. Do not let anyone disturb us!" The prince slammed the door, breathing heavily as if coming in from battle. Striding back, he slapped a leather costume sewn in the shape of a naked woman—an Eve costume, I guessed.

On the stool, Garth sat strangely calm.

Prince Arden took in some air at the barred window, then leaned his shoulders against the bars, the wind from without blowing his hair forward across his cheeks. He was as dark as Garth was sun-browned.

"Say what you have to say now, brother. No one else is listening."

Brother? I pressed my hand over my mouth to suppress a cry, my cut chin stinging fiercely. Had I heard him right? *Garth is Bion Pendragon?* The thought dizzied me. I lowered my head to keep from blacking out.

When I looked up again, the two men faced each other, one man in princely garb, the other in green.

"I see you let a woman do your mending for a change," Prince Arden remarked smugly, eyeing my needlework on the prisoner's sleeve.

"Never mind about that." Garth rolled up the sleeve I'd fixed the stormy night in Margaretton. Something green and shining. My eyes fixed on his left arm, where dragon scales ran from just above his wrist to his elbow. In the candle glow the man's scales seemed to move like rippling water.

Seeing them, the full force of it hit me. I'd stayed with Prince Bion in the huntsman's lodge—ridden Kingsway Road traveling as his wife! God's teeth! How was I to conceive of it, understand it, swallow it?

The brothers were close enough for me to notice similarities in their look and coloring. I knew now Garth, or rather Bion's dark skin had none to do with too much sun as I'd once supposed, but was passed down from King Kye, whose mother was Persian.

Prince Arden said, "Come on. Door's shut like you asked. Tell me where you hid the stolen treasure."

Garth who is Bion sighed. "You cannot steal something that is already yours, Ardy."

"You know what I mean, Bash."

"I'll return all of it as soon as you're crowned."

"Now! I order you!"

"When it's safe."

"Safe from what?"

"Sackmoore."

"He's done his best to hold the kingdom together while I was gone. He doesn't deserve your disloyalty."

"He deserves every bit of it," said Bion. "Do you want to know why I hid our treasure?"

"Of course I do."

I peered through the devil's eyes, waiting. I already knew Bion hadn't strictly broken the law, stealing treasure from his own strong room. Still, why had he done it?

"I'm sure Sackmoore told you I stole it as a means to gain the king's crown myself."

Arden was silent.

Bion studied his face. "This isn't England, brother. I've not been acting as rightful king while my older brother was away. King Richard the Lionheart has his hands full back at home with his younger brother, John, but you shouldn't worry over me. I waited for your return. I'm glad you'll be king here."

"So you say."

"I do say."

"Then why hide the treasure? Tell me that."

"I caught Sackmoore using our treasury to fund soldiers."

"The king's regent had every right to pay our knights."

"Maybe, but was he supposed to raise his own army? One loyal only to himself?"

"Rubbish."

"Nevertheless, I stole the treasure for you."

"For me?" Arden slapped Bion's chest. "You always treated me like a lackwit. Now you ask me to believe you—"

"Ardy, listen! Sackmoore's been after the throne from the start, if not through battle, then through his daughter."

"You're mad, Bash!"

Bion saw the candles guttering. Crossing the room, he scooted the table with the jarred candles out of the wind. "Lord Sackmoore saw how it was between you and Lady Adela. All of us could see your growing affection."

I winced. Prince Arden and . . . the witch hunter were lovers? I'd had enough of a shock already learning Garth was Bion, now this. It was beyond me. How could anyone love that monstrous fiend?

Prince Arden blushed at the mention of Adela. Even in the dim candlelight I saw his cheeks darken. "Make your point, brother."

"Lady Adela's kidnapping was planned."

"What?"

"Lord Sackmoore wants his daughter crowned."

Prince Arden snorted. "I can see that, Bion. I'm no fool."

"But you don't know he hired cutthroats to abduct Lady Adela."

"That's a lie. Witches abducted her. Everyone knows—"

Bion put up his hand. "He paid cutthroats to take her, brother. He did it to break it off between you two. To assure his daughter's place on the throne, he ordered them to maim Lady Adela's face, destroy her beauty, so you'd find her repugnant and—"

Prince Arden flew at Bion. Crashing to the floor, they rolled over and over, their hands about each other's throats. I gasped as they tumbled toward me.

"Take it back, you bastard!"

"It's true."

"Take it back!"

"No."

Struggling, they rolled over again. God came crashing down on top of them. Bion bucked the mask off with his head. Sitting on Arden's chest, he pressed his brother's arms against the floor. Arden kicked up with his feet, overturning Bion. I saw his fist fly, heard the horrible crack as Arden punched Bion's jaw.

I bit my fingers to keep from screaming, my own jaw aching as if I'd been punched, so many memories of it, too many memories. It was all I could do not to leap out from behind the mask and stop the fight. Arden saved me from giving myself away by jumping up and staggering out, slamming the door behind him with a bang.

"You'll be back," Bion said to the ceiling, feeling his sore jaw with his hand. Suddenly I too wanted to flee. To breathe and think and wonder and curse and think again, but before I could escape, keys rattled outside the tower door.

We were both locked inside.

Chapter Thirty-three

BION LAY MOTIONLESS a long while as if his brother still held him down. I stayed hidden, unsure of what to do next. It had been full dark a long time when he arose at last and went to the small table. Squatting on his haunches, he studied the flames in the glass jars, a worry line creasing his forehead. He reached into one of the jars and dipped three fingers in the pooling wax near the flame. Bringing hand to lips, he blew till the waxen fingertips hardened, turning white. A child's game? One I used to play anyway when the blacksmith wasn't looking. But there was more.

Bion closed his eyes as if in prayer or thought, then peeled the wax from his fingers and cupped them in his hand. They rocked like tiny cradles on his open palm as he crossed to the window and gave a low whistle. He stood black against the blacker night, peering out as if studying the ocean stretching far beyond the castle cliffs, or as if he awaited something. Waiting, yes, waiting as it turned out, for a will-o'-the-wisp answered his whistle and flitted through the bars. Amazed I bit my tongue to keep from gasping and giving myself away. (Sharp pain that last time kept me from clamping my hand over mouth and stitched chin.)

Bion held out his hand. "Take these to Onadon," he said. The bright will-o'-the-wisp gathered them in her tiny arms, flitted about the tower room, then straight through the devil's eyes.

"Tess?" was all she said—all the tiny tattler had to say for me to be discovered.

Prince Bion was over in a flash, pulling the heavy devil's face aside. "Tess?"

The wisp flew out the window with her prize while Bion stared at me, stumbling over his words. "What are you doing? How did you . . . Who cut your chin?" The last he said in anger as if he'd pound the one who'd cut me.

"My lord." I stood, covering the bottom half of my face and whispering into my hand. "I slipped and fell on the ice."

"It's quite a war wound, but there's no need to whisper. My brother has the guard stand at the base of the stars. There's little room for a man-at-arms at the top of this stairwell."

He glanced at my hand. "You can drop your hand too. I've already seen the cut." The worry line returned. "How much did you hear?"

"Everything, Your Royal Highness."

A fly buzzed past, landing above us on the serpent's felt tongue.

"Call me Garth or Bion if you will."

"Or Bash?"

He flashed a smile at that, but it vanished soon enough. "Truly, drop your hand, Tess. You've seen this, so we're even." The sleeve was still rolled up. Blue-green scales scalloped down his arm shimmering in the candlelight.

"Come away from the masks." He righted God knocked over in the brawl, and stood the stool up again for me to take a seat. I chose to stand. There was no hearth in the tower room. Now it was night, I could feel the chill even in my flit gown and cloak. I wondered how he slept here on the cold planked floor. Had he blankets in the wardrobe?

"You put yourself in danger coming here, Tess. Tell me how you managed it. Tell me quickly. I want to trust you as I did before."

I saw no reason to hide the truth if the man was in league with Onadon. "I came by invitation as one of the Irish princesses."

"You're half fey." He heaved a sigh. "I thought you might be, but then when you agreed to ride south with me for Alice, I wasn't sure."

"Was that some test? I agreed to go south to right a wrong I'd done."

"Of course, but I also knew the half-fey princesses would yearn to go north to DunGarrow."

"I did . . . yearn. But I had my friends to think of. Doesn't anyone consider loyalty important anymore?" I'd always thought myself loyal. It had made betraying my friends that much worse. But I shouldn't have barked at the prince. "Forgive me, Your Royal Highness. I shouldn't speak to you that way."

"Sit, will you?"

I took the stool he offered. There was another reason I'd gone south. I'd wanted to ride dressed as Garth's wife, trying on a role I'd never thought to consider until I'd met him. I was drawn to Garth as much as DunGarrow back then, though I'd not admitted it to myself at the time. If I was confused then, I was more so now.

"So you suspected I was fey when you took us in?" I was trying to piece it all together.

"At first I saw four starving people hounded by the witch hunter. Later I began to wonder, if you or Poppy . . ." He ran his hand through his hair. The locks fell again across his forehead. "Poppy enspelled me in a way I found distressing," he confessed. "Her beauty was too overpowering."

He admitted she'd charmed him, but I was glad to hear he'd not welcomed it.

"She's here too."

"The two Irish princesses." His laugh was bittersweet, then he shrugged. "I agreed it was a good thing for the fey to bring princesses here. Give them a chance to meet my brother. Sackmoore wants his daughter on the throne, his hand in the affairs of state. He wants to destroy Dragonswood, even though it's a sanctuary my grandparents Rosalind and Kye spent their lives building."

He walked a little in the room. "After I began to suspect

you or Poppy might be . . . If you were the ones chosen by the fey, I didn't want to stand in the way of it."

Was that why he kept deserting me at the lodge when he knew I wanted to go with him?

He turned and saw my face. "What's wrong now?

"Nothing, Your Royal Highness."

"Back to formalities? I thought we went over that."

"I told you. Nothing."

He rolled down his sleeve. "You have your secrets, I suppose. You had them before."

"And you, king's huntsman."

"Don't forget thief," he added with a flicker of a smile.

He'd ridden off again and again. I could not leave the point hanging. "You said you did not want to stand in the way?"

"The fey need this marriage. I thought if you were indeed fey, if I left you alone, you might resume your journey to DunGarrow. I was right in that, I see," he added.

Keys rattled in the door. I leaped behind the God mask as the guard came in with a tray. He set it on the table and quit the room.

"Come out from behind God," Bion said.

I crept out.

"Share my dinner with me, Tess."

He offered me the stool again and sat cross-legged beside me on the floor.

I'd not eaten since my small breakfast on the ship. "It's not enough for two. You must be hungry. You go on."

"Eat with me or I won't eat at all."

"You're a stubborn prince."

"Not half as stubborn as you are."

We lingered over the small bowl of stew and split the single piece of bread. "Is this how they feed a prince of the realm?" I said bitterly.

"It's how they feed a thief in the tower. And I'm sure it's better than what those in the dungeon get."

I nodded, remembering Osric's filthy cell.

Wind gusted through the window. The scent of the sea was on it. Prince Bion looked out as if he also caught the scent, a cold freedom in it and the dangers of the ocean. Smells like these had awakened my grandfather's sea lust. I put my elbows on my knees and leaned over, suddenly tired. My head pounded trying to think it all out. He'd left the lodge to clear the way for me so I could go to the fey. Had he wanted that for me? Or did he wish I'd stayed with him? I had no way of knowing.

"Do you need water?" Before I could answer, he dipped from a bucket below Eve's hung skin, and brought the filled tin cup. I drained it in three thirsty gulps, the metal stinging my teeth.

Bion reached for it, his cool fingers brushing mine. I held on a little longer and caught his eye. "Did the fey know you took the treasure?"

Chapter Thirty-four

BION HELD THE cup between us longer, his look intense. "Ore and I worked alone, Tess," he whispered. "No one knows about Ore's part in this aside from you and one other unless you told someone of it."

His eyes were on me, hoping, fearing, and the gaze lightened with my answer.

"I've told no one what I saw, Bion." I'd said his name aloud and did not mind the taste of it in my mouth or the look he gave me after. He went to fill the cup again, drinking himself this time before bringing me another cupful.

He'd said one other. "Who else knows?"

"The dragonlord, Kahlil."

Somehow this didn't surprise me. "Ore attacked us on the road." I recalled the way she'd swept down so low, she'd knocked me from my horse.

"She was alarmed that I'd left the lodge to travel so far south with a lady when we had the king's treasure to guard."

"I can understand her concern."

"Women will stick together," he said with a sigh.

I laughed at that, then all was silent awhile, God and devil, prince and fey girl, mute in the candle's glow. Only the serpent seemed to speak, his orange felt tongue lifting in the wind.

I drank more slowly this time, tasting the freshness of the water and remembering Ore's blue eyes. "Is Ore the same hatchling Princess Rosalind raised?" I knew the youngest was blue-eyed.

"She is the same. My grandmother watched her and Lord Faul's other three pips hatch from their shells in his den on Dragon's Keep. Can you imagine what that must have been like, Tess?"

"I thought of her story often growing up, and tried to imagine her living there," I whispered. Our shadows wavered on the wall in the dim candle glow. "You said your grandmother walked the coals. Now I know who your grandmother was, I see you were telling the truth." Princess Rosalind was thought to be a witch when she first returned home from her time with the dragons on Dragon's Keep. Who but a witch could dwell with dragons and live? Or so it was thought back then. She was imprisoned and witch-tested before she was proved innocent.

It was still hard to believe I'd just shared a meal with Queen Rosalind's grandson. That I'd eaten from the same bowl; drank from the same cup.

"Are you all right?"

"I am still getting used to who you are."

"I'm the same man you met in the wood, Tess."

"Hardly that!"

"And should I treat you differently, now I know you're half fey?"

I pressed my lips together, unsure of how to answer him. If he was the same man I met in the wood, it was not so for me. I had changed since he'd found me hiding with my friends in the cave. I knew a little more of who I was now I'd met the fairy folk. I didn't have to feel ashamed of my attraction to Dragonswood, or be quite so afraid of my fire-sight. Still, I couldn't think how to share this with him. Looking up from my lap, I caught Bion's intent gaze.

"You have some fey powers, Tess. You proved this by coming in here unseen, but you've not explained how you—"

Before he finished, I stood and pulled the sponge and vial from my waist pouch. "Sleeping potion. I drugged the guards."

"Delightful," he said, a boyish look on his face. "So the one my brother shouted 'Get up, man' to down at the bottom of the stairs wasn't just sleeping on the job."

"I'm afraid not."

"The poor man was likely discovered by a fellow guard and sacked."

"I'm sorry for that." I chewed my bread. Sorry, yes, but I would do it again to be with Bion.

"Any fey powers I should know of?" he asked.

I sat again, squeezing the sponge in my hand. I'd shared my power with Grandfather long ago, no one else. It was time.

"Remember when I said I'd had the nightmare about Princess Augusta? It wasn't a dream."

"Go on."

"I saw her in the fire."

"Fire-sight," he whispered. "How many times in your life?"

"Often enough. I saw you in the blaze."

"Me?"

"Twice before I met you."

His face grew very still. "What was I doing?" he asked cautiously.

"Waving your sword."

"Was that why you were so frightened when I found you and your friends in the cave?"

"I had any number of reasons to be afraid of you back then, but that was one," I admitted.

Bion drew his knees up to his chest. "Now I know how you entered the tower. You must also tell me why. What made you climb the stairs? Did Onadon send you?"

"My father doesn't know I'm here. I came on my own."

"Then how did you know where to find me?"

Suddenly my hands were damp. I wiped them on my gown, remembering the feel of death. "I searched for you first in the dungeon. Osric the soothsayer told me to look in the tower."

"Poor man. How is he?"

"He . . . died," I whispered.

Bion sat heavy with the news. "I knew him since I was a boy."

We talked on in the night about his boyhood. I was hungry to hear all—to piece together a new understanding of the man I'd known as Garth, to see Bion for who he was. In the passing hours he quizzed me about my life back at home, before I'd had to flee the witch hunter. He'd shared much with me, but I couldn't return his openness. I spoke little of my time in Harrowton. "I was unhappy," I admitted.

"There's something I've been wondering about," he said. "You said that Onadon didn't send you, that you came on your own to the tower. I assume you guessed I was the prince and so determined to find me?"

"I didn't know who you were other than Garth Huntsman, liar and thief, when I came."

"Tess. You climbed up here to free a thief?"

"I rescued Tom from the sheriff's cell. Why not help a man who'd risked his neck to save me and my friends?"

"You're brave, Tess, if a little foolhardy. You'd be condemned to death if you were caught trying to free a man who'd stolen the king's treasure. Why put yourself in so much danger?" He looked up from the floor, his dark face brushed silver with the pale predawn light creeping through the tower window.

"I had to come. I had no choice after all you did for us." I fought the urge to touch his cheek. His face was unshaven and would be rough as dry lichen. I knew it would be warm. *Don't. He's a Pendragon prince.*

The faint light beyond the barred window was changing hue. It was hard to believe we'd talked till dawn. All the folk at the castle would be roused from their beds before long. "Listen, we haven't much time. When they come with your morning meal, I can help you escape."

"I can't run, Tess."

My breath caught. He couldn't mean it. "I'll use the rest of the potion to put the guards to sleep. We can plan a way."

"I'd go if my brother allowed it, but I cannot leave the way things are. I have to stay here and be my brother's conscience."

"What, be his conscience when he locks you in the tower? Why? I saw the way he treats you. You're in danger."

"I'll be in greater danger if I go without his blessing. Leave Pendragon Castle now and Sackmoore will have Arden's ear with no one to counterpoint. Sackmoore will convince Arden I've fled to raise an army against him and claim the crown myself. My brother will believe it. He half believes it now. It is how my brother thinks."

I knelt on the floor. I'd been uneasy sitting with my head above a prince of the realm. The thick wood was hard on my knees and I was too close to him by this, so much so, that my cloak fell across his knee, but I didn't draw away and call attention to it. "Why would he believe Lord Sackmoore over you?"

"We might be brothers, Tess, but we've not been close for a long time. Arden's bullheaded. He blamed Augusta for our mother's death and refuses to see her. I can't make him change his mind about her. As to kingship, my brother craves the throne so much, he can't believe it when I tell him I don't feel the same. He's always seen me as a threat. Lord Sackmoore knows it and plays into his fears."

He fingered my cloak, the flit weave soft as silk, hued pink and lovelier than he had seen on human folk, even royal ones. I read that in his look as he examined it. "I wrote to Arden while he was away, but I know Lord Sackmoore also wrote to him, filling his head with lies about me, adding fuel to a fire that was always there, when all I truly want is to live year-round with my sister in the modest castle on Dragon's Keep. I'm happy there as I am in Dragonswood. I was never quite at home here at Pendragon Castle."

He looked at me. "I'm boring you with this."

"No, not at all." I was glad to hear he wanted to live

free on Dragon's Keep, to be with his younger sister, and the dragons there, but his confession came with a pang. *All I truly want,* he'd said. He'd not mentioned wanting a lover or a wife.

"What can I do to help you, Garth?" The old name was a slip of the tongue, but he grinned at my mistake. His smile was sunlight to me. "It's hard to get used to the new name. Forgive me."

"Tess. What is there to forgive?" He leaned closer, touching my neck just under my wound.

"Does it hurt much?"

"No," I lied.

I should have said yes. Wouldn't he have held his hand out longer then? But the gesture lasted only as long as a single breath. Some folk believe when the breath leaves the body, our spirit can flee by it. I am not sure of this, but I felt something go out of me in that breath when his hand fell.

"How," he asked, "with your chin sewn up, were you introduced at court? I only wonder . . ."

I blushed. "The fey cast a glamour over my face." I knew the spell went against their agreement with Bion. "It was only to cover the wound and no more," I added.

"You need no glamour. You have all you need."

I was drinking this in when he added, "There's nothing you can do for me just now, Tess. They will bring my breakfast up soon. I'll distract the guard long enough for you to creep out the door. Failing that, you can use your potion. Once you're back downstairs, you can continue to play your part as an Irish princess."

"I don't want to."

He looked stern. "And if I order you to?"

I sparred back, look for look. One candle burned out. Smoke rose in gray rivulets from the wick. I thought of the wisp he'd called to the window.

"Tell me what you made with the candle wax."

"You're stalling, Tess."

"Tell me," I insisted.

"A message," he said simply.

"There was no writing on it."

"In thought and fingerprint there is message enough for Onadon to read, but it's no more than what transpired between me and my brother, so you saw and heard it all yourself."

"All of that was in those three wax petals?"

"All I could think to put in them before the warm wax dried."

"I didn't think the Pendragons had such powers."

"Just a little thing I learned from Onadon," he said, eyes twinkling.

"So my father's read the wax and knows you're in danger."

"He knows, but can do little about it. My brother needs persuading." He leaned back on his hands. "He has to learn to trust me again. Would magic do this? Would violence?"

I knew he was right; neither magic nor violence could be used to sway Arden back to his brother's side.

"You could do what he asks," I said.

"Return the treasure, you mean?" He sat up straight. "Do that before he's crowned and Lord Sackmoore takes control again."

"I don't want to leave you here in the tower."

"And I don't want you getting into any trouble over me. It's best if you go back downstairs and do what you came here to do, Tess."

What I came to do? What did he mean by that? Did he still think I'd come to marry his brother? Red light streamed through the window bars now it was truly morning. Again time pressed in and I had no answer. Two gulls flew past, dipping on the sea air.

"I should tell you I'm not in agreement with my father's plans for me."

"You came here of your own free will, didn't you?"

"I did not come to marry Prince Arden. I came to free you."

He took this in, shaking his head a little. "It's risky enough now for you at the castle as it is, Tess, more so if you're entangled with me."

"Still, I would help."

"No."

"Yes."

"You would disobey a prince of the realm?"

We glared at each other, my happiness growing as I took in his intense expression, for I knew I wouldn't back down.

"This is what you want?" he asked.

"It is what I want."

Bion jumped up to pace, the two remaining flames still burning in the jars leaned this way and that in the air he stirred. It was a long while before he spoke, but I'd grown used to his silences. I studied him out of the corner of my eye, dressed still in his huntsman's clothing, a green man in a gray tower. He muttered to himself, though I heard nothing but the gulls outside and the sea pounding rocks below.

"The fey worked closely with the dragons on their plan to bring a half-fey maiden here to the castle." He was at the window looking out, speaking as if to the dawn. "Onadon introduced you to Lord Kahlil before he brought you here, am I right in this, Tess?"

I spoke to his tense back. "My father took me to God's Eye."

"How did you fare with Lord Kahlil?" He still hadn't turned, asking the air, the sky opening up as the light grew brighter in the east.

"I spread salve on his scales to ease his itching, and some on his burned wingtip."

He turned. "After the way you went green in Tom's sickroom?"

So Bion had noticed my reaction. "I can't account for it, only say I didn't mind salving the dragonlord's scales."

"Was Lord Kahlil pleased?"

"He was," I answered shyly. My palms felt moist as if the salve were still thinly spread across them.

"So you do not fear him too much?"

"I fear him enough," I answered truthfully.

He smiled at that. "Only a lackwit would say he's fearless around such a dragon. Tess," he said, "would you be willing to slip away from the castle, go to Lord Kahlil, and tell him where I stand now with my brother?"

"Why?"

"The dragonlord is very old. When you live nigh on a millennium, you see much. If anyone will know what to do to prevent a war, it's he."

"Will there be a war?" I asked, startled.

"Lord Sackmoore would like nothing better."

Chapter Thirty-five

I T WASN'T TOO long before the guard brought
Bion's breakfast tray, a paltry meal of cold gruel. Bion
took the food and spoke to the man, giving me a moment
to sneak out the door and down the steps. Shivering back
in my solar, I searched my trunk and slipped on my fiery
gown as if to warm myself in its flame. I did not know
why I should choose it now except that I was off to see
the old dragon. I wore it like one stepping into her own
fire-sight. Refastening my belt, I tucked in my knife. To
guise the shimmering flit-cloth, I put on my old travel-
worn cloak, then snatched my rucksack from the trunk.

The courtyard was still bustling with castle guards, servants unloading wagons, and entertainers come to put on
a show for Prince Arden's pleasure. Many folk huddled
excitedly near the dovecote, where a performing bear was
tethered to a post by his foppish trainer. I felt sorry for the
bear but could do nothing for him.

In the stables I ducked behind a stall until the stable

boy led one of the horses outside. There were two doors, I would use the second. No time to saddle a horse. I took the closest one and led him out, walking as discreetly as I could through the busy courtyard. I turned my hooded face away when I spied Jyro juggling knives not far from the dancing bear. His show proved riveting enough to entertain the guards. I made it across the drawbridge. If I ever had the chance to thank Jyro for this eye-catching act, I would.

Down the road, I used a log to mount the gelding, then clung to his mane as he took off. My stitched chin throbbed. Nevertheless, I kept him to a canter. The lake lay south along the coast. I was hungry when I reached the shore at last. No time to think of food.

Lake Ailleann was mist-covered as it was before, though little fog came up from the sea today and no clouds hung over Dragonswood beyond. The pearling mist had a magical quality; spun to hide the dragonlord's lair? I searched for the boat Onadon used when last we crossed and found it hidden in the rushes halfway round the lake. A slender elm grew there strong enough to tie my mount, but he had no reins, and I didn't have my father's magic skill.

"Beelzebub! Will you stay if I dismount?"

I slid down and rubbed his neck. "You have been fairy filched, sir. Did you know?" I looked about. "There's good grass here for a meal," I said. "And lake water to drink. I've no summoning finger like my father, Onadon, but will you stay?"

Reluctantly I let go of his mane. He shook his head, bowed, and tore a hunk of fresh grass as I climbed in the rowboat.

A SLOW FIRE burned in Kahlil's cave. Even dragons with their own inner fires had to warm themselves in November, I supposed. In the firelight I saw his scales had a healthier greenish sheen. He was better.

I bowed as I'd seen my father do on our first visit. Would this old one know how to help us?

"Prince Bion sends his greetings, Lord Kahlil."

The dragonlord bid me add wood to the small cave fire. I'd caught him mid-meal, half a roast boar impaled on his talon. He finished it off, crunching the bones with delight, and said, "Tell me, how is the boy?"

I didn't mind him calling Bion a boy. We must all seem young to one who'd lived so long. As I recounted all that happened since I'd arrived at the castle, he used his smallest talon to pick stray bits of meat caught between his teeth.

The dragon made a rumbling growl when I described the fight, then he scratched a little, listening until I was done. I was tired from my sleepless night with Bion and my long ride besides. Lord Kahlil asked no questions right away, but read my weariness. One eye swiveling back, the other on me, he clawed wine and goblet from the recesses of his cave.

It is a grand thing to see great black talons pinch a wine jar and tip a slender red rivulet into an even smaller golden chalice.

As I drank, lights swarmed in from outside. Thirty or more will-o'-the-wisps flitted along the dragon's scales, each tiny hand spreading pine-scented ointment. (I knew this only by the smell. Their hands are very small.) When done, the will-o'-the-wisps settled along the dragonlord's head and shoulders—a crown and mantle of glowing light. Anon he shook them off and bid them leave us for a while.

"Bion is both wise and foolish to stay in the tower," he said.

"I tried to convince him to run, my lord. He could have escaped with my help, but he refused."

"Love binds the prince to his brother," the dragon said. "It's dangerous to remain in his brother's custody, but Bion's right in thinking Lord Sackmoore would turn Arden against him if he ran. Your part in this interests me," he added, pouring more wine.

The wine lessened the pain in my chin to a distant ache, but rolling it along my tongue awakened hunger. "My part interests you, sir?"

"You went straight to the dungeon to rescue a man you thought to be a thief."

It wasn't a question, but I answered anyway. "I did."

"So you would have freed the thief who'd stolen the crown jewels, even if it was an act of treason?"

My body shook. *I'm tired,* I thought, *worried about Bion, undone with wine.* But I was also afraid. I'd known the blacksmith's wrath, but a dragon's . . . Why had Bion sent me here? "I didn't want to break the law or to dishonor the king, my lord, but—"

"Yesss?" he hissed, his tongue flicking out.

"I owed the man a good turn after all he'd done for me and my friends. I couldn't just leave him there, could I?"

The dragon lowered his head, narrowing his large golden eyes.

I choked out a few more words. "I also planned to convince the huntsman to return the treasure. Everything changed when I learned who he was."

"And why he stole it," Kahlil added.

I nodded. "Sackmoore was using it to build his own army. Bion said he wouldn't return it until his brother's crowned."

"You were right and wrong in breaking the law," he said.

I stood, the cave swaying a little. Bion was both wise and foolish to stay in the tower. I was right and wrong to break the law. Was this the wisdom of dragons? If so, how was he going to help us?

"Sit again by the fire and tell me more," said Kahlil.

I teetered on my feet. "More of what, sir? I told you

what took place in the tower. All that I can remember and I swear I left nothing out."

One large yellow eye peered back whilst the other focused on me. "More about yourself, Tess. And if you're hungry, I've finished off the meat, but I have some other man-food here." In the cave behind he felt along the ground with his back leg. There was a clank of coin in the dark, but he brought forth an onion and two fat turnips pricked at the end of his talons. Breathing fire over them, he roasted them as he had the boar, then set them on the stones by my fire, adding a knife that I might slice and eat the vegetables hot. I had my own knife with me, but didn't refuse his.

"I have run out of cheese," he admitted.

"Thank you for your kindness, my lord. This is all I need." I said my prayers and supped. Midway through the meal in a generous moment or calculating one, the dragonlord poured me a third cup of wine. Warm within and without, I began to answer his probing questions. Checking no words at the crossroads of my mind, I let my story trip along my inebriated tongue.

By this means and through weariness besides, I found myself speaking earnestly of my life in Harrowton before my arrest. Why I divulged this or what it had to do with Bion's trouble, I do not know, but soon I was telling Kahlil of my life, of Mother and her lost babes, of the blacksmith's angry fists. My hand went up to my cauliflower ear. Tears came.

I'd never let the blacksmith see me cry. I took my tears to the wood and climbed a friendly tree to shed them. But I couldn't keep them back now. Half human and half fey, neither and both, the longing for my place in the world was an ache I'd grown used to, and the ache was more my home than any place I'd found, except for my short stay with the huntsman. Even that was taken from me now I knew Garth was Bion.

All I truly want is to live year-round with my sister in the modest castle on Dragon's Keep. The prince had no intention of returning to the lodge. No desire to look for what we might have had there together. I didn't say these last few words aloud. They'd been Bion's things to say, not mine, and he did not want them.

Dragons cannot cry, but he did not turn his back when my tears came hot with anger, then cool with sorrow, then empty of both. I felt hollow when all was said, and lighter somehow.

Chapter Thirty-six

I AWOKE IN the cave, blanketed in shimmering green dragon scales, thicker than flit cloth, yet surprisingly supple.

"I would have awakened you if you hadn't risen on your own soon," said Lord Kahlil. "You slept all day and through the night like a cat. Are you rested now? There's much to do."

"You know how to help Bion, my lord?" I asked, rubbing the sleep from my eyes.

"Prince Arden has to be told the truth about Lord Sackmoore."

I gave a little huff. "Bion already tried that, sir."

"If Arden won't believe his brother, whom is he likely to believe?"

The fire had gone out long ago, a few red coals remained. Dragon scales about my shoulders, I hugged my knees to my chest the way Bion had, sitting on the floor in the tower, and blinked up at the dragon. Was he asking me to supply the person? I shook my head.

The dragonlord raised his index talon. "Lord Sackmoore himself could tell him, but is he likely to confess?"

"No."

He put a second talon in the air, counting off as he spoke. "Would the Gray Knight tell Prince Arden the truth?"

"Not likely, since he serves Lord Sackmoore." These were obvious questions any simpleton could answer.

He raised a third talon. "So we come to the one person the prince would listen to in earnest and believe, and that is Lady Adela herself."

"What?" I stood, seized with trembling, my dragon scale blankets dropping to my feet.

His wrinkled eyelids narrowed. "Think, Tess. If Lady Adela knew the truth about her uncle, she would turn against him. Once she tells Prince Arden her uncle was behind her abduction, that crime alone would be enough to reveal the man's true nature. Arden would imprison Lord Sackmoore, or worse."

I stooped and folded the scales, more to busy my shaking hands than anything else. My heart thumped in my chest.

"While you slept I sent some will-o'-the-wisps across the sea to Dragon's Keep. You knew of blue-eyed Ore. I assume you know of her older sister, Eetha, the other female pip Princess Rosalind raised when she was a girl?"

I nodded, too angry yet to speak.

"My wing's not ready to fly with you riding on my back," he said. "And Chawl, Eetha's older brother, stays on Dragon's Keep, but Eetha can take you."

"T-take me where?" I stuttered.

"To Lady Adela. You'll have to hurry, Prince Arden's crowned tomorrow."

A pox on him. "No."

Every bone of my being was in that *no*. "The woman thinks I'm a witch. She tortured me, threatened my friends, made us run. All the cruel things that happened to us and to Tom were because of her." I was choking on the words, my throat tightening so I could barely breathe.

"She does not think you are a witch, Tess. She never did. Have you noticed what's been happening all up and down the countryside these last few months?"

"What do you mean?"

"You recall how Lady Adela used to hunt older woman as well as young? After King Kadmi died, she turned her attentions on the young. Why is that? Why be consumed with young girls attracted to Dragonswood, girls who were accused of displaying magic powers?"

I remembered how she'd let Joan Midwife speak at my trial. The lady had seemed less concerned about Joan's crimes, more fixed on mine.

The dragon went on in a craggy voice. "Lady Adela heard the troubadour's song. All the people were meant to hear it to prepare them for a fey maiden on the throne.

But the words enraged Adela. She would do anything to stop a half-fey girl or any other maiden from marrying the man she loved."

I glanced up at his burning eyes. "What?"

"You know Arden and Adela were lovers, Tess. You heard all about that in the tower. Tell me now why she arrested you and the others." He tapped his black talon against the rocky floor, waiting for my answer, *click, click, click.*

"She did not think me a witch," I said, piecing it together slowly as one would stitch a long tear, carefully aligning the ragged edges. "She thought I might be half fey, and if so, if the song was true about a half-fey girl marrying the prince, *her* prince, I'd threaten her chance to win Arden back when he returned."

"You and the other girls, all threats as you say. And," Kahlil added, "there's no doubt Lord Sackmoore made sure Adela had all the funds she needed to round girls up. He wanted the half-fey girls destroyed to make his daughter queen."

Overwhelmed, I rushed outside and leaned over on hands and knees. The ground spun, my stomach lurched. Stumbling, I made my way to the pond on the little isle, the beech trees skeletal in the rising mist. I thought of what she'd said when she'd tightened the thumbscrews.

There are two reasons a girl enters Dragonswood. Either she goes to join with Satan, or she's drawn in by the fey.

So she'd known. All along, she'd known. Heat inflamed

my body. I pulled off my slippers and waded in the murky pond.

Lady Adela had looked at me with her fey eye. *What are your powers?*

I don't have powers. The lie had hung between us. She'd seen I was half fey, scented my magic.

My feet sank in the oozing mud. Had it been the same with Tanya? Did calling us witches simplify her mission? The girls she sought would have powers, perhaps not those witches were said to have, but close enough. Why not keep it simple, have the folk point out any girls with powers, any girls seen in Dragonswood. Folk liked witch hunts. There was drama in it, and righteousness, and sport.

I walked around the pond and sat in the rushes. On the surface a large green rock moved, dipping up, then down, coming slow across the water.

"You saved me, I think," I whispered to the turtle. "You or your brother. I never thanked you for it." I slid my feet deeper in, but the turtle ignored me and swam past. "Well . . . thank you anyway, sir."

I was a little calmer, if muddier, when I went back into the cave and bowed to the dragonlord. "My lord, I understand the reason for your plan. She might convince Arden. She of all people might change his heart, but you know I can't go to the witch hunter. She'll arrest me."

"She cannot arrest you, Tess."

"There's a bounty on my head, my lord," I reminded.

"The lady's a captive."

"Adela?" I couldn't imagine anyone holding Lady Adela against her will. I have to admit the part of me that sought revenge was warmed by the news. "Who holds her? Where?"

"The Gray Knight keeps her on Black Swan Isle."

I knew Lord Sackmoore had a castle and lands on the tiny offshore isle. "Why take her there?"

"Sackmoore wants her and the prince kept apart."

"How long have you known this, my lord?"

"I knew the day their ship reached Black Swan. Will-o'-the-wisps may be small, but they can fly many miles over the sea."

"Let the wisps tell her the truth about her uncle, then."

Lord Kahlil lowered his head. The nearness of his toothy jaw unnerved me. I thought of the iron spikes in the castle portcullis gate. "Would the lady have reason to believe fairies, Tess?"

"Would she believe me?" Anger and fear sharpened my question to a shriek.

Smoke twined from the dragon's nose. "I think she might if you made it clear you have no desire to marry the man she loves."

I thought of Prince Arden locking Bion in the tower, knocking him to the floor when Bion tried to tell him the truth about Sackmoore, and punching his brother in the jaw.

"I would never marry Arden."

"Not even to be queen?"

"Not even to be queen."

"Just so." Lord Kahlil's left eye swiveled up. Flicking out his long tongue, he furled a bat and drew it into his mouth with a soft crunch.

I ran my hand over the dragon scale blankets I'd slept under. *From a boy, the younger prince Bion showed no fear of dragons. The same cannot be said of Arden. I say Tess is better suited to Bion.* Had he known even then that I loved Bion?

"Onadon wanted you on the throne, Tess. He'll be disappointed, but I am not."

It saddened me to think I'd let him down. I'd wanted so much to please the father I'd been apart from all these years. Poppy too would disappoint the fey. Steeped in my host's wine, I wasn't sure how much I'd said the night before. "Did I mention Poppy last night?"

"You didn't. Is she pleased with Pendragon Castle? Is Tupkin minding his manners?"

"Tupkin? Why bring him up?"

"He goes everywhere with her. He was a nuisance here."

I smiled in spite of myself. "He can be a pest."

"He kept leaping up and swiping the air, trying to catch a will-o'-the-wisp in his claws. He didn't, of course, they're much too quick for him. What did you want to tell me about Poppy?"

I signed. "She has no interest in Prince Arden either, sir. She's met someone."

Lord Kahlil flicked out his tongue, waiting.

"A fey man named Jyro."

"The juggler?" The dragon's laugh was deafening as a landslide. His enormous mouth opened to a red cave. His ribs shook. I covered my ears until he was done.

"Yes," he said. "Of course she likes him. Jyro spied her the night we rescued Tanya. The boy talked on and on about her."

"She saw Jyro that night too."

"Mmm," he rumbled.

Were they meant to be together even then? I dismissed the thought; too romantic for my blood, though Poppy would have liked it. "She's set on Jyro. I don't think she can be convinced to marry Prince Arden now," I said. "Where does that leave the fairy prophecy?"

I looked up in his eyes, shining gold as the flit hives; they were very old, vivid with life, altogether wild.

"The prophecy says *The Prince shall wed a Fairy child.* It does not say which prince, does it? There are two."

"A fey queen would protect Dragonswood. My father said so. They all think so, and Prince Bion isn't going to be king."

The dragon swiped and munched another bat. "Can you see the future?"

I saw things in the fire-sight; small, blazing glimpses. They did not predict earthquakes, wars, a kingdom's future. Thus far the visions had been more personal and seemed meant for me alone. "No, my lord. All is dark."

"Not so dark, Tess." Kahlil scratched under his wing. "I doubt Prince Arden will be interested in Lady Lizbeth. You told me Prince Arden tackled his brother. It was what Bion said about Lady Adela's kidnapping that set him off, wasn't it?"

"Aye, it was."

"Yesss," he said extending the *s* into a thoughtful, serpent's hiss. "Love will win out, I think, if you bring them together."

"She is my enemy!"

"Set that aside, Tess."

"Aside? Set it aside? She tortured me. She nearly had me drowned. I had to run and take my friends with me lest she arrest them all, and she had Tom dragged through town behind—"

"I heard this all last night." It was the only time he'd interrupted me.

I looked up. *Of course Kahlil knows it all. He dropped the turtle in the millpond, scorched his wing saving Tanya, and here I am arguing with the ancient dragon.* "You don't know what you are asking, my lord."

"I know what I am asking. I also know whom I'm asking."

"I won't go to her. Find another." I grabbed my rucksack and quit his den.

The dragon scales cloaked me against the chilly day.

Fog swirled around rocks and trees as I circled the pond and settled in the lee of a standing stone.

Saints! I'd be a fool to go to her or help her in any way. I was glad she was locked up. I hoped they'd hang her by her arms from a ceiling hook. There must be more than one way to turn Prince Arden against Lord Sackmoore. Surely I could come up with something better. Wandering down narrow paths through tangled greenery, I circled God's Eye's rocky shoreline, returned to the small pond near Lord Kahlil's cave a little more refreshed, but with no clear plan. *I shouldn't have to go to her. There has to be another way.* Perhaps if I wrote down some thoughts, made a list?

I had the quill and small ink block from the hunting lodge with me in my rucksack. Princess Rosalind had used dragon scales to make her book on Dragon's Keep. Lord Kahlil's scales were large and cumbersome, plenty of room to write. A bit of rubbing and some drops of pond water made a good, black ink.

One scale wrapped about my shoulders, the other on my lap, I set my thoughts down beginning with the argument in the tower, I teased out clues. Partway down the scale an idea emerged. What if we found one of the women Lord Sackmoore paid to abduct Lady Adela? As the story went, the knights killed the cutthroats guised as witches when they rescued the lady, all but one, as I recall. Find her and she could tell Arden the truth about Adela's abduction. But how could I hope to find the kidnapper who'd survived, and even if I did, why confess her crime knowing she'd be hanged for it?

God's teeth! Was there no solution?

I leaned against the standing stone, the lake mist still rising thick as dragon smoke around God's Eye. Rewrapping the small ink block and slipping it back in the rucksack, I washed my inky fingers in the pond. Black ink coiled in the water.

How could I help Bion without going to my enemy?

A sudden tempest swirled around me. I held my writing scale, my cloak flying out. It seemed as if I had unleashed my fears and by this, brought on a storm. But it was dragon wings made the gale that blew my hair back. From the mist, a female dragon came into view, circling once before landing outside the dragonlord's lair.

Her back was to me and her curving tail encircled half the pond, the tip dipping down in the shallows where frogs leaped, suddenly disturbed. My chest pounded, but I got to my feet. She was larger than her little sister, Ore, who'd been the runt of the hatchlings. Her golden right eye swiveled to take me in while her left turned the opposite way, scanning the cave entrance as Lord Kahlil emerged.

As he stepped outside, I was reacquainted with his impressive size. Twice as long as Eetha, Lord Kahlil was nearly as large as the *Malarkey*.

Eetha bowed to him, her snout blowing dust at his feet. Her father had been the famed dragonlord Lord Faul.

Lord Kahlil returned Eetha's greeting with a single nod. His great age showed in his darker scales, battle scars, and wrinkled eyecups. Even so he looked stronger than the younger dragon. *He is a great warrior who has been only a short time at peace with men,* I thought. *I'd fear him more if I didn't already know him.* Spying him in full view here on the ground, I wondered at my foolhardiness to have argued so heatedly with him back in his cave, like a vole standing firm against a tomcat.

"My lord, the will-o'-the-wisps told me Bion is in trouble," Eetha said.

"Prince Arden locked him in the tower."

"Shameful!" Eetha whacked her tail, the tip-most splashing water down my front. I wiped my face with one hand, clung to the lettered scale with the other, holding it up like a shield, writing inward so the ink wouldn't run. The dragon did not ask my pardon for the splash. I did not expect her to.

"We should take Arden back to Dragon's Keep," she said. "Bion should be king."

"It would only start a war, Eetha. Arden is already convinced Bion wants the crown."

"Doesn't he?"

Lord Kahlil shook his head.

"Then we should free Bash from the tower." I heard her care for him in the way she spoke his nickname.

Lord Kahlil pointed with a talon. "Tess has already tried to free him. Bion refuses to go."

Again Eetha whacked her tail. This time I jumped back to miss the splash.

The dragonlord kept me in his gaze "Tess? Come by."

I stepped around the pond, standing to their right away from the water.

At last Eetha acknowledged me. "You are the half-fey girl the will-o'-the-wisps told me about," she said. "I am Eetha."

"Good morrow, Eetha." I curtsied best I could, still gripping the scale. I'd met Ore, now Eetha, two of the four Princess Rosalind raised. It was an honor even if she *had* splashed me twice.

"I see you write on dragon scales as Rosie once did." If dragons smile, then she was smiling.

I was glad she was not offended that I'd used a scale, and warmed to hear her call the queen by the simple name Rosie.

"She might use the skill to help free Bion," said Lord Kahlil.

Startled, I dropped a scale, picked it up again. "What, my lord?"

"You said you are afraid to face Lady Adela."

"I said I refused to face her," I corrected.

He ignored my remark and went on. "I know the risks you would be taking, Tess. Even if you did choose to go to her she might not listen to you, but if you acted as a messenger and delivered a written message about Lord Sackmoore's deceit, she might read its contents. After that she'd be willing to help."

"It would put me in danger." I was shaking all over.

The dragon narrowed his eyes and gave a low growl. "Bion is in danger," he said. "Will you do it?"

His question went to the heart. "For him I will, sir."

"Write your letter," he said. "Let there be no guise in the words, only truth about Lord Sackmoore. Convince her he was behind her kidnapping and she will do the rest. Now Eetha," he said, turning back to her, "here is our plan."

Our plan, he called it. How generous of him, to be sure!

But Bion was in danger. For him I used my ink block to mix new ink, for his eyes and wicked smile, for his moods and corners, for his hands that whittled a doll for Alice, that offered me drink in the tower, that touched my neck as he asked if my chin still hurt. But mostly for the man who had taken in four starving strangers even though our presence had endangered him, the man who would not give up on his brother, though his brother had given up on him.

Chapter Thirty-seven

I T IS A mighty thing to ride on a dragon's back. Flight beyond dream.

Straddling Eetha's broad, scaly neck, I held her upright spiny pads, and clung hard with my knees as she rose over God's Eye. Lake Ailleann shrunk below us till it seemed button small. Riding the gusts beyond the shore, Eetha wheeled south along the water for Black Swan. My body thrummed with her flight, lifted as she lifted, soared as she soared.

When the moon hung lantern bright above, I saw my reflection below us in the sea and wondered at it. Just one of me, yet I'd taken many forms. Tess shaped by the blacksmith's blows, outsider in the human world. Tess jailed as a witch, cast in the millpond, stinking leper. Huntsman's guest, pretend wife, fey man's daughter. Now Tess, Prince Bion's champion. Dragon friend and dragon rider. I'd thought the woman skimming over the water in my firesight was a fey scout, but it was myself I'd seen long ago.

I was high above the world. How wide the sky. How vast the ocean. How free I felt flying to my enemy.

Tiny islands dotted the coastline below. With the exception of Dragon's Keep, which is a quarter the size of Wilde Island, most isles near our shores are little more than single hills with slim beaches where seals and sea lions gather.

Black Swan was large enough for a lord's castle, forest, farm, and pasture. Enough land for serfs to till soil and host a small town with its own craftsmen.

Dragon wings can be loud as a garrison thundering down a road, or quiet as a breeze. I'd discovered this when we crossed the sea, and was grateful for Eetha's skill as she soared above the western quay. Sentries stood watch at the dock where a single ocean vessel was moored. The ship the Gray Knight and Lady Adela arrived in, I supposed. If there were other smaller fishing boats on the isle, I did not spy them. With the surrounding sea, it was a prison sure if boats were outlawed here. I wouldn't put it past Sackmoore.

We approached Lord Sackmoore's castle from the back side. It was built in the very image of Pendragon Castle, though much smaller. A high guard wall enclosed the expansive lawns and gardens. The moat's surface caught the white moonlight. The drawbridge was up.

Black swans swam on an oval pond. The nooks in the garden maze nearby hosted artfully clipped junipers, each trimmed to the shape of a living creature. One bush was a bear standing on his hind legs. Another nook housed a giant rabbit the same size as the bear. I had never seen the like.

Eetha landed in a stand of cypress trees just inside the guard wall. Three windows on the second story were still lit. The will-o'-the-wisps told Lord Kahlil the lady was held against her will, but there was no need for a tower or dungeon cell on this island. She had no means of escape. I almost felt sorry for the woman—almost.

My fingers ran along the edge of the dragon scale scroll tucked in my belt. This was the final draft. The dragonlord had torn the letter eight times before approving the ninth. "Eetha, the lady has three deerhounds."

Eetha wrapped her tail about her clawed feet. "Are they with her on this island, do you think?"

"I don't know, but the dogs, at least, will scent me even if I'm well hidden."

"Go carefully then," said Eetha.

A kind thing to say, but no real help. Still, Eetha couldn't go any closer herself, large as she was. I had to go in alone. Wrapping my cloak about my front, I covered the wretched letter. Only the image of Bion in the tower made me leave our hiding place. Past pond and maze, I crouched behind the courtyard fountain to study the upper-story windows. Only two lit now. Tugging cloth from my pack, I tied a veil over the lower half of my face. It covered my stitched chin, but that wasn't the reason for it. I had no desire to be recognized. Lady Adela would see a secret messenger, nothing more than that.

Scurrying to the door, I checked it, found it locked, and retreated to the fountain again. I was hunched there wondering what to do next when a familiar pock-faced youth led Adela's dogs out on their leashes. The deerhounds were alert to intruders. Ears pricked and noses sniffing, they howled. With snapping teeth they lunged for my hiding place.

The boy dragged behind, shouted, "Stop, ye bloody turds!" A window flew open. Overhead Lady Adela called down, "Curse my darlings again, knave, and I'll whip your pimpled hide! Now take them out to the lawn, and be quick about it!"

"My lady. Yes, my lady," the boy called, still trying to yank the barking dogs straining at the end of their leashes toward the fountain. Running this way and that, they had bound their tethers into a single braid.

The boy had had no time to shut the door with the "bloody turds" dragging him bodily after me. But he had them more in hand now. Dashing for the door, I slipped unseen into the kitchen, where I ducked under a chopping table to catch a breath. I was hiding amid rushes, meat bones, and onion skins when a man stormed through with his candle. The Gray Knight, I guessed, though I saw only his slippers and hose. He slammed the door, muttering, "Damn dogs!"

The kitchen went pitch dark when he left. Under the table my heart thudded, but I gave honor where honor was due. The deerhounds had done all, opening the way, showing me the lady's room. I whispered, "Thank you, darlings," before leaving the kitchen to climb the servant's stairs. The chamber door was half open. Silently I crept in.

Lady Adela leaned over her parchment at her candlelit writing table. She did not notice me in the dark corner. Sighing deeply, she dipped her quill, and used one hand to keep the page from curling. A silver cup of sand was to her right. It irked me to see her at her desk, a frown of concentration on her face. Had God construed a scene to taunt me, a kind of holy joke? Lady, page, quill, and candle were all too familiar.

Night after night at home I'd hunched over my small table drawing things I'd seen in Dragonswood, the foxes, deer, owls up in the branches, the will-o'-the wisps, and the fey scouts riding dragonback. Confined to the blacksmith's house, pen and parchment had been my one consolation. Hadn't I held the curling corners of the page just so? Sprinkled sand on the ink to speed the drying process before I hid my drawings? Not only that, I'd written letters for extra market money when I could, so the tools of my beloved art and my small livelihood had been the same.

Show her mending, needling a tapestry, even reading by her fire, anything but this. A holy joke indeed. It was like seeing my own reflection across the room.

She was dressed in green velvet, her sleeve rolled up to write. Ink stained her wrist, a blot cloth bunched beside it. She'd always worn her hair pinned up or in a long plait down her back. Now it was undone. Black locks spilled over her shoulders and down her back. She looked younger by it, and frailer.

Witch hunter. Torturer. Remember who she is and do what you came to do.

Steeling myself, I whispered, "I have a message for you regarding Prince Arden."

She turned, gasped, and dropped her quill. Bounding for the door she shut it carefully with only the slightest click. My heart sped. I was shut in with *her*.

"Who are you?" She eyed my veiled face, tattered cloak, and muddy shoes.

"A messenger with a letter for you." I did not address her as *my lady*. She didn't deserve it.

She put out her greedy hand, ordering in a whisper, "Give it to me."

She does not see Tess, condemned witch girl. She sees a messenger. "The letter is not from Prince Arden," I warned, "but I'm here in his cause and yours. You can help him, if you wish to."

"Of course I wish to help him!"

A pox on her. My hand went for my knife belted by the scroll. Attack me and she'd feel my point. I pulled the scroll from my belt. She unrolled it, pinching the strange greenish page between her fingers, never having felt a dragon's scale, I guessed.

Her lip curled. "What . . . is this?"

"Later," I said. "Read it. We haven't much time."

The lady sat again and read. Moans increased to bursts of fury tightly leashed by teeth and tongue lest the Gray Knight come in and catch us together. I could tell by the sounds what part of the letter she was reading. Later she put her hand to her mouth and rocked to and fro.

I was well aware Lady Adela would have dropped the page and strangled me if Lord Kahlil had not forced me to rewrite the letter multiple times. Shredding the first eight drafts, the scale growing smaller after each shredding, he'd handed it back saying, "Again, Tess. More to the point. Less angry spleen."

By the last draft I'd managed to refrain from addressing the intended reader as Lady Pustule, Lady Leech Mouth, Mistress Cesspool, Demon Torturer, and such. In this way the dragon scale had been torn down to a tidy page the witch hunter read now, both front and back.

She turned it over to read a second time. There was a lot to take in. I was sure she'd believe the news of her uncle Sackmoore's part in her abduction now his knight held her prisoner here. The back side of the letter she read now was a list of demands. She must read them aloud to the messenger (myself), swear by them, and sign the bottom of the scale if she wanted to see Prince Arden.

Adela stood, trembling. "I will swear by all."

I made her kneel to read the words on the back side aloud. I was proud of the demands I'd laid out with the dragonlord. She read them in a hurried whisper lest the Gray Knight hear:

"I, Lady Adela agree to abide by the demands below.

"First, I swear that if I am taken by this escort to Prince Arden, I will tell him the truth about my uncle, Lord Sackmoore, that he had me abducted and maimed to cut me from Prince Arden's affection, and later sent me away from my former life at Pendragon Castle, and funded my witch hunts. I will also tell Prince Arden of my uncle's gross misuse of the royal treasury before it was taken into safekeeping, using the king's money to fund a secret army of his own to back his attempt for the crown. I will tell him my uncle organized raids on Dragonswood, done in the prince's absence, which were against the law.

"Second, I will persuade Prince Arden to free his younger brother, His Royal Highness Prince Bion, from the tower and drop all charges against him. Lord Sackmoore says Prince Bion stole the royal treasure to crown himself king. Prince Bion only guards the Pendragon treasure to keep it safe from Lord Sackmoore. He vows to return it when Prince Arden's crowned, my uncle jailed.

"Third, if I should win out and by good fortune marry Prince Arden . . ." She stopped here, choking up with emotion, then took a breath. *"And by good fortune marry*

Prince Arden," she said again, "*and become queen of the realm, I swear to put an end to witch hunts on Wilde Island.*" She frowned a little here, but went on. "*Finally, I swear to convince King Arden to adhere to the laws set down by Queen Rosalind and King Kye, regarding Dragonswood protecting all those who sanctuary there.*

"*I swear by Almighty God, the Blessed Virgin, and Holy Trinity to adhere to all listed above, doing right by all on our fair island where human, fey folk, and dragons are bound to live in peace. May God have mercy on us all.*"

She looked up at me.

"Do you swear?" I asked.

"I swear. Hurry, now," she whispered. "Take me to the prince."

"Sign it first," I insisted. Her humility, honed from need to see her lover, kept her at my feet. I thought of the pitiless torture she'd put me through, the hardship she'd pressed on me and my friends. *She should beg for my forgiveness.* Ah, I'd have kept her kneeling there a good deal longer if I could have. But I had Bion to think of, so I placed the dragon scale on her writing table.

On her knees, she signed.

Snatching the document, I rolled it up and said with leaden voice, "Follow me."

"What then?" she asked.

"You will see."

"Do you have a ship?"

I didn't answer. We crept downstairs and out the kitchen door. The boy and dogs were far away on the lawn as we slipped past the fountain and out behind the maze.

I pointed to the stand of evergreens. "Run."

She raced, her cloak flying, her limp more pronounced than ever as she ran. I feared the dogs would spot her, but there was little space between garden maze and woods. She made it to the trees.

Following, I found her facedown on the ground where she'd fainted at the sight of the dragon. Her arms were spread out wide as a holy pilgrim come to confess at the altar. I would have liked to leave her there with her face planted in the earth.

Eetha said, "You should have warned her, Tess."

I turned Adela over and slapped her cheek to wake her. Next I caught her startled scream inside my hand.

"Hush," I whispered. "This is Eetha. She's known Prince Arden and Prince Bion since they were babes. She is here to help us."

Lady Adela stood and brushed the grass from cloak and gown. Her face was despoiled with mud.

"Forgive me, Eetha. I was . . . startled."

"I forgive you. I am large and impressive," Eetha said immodestly.

I laughed. Then the she-dragon lowered her long neck that we might both climb on. Adela was frightened, but I did not help her clamber up behind me.

Over sea and under stars, Eetha flew us back to Wilde

Island. When she landed by the cave on God's Eye we dismounted, shivering in the fog that always cloaked the little isle. Eetha urged us both into the cave, where a warming fire waited, before she flew skyward again to hunt.

Inside, Lord Kahlil offered food and wine. The steaming turnips were bitter, but I ate hungrily, knifing them and slipping bites under my veil. I'd no wish to shed my facecloth before my enemy, and was glad to have a knife in hand with her close by.

The lady was exceedingly nervous before the dragonlord. It was gratifying to see my enemy so undone. Silent in his den, Lord Kahlil watched us, smoke curling from his nostrils. Lady Adela's eyes flitted from teeth to talon and back again. Was she expecting torture? She deserved it.

Anon Eetha returned with her kill. Breathing fire, she roasted the venison outside before serving Lord Kahlil. The dragonlord ate first, then Eetha. Last we were served. Adela, still too fear-struck to eat, left her strip of meat and steaming turnip on its stone.

Meal done, Lord Kahlil picked his teeth awhile before pointing a damp talon at me. "Leave us, Tess."

I jumped up, the name Tess reverberating in the cave. Adela glared. I quit the den. How dare he reveal me to my enemy? Hadn't we agreed I could keep my disguise as long as I liked?

I was by the pond huffing when Eetha came out after me. We were close enough to the cave mouth to hear the voices within, one deep and rough as cinder rock, the other higher pitched and wavering with fright. Leaning in with my good ear, I still couldn't make out what they were saying.

"Come, Tess, tomorrow's coronation day. If things are going to unfold as planned, you'll need your rest."

"I can't sleep."

"Then you can rest while I sleep," she snapped. I followed her to a grassy spot. Things had happened so quickly since I'd arrived on God's Eye. I could hardly believe Wilde Island would have a new king tomorrow. Eetha lay under a yew tree, patting the ground beside her with her claw. Agitated, I sat near her warm body.

"Why so angry, Tess?"

I supposed it was easy enough to read my mood. "Adela's a demon." How much would Eetha know about the witch hunter, having lived on Dragon's Keep? I told her all the terrible things she'd done to me and my friends. Eetha listened, breathing softly; her exhale made a whistling sound like songbirds in a far-off wood. "I don't trust her. What if she sides with Prince Arden and Sackmoore and keeps Bion locked up in the tower?"

"Didn't she agree to our demands?"

"Swore to them and signed the scroll."

"Then why would she go against her oath?"

"I told you, she's a bloody fiend!" I curled my fingers round my thumbs remembering the pain.

"Lie down, Tess." Eetha rested her wing over me, shielding me from the gusts coming up off the lake. On my back, looking up at her elegant wing scales that held the same filigree patterns as I'd seen on the undersides of leaves, I wrangled with my thoughts. How could I help Bion escape if Lady Adela betrayed us? If I made it back into the tower with the last of my sleep potion, and opened a way for Bion, would he even come? I looked at my companion. Her eyes were still open.

"Prince Bion's still in danger, Eetha."

"Bion knows what he's doing, Tess. Be sure of it. He was fearless as a boy. I'm the one who named him Bash," she added proudly. "Such a ferocious toddler he was, always climbing up my leg to slide down my tail. Before he could lift a sword, Bash sparred with us, using nothing more than a stick, the little imp." She gave a low chuckle. I thought of him fencing with Ore in the cave as she went on. "Lord Kahlil took him flying when he was but five years old. They both got a scolding for it."

I laughed. "Who scolded them?"

"His mother, Queen Lucinda, of course."

I sighed and folded my hands across my belly. "One night at the hunting lodge, Bion showed me his mother's pearl necklace. He put it in my hand so I could hold it up to the window in the moonlight."

"He did?" Eetha sounded impressed. Her eyecup swerved to look a little more closely. She kept it on me as I told her of our ride south together to fetch Alice, of the time he'd climbed a tree to sit with me until I was ready to come down.

"Tess," she whispered. "The man loves you."

Her quiet words ghosted up over God's Eye. I remembered the feel of his fingers on my neck, the lightest touch like a passing breeze. Eetha's words had sent a river through me.

"How can you know something like that?"

"Read his actions, Tess. He climbed the tree to speak with you, told you openly about his sister on Dragon's Keep," she said. "She's dear to him. He doesn't share his love for her with just anyone."

"I didn't know she was his sister back then."

"Then he risked even more to speak of her that way."

I'd never had a sister who'd lived more than three weeks, but I'd loved the little ones fiercely and would have done anything for them.

There was a long silence. So long I thought she'd drifted off, but as the yew creaked in the wind she said, "There are few of our kind left, Tess. Our numbers dwindle even with Dragonswood sanctuary and our caves on Dragon's Keep." She paused. "In her long life, a female dragon might lay only two clutches, Tess. I'm ready to have my own clutch. My first," she admitted. "I have chosen Shiraz, a fiery orange dragon from Persia, though he does not know it yet."

Together we gazed up where a small rent in the mist revealed black sky, a star. "We dragons are not like the fey; we mate for life."

Eetha did not ask if I loved Bion. She did not have to.

Chapter Thirty-eight

AT FIRST LIGHT, I sat up under Eetha's wing. *The fourteenth of November. Coronation day.*

I tapped Eetha's side. She roused and shook herself awake. We hurried to the cave for a last word with Lord Kahlil. Eetha went in, but Lady Adela stood at the mouth of the cave barring my way. Her face was streaked with dirt and tears.

"I hope you will forgive me, Tess."

I was speechless.

She eyed my chin now I was unveiled. "Who did that to you?"

"No one. I did it myself. I slipped on the ice." Why even answer her? I didn't have to.

"Who doctored you?"

"The fey," I said with some pride.

"Lucky for you they did the work. I've never had any trouble with the clever glass eye they made especially for me."

I didn't like to think the fairies had willingly given her the gift. She did not deserve their help, in my opinion. But then, they'd fashioned Adela's fey eye before she'd become a witch hunter. Perhaps they didn't know she'd use it to cower the population and frighten poor innocent girls out of their wits?

She was peering much too closely at me. "The fey know how to speed up healing. Such fine thread. What did they use?"

"Flit silk. I doubt you've heard of it."

"Well they've done their job. I can see the stitches are ready to come out. Let me do it." She reached for the small pouch hanging from her waist. "I have some skill with wounds."

"Skill with wounds?" I snarled, backing away. "Don't touch me."

Her velvet waist pouch was already half open. "Are you sure? It will only take a moment."

"Leave me alone."

"Let her," Eetha called from inside the cave. "She's right. The stitches should come out."

Maybe so, but the witch hunter didn't have to do it. "Have you a mirror?" I asked. She might have a small one in her waist pouch. "I'll take them out myself."

Adela shook her head. "We left the solar too quickly for me to think to bring a mirror or a brush." She fingered her tangled hair. "I have only what I use to trim my nails."

In the end I insisted Eetha come out to watch.

"Chin up," said Adela.

I sat stone silent as she clipped and pulled the threads out. Our eyes met. Hers were blue as water hyacinth, the glass one slightly darker than the real. I looked straight into her fey eye. Let her see me for what I was. I welcomed it. Her hands were steady tugging the flit threads with such care it did not hurt at all after the first stitch. Her tenderness stupefied me. Was she hoping I'd forgive everything by this?

As soon as she was through, I jumped up, gave no thanks, and marched inside to Lord Kahlil. Adela spoke to my back as I left. "I hope you can someday forgive me, Tess."

Someday? When Satan sits at the right hand of God.

In the cave, I shouted, "God's teeth! What did you say to her last night?"

"That is between the lady and myself," the dragonlord said. "It does not have anything to do with you."

"It does!"

"Not everything concerns you, Tess."

Eetha stepped inside and tipped her head. "She's as wild as Bash." Both the dragons laughed. I turned and was halfway to the entrance when Lord Kahlil called me to a halt. "Wait, Tess. Bring the lady this."

He handed me a large blue velvet bag. I looked at it suspiciously. "What's inside?"

"Bargaining chips."

I opened the sack. A king's crown and scepter winked up at me from the dark maw. "Why would you entrust a witch hunter with these precious things?"

"She wants to bring them to the coronation."

"Of course she does! I won't hand them over."

"It's time to go," said Eetha.

Sack in hand, I followed Eetha out. Lady Adela was crouched over the pond washing her face. Her cheeks were blotched when she looked up. "He hasn't seen me since the day . . . I don't know if I can show Arden my face. What if he—"

"You are not completely unsightly," I said coldly. I clutched the velvet bag. The crown and scepter had not gone with the rest of the stolen treasure, it seemed. Bion had stashed them here for safekeeping until coronation day.

Lady Adela's face still dripped. "My glass eye," she said, pulling back her hair, then letting it fall down again. She turned her back. Her shoulders were hunched.

"We will be late if we don't leave soon."

She wiped her eyes. "Yes. All right, I will come. We must be brave, mustn't we?"

"Do as you like," I snapped.

WE WERE LATE. Almost too late. Spying down from a rent in the dark clouds, I saw the amphitheatre already full to bursting with the population. The ceremony had begun. Prince Arden was enthroned center stage under the colorful cloth awning. The bishop and his priest were there with a handful of knights and Lord Sackmoore. Just below and to the right of the stage, Prince Bion stood with armed guards at his back. Not far from him I glimpsed my father and the fey delegation dressed in their finery.

I saw all in an instant, for just then Eetha called, "Hold on," and knifed through the clouds. A storm broke with our coming as if she'd winged in the rain. Showers hit the stands where frightened people jumped up screaming at the sight of the dragon. They crushed one another on the steps trying to race down.

Prince Bion shouted, "Stay, people. Do not be afraid."

His voice carried up through the amphitheatre. Some still ran down the stairs and out, but others stayed. On stage Lord Sackmoore waved his arms. "Get back, dragon!" He and his knights drew their swords shouting more threatening warnings.

Eetha landed smoothly and lowered her head just long enough for Lady Adela and me to climb onto the stage. Then Eetha stepped off the platform. The crowd in the stadium seats climbed higher, so only Prince Bion with his guards, and the fey guests stayed at ground level with the dragon.

The knights encircled Prince Arden, swords up to protect the future king. Seeing Lady Adela, Arden called, "Wait! Don't harm them!"

Adela went boldly forward. I followed, keeping her in my sights. We'd delivered her as promised. I was here to make sure she kept her word.

"I have your king's crown, Your Royal Highness," she

said, trembling. Adela reached for the velvet sack in my arms. We had it between us now, my hand on it and hers.

Lord Sackmoore leaped in front of us. "What trickery is this? You disturb our holy occasion!" He thrust a hand out. "Give it to me."

"No, Uncle. It belongs to Prince Arden." She took the smaller crown from the priest's satin pillow and replaced it with the true one.

"Thieves!" said Sackmoore. "Arrest them both."

"Wait," cried Lady Adela as the knights surrounded us.

"Please, Your Royal Highness," I pleaded, "hear the lady out. She brought the true crown for your coronation in good faith. Your brother promised your crown would come in time and here it is."

"On my word, I promised you," Prince Bion called from below, rain streaming down his face. He was wet as a dog and smiling up at me.

"Will no one offer Prince Bion shelter?" I said. I was ignored. But Arden waved his knights away from us.

Then he stepped a little closer, not to touch his king's crown, but to brush back Lady Adela's hair. "You wear it the way you did as a girl," he said.

I was close enough to hear the fond remark.

"I had no time to put it up and . . ." She paused, blushing. "Thank you," she said. "Please, if I might speak with you," she added.

"Soon, Adela."

"Now, please," she insisted. "It must be now, before you are crowned."

"What can be so needy of attention?" He frowned. Still, he didn't sit again to continue the ceremony or wave the lady away.

"It is just this. My uncle was the one who ordered my kidnapping. He had me maimed so you would no longer want me."

"That is a lie!"

"Shut up, Sackmoore!" He pointed at the man. The knights moved in.

Arden asked, "You are sure this is true, Adela?"

"I know it's true. My uncle imprisoned me on Black Swan. I only now escaped with the help of this girl, Tess, and the dragon, Eetha."

Sackmoore's mouth twisted. "Prince Arden . . . Sire. Witches attacked my niece, poor girl. She's not been the same since. I tried to warn you in my letters. Feel sorry for her as I do, but do not let yourself be fooled. She has lost her mind."

Prince Arden whipped round, drew his sword, and slashed Sackmoore's cheek.

I jumped back as the man hunched over, face in hands, blood dripping onto the stage. The prince wiped the bloody weapon, then held the clean blade in the air for all to see as the knights dragged Sackmoore from the stage.

The crowd cheered. Handing the sword to one of the

remaining knights, he went down on his knees before the bishop. The bishop anointed the future king with holy oil. All seemed to hold their breath as he placed the crown on Arden's head.

Trumpets sounded. Shouts went up. "Long live King Arden! Long live the king!"

I pulled the scepter from the velvet bag. The cheering heightened to a roar when I passed it to the king. Standing with his arm around Lady Adela, he held it high. King Uther Pendragon's daughter, our first Wilde Island queen, brought the scepter here nearly seven hundred years ago. Here was proof of our sovereign's Pendragon bloodline. The fist-sized golden dragon perched atop the staff was ruby-eyed and diamond-toothed.

Even in the rain, I caught the sound of dragon wings. Lord Kahlil and Ore flew over the stadium bearing a great bundle between them. Skimming in lower, they dropped the bundle on the stage with a thump. It landed at King Arden's feet.

"Our treasure, brother," Bion called from below. "Protected by the dragons until you were crowned."

Lord Kahlil and Ore circled over stage and treasure bundle as the new king untied the knotted cloth and peered inside. From where I stood I saw golden gleams and silver. Red stones that must be rubies, emeralds, sapphires, more. But the one I thought of was the smallest of these, and the plainest. Where was Queen Lucinda's pearl?

"The king's treasure is returned!" Arden shouted.

All was pandemonium. The cheering crowd, the lashing rain on tarpaulin, stage, and amphitheatre, the heavy gusting wind: All ran together to one resilient roar. Lord Kahlil and Ore landed next to Eetha at the foot of the stage. Three dragons raised their heads and spewed blue fire up into the rain. Flame and water sparked overhead like fireworks. Shining blue light filtered down in fizzling sparks on the crowd below.

On Bion's right, Onadon and Elixis gazed up at the flames. In that moment of distraction Poppy made her break. Deserting her fey father, she raced, screaming joyfully, into the revelers who swarmed down to the ground level. She grabbed a brightly dressed man waving a pole adorned with colorful ribbons and held on as Jyro dropped the pole to spin her round and round.

One fey princess gone into the arms of another, the second was on the stage with Lady Adela. Onadon looked up at me. He did not point a finger; still, I was bound by his powerful gaze. His eyes said, *You betrayed me*. I saw no love or forgiveness there. My father didn't know how carefully we'd worded the demands in Lady Adela's letter. That I'd made her swear if she was queen she'd protect Dragonswood. If she failed to win her man, Bion would step in to guard the sanctuary.

Father's cool green eyes were hard. I held him look for look. I'd been his choice, his champion. I'd wanted to love him as a daughter loves a father. But he had not seen me for who I was. He still did not see me.

A child raced through the crowd. I caught sight of Alice's dimpled face as she bounded toward the edge of the stage, her curls bouncing even in the downpour. So Meg and Tom had come to the coronation! I spied Meg below, chasing Alice in her sodden cloak. Tom ran behind. Both parents shouted through the boisterous mob.

The audience had given the dragons a wide berth at the foot of the stage, so the small area was open enough for me to see Alice speeding toward Bion, holding her doll up as our new king had raised his scepter. She held it in the air to Bion, for he was its maker.

I guessed from my place on the stage the doll was broken. The child had a second wooden piece in her other hand.

Dragon's blue fire overhead, the revelers still cheering, I saw Bion go down on his knee before the little girl. He kept his hands behind his back and did not take the doll Alice held out to him. I wondered at it until I heard King Arden calling down, "Guards, release my brother." And I saw the knight slit the cords on Bion's wrists.

Once unbound, he brought his hands round to Alice. The child's back was to me. I could see Bion's dripping hair and earnest face as he spoke to her. The tumultuous crowd moved in waves, the wind and rain were deafening, but the world went still for me and silent in the eye of the storm where Bion knelt with Alice.

I am a girl who has known mostly the back of a man's hand, and not the front of it. My heart filled with a terrible crushing ache as I watched him touching the doll so and so with his forefinger, showing Alice where he might mend it. The child nodded, listening to the words I could not hear. By now I had stepped out from under the awning, though I did not remember moving out. Slanting rain pelted my face. There was no wounding in it, only a wildness as raw as any hard November rain that swells rivers and crumbles hillsides.

Bion stood with Alice in his arms and handed her back to Meg. My shoes were at stage edge, my heart somewhere outside of me in the rainstorm. Bion was free now to live as he chose. *All I truly want is to live year-round with my sister in the modest castle on Dragon's Keep.* Was that all, truly all?

I leaned out, wishing to be drenched as Bion was drenched. The sky letting down all its fury and celebration on us, the water slapping and clapping and taking the last traces of Sackmoore's blood from the stage.

"Tess?" he shouted up.

"Bash?"

"Come down." He waved his arms, laughing and stomping in a puddle. I jumped from the stage, and stomped. Freezing water splashed up my legs.

Mud and rain and glorious shouting all around, still we were yards apart. Stepping up, Lord Kahlil drew us closer together with his wing. Under this broad tent, Bion cupped my face. His wrists were raw with rope burns. I encircled them with my fingers to cool the sores. His sleeves were rolled back. I kissed the dragon scales on his left arm. He drew me closer. His hands cupped my cheeks. Open hands. The front and not the back.

KING ARDEN AND Lady Adela were wed a few months later and there was much celebration all over Wilde Island for the new king and queen. But Prince Bion chose another way.

In the enchanted woodland wild,
The Prince shall wed a Fairy child.

In the woodland we were wed, surrounded by the fey folk and three dragons: Eetha, Ore, and Lord Kahlil. Lord Kahlil himself married us. A night wedding in the glow of bonfires set by dragons. The pearl ring set in gold was the one Bion first showed me at the window, the one Ore swung over a carpet of blue fire, the smallest jewel in the king's treasure that was his mother's pearl and mine.

Dragon, Human, and Fairy,
Their union will be bound by three.

If the prophecy came true that night, our union binding three races together at last, I could only wonder at it. Vows said in such a magical place are binding. But the true moment of union for me was a silent one when Bion held my chin, his thumb resting lightly on my scar; a hand I knew would never strike, but gently touch a scarred girl both human and fey. Lifting my chin he gave his kiss both long and sweet.

Epilogue

DRAGON'S KEEP

Month of August AD 1195

"Tess?" Bash calls from below my tree. "Will you come down? The birthday feast is almost ready."

The last light of the summer's day spreads tangerine across the cliffs and ocean. I am reluctant to climb down my favorite pine, but I see the blankets and food baskets on the beach to celebrate our son's second birthday, the bobbing wine casks chilling in the river. Jackrun toddles up to the base of my pine. He tugs his father's hand, wanting him to come back to the beach and play.

"I'll join you soon," I call down.

Bash takes Jackrun up in his arms and crosses the sand to meet the fey folk who have stepped out of the wood to join our celebration. I breathe the tangy sea air. Far off on the flat rocks dragons bask alongside seals in the fading sun. Lord Kahlil used to summer here when my husband was a boy and live the rest of the year on God's Eye; by this he stayed close to the princes as they were growing up. Now Lord Kahlil lives with us on Dragon's Keep year-round. Jackrun's birth brought him here, contention between him and the Wilde Island fey keeps him here.

Elixis and Onadon know he supported my love for Bion, and Poppy's choice in Jyro, and didn't press either of us to fulfill the prophecy as the fey envisioned it. They are angry, firmly unforgiving. They mislike Queen Adela and do not trust her. In that one thing, I'm in agreement with my father, Onadon. My suspicions of her remain, but so far she's kept her promise, the boundary walls have not been breached.

The sun's warmth fades. Near the old dragon, Eetha's orange-scaled mate, Shiraz, sleeps on the flat rocks with their pips.

The back steps running from our castle to the beach are overgrown. I spy Jyro bounding down them with a wooden cradle. Poppy follows more slowly, their infant son snugly wrapped in her arms, and Tupkin, as ever, at her heels. I climb down the tree barefoot, race through sand, take up my son, and swing him around, shouting his name aloud. He screams with delight. I hug him close to my chest. The feisty little boy protests. Jackrun thinks he is getting too old for such cuddling. This saddens me some, but another child is growing in me and will, by God's grace, be here by winter's snow.

Princess Augusta races up the beach in her little copper-colored party dress made of shed pip scales and tugs my son from my arms. She is seven, just five years older than her nephew, Jackrun. He is heavy for her and she stumbles a little. But I stand very still now that my child is in her arms.

A wonder comes on me. *Here is my fire-sight come to pass.* Long ago in the flames I'd seen myself on a beach, holding a child, seen the dragon-faced girl snatch the child from my arms. I stand so still my feet root deeper in the sand as the waves suck away from my ankles.

So many things I feared have come true. They have not destroyed me. Princess Augusta shows Jackrun the sack of walnuts Cook gave her for our feast. Her scaled forehead and golden dragon eyes have never bothered Jackrun in the least. My son takes a walnut and throws it in the sea.

"No, they're not to throw, Jackrun!" Augusta scolds. Both laugh as they try to fetch the walnut tumbling shoreward on a fresh wave. I splash in, catch it, and give it to the princess. Her dragon eyes are even more golden in the fading daylight reflecting up from the water. Taking the walnut from me, she races back to Jackrun. King Arden's come just once to meet his little sister. He and Adela haven't sailed to Dragon's Keep since the birth of their first child. If they shy away from our rough life here, Bion and I revel in it.

We lived in the lodge when we were first wed, but try as

I might, I couldn't stay in Dragonswood. The fey shunned us for going against them. I felt the blacksmith's anger all my life; I will not live under Onadon's. Some fairy folk left to join us on Dragon's Keep. No boundary wall around us but the sea.

In the damp sand, Bion and Jackrun are building a sandcastle with Augusta. My grandfather comes slowly down the beach steps, leaving his map room to join us for his great-grandson's birthday. I walk along the shore to where Eetha stands at the water's edge. She flicks her tail in worried irritation as her most daring pip, Babak, wades in the water. Everyone knows dragons hate to get wet, so she is endlessly surprised by Babak's interest in the sea.

"He is only in knee-deep, Eetha. He won't drown."

"I cannot understand it," she says, cocking one eye my way and keeping the other firmly on her son, who splashes happily in the shallows. "His brother and sisters are sensible dragons. They do not like the water any more than their father or I do. Where does Babak get this fixation?"

We watch Babak, whose scales are a complex pattern of copper and green patchwork like a calico cat's. His unique coloring differs from his brother and sisters, who are all copper-scaled like their father.

Eetha's brother Chawl spirals down with Ore. The rest of our feast has arrived. Lord Kahlil and Shiraz light the bonfires. The dragons roast wild boar on their talons to share with all. I back away from the smoke. Bash runs his finger down my neck. I feel a brushfire cross my skin. We never tire of touching each other. I run the back of my hand across the dragon scales along his arm. We will sneak off to our tree house when the feast is over.

The fey have brought fine cakes with elaborate icing all on shimmering glass trays. Will-o'-the-wisps flit overhead. Tupkin leaps up trying to capture one. I hear their laughter, flying down lower and lower to tease Tupkin, only to flit away.

Babak shakes sea water from his scales and joins his brother and sisters, cracking walnuts between their tiny black talons. Jackrun tries to do the same with his pudgy fingers and screams with frustration.

"Try this," Grandfather says, smashing a walnut against a rock. He hands Jackrun another walnut. Jackrun hammers. Bang. Bang. Bang. The nut will not crack, but he does not give up. Bang. Bang.

Grandfather raises his tufted brows, giving Bash and me a quizzical look. We laugh at our determined son and shake our heads. Poppy nurses her babe under her shawl.

"This is what you have to look forward to, Poppy." Her son's head pokes out from under the wool, revealing a shock of hair as fiery red as Jyro's. I think of Alice's curls and ache. Meg died last winter. Tom said she passed a week after the fever took her. I try to imagine Tom and Cackle raising Alice alone at the lodge. It isn't right. The child should have women about her, a playmate in Princess

Augusta, who is just a year older than Alice. I invited Tom to bring his daughter here. No word back yet.

Mother too won't visit. I've sent her invitations and a sound ship to escort her. The blacksmith will not let her go. Poppy places her sleeping babe in the wooden cradle. She hums as she rocks him. I painted vines and will-o'-the-wisps around the cradle's top, and a dragon encircling it.

Most of my gowns are splattered with shades of yellow, green, and crimson. I painted murals on the inner castle walls, and adorned furniture like this cradle, but I like working on dragon scales the best. We are in good supply here, since the dragons shed them often.

A short letter from my mother was tucked inside the cradle along with a handmade blanket. I read it again and again, and know the words by heart.

My Dearest Tess,

How good to hear that you are well and happy. Our son, Paul, is two years old now and a blessing to us. John Blacksmith has crafted him a small hammer. Paul pounds everything with it. He dents our pans and furniture and makes his father laugh. Your Jackrun sounds a strong lad too. We cannot journey to Dragon's Keep this year, but hearing your good news that you expect a second child, we send this cradle.

God's Blessing, your mother

No words from the blacksmith, but was this cradle word enough?

We sing a song to Jackrun. After the meal we all partake of the birthday confections, trying the fine sweets the fairies brought. Jackrun chooses a little round cake, shoves the entire thing into his mouth, and laughs, spewing crumbs. After a few more pieces, Jackrun's clothing is smudged in decorative icing as colorfully patterned as his friend Babak's scales.

My son strips off his shirt and trousers. I see the familiar dragon scales running down the back of his plump right leg.

And when these lovers intertwine, three races in one child combine. I wonder this part of the prophecy should come to pass in our son. He is not a king's son as the fey had hoped. Nonetheless, he is the first to combine dragon, human, and fairy in his small frame. Lord Kahlil says our story is not over. I've seen his thousand-year-old eyes taking in our little boy. There is pleasure and concern in his look, but when I ask him what he sees, he does not speak.

Jackrun races down the beach after Babak. Eetha follows them, her long tail making serpentine marks in the sand. Babak trots up to a smooth driftwood log and shows his newest dragon power, blowing a small orange flame. The flame is too short-lived to light the log, but his mother slaps her tail in approval. I shout, "Good for you, Babak," and clap alongside Bion. Not wanting to be outdone, our son roars at the log as if to produce his own fire. We laugh at his attempt, but I swallow my laughter seeing a small, bright flame shoot out of Jackrun's mouth.

Poppy screams. The rest of us stand silent, stunned as Jackrun proudly roars flame again alongside Babak.

"Jackrun!" I race across the sand.

Bash runs ahead and sweeps our son up in his arms. Jackrun is coughing smoke. His face is red. We bring him back to our gathering and give him water. He drinks two cups, then laughs. I am frightened, but I try and smile before I take Bash aside. "Have any other Pendragons ever breathed fire?" I whisper.

"Mixing bloodlines always brings some risk."

"Tell me."

Bash shakes his head. "It seems our son is the first."

"What does it mean, Bash? What will it mean?"

"Don't let it frighten you, Tess," he whispers into my ear. "He's our son. He will learn to control it."

But I'm trembling now and he can feel it. "A boy who's dragon, human, and fairy: What other strange powers might he have?" My power set me apart. Hidden as it was, the midwife still caught me enthralled by the fire, the witch hunter tortured me, my own townsfolk called me a witch. I won't punish my son for breathing fire. But I am afraid for him, for us.

Bion lifts my hand. Kisses my pearl ring. "Whatever powers come, we'll raise him here on Dragon's Keep. Our son, Tess. Ours together."

"Yes, ours together." I feel his strength as he lightly runs his fingers along my chin.

Babak and his sibling dragons tumble snout over tail in the sand. Jackrun jumps up. I think he will run after Babak and the others, but he goes to Lord Kahlil, who has just finished eating and is still licking meat juices off his talons. Jackrun thrusts out his small hands, lifts his bare foot, and begins to climb the dragon's tail.

I call, "Leave him be, Jackrun." But the dragonlord is used to this game. Beside me my husband sighs.

When Jackrun slides down the long tail, Kahlil grabs the sliding boy, coiling him in the tip. He throws him into the air and catches him.

Jackrun squeals with delight. "Again! Go again!"

Bion puts his arm around me. This son of the prophecy has a long life ahead of him. We watch our boy together.

Lord Kahlil flicks his tail.

Jackrun flies.

Acknowledgments

I'm indebted to the many friends, colleagues, and mentors who helped with this book. Warmest thanks to my intrepid editor, Kathy Dawson, whose editorial genius and clear vision helped guide Tess's tale from first to last. Thanks also to the people at Dial Books, who are committed to excellence, and to my agent, Irene Kraas.

Fellow authors Justina Chen and Indu Sundaresan gave unswerving advice on the manuscript, as did Sarah Bond. Thanks also to the Diviners: Peggy King Anderson, Judy Bodmer, Katherine Grace Bond, Dawn Knight, Holly Cupala, Molly Blaisdell, and Nancy Carlstrom, critiquers who shore up my weaknesses and add to my strengths; to gifted photographer Heidi Pettit, for the festive book launch party photos (http://litart-photography. smugmug.com/), and ongoing gratitude to the librarians and independent booksellers who offer voracious readers delicious books.

Speaking of books, my shelves are crammed with informative and sometimes alarming titles necessary to writing this medieval fantasy with an eye to historical authenticity. I have far too many reference books to list here, but these few I found invaluable.

Nigel Cawthorne. *Witches History of a Persecution.* Edison, New Jersey: Chartwell Books, Inc., 2004.

Karen Farrington. *Dark Justice: A History of Punishment and Torture.* New York: Smithmark Publishers, 1996.

Joseph & Frances Gies. *Life in a Medieval Castle.* New York: Harper & Row, 1974.

Vicki Leon. *Uppity Women of Medieval Times.* New York: MJF Books, 1997.

Sherrilyn Kenyon. *The Writer's Guide to Everyday Life in the Middle Ages: The British Isles from 500–1500.* Cincinnati, Ohio: Writer's Digest Books, 1995.

Roger Virgoe, editor. *Illustrated Letters of the Paston Family: Private Life in the Fifteenth Century.* New York: Weidenfeld & Nicolson, 1989.

David Macaulay. *Castle.* New York: Houghton Mifflin, 1977.

Christopher Tyerman. *Who's Who in Early Medieval England.* London: Shepheard-Walwyn Publishers Ltd., 1996.

Lady Wilde. *Irish Cures, Mystic Charms & Superstitions.* New York: Sterling Publishing, 1991. Note: Lady Wilde, 1826–1896, Oscar Wilde's mother.

Annette Sandoval. *The Directory of Saints: A Concise Guide to Patron Saints.* New York: Signet, Penguin Group, 1997.

Madeleine Pelner Cosman. *Medieval Wordbook: More than 4,000 Terms and Expressions from Medieval Culture.* New York: Barnes & Noble, 2007.

Scott Cunningham. *Cunningham's Encyclopedia of Magical Herbs.* St. Paul, Minnesota: Llewellyn Publications, 1987.

A. C. Cawley, editor. *Everyman and Medieval Miracle Plays.* London: Orion Publishing Group, 1993.

A special thanks to fellow novelists who bring medieval life and times alive in their historical fiction, mystery, and fantasy books. For Karen Cushman's excellent medieval novels for young readers, Ellis Peters's wonderful Brother Cadfael mystery series, Barry Unsworth's *Morality Play,* and Juliet Marillier's Sevenwaters series and Bridei Chronicles. Without these reference books and novels within arm's reach, I could not have delved so deeply into Tess's world.

TEEN
FIC
CAREY,J

Carey, Janet Lee.

Dragonswood.

DATE			